BEYOND

THE

WILD

RIVER

SARAH MAINE

HODDER

First published in Great Britain in 2017 by Hodder & Stoughton
An Hachette UK company

First published in paperback in 2017

2

Copyright © Sarah Maine 2017

The rig... ...Vork has been
asserted ... ...ents Act 1988.

Aberdeenshire Council Libraries		
4012405		
Askews & Holts	17-Jun-2019	
AF	£8.99	
HQ		

...oduced,
stored i... ...means without
the pri... ...culated in any
form of ... ...and without a
...aser.

...nblance

A C... ...ish Library

Paperback ISBN 978 1 473 63969 0

Typeset in Adobe Caslon Pro

Printed and bound by CPI Group (UK) Ltd, Croydon, CR0 4YY

Hodder & Stoughton policy is to use papers that are natural,
renewable and recyclable products and made from wood grown in sustainable
forests. The logging and manufacturing processes are expected to conform
to the environmental regulations of the country of origin.

Hodder & Stoughton Ltd
Carmelite House
50 Victoria Embankment
London EC4Y 0DZ

www.hodder.co.uk

To my father and mother, and Ian, for those wilderness days

BEYOND
THE
WILD
RIVER

Prologue

The gunshot lifted the rooks from the branches.

James was already running fast through the woodland when he heard it, and he plunged on, cursing now and desperate, careless of skin and clothes that caught on twigs and brambles. He reached the edge of the trees in time to see Jacko fall to his knees, head thrown back, his hands clutching at his chest.

The rooks were etching a ragged halo in the sky as James broke cover and ran to where the poacher lay beside the bulrushes, a booted foot in the shallows. He sank to the ground beside him. '*Jacko!* Jacko, hold on—!' But the old man's breath was just a wheezing rasp, and his eyes were closed. Blood oozed between his filthy fingers, and spread over his shirt. '*No!*' It could not end like this. The circling rooks protested their own outrage, while a coot scuttled to safety amongst the reeds.

James stared down at the wreck of a man, once his champion, protector, and friend. And guilt flared. Oh Jesus, how complete was his own betrayal . . .

'Good God! There's another of them.'

A man's voice carried clearly from the other side of the river, and James looked up. Then he fumbled through Jacko's torn pockets for something, anything, to stem the flow.

Hopeless. 'I'll get help.'

Jacko's eyes opened and gleamed briefly. 'From them?' And he gave a croak of a laugh.

1

James lifted his head again and looked across the river, his brain sharpening into the moment. Two men in sporting tweeds stood on the opposite bank, looking back at him, motionless. House guests? One had a gun half-raised, and James's head began to pound. What had happened here? Had *they* shot Jacko? Reckless he was, half-crazed, maybe, but the old poacher offered a threat to no one but himself.

Then James saw a third figure, hidden by the shadow of an ancient oak, and he cursed, sickened with sudden comprehension. It must be one of the keepers, probably McAllister himself. He would gun Jacko down without a thought, and so settle a conflict decades long. That, he *could* believe.

Then the man stepped out of the shadows, and James's heart stopped.

It was not McAllister, nor one of his men.

It was Ballantyre.

Thank God! But the relief withered, stillborn – for Ballantyre did not move; he simply stared across the river at James, and James stared back.

'Run.' Jacko's voice was a hoarse whisper, his fingers pawing at his sleeve, but James's eyes were still fixed on Ballantyre, locked with his across the river's gentle current, frozen into the moment. '*Run.* I tell you. Run fast, lad, and as far—'

And then the rooks, dark witnesses, broke their circle and flew off, their protests fading into the soft autumn evening. They regrouped briefly above the great roofs and chimneys of Ballantyre House and circled once, as if in judgement, then disappeared into the gathering mist. And the house stood solid on its raised terrace, above the neat lawns and gravelled paths which led down to the river, quite indifferent to the passing moment.

What happened next happened fast. Only later would memory replay the events in James's brain, scene by scene, endlessly over the years, as he sought the sense in it.

Jacko's body had crumpled in his arms, a spent force, his wild spirit flown with the rooks – and then: bang! A second shot had whistled past James, its wicked breath fanning his cheek.

Somewhere, someone gave a furious roar.

It needed no more. Old instincts, buried deep, took hold as James rose and spun in a single movement and then tore, half-crouching, back to the shelter of the oak woods, a fox streaking to sanctuary, to the echo of the rooks' reproaches.

Chapter 1

Every few minutes the beam of a giant arc light swept the roofline of the White City, cleaving the Illinois night sky to startle the grebes that rode the lake's dark swells. It lit the sleek undercut bow of Mr Larsen's steam yacht *Valkyrie*, which rode at anchor, adding lustre to her varnished hull, and it reached Evelyn Ballantyre as she leant over the port rail, staring down at the jagged reflections. She began counting the seconds between each raking shaft. One, two, three – and as the beam swept away again, she raised her head, following its course over the ripples to the pier a hundred yards away, where it lit the promenade with its booths and stands, shuttered now for the night, before rising again to illuminate the improbable cityscape of classical domes and colonnades, every roofline a string of stars.

The White City . . .

Briefly, the beam lit the aft deck where her father sat with Mr Larsen, their host. They were elegant in evening dress, taking their ease under the yacht's striped awning until the evening's engagement should begin.

'Alright, my dear?' her father asked, lifting his head and looking across at her. She nodded briefly and turned back to the lake. She had sat with them earlier, then risen, excusing herself with a smile that neither man noticed, and drifted over to the rail to watch the extraordinary spectacle as the miracle of electricity transformed the scene on shore. Their conversation had been dominated, as ever, by the day's newspapers with their daily accounts of bankruptcies and suicides, and she had found it tedious. How could there be *anything* new to say?

She frowned down at the toes of her sequinned shoes. It was a new pair, and very fine they were, very costly, purchased during a brief shopping trip after disembarking in New York en route to Chicago. The sequins glittered as the arc light swung back, evoking a glamour that, as yet, had no substance.

The White City. Back in Scotland, when she first heard the name, it had conjured up an ethereal, mysterious place of great wonder, and looking across the shore now, she thought it lived up to expectations. But there had been nothing ethereal inside the noisy Machinery Hall, where they had squandered their morning, nor in the Mines and Mining Building that afternoon. Her father, inevitably, had been fascinated by both places, engrossed by what he saw, probing for information about costs and returns while she stood by with nothing to do but wait and study the extraordinary fashions of the few women there who, like her, attended their male companions.

Mr Larsen had left a selection of souvenir guidebooks and programmes in the yacht's saloon, and she had browsed through them with a keen interest. 'The world has come to Chicago,' he told her with a smile, 'so prepare to be amazed.' She had browsed through the *Illustrated Guide to the World's Fair and Chicago* and *The World's Columbian Exposition*, which informed her that, quite apart from the main pavilions, there was a Japanese garden and a Chinese pagoda to see, a group of Esquimaux and a Red Indian encampment, as well as the well-publicised attractions of the Midway Plaisance. But her father had skimmed over those pages, focussing instead on the dullest of the exhibition halls, not for a moment considering what *she* might want to see.

Tomorrow, though, when the rest of their party arrived, she and

Clementina would leave the men to their machines and explore the wonders of the Woman's Building together. A whole building designed entirely by women, Mr Larsen had told her, filled with the creations of women, lined with murals which celebrated the different spheres of womankind, and with exterior ornamentation, the work of a sculptress her own age.

She glanced again at her father as he sat there, complacent and urbane, and considered what *she* had to show for her nineteen years. Buried in the rural fastness of a Borders estate, miles from Edinburgh, she was left for weeks on end with only the dullest of companions, an occasional drawing master and an enfeebled tutor who taught her classics. Did her father ever consider her feelings, or her future? Did he simply assume that she would marry some neighbour's son, as Clementina had done, and live out her days on a similar estate, while the world passed her by?

The thought terrified her, the sheer relentless boredom of it.

And could he not see, for goodness' sake, that it was boredom, nothing more, which had led to the Incident?

She gazed down at the water again, seeing how the reflections fractured into zigzags as the raking light swept towards the *Valkyrie*'s hull. A simple friendship, nothing more, born of loneliness and a deepening frustration – it had meant nothing! But the shock of her father's discovery had spurred him into action, and the outcome had left her more delighted than she would allow him to see. Nothing more had been said about it since that dreadful day when she had stood before him in his study and been asked to account for herself, but she knew that he watched her now with an unnerving intensity and a speculative eye.

Behind her, she heard him laugh at some remark of Mr Larsen's and raised her head to look again towards the enchanted shore. He watched her, yes, but he saw nothing.

The two men talked of visiting the Electricity Building tomorrow morning, before George and Clementina's train arrived, and Mr Larsen had chuckled at her expression. 'But we will see the Midway Plaisance too, my dear, I assure you, and Mr Ferris's great wheel. Will we take a ride, do you think? Have you courage enough?' She had returned him a tight smile. Did he consider her a child to be placated by a promised treat?

The giant wheel was visible now above the rooftops, lit by a double row of sparkling lights, an extraordinary sight, and she felt another stab of impatience for the evening to begin. But *still* they talked . . . What more could be said? There were financial and political catastrophes exploding around them, she had been told, and yet the two men appeared to be calm, so she could only assume that they had suffered no great losses. So why the endless debate?

'It won't be long now, my dear, I promise you,' Mr Larsen called across to her. 'Keep a lookout. The Wizard said to watch for the magic.'

Mr Larsen was a banker, one of a very small number of her father's business associates who visited Ballantyre House, crossing the Atlantic regularly once a year in pursuit of the bank's business, and Evelyn liked him. He was a genial man, generous of spirit and proportions, and he would discuss books and paintings with her, seeking her opinions, exploring her tastes. But invariably, as she struggled to express views half-formed or ideas newly considered, her father would take him away to spend hours closeted in his study, or out on the terrace with their papers and cigars, locked in endless discussion. *Thick as thieves*, she once heard the housekeeper remark as she sent afternoon tea out to them.

Not thieves. Oh *no*. She looked back out across the lake's gun-metal surface as the familiar sickening sensation churned her insides. Her father was respected throughout the county, a magistrate who upheld the law, dealing out the Queen's justice to thieves.

And poachers . . .

Quickly she shifted her gaze to the yachts moored close by and began counting their bowsprits – anything for a distraction. Eighteen, nineteen – there must be twenty of them, which, Mr Larsen said, had formed a flotilla from the New York Yacht Club. And now they rode there, pulling at their warps, tethered like restless thoroughbreds, magnificently *en fête*, dressed over all with bunting and flags, as sleek as their owners. Glossy paintwork bounced the light to brass deck rails and fittings, scattering it across varnished decks, while the aroma of expensive cigars wafted across the water towards her. Perhaps the same anxious conversations were being repeated there too, punctuated by demands to liveried servants who hid concerns about unpaid salaries behind an unctuous servility.

'Now what is the lovely Evelyn thinking, I wonder?'

She was familiar with the banker's avuncular gallantry, which was offered with a sparkling eye and traces of the singsong accent of his native Aalborg as he joined her at the rail. She smiled slightly and shook her head.

From the corner of her eye she could see her father, still seated, drawing on his cigar, watching her through narrowed eyes. Was he asking himself the same question—

'I'm trying to make sense of it all,' she said – and that would be the answer she would give him too, if he ever troubled to ask.

'Ah. The *sense* of it—'

Well-bred laughter floated across the water from the other yachts, and Evelyn gestured towards them. 'Where's the panic and the collapse you describe? The desperation—'

Mr Larsen grasped the rail and looked gravely across the row of lifting bowsprits to the largest yacht, the *Morgan-le-Fey*, which rode complacently in their midst. It had led the flotilla through the Erie Canal and belonged to the Wizard, he had told her, who would be their host for the evening.

'There's panic in the heart of every man out there, young lady,' he said eventually, then pulled out and consulted a pocket watch, its heavy gold chain stretched tight across his corpulent chest, adding, 'except in whatever organ provides that function in the Wizard.'

She heard her father laugh. 'And I don't see panic in the eyes of Niels Larsen either, thank God,' he remarked, tipping his head back and blowing blue cigar smoke into the night sky before rising to join them.

'But the money to build the Exposition,' Evelyn insisted, 'and these yachts, and the clothes, and the jewels— Where did the money come from, and where did it *go*?'

'That, my dear,' replied the banker, 'is what they are asking themselves.'

And then, without warning, the quiet of the evening was torn apart by a mighty whoosh and the gunfire-crackle of fireworks as a dozen rockets shot into the sky from the bow of the *Morgan-le-Fey*, blazing trails of light through the blackness. An appreciative sigh spread across the water, and those who had languished on aft decks rose as if called to worship, and within minutes the first of the launches set out.

'The supplicants go to entreat, and the hungry to feast . . .' her father murmured beside her, but panic was choking her senses. At the first salvo she had gone rigid, gripping the deck rail, her eyes screwed shut, her heart had stalled, but it now began to race and her breath came in shallow pants. She forced her eyes open again and stared out across the water, fighting a rising nausea and focussing on the dark shapes of the launches as they cut through the yachts' reflections, heading for the *Morgan-le-Fey*. And as the night sky exploded with starbursts and rockets, the air grew heavy with the smell of cordite.

———

She still felt shaken half an hour later when she was handed up out of the launch onto the deck of the *Morgan-le-Fey*, flinching as the last of the rockets blazed above her. They were amongst the last guests to arrive, doubtless gaining some mysterious advantage thereby, and the deck of the yacht was already thronged with people. The party goers were stylish, sleek and burnished like their vessels, and were putting on a fine show. Few of them were under forty, Evelyn decided, as she watched them mingling beneath the swaying shadows cast by rows of Chinese lanterns strung between mastheads, accepting drinks and exotic delicacies from servants who glided along the decks to serve them. And in the midst of them all a tall, broad-shouldered man was holding court. He caught sight of their party and beckoned them forward with a lordly gesture.

So this was the Wizard—

His real name was Jeremiah Merlin and he ran a powerful banking empire, Mr Larsen had explained to her. 'A financial wizard of legendary status.'

'Ha!' her father had retorted. 'As Beelzebub is legendary, I suppose. And his name's a travesty.'

'How so?' she had asked.

'The merlin is known as the dove falcon, my dear, but Jeb is more of a vulture, picking over the carcasses.'

Larsen had laughed. 'You'll keep that view to yourself tonight, my friend.'

'If I must.'

And so it had been all civility and good breeding as their host greeted them. 'Your first trip to America?' he asked her, touching her hand briefly and turning back to her father before she could reply. 'I hear your name mentioned a great deal these days, Mr Ballantyre—' He let the sentence hang there, to become a question. 'There are rumours—' he prompted, his eyes, heavy lidded, shifting between the two men. Her father blandly remarked on the splendour of the yacht by way of response, a deflection which clearly displeased their host.

'Rumours, Niels?' she heard him murmur as they moved away, their place taken swiftly by a thin, anxious-looking man.

'There are always rumours, my friend.' Mr Larsen took her arm and guided them to a space beside the rail where a dark-skinned servant brought them drinks. Evelyn looked about her, at the almost theatrical swirl of people and lights, and he smiled at her expression. 'Extraordinary, isn't it? Two hundred and ten feet of white pine deck, mahogany fittings and yards of gleaming brass. Schooner rigged, of course' – he glanced up at the masts – 'although I've yet to see her under sail for more than half an hour; Jeb prefers a twelve-knot cruising speed and knows his engine can outstrip us all. Ten staterooms, I'm told, six bathrooms, a billiard room, a music room, library, and a deck large enough to hold a small orchestra, and still have room for dancing.' He raised his cocktail glass to the light and showed her the etched design of a magician's wand under an arc of stars, above the shield of the New York Yacht Club. He took a slow drink, looking at her father over the rim. 'You'll have to watch him, Charles.'

'I will.'

'Not a grain of compassion.'

'I'm rather depending upon that.' Evelyn looked up at his quiet words and saw that he was watching Mr Merlin, who had brushed aside the supplicant who had taken their place, and was shaking another's hand. 'His father was a butcher from Carlisle. Did you know?' And he turned back to lean over the rail in contemplation of the lake water.

The rest of the evening was a deadening succession of polite encounters with business associates of Mr Larsen's. To her surprise, many of them knew her father, or at least recognised his name, and she was impressed by the deference and respect they showed him, while he, urbane and assured as ever, politely introduced her to them, his hand under her elbow. And with the same fixed smile she repeated the same answers to the same questions, and found them almost invariably ignored.

At one point a small round man shot across the deck to join them. 'Ballantyre! What the devil brings you here?' A large diamond on his little finger caught the lantern light.

'Fraser. Your servant,' he said, and presented the man to Evelyn as another business associate, originally from Perth, with whom he shared common interests on both sides of the Atlantic.

Evelyn found herself briefly under scrutiny, before being asked again if this was her first visit to America, then he too turned back to her father. 'What did you say brings you here, Charles?'

'I didn't.'

The little man chuckled, looking shrewdly at Mr Larsen, then back at her father. 'There are rumours, you know.'

'I've just been told there are always rumours,' her father replied.

The little man searched his face again and then turned back to Evelyn. 'I last saw your papa in an Edinburgh boardroom, young lady, with a bunch of hardened Calvinists who believe that the abuse and neglect of orphans achieve their redemption.' He swung back to her father. 'How did that matter resolve itself in the end? Did the governors suspend the warden?'

'He'll stand trial for the boy's murder.'

Her father's face had hardened and the little man whistled.

'Will he, by God! I thought they'd find a way to cover the whole thing up.'

'They tried.'

Evelyn looked across at her father and felt that familiar flutter of confusion and pain. The world thought well of Charles Ballantyre, seeing in him a man of unshakeable integrity, a champion of penal reform, a generous benefactor who used his money and his influence to further just causes. This much she knew.

She dropped her eyes to avoid his.

Once, she too had thought well of him—

———

Things used to be so different between them, easy with understanding, and bound by an unquestioning love. As a child she would kneel on the cushioned seat in the window of the music room at Ballantyre House, palms pressed to breath-steamed glass, and watch for him on days when he was due back. And seeing him, she would run out onto the gravelled drive, curls a-tumble, and he would dismount to sweep her off her feet, crushing her to him, or better still, he would lift her up in front of him, her short legs straddling Zeus, the great black stallion, as he held her tight. Later they would quarter the estate, stopping to talk to the lodge keepers or to the farmers, who would answer his enquiries in tones of respect and liking. And later still they would stroll together along the riverbank, through the scented evening, she skipping ahead or walking beside him, her hand in his. They would stop to watch the fish rise to kiss the water's surface, and his eye would gleam in anticipation of the next day's sport, pointing out the riffles which might hold promise. And as the heron lifted from the reeds to flap slowly homeward he would talk to her – describing how other children lived, how many went to bed hungry, had no schooling, no chance in the world, explaining that money and influence were a privilege and should be used to bring hope, and she would listen and nod, striving to understand the complexities of a world from which his devotion protected her.

And sometimes she would ask him about James Douglas—

———

The little Scotsman soon made his excuses, and as they watched him stroll off down the deck and inveigle himself into another group of guests, Mr Larsen quietly remarked, 'Testing the water,' and her father nodded.

'What do you mean?' she asked, frustrated by their habit of communicating by glances and cryptic phrases, which left her in ignorance.

'Not now, my dear,' her father murmured and turned aside, tapping his cigar into an ashtray marked with the yacht's insignia. Mr Larsen did not hear him, however, and explained in a low voice that there had been a strike at the factory Fraser owned in upper New York state, and several strikers had been badly beaten. One subsequently died, and the incident had caused a political furore; Fraser's inhuman work practises had been exposed, and his handling of the matter was widely condemned.

She watched as the little man successfully infiltrated himself into the centre of the group. 'He seems to have been forgiven,' she remarked.

'Appearances deceive, my dear,' her father murmured, following the direction of her gaze. 'And memories are long.'

'Could he not have prevented it?' The man was now slapping another on the back and laughing rather loudly.

'He was in Leith receiving honours for his work in the slums,' he replied, his tone dry.

'And returned here to newspapers crying *hypocrite*,' Mr Larsen added.

The word crackled in the air and she caught her father's swift glance at her before dropping her eyes to her lap, and she began playing with her buttoned glove. But it hung there between them like a poison gas, evoking that dreadful scene in her father's study back in Edinburgh.

⟶ *A month earlier* ⟵

'And who was the woman *you* were with?' Pink-faced, she had tried attack as a means of defence.

'That does not concern you.'

'Not someone you'd think of bringing home to tea?'

'No, shrew.' His eye had gleamed momentarily. 'But then I'm not a nineteen-year-old girl with a reputation to lose, prey to any sort of chancer. And it isn't my conduct . . .'

'A chancer? Patrick was not after money!'

'He was, my dear. One way or another.'

'*No!*'

He had stood opposite her, the oak desk dividing them, grim faced and sardonic, but resentment had made her reckless. 'And I suppose your friend was not? After money.' His eyebrows had shot up and she had sensed an advantage. 'It's the *hypocrisy*, Papa.'

It was as if she had struck him. He had blanched, his face rigid, and there had followed an awful silence while they stared at each other across an abyss that was wider than either wanted to acknowledge. Then his features had twisted in an odd expression. 'Yes, but I'm beyond redemption. You, child, are not.'

The evening on the yacht ended with a concert held, she decided, so that Mr Merlin could substantiate the claim that his deck could accommodate an orchestra. She said as much in low tones to Mr Larsen, who chuckled and squeezed her hand while the voluptuous strains of a Strauss waltz filled the air. Some couples were dancing – how extraordinary, she thought, that these expensive-looking people could dance and laugh while, if what Mr Larsen had told her was true, their fortunes were vanishing into smoke. Was it all a charade, and, if so, to what purpose? Defiance or delusion? Or did they feel protected against disaster, here at the Wizard's court?

Her father had abandoned them some time ago but she glimpsed him now, in the shadows of a bulkhead, talking to their host. He was half-hidden from view, and so did not see the man-servant who approached, bearing a silver salver. He addressed Mr Larsen.

'A telegram, sir, for Mr Ballantyre, sent over from the *Valkyrie*.'

Her father rejoined them a moment later, and Mr Larsen gestured to the telegram. He took it up, read it, frowned, and then passed it to Mr Larsen, who absorbed the contents and silently passed it back.

She felt a quiver of fear as their eyes met and held. 'What is it, Papa?'

'Just business, my dear,' he replied softly, before reading it again, and then folding it thoughtfully, sharpening the crease between forefinger and thumb, his gaze unfocussed. A moment later, when the music stopped, he leant forward to address Mr Larsen. 'We *must* find the man before someone else does. There's too much at stake.'

'But where to look—?'

'Kershaw will find him, if anyone can.'

'And you trust him?'

'Best agent I ever had.'

Evelyn listened as they began to discuss contracts and agreements, mineral rights, and claim registration – understanding not a word of it.

'I don't like it,' her father concluded, his face hawkish and grim. 'And I smell a swindle.'

And so the evening was ruined, and all Evelyn could do was listen in dismay as they arranged matters between them. Business, man's work. And on the launch back to the *Valkyrie* she knew she had been forgotten. There was an early train, she heard Mr Larsen tell her father, which would take Charles to a port from where he could pick up a lake steamer and arrive in Port Arthur a few days ahead of the yacht in order to assess for himself how matters stood.

She stepped out of the launch, tight lipped, and turned to go below, and only then did her father seem to become aware of her. He caught her arm, pulling her round to face him, and lifted her chin with a forefinger.

'It can't be helped, my dear,' he said, demanding eye contact.

'Can't it?'

He pulled a wry face. 'No—'

Mr Larsen looked on sympathetically. 'We'll manage just as well without him, I promise you, and I can spoil you without fear of paternal censure. And besides, your friends arrive in the morning.'

'And once Clementina is here you won't care a bit—' She gave him a smile that was not a smile, released her arm from his grip, and went below.

Chapter 2

Closing the cabin door behind her, Evelyn leant against it a moment, and stared at her turned-down bed. A weary-looking girl rose from the chair, awaiting instruction, and Evelyn let her unhook the fastenings of the unfamiliar New York gown, and then dismissed her with a brief smile.

Surely she could undress herself—

Mr Larsen's yacht was not as large or splendid as Mr Merlin's, but he had seen to it that she had been provided with every luxury. Her cabin had a fitted dressing table, a neat affair of walnut with gleaming brass cockleshell handles, and she sat at it now and began pulling the pins from her hair and stared at herself. A pinched and petulant face stared back, and she ran her fingers through her hair, shaking it free, then began to brush, ignoring the stinging hotness behind her eyes, blaming the tears on the tangles.

A slip of pink paper on a silver salver, that was all it had taken and he was away, leaving her behind, as incidental to his life here as she was at home, despite all his promises. She rose, washed quickly, and then climbed into the odd little box-bed and pulled the quilt up under her chin, but found there was little warmth in the silky fabric.

After that afternoon in his Edinburgh study, he had forbidden her to leave the house unescorted. Alarmed by his manner, she had dared not disobey him while, behind the scenes, he had acted swiftly, not consulting her until all the arrangements had been in place.

'You will accompany me to New York next month, my dear,' he had announced over braised lamb a few days after the Incident, and she had looked up. 'Once my business there is concluded we will travel by train and meet Mr Larsen in Chicago. He intends to join a flotilla of vessels going to the World Fair, and has invited us to stay on board his yacht. The world is going to Chicago, he tells me, and so we will go too.' He had watched her as he refilled his glass, a hint of amusement playing around his lips as he registered her reaction, and he gestured to her neglected plate. 'Not hungry?'

She had begun cutting up her food, chewing it carefully, not meeting his eyes lest he saw the thrill of excitement running through her. At last, she would see something of the world beyond Ballantyre House and Edinburgh—

And he was taking her with him, not leaving her behind. 'When we have drunk our fill of those wonders,' he continued, 'we will sail north to Canada—' She frowned, still chewing steadily. Her father had business interests in Canada, in the railways there, and so, she understood, did Mr Larsen.

'— where we shall go fishing.'

She had swallowed abruptly and stared at him. '*Fishing?*'

'Fishing,' he repeated, 'in the world's finest trout stream.' His amusement was evident now as he returned her look, then reached out to spear a potato. 'A fishing *expedition*, in fact. Tents, canoes, campfires and all. And if that sounds like dull stuff you will be able to complain about it to Clementina. She and George will join us in Chicago and sail north with us—'

She looked back at him, aghast. 'But – Clementina, in a *tent*?'

For a second they had shared the thought of the elegant, and very feminine, Lady Clementina Melton living in a tent.

He laughed. 'George is at least thrilled at the prospect and has succeeded in convincing Clementina that she will enjoy herself. Her presence will not only give you company but will also lend you respectability – a commodity you apparently hold in some contempt.' It was the closest he had come to mentioning the Incident again, and she had lifted her chin defiantly, encountering a look of grim humour. 'If it's excitement you were looking for, my dear, you'll find more of it on the Nipigon than behind a hedge in the West Gardens.'

After that it had been all bustle and haste to get prepared and she had hardly seen him. It had been a rough ocean crossing, marred for her by seasickness, but he had come to see her each day, and stood over her: 'Poor child, no sea legs yet?' and by the time she had gained them the skyline of New York had come into view.

From there, they had come here.

And tomorrow, he would be gone again—

She clasped her hands behind her head and stared bleakly up at the plastered ceiling of her cabin. It seemed now that it had always been like that. Business had become king, and was an unforgiving ruler. It had been the same in New York where, upon arrival, she had found herself passed into the care of the wife of one of her father's associates while he had disappeared to execute his business in the city. This had clearly been organised in advance, and the fact that he had omitted to tell her had fuelled her resentment.

Her chaperone, a rather overblown woman of forty, had whisked her away, clucking with disapproval over her appearance, and taken her on a whirlwind shopping expedition to redress the shortcomings of her wardrobe. Evelyn had been agog as she surveyed the contents of the glittering emporia, the trim salesgirls and the elegant customers, and her companion had encouraged her to spend her father's money but had done so with such a pushy, unwanted, familiarity that she had resisted from sheer perversity.

Now she wished that she had been more reckless—

Perhaps an outrageous bill would have secured his attention, as her altered appearance and increasing frustration clearly had not.

Her newly styled hair and modish dress had done no more than elicit a 'Very pretty, my dear' – and he had remained quite oblivious to her, as he was to anything beyond his own world. A world of business. A man's world.

She turned on her side to stare at the curtained portholes. *Just business*, he had said tonight, and that impenetrable shutter had descended. Business created wealth, and wealth bought comfort. They were very wealthy, that much she understood, and so her life was very comfortable. Nothing was expected of her except that she adorn her father's household until, presumably, he passed her on to some other man who would be her husband. And she could see no escape.

He never seemed to want to talk, really talk, about the things that were important, and sometimes he was away from home for months; and even when he was at home, he was unapproachable, hidden away in his study, engrossed in papers with instructions that he should not be disturbed. Amassing wealth had become his obsession in recent years – and it measured poorly against what they had once had, and had lost. Her mind shied away from dangerous territory and took refuge in a safer grievance, remembering how he had cancelled a promised trip to the World Exposition in Paris four years ago, and had sailed for Cape Town instead, returning with exotic gifts which had done nothing to ease the hurt.

Recently, as her resentment hardened, she had begun to grasp the extent of her father's investments: in South Africa it was gold mines, and in Canada it was railways. And she was beginning to understand how closely he was associated with Mr Larsen, and with Larsen's bank. And the banker had become a more frequent guest at Ballantyre House. Perhaps they met at the house in Edinburgh too, but she doubted it. Edinburgh was where her father pursued his civic and philanthropic interests, went to the theatre, saw his friends. And his women—

She lay there feeling quite defeated and listened to the gentle slap of the waves against the hull, and allowed her mind to unlock, just a little. If she wound her memories back to when this obsession with business had begun, and to when things had changed so dreadfully between them, she was brought back to that day five years ago, to the day the poacher had been shot.

Chapter 3

'Oh, but this is all *too* splendid, Mr Larsen!' Larsen ushered his new guests into the *Valkyrie*'s saloon and Lady Melton looked about her. 'So trim and so *elegant*.'

Larsen watched with some amusement as she trailed her fingers over the furnishings, pausing to adjust her hat in front of the gilded mirror, her eye skimming the leather-bound books which lined the bulkhead.

'Don't you think so, George?'

Trim and elegant, indeed. How on earth had Ballantyre persuaded her to come?

'My wife is terribly nosey, I'm afraid,' her husband said, with an engaging smile. 'She'll be into everything unless you explicitly forbid it.' Sir George Melton had that lean, angular look which characterised Englishmen of his class. Quiet, but shrewd, Larsen reckoned. Several years, maybe even a decade, older than his wife. Larsen knew the type well: they inhabited English country houses and were lethal with sporting guns, cards, and women, capable of drinking all night and yet be out exercising the horses at dawn.

Ballantyre had said he was a keen fisherman too, and that was all Larsen had needed to know.

'You have the run of the ship, dear lady,' he said, bowing, then twinkled at Evelyn. 'And Evelyn's been looking forward to your company.'

His friend's daughter returned him the same tight smile she

had worn all morning. It had been pinned in place as she stood beside Ballantyre on the station platform waiting for the Meltons' late-running train. Larsen had been aware of his friend's quick glances towards the station clock as the minutes ticked by; and in the end there had been time for only hasty introductions and explanations as the guests' trunks and boxes were unloaded.

Evelyn had stood by impassively, saying little as her father apologised for leaving them in this manner. 'It's too bad, but of *course* we'll look after Evelyn,' Lady Melton had said, tucking Evelyn's hand companionably under her arm. 'You'll miss the voyage up through the Lakes, though—'

'But not the fishing, I gather,' her husband remarked with a dry smile.

'Not a chance.' Ballantyre had glanced once more at the railway clock and picked up his valise, his coat draped over his arm. 'I must go. My apologies again, but thank you, Clementina, I'm grateful, and if you can persuade Evelyn to forgive me, I'll be forever indebted. Niels, what can I say—?'

'Nonsense. Away with you!'

Ballantyre's eyes had lingered on his daughter and then, abruptly, he had dropped his valise again and pulled her to him muttering: 'Evie, my dear child, *do* stop hating me,' and had planted a kiss on her forehead.

A strange stricken look had flickered over the girl's features. 'I'll come to the carriage,' she said.

'No, you won't.' Ballantyre had released her and pushed her firmly towards Lady Melton before scooping up his valise. 'I shall have to dash.' And with that he had set off down the platform and stepped swiftly onto the carriage. He waved once, a gesture lost in the steam blown back down the line as the train departed, and Evelyn was left standing with her hand half-raised.

Larsen glanced at her now as she sat staring out of the window, while Lady Melton continued exclaiming over the smartness of the saloon. There was surely more to this breach between father and daughter than a quarrel over some half-grown youth from the peat bogs; or had she fancied herself in love with the scoundrel, poor child—? Ballantyre had left Larsen with the impression that the matter had been nipped in the bud, before any damage was done.

It would be wisest, perhaps, to leave her with her friend, he decided, and he turned back to George Melton. 'The wheelhouse and engine room might interest you, sir, while Evelyn helps your wife to settle in. Then we'll have a light luncheon on deck before going ashore.' He ushered his guest through the door. 'I had a new compound engine fitted last year, more speed, you know, and less vibration—'

Clementina swung back to Evelyn as soon as they were gone, her eyes asparkle. 'My dear, show me *everything*!'

The stateroom allocated to the Meltons was, of necessity, larger than Evelyn's and every bit as luxurious. 'My, oh my!' Clementina looked about her, approving the neat desk and dressing table, bending to examine the drawers beneath the double box-bed. 'It's like a doll's house. Everything so neat.' She inspected the pens and stationery on the desk, and cooed over all the little luxuries, picking up and putting down hand mirrors and brushes, admiring a china pot filled with rose petals. 'What a treat this is going to be! And what a lovely idea of your papa's to invite us along.'

Something in her tone made Evelyn look up. Had Clementina been told about the Incident? She felt herself flush with indignation at the thought and turned away, pretending an interest in the door which opened onto the tiny bathroom and water closet. Clementina squeezed past her to see. 'A shower too. Gracious! I shall have to get George to try it first though. The one we had in New York was quite terrifying!'

Clementina continued to chatter about the wonders of New York, about the tall buildings and the stores they had visited, and theatres, and the strange people on the streets as she unpinned her hat and smoothed her hair, stretching her neck towards the mirror to examine her complexion. 'I could have stayed there forever, couldn't you? All those marvellous shops! But George said I was bankrupting him – and I'd no idea that I'd be coming to such luxury here. What a lot of money these Americans seem to have.' She picked up the silver-backed hand mirror and gave an imagined blemish a closer look. 'And what a lovely man your Mr Larsen is. George says he's rich as Croesus—' She put her hand to her mouth, and made a little moue of self-reproach, looking at Evelyn over the top of the mirror. 'But then again he *is* a banker . . .'

Her Mr Larsen? What on earth was she thinking? Her friend seemed taller and thinner than Evelyn remembered, more angular. More adult. 'He's an old family friend,' she said. Clementina lowered the mirror and gave a gurgling laugh which sounded much more like her old self. 'No, silly, I didn't mean *that*! Far too old for you. But when we get back you must come for a long stay and I'll see that you meet all sorts of people' – so something *had* been said – 'and we must persuade your papa to open up Ballantyre House again. The shooting parties he used to have were quite legendary. I was always too young but George used to go.'

And then they stopped happening—

Clementina's childhood home had been on an estate just twenty miles from Ballantyre House, and Evelyn had seen as much of her as anyone during her adolescence, although almost five years separated them. All too soon, however, her playmate had grown taller, started to put her hair up, and had glided away. Her marriage to George Melton Bart had been considered a good one, and had taken her south of the Border.

'What has Papa said to you?' Evelyn asked, and she saw her friend pause.

She began patting the cushions on the bed.

'Why, whatever do you mean?' She turned back to the dressing table, smoothing her hair again and glancing obliquely at Evelyn through the mirror.

'You know perfectly well what I mean,' Evelyn said. Clementina had never been any good at dissembling. 'I'm not a fool, you know. Tell me what he said.'

Clementina looked cornered, then shrugged and sat down.

'Oh, for goodness' sake! Only that he was concerned that you should meet the right sort of people and have a chance to see a bit of the world. And would we come along.'

Resentment surged. 'Did he say I'd been meeting the *wrong* sort of people?'

'Had you?' Clementina's arch expression made her turn away.

She felt ashamed of the incident now. Agreeing to meet Patrick Kelly had been a mistake. In truth, she had been relieved by his sudden departure from her father's household, following their discovery. It was one thing, she had found, to chat to him along the rides through the estate at home, but quite another to meet him, clandestinely, once they had arrived in Edinburgh. He had sat too close on the park bench, his eyes had been too bold, and she had not expected him to take her hand – she had, in fact, been very glad to see her father appear on the gravelled path between the two high laurel hedges, despite the scene which had erupted.

'So who was it?' Clementina's eyes sparkled with curiosity, but when Evelyn told her they widened in horror. 'A *groom*! Evie, what on earth were you thinking? Madness— And how damaging!'

Damaging! Anger surged over resentment. 'There was no harm in it. We were just talking, quite openly, in a public place—'

'In a *public place*!' Clementina's horror intensified. 'Oh Evie! I trust no one saw you!'

'It wouldn't have mattered if they had as I don't know a soul in Edinburgh, and no one knows me.' She made to rise, but Clementina pulled her back down.

'Since you will have it, your papa simply wrote to me saying that you'd made an error of judgement, and asked if I'd take you under my wing, so to speak, when we get home. He blamed himself, you know, not you—' There was a tap on the door and an announcement that luncheon awaited them on the aft deck. 'But no harm's been done, and no one knows, not even George.'

———

Larsen smiled at his young friend as she slipped into her seat beside him under the striped aft awning. He thought that she looked better already.

'This is too delightful,' Lady Melton was saying. 'Such a treat! Everyone was wildly jealous when I said we were coming to the Exposition. George is more excited by the fishing, of course, and has had his nose in Hardy's catalogue ever since we had Charles's invitation.'

'Expositions come and go, my love,' Melton said with a smile, 'but a chance to fish on the Nipigon—'

'— is quite another matter.' Larsen raised his glass in agreement. Melton had a slow attractive smile, and he had already taken to the man. 'I hope you didn't spend too much money, though; the Nipigon trout are unsophisticated creatures – they'll rise to anything. The skill is in the fight that follows, and then all you need is a firm grip and grim resolve.'

He reached over to pour drinks for the ladies as Melton replied, 'I treated myself to one of those new split cane rods with a steel centre—'

His wife turned to Evelyn. 'You've no idea how *much* there is to talk about when it come to fishing – rods, lines, guts, flies. Although I expect your papa must be just as bad.'

'Does he still tie his own special flies?' asked Melton, smiling across at Evelyn.

'I believe he does,' she replied, and Larsen saw that odd shadow cross her face again as she took a devilled egg. He turned the subject back to the Exposition, describing the wrangles over its planning and construction, the conflict over the halls and their exhibits. Then he gently teased Evelyn for her opinion of the Mines and Mining Building and was at last rewarded by a smile. 'Admit it, my dear. You were bored to tears.'

'Of course I was,' she said, with that delightful little lift of her chin.

'I should think so too! When there are all these lovely promenades and courts,' said Clementina. 'But never mind, this afternoon we'll explore it properly.'

———

After lunch, *Valkyrie's* launch took them through the gleaming whiteness of the Triumphal Arch and dropped them at the landing provided there for lake visitors. 'The idea of the Exposition is to celebrate four centuries of progress since Columbus landed,' Larsen explained as they walked beside the still waters of the Basin. 'Unfortunate timing, perhaps, given recent events, but I reckon it's easier for us to look back rather than forward in these troubled times.'

'Yes,' said George, gazing about him. 'The past can be a safer place to inhabit.'

Was that so? Evelyn looked down the length of the Basin to the fountain at the far end, twirling her parasol. The past was a place she rarely dared to venture.

Yesterday, she had stood with her father and Mr Larsen beside the huge fountain and her father had gestured with his thumb. 'So what's this all about, then?' he had asked, examining the elaborate statuary. 'A Winged Victory, some burly nymphs rowing—'

'Arts, science, and industry driving the barge forward,' Mr Larsen had replied, with a smile to Evelyn. 'Classical allusions, my friend, as I'm sure you are aware.'

'Ah! America, the successor to Rome.'

'Exactly.'

'Does the irony not strike them?' And he had turned away to watch the progress of a well-turned ankle along the edge of the Basin.

Mr Larsen had rolled his eyes at Evelyn, and tucked her hand under his arm. 'What makes your father such a cynic, my dear?' he had asked, and she had had no answer.

This afternoon, George seemed more impressed than her father had been. 'It's the sheer scale of everything,' he said, looking up at a colossal gilded statue which rose from the Basin, symbolising the unity of the Republic. Yesterday her father had scoffed at that too. '*Unity*?' he had said. 'What do the prairie farmers in hock to eastern insurance companies have to say about unity, I wonder? Have they asked the strikers . . . ?'

'My dear fellow.' Mr Larsen's eyes had gleamed appreciatively. 'You make the task of guide most unrewarding.'

'Do I?'

But Evelyn had looked at him, thinking she had not seen this side of him for a very long time. The old passion—

'And now, my dear.' Mr Larsen broke into her thoughts. 'Who is for the delights of the Midway Plaisance? I suspect that Lady Melton will wish to join us, but will you, sir?' George begged to be excused, saying that he would find his way to the Electricity Building and join them later back on the yacht.

Mr Larsen offered an arm to each of the ladies and led them through the gateway to the now famous Midway Plaisance.

'Where shall we start?' he asked them. 'Shall we stare openmouthed at the camels, or watch men in silken robes smoking hookahs outside the Turkish Theatre? Will you be outraged by the half-naked Samoan villagers, I wonder . . .' The Midway had been something of an afterthought, he told them as they proceeded down the main thoroughfare, and was hugely popular.

But the long summer's heat had given everything a rather faded appearance, bleached and tired. Evelyn found herself jostled by the crowd and began to feel oppressed by the noise and the constant buzz, overlain by exotic wailing music and the cries of the vendors, while above them snapped the flags of many nations. And there was a weariness in the drooping shoulders of the hawkers and showmen, a bored indifference as they tried to entice them into the exhibits, returning their sour faces and surly frowns when they resisted. Already several of the bazaars and emporia were advertising CLOSING OUT SALES, ALL GOODS HALF PRICE.

They stood for a while and watched a group of Esquimaux, clad from head to toe in thick furs, wilting under the relentless late August sun as they halfheartedly lashed at their mangy huskies. 'Poor things . . .' said Evelyn, watching as the men urged them to pull the sledges along dusty tracks, the animals panting, their tongues lolling and eyes dull. 'They look ready to drop; the men too—'

'The authorities threatened to withhold their food unless they wore their furs . . .'

'No!'

'. . . so the Esquimaux took them to court.'

'And did they win?' Evelyn asked as they moved away.

'A few concessions, nothing more. They are exhibits, you see—'

Larsen led them towards the Street in Cairo, where camels and their riders were bedecked in colourful blankets and robes. 'You want ride? Special price for lovely lady—' A Moor plucked at her sleeve, his face too close, while the camel swayed on spindly legs, chewing indifferently and breathing foul odours. Mr Larsen waved the man away.

The Ferris wheel, however, was quite another matter, and she waited with eager anticipation while Mr Larsen negotiated their tickets, paying extra for a private car to accommodate them. As it rose to the top, the whole complex of the Fair, with its halls and pavilions, basins, lakes and waterways, was laid out below them. Evelyn looked down onto the dome of the Moorish palace, and out beyond to the grey plane of the lake. A cooling breeze reached them through the open window.

'It really is a marvel,' exclaimed Clementina. 'But what will happen to it all when the Exposition closes?'

'They'll clear the site.'

'But the buildings, I mean?'

'They'd not last the winter.'

'Surely—'

'It's an illusion, ma'am. Straw and plaster over frames of timber and steel, then white paint and gilding. This time next year Jackson's Lake will be swampland again.'

Evelyn absorbed and considered this information as they began the descent. An illusion? Counterfeit— And she thought of the brittle laughter on Jeb Merlin's yacht the night before, and the anxious eyes. Straw and plaster, white paint and gilding—

The illusion shattered as they neared the ground, where the hot smell of humanity rose to greet them, overlain by the smells of animal dung and greasy food. They stepped out of the Ferris wheel car to find the afternoon had grown sultry.

'Tomorrow, the Woman's Building, I think,' Mr Larsen said, steering them towards a table in the shade. He disappeared, returning a moment later followed by a waiter bearing lemonade chilled by ice from a giant icehouse, and handed them souvenir fans. So they sipped their drinks, refreshing themselves, and began to talk of returning to the yacht.

It was then that the little drama took place. Their route back ran past the wigwams of the Red Indian Encampment. Evelyn stopped before a small wooden cabin which had been tucked into a vacant space nearby, and read a tatty poster pinned to its side. HERE, DECEMBER 15TH 1890, THE LAKOTA CHIEF SITTING BULL WAS KILLED WHILST RESISTING ARREST FOR PLOTTING A BLOODY INDIAN UPRISING. EIGHT POLICE OFFICERS DIED THAT DAY IN THE COURSE OF DUTY.

'And a great many more Lakota Sioux . . .' muttered Larsen.

'Just three years ago!' Clementina looked at the encampment in sudden alarm.

A dejected figure in dirty rawhide sat on the cabin door-step, scratching the dust with a stick. Was he too an exhibit? Evelyn wondered, unsettled by the thought. And then suddenly the cabin door behind him was flung open and two figures can-noned out onto the threshold, locked in combat, kicking and biting, cursing and tearing at each other's hair; an empty spirits bottle rolled out behind them. The first man leapt to his feet and attempted to pull them apart, shouting angrily, but they flung him aside, sending him stumbling into the crowd which had quickly gathered. He tripped, lost his footing, and fell against Evelyn, knocking her from her feet, and then landed sprawling on top of her.

It all happened so quickly— She heard a shriek as she went down under the weight of the man, and lay there gasping, inhaling a mixture of stale alcohol and the musky odour of his hot skin. De-lighted by the unfolding drama, the crowd closed in. The man had already begun to scramble to his feet when he was pulled abruptly off her and she heard an outraged voice. 'Filthy brute—!' And then the sound of a blow, and she saw the man sent sprawling in the dust. A stranger knelt by her side and placed his folded jacket under her head. 'Are you alright?' Dazed still, she looked up into a pair of startling blue eyes beneath a mop of fair hair.

'*Evelyn!*' Mr Larsen had pushed his way through the crowd. When she saw that he too was preparing to kneel, she sat up, mortified by all the attention.

'No. Don't. I'm fine.' The fair-haired young man helped her to her feet and restored her parasol to her, repeating his concern. 'Let me find you a seat. A drink? Some shade?'

'Honestly, I'm quite alright.'

Then a whisper of anticipation went through the onlookers and they parted as the Indian came towards her again, his face and shirt blood-stained from his bleeding nose.

'Stay back, damn you—' Her rescuer took a step forward, raising his fist again, but the Indian stared unflinchingly back at him before switching his attention to Evelyn, and he held out her fan. It was broken and soiled, and he apologised with a quiet dignity. Then, called from somewhere, two of the Fair's special constables pushed their way through the crowd, and seized him by the arm.

'It's alright, ma'am, we have him. There's been trouble here already.' One of them produced a pair of handcuffs.

'No, wait—!'

The constable turned to Mr Larsen. 'Are you pressing charges, sir?'

'It was *me* that was knocked down—' Evelyn protested, suddenly furious. 'And of course he isn't!'

The Indian began to struggle, resisting arrest. 'No, you don't, my friend,' the officer said, but in restraining him he dropped the handcuffs. Without thinking, Evelyn picked them up and held them behind her back.

The constable, taken by surprise, must have loosened his grip, for his prisoner gave a final twist and sprang away, pushing through the crowd, and vanished.

'Good! He had done nothing—' Evelyn thrust the handcuffs back at the constable and began brushing the dust off on her skirts. The crowd appeared divided by this outcome; she glared at them and they began to disperse.

Mr Larsen took her elbow. 'Come away now, my dear. Thank you, constable, but the lady is correct.' He turned back to the fair-haired man who had been watching the proceedings with interest from the sidelines. 'And thank you, sir, for your well-intentioned intervention—'

But Clementina, who had been hemmed in by the crowd, now stepped forward and put out her hand. 'Good heavens, *Rupert*! It *is* you! I thought it *can't* be . . .'

'But it is.' The fair-haired man smiled and, taking both her hands, gave her a peck on each cheek. 'Large as life—'

Introductions were swiftly made. 'Mr Larsen, this is Rupert Dalston, who lives not twenty miles from us. Imagine!'

Mr Larsen knew his father, Earl Stanton, it transpired, so there were exchanges of incredulous wonder that they should meet here, so far from home, and in such circumstances.

'Actually I spotted Clementina a little while ago,' the young man confessed, 'and I've been shamelessly stalking you these past fifteen minutes. Not seeing old George anywhere, and not knowing your companions, I hardly liked to approach—'

'Earl Stanton is a friend of your papa's too, my dear,' Mr Larsen told Evelyn as she continued to dust off her skirts.

The young man stared when they had been introduced. 'Good Lord! You're Charles Ballantyre's daughter—' He looked quickly around. 'And is your father here too?' Explanations were given, and his smile spread. 'We used to come to you to shoot, you know, years ago. But you were probably still in the schoolroom.'

He had a beguiling, lopsided smile. 'I expect I was,' she replied, and smiled back.

'Join us for dinner tonight, young man. We dine at Delrio's,' said Mr Larsen, and the invitation was warmly accepted. 'And come aboard for a drink first. I'll send the launch to collect you.'

Chapter 4

Larsen sat under the stern awning later that evening, dividing his attention between pipe and newspaper, and then put both aside to enjoy the spectacle of the setting sun, and to wonder how far Ballantyre would have got. The man was nothing if not driven! The first hint of a setback to his enterprise and he was off like a shot. And here *he* was, his first day *in loco parentis* and already put on his mettle. Brawling Indians and now a niggling concern that he was doing the right thing. He was out-of-date and out of practice; what *was* the correct way of dealing with young girls and young men who had never met? It had always been his dear departed's province, and his own daughters were long grown and gone, mothers themselves. But there was surely no harm in offering a dinner invitation since the families were long acquainted, and the Lady Melton was able to vouch for the young man.

Evelyn came up on deck but failed to notice him, hidden as he was by the raking shadow of the awning, so he was able to study her unobserved. He thought of the portrait of her mother, which hung in the hall of Ballantyre Hall, and the smaller, more intimate one on Ballantyre's desk. Caroline Ballantyre had been slightly darker than her daughter, and Evelyn had her father's eyes, tawny and very clear, as well as his resolute chin. She was going to be every bit as attractive as her long-dead mother.

Beauty, combined with wealth and an undoubted naïveté, attracted predators, though, as her father had recently learned. The

cryptic message *undesirable swain* on the telegram asking to alter
the original arrangements had told Larsen all he needed to know,
and upon arrival Ballantyre had described how he had come upon
his daughter seated beside a young man – 'a groom from my own
stables, damn him!' – in a shady corner of the West Gardens below
Edinburgh Castle. Larsen had listened sympathetically but had
been unable to suppress a roar of mirth when Ballantyre went on to
recount the difficulty which had arisen from the fact that Ballantyre
himself had been escorting a delightful dancer from the Royal Theatre into the same secluded spot at precisely the same time. 'Disconcerting for all concerned,' he had said, a wry smile acknowledging
Larsen's laughter. 'And a devil of a scene when I got her home.'

Larsen had wiped his eyes with his handkerchief. 'I can imagine, and it's often the Irish in these cases, don't you find? Groom
or a coachman. Opportunism and opportunity, I suppose, and the
fatal charm of that race.' Ballantyre had made a grimace. 'But I'm
delighted that it gave you a reason to bring her with you, Charles.
You should have done so anyway.'

'I know. And then the whole wretched business might have
been avoided.'

It had been one of those rare moments when Charles Ballantyre
revealed the private side of himself, and Larsen had offered him his
silence, a space for further confidences, should he wish for it. He
liked Ballantyre enormously, and felt towards him as he felt towards
few men, in awe of his energy and his intelligence, and over the
years he had developed an almost paternal concern for the younger
man's well-being, which went far beyond their business dealings.
Perhaps he saw himself in Ballantyre, that same drive and determination which had once spurred him on – and so it pained Larsen to
see his friend looking so strained and weary. Ballantyre was a fine-
looking man, tall with a lean, athletic form, but his face had become
almost gaunt, making his eyes appear more hooded. Something was

troubling him, something more than either the bank's business or his fledgling daughter's rash behaviour. Something deeper.

And he kept it close.

'I've neglected her, Niels, these last years, let her slip away from me.' Ballantyre had rested his forearms on the rails, watching zephyrs pass over the surface of the lake, roughening it to hammered silver. 'I turned my back and she'd grown up. I should have been more aware – but at least I was able to save her from her Irishman.'

Larsen had let the silence lengthen. 'Did you have to pay him off?' he asked eventually, and Ballantyre had snorted.

'My dear Larsen! He left with his hide intact and a very clear understanding of what would happen if I ever clapped eyes on him again.' Larsen raised his eyebrows, and Ballantyre had smiled slightly. 'Though, to be fair, I think the association was in its infancy. Evelyn swore she'd only met him alone that one time, and the lad said the same, adding, rather defiantly, that he'd felt *sorry* for her as she'd seemed lonely.' Ballantyre had looked bleakly out across the waters of the lake. 'And that's the bit that stings, as I think he was probably right.'

Larsen had said nothing.

And now he reached again for his pipe and looked across at Evelyn where she leant against the rail as he carefully refilled it. Ballantyre might have protected her from her Irishman, but she was prey worthy of more than enterprising stable boys.

———

Evelyn watched the hawkers as they closed up their booths along the promenade, the more determined of them pursuing visitors as they left. She took deep breaths, grateful for the cooler air out on the lake. It was close and rather stuffy below, so she had come up on deck but still felt unsettled by the afternoon's incident. It had all happened so quickly! First the fight and then being knocked to the ground – and then the horrid aftermath. She could still see the resentment deep in the Indian's eyes as he came towards her, his face and shirt bloodied, and his expression had struck a chord in her memory. She had seen his face darken at the constable's accusation, knowing he had already been judged and condemned, and that there was nothing he could do but flee.

As another man had fled—

And then the fair-haired man had appeared. Clementina's friend. The Honourable Rupert Dalston. He had offered no apology, although later, at the landing, he had been fulsome in his regret for having misjudged the situation and had applauded her for her own action in taking the handcuffs. 'Very plucky of you – and *absolutely* the right thing to have done,' he had said, smiling as he handed her down into the launch before excusing himself, promising to join them later.

Clementina had spoken warmly of him when they had gone down to their staterooms: 'Just fancy! George will be astonished when we tell him. They're very old friends, you know, although George is better acquainted with his older brother. Rupert is quite charming, and, you'll find, *just* the sort of man you ought to meet.'

What a pity her father was not here to see her, she thought, as the last of the booths shut for the night, doing *absolutely* the right sort of thing, and meeting *just* the right sort of man. 'Evelyn, my child!' Mr Larsen's voice startled her and she turned to see him sitting under the shadow of the stern awning, beckoning to her. 'Come and join me, and tell me that you really are unhurt.'

'Of course I am.'

'Good girl.' She sat down beside him and he tapped the newspaper with the stem of his pipe. '*Another* railroad company has just declared itself bankrupt! I've almost lost count of how many. Years of gross folly catching up with them all, and now the consequences to bear!'

They sat in silence for a few moments until she became aware that he was smiling gently at her. 'Life without Papa becomes more bearable now, perhaps, with your young friends about you?' She returned him a little smile. Papa was not so easily forgiven. 'It was unfortunate what happened this afternoon, but he would have approved of your defence of that young Indian.'

'Would he?'

Mr Larsen shifted topics. 'Now tell me, my dear, whether the Midway lived up to your expectations?' She dissembled, not wishing to appear ungrateful, and commented instead on the fine views from the top of the Ferris wheel. 'Yes, indeed' – he nodded – 'and from there the illusion remains intact.' His pipe had gone out so it took his attention for the moment. 'And the rest?'

'It was all very interesting, of course, but making real people into exhibits, and then treating them so badly seems wrong . . .' He glanced up at her from under his bushy eyebrows as he struck a match and held it to his pipe. 'It's like a *zoo* for people – they must hate it.'

'I'm sure they do.' He flicked the match overboard. 'But why are they there, do you think? These odd people with their strange animals and their exotic dress? To inform us, or to entertain? Like us, but different. More primitive—'

She looked across at him. That Indian had not been primitive, he had understood only too well what he was up against. 'I don't know,' she said.

Mr Larsen returned her a wry smile. 'Perhaps they serve to confirm our own superiority, my dear, and provide an excuse to civilise them, and to educate their children that this is how it should be. They console us.'

It was the sort of thing her father would say. 'And is it? How it should be—?'

'I imagine you know the answer to that, my dear,' he replied through a cloud of pipe smoke.

Lights had begun to appear along rooflines and pediments back on shore, creeping over domes and columns, restoring an illusion which was becoming more difficult to sustain in daylight, but its *faux* beauty confused her now, just as the day's incidents had done. 'Straw and plaster,' her host murmured, following her gaze. 'A stage set, and a display of confidence which cloaks a troubled nation, made foolish by the realities. Your father was right.' More lights appeared, sparkling bright against the blue-black sky, and the hum of the evening promenade drifted towards them on the breeze, while overhead the beam of the arc light began its nightly scrutiny. And then he leant towards her, his eyes suddenly hard and intent. 'You begin to question it all, I think. Excellent! You have your father's brains – so make sure you use them, for just beyond the fairgrounds there are children who go to bed hungry, while their mothers lie sleepless and their fathers take their own lives in despair. Those who were lured here by high wages to build the Fair will be queueing for food handouts this winter, begging for relief while the politicians squabble in their drawing rooms.'

Evelyn recognised in his words the same fervour and conviction she had once associated with her father, and quite suddenly she found she missed him dreadfully.

Then Mr Larsen shook his head, as if in self-reproach, and took her hand, squeezing it in his. 'But what am I thinking, God forgive me! You're young, my dear child, and so it's your *duty* to be idealistic! Forgive an old man's ramblings – I should bid you instead to enjoy the beautiful White City with your young friends, and be hopeful. Hope is sometimes all we have to sustain us.' He summoned one of the servants, sending him back for champagne, and they talked of other things and watched as a small launch set out from the shore and headed towards them. 'It is well, I think, that you've found another companion here. I know his father a little, and I also know that your father has been a good friend to him over the years.' The launch drew closer, and then the champagne arrived, and he took a glass, his eyes warm and wise, but he held it a moment before he gave it to her. 'Try to forgive your papa for leaving you these few days, my dear. He's at the stage of life when a man is driven by his work, and these are troubled times.'

There was a slight bump as the launch came alongside and the deckhands stepped forward to receive the visitor.

Later that evening Evelyn sat eating a syllabub, looking out of the window of the restaurant where Mr Larsen had taken them, watching smoke drifting from the funnel of a steamer as it pulled away taking the last of the sightseers back to the city. Rupert Dalston was sitting opposite her and had been entertaining the party with stories of hunting tigers in Nepal, from where he had recently returned. 'In the end we only got one, and that was because it was sick, or weary of life, I expect. Tigers are dashed hard to hunt these days, you know, unless you employ beaters for days beforehand to find the creatures.'

Evelyn had been only half-listening, her attention taken by the smart clientele who surrounded her, and the Tiffany lamps which cast a seductive glow on fine crystal and silverware. Haughty waiters glided among the tables. But Dalston's last comment drew her back. 'That hardly seems fair,' she said.

George Melton agreed. 'It isn't.' He had been on an expedition himself in the same region, he told them, some years back. 'Sometimes they even tether a goat in a clearing as bait to bring the tigers into the open.'

'But that's a dreadful thing to do!'

'Or else the creatures are driven practically to the doorstep, then shot by so-called hunters who hardly stir from their verandas. Permanently half-cut.'

'George! I protest! We went out and actually hunted the brutes,' countered Dalston. 'Besides you employ beaters on your estate back home, don't you, so what's the difference?'

'Game birds are raised for the purpose,' Evelyn answered for him. 'They aren't wild noble creatures like tigers. Killing *them*, just for fun, is cruel and . . . and unworthy.'

'Unworthy? *Unworthy* . . .' Dalston sat back in mock dismay, then leant, conspiratorially, towards Clementina, his eyes still on Evelyn. 'But, you know, she hasn't a leg to stand on, I bet she's been out there stalking deer with her papa and his cronies. Aren't they killed *just for fun* each season?'

'Yes, but we do eat them,' she responded, and Dalston acknowledged the hit. She was finding him lively company and felt very sophisticated in her newly purchased New York gown. 'Did you eat your tiger?'

'Lord, no!' He sat back again, contemplating her with an amused smile as he stretched forward and helped himself to a grape from the centrepiece, signalling for his wineglass to be replenished. 'Would *you* eat cat?'

'So why hunt them?' she persisted, emboldened by the smile in his eyes.

'For the thrill, of course.'

'Poor tigers—' She nodded at the waiter to refill her glass as well.

'Nonsense! It's what we do, isn't it? Back home we construct a whole social season around killing birds and animals. All those niceties of dress and deportment, you know, all the little rituals. Hunt balls and the like? Eh, Miss Ballantyre?' He raised an eyebrow at her. 'And all to stalk a stag in style or chase a fox with finesse.' He reached for another grape, then paused. 'Now there's a point, do you serve *fox* for dinner at Ballantyre House?' He sat back, his smile mocking her.

'Behave yourself, Rupert, and leave the poor girl alone,' Melton drawled.

But Dalston shook his head, pushing back a lock of hair which had fallen across his forehead. 'I merely defend myself, George. Now, where was I?'

'Not eating old cat,' murmured their host, who sat crumbling a piece of cheese and watching them with a benevolent expression. He shook his head at the waiter, who hovered again with the champagne.

'Just so. Although, in fact, I'm bored to death with the whole business, which is why I decided to go out west this summer and hunt buffalo. Now there's sport, if you will, altogether more the thing! Tearing along on horseback beside the beasts, not knowing if one will turn and attack you. A much more even contest, don't you think, Miss Ballantyre?' He raised his glass to her. 'Am I absolved?'

'Certainly not!'

'Man the hunter, the primeval urge . . .' Mr Larsen spoke softly, and Evelyn glanced across at him.

If there was irony in his words, Dalston did not see it.

'Exactly!' he continued. 'At home everything is so ludicrously staged, the whole absurd business! What with raising the birds, employing keepers to protect them, water bailiffs patrolling the rivers, then courts and gaols for the poachers . . .' He continued in the same vein, but Evelyn was no longer listening. Her eyes had become fixed on the flickering table lamp, seeing in its shadows the cart in the cobbled courtyard with the dreadful bundle wrapped in a tarpaulin, and the shocked faces of the servants as she was pulled away from the landing window.

Then the whispers and half-heard conversation. And then the dogs—

Her father, as she had never seen him, white with fury.

And then a name.

Chapter 5

A knot of tension coiled and tightened in James's stomach as the canoe began to buck and lift on the quickening current, and the river beneath him became a living thing. His jaw was clenched tight but every other muscle was working as they approached the converging cliffs and white water began to leap and boil.

'Holy Mother of God . . .' It was a prayer, not a blasphemy, spoken in awed tones by the man behind him. A lion in the board-room, no doubt, but the rapids on the Nipigon had reduced the steel tycoon to a terrified wreck, his knuckles white as he gripped the sides of the flimsy craft. James could almost smell his fear. He allowed himself a grin, savouring the moment, and set it in balance against a week of condescension and insolence from the angler and the rest of his party. While the Ojibways and French-Canadians could feign a lack of understanding and carry out many subtle forms of retaliation, James could only thicken his Lowland accent and play the dullard. And this had gained him the boss's censure: 'I don't give a damn,' Skinner had said. 'If he wants his boots pol-ished, you polish 'em. If he wants his boots *licked*, you lick 'em, and thank God it's not his ass. Go on, you heard the man.'

A great leveller, the Nipigon River. James felt his own heart racing as excitement kicked in, killing his fear, steadying his brain. He had never known the river so fast, swollen by two days of heavy rain which had fallen up north into Lake Nipigon, from where it charged thirty miles downriver, forcing its way over a series of

47

rapids and through narrow gorges to the greater lake below. And the canoes shot like arrows through the rocks, spared destruction by the skill of the men who were now his companions.

'Is that the worst of it?' the man behind him quavered as the river widened and the current began to slacken.

'Next lot in about half an hour.'

'Are they as bad?'

'Mr Wallace, that was nothing.' He glanced over his shoulder and caught an appreciative gleam in Louis's eye as he angled his paddle in the stern. In Louis's sure hands James knew they would take the rapids safely, and with considerable style, but he saw no reason to tell the man behind him. Let the river exact his sweet revenge.

The anglers had come up from Buffalo two weeks ago and this evening they would be delivered back to their train at Nipigon station, and would doubtless spend the journey east honing their experiences for audiences back home, omitting the grumbling and discord – and the fear. And then there was only one more party to take upriver this year: a rich American banker with four or five guests, two of them women. *Women?* The guides had looked at each other in disbelief when Skinner had told them. Why would women choose to endure the discomfort of a bug-infested fishing camp miles from civilisation, for God's sake? Surely Nipigon's legendary brook trout were an exclusively male obsession—

And yet James could remember horse-faced women in pantaloons standing thigh-deep in the River Tweed beside their menfolk – in another world. So why not here?

He rested his paddle a moment and breathed deeply, inhaling the spicy odour of cedar and hemlock, and was filled with a profound sense of well-being. There was a beauty to this place, wild and unspoilt, vivid and sharp. Between the roar of the rapids there were stretches of exquisite calm water where the river widened along its course to form narrow lakes which sparkled with a piercing clarity, their shorelines now gloriously aflame with low-growing maples and huckleberry. But did women seek beauty in such places?

Louis's low growl brought him back to the moment as, once again, the banks began to converge. Ahead of them the river twisted towards a dark incline, drawing them relentlessly on to where it would explode once more into a chaos of white water. James sat forward, tensing, and heard a low moan behind him. 'Alright there, sir?' he called cheerfully over his shoulder. If there was a response, it was lost in the roar of river water boiling over granite and grey-wacke as the birch-bark canoes were tossed like aspen leaves on a fast mill race. The other canoes came close, shouting out a challenge as they jockeyed for position. And in the next instance, James knew a jolt of wild joy as Louis stood and then, unblinking, stole a march on them all and led them through the submerged rocks beside great curls of purple water. James yelled a defiant insult at Death, who hovered unseen above the pines, and Louis answered with a whoop of triumph.

All too soon, the mad hurtling moment was over, ending in a deafening roar and drenching spray before the river widened and the current slackened. James's pulse slowed with it and he exhaled a long breath.

'Oh God. Thank the Lord.' The hoarse words from behind fuelled James's scorn. Had the man expected to die, imagining his body bloodied and broken, floating past the sumac and maple on the rocky riverbank? Gutless, he was— But the thought allowed a banished image to intrude, that of another body fallen beside bulrushes on the bank of a different river, three thousand miles away, and James saw again the scuttling coot, the booted foot in the shallows, and felt the grief.

And then the bewildered fury.

He shut his eyes, driving the image away, back to that closed place of a life that was done with. This was where he belonged now, in this wild place. It had offered him sanctuary and he was his own man here, never again prey to another's deceit and base duplicity. And, as the image receded, the pain of it was replaced by a blood-rush of delight, and he turned to grin at Louis. They sat, paddles resting on the canoe's side, and listened to the sound of Mr Wallace, steel baron and boardroom lion, vomiting violently over the side.

———

'Et bon débarras!' The eastbound train pulled away from the station and was immediately swallowed by the forest. Louis sent it on its way with a primitive gesture and spat on the rail, then draped an arm across James's shoulders, uncurling his fist to reveal their derisory tip. *'Sont chiches, aussi.'*

Smoke and steam drifted back down the track towards them.

They headed down the dirt track towards what remained of the International Hotel. Only the brick-built bar at the back had been spared from a recent conflagration, but that, after all, was what really mattered. It had long been a popular haunt of railwaymen, bush workers and prospectors, and, more recently, small groups of commercial fishermen who Skinner complained were ruining his business, damaging fish stocks. More prosperous visitors, and an increasing number of tourists, preferred the Nipigon Hotel, where there were some pretensions of elegance. There were fears that a rebuilt International might follow the same example, but for the moment the old bar still offered its shabby comfort, cheap drinks, and easy company. Its distempered walls had long since faded to the shade of pale tobacco, fire-blackened in parts, the whole place reeked of pipe smoke and spilt whisky – and suited the river guides very well.

Pushing open the door, they were greeted by a warm fug which issued from the pot-bellied stove in the corner, and James went over and held his hands to it. Last night the temperature had dipped low for the first time; the seasons were changing. Just that one more party to take upriver and then—

Then what? Back to Port Arthur to face six-foot snowdrifts and a frozen lake, bleak rooms and the sort of cold that tore the flesh off your fingers and froze your eyeballs. And a hunger which hollowed out your stomach; there were times last winter he thought they would surely starve. Would they find work to tide them over until spring? The question was already beginning to gnaw at him. He looked over to Louis, who was rapping on the bar for attention. Thank God for Louis; without him the prospect of winter would be unbearable.

He grinned as he watched him now, describing yesterday's trip downriver, leaning across the bar in mockery of the steel baron vomiting over the side before suggesting, equally graphically, that the man had also filled his breeks. He had, as ever, an appreciative audience.

They had met at knife-point four winters ago in a cold warehouse behind the docks in Montreal where James, starving and desperate, had forced entry to take shelter. Exploring deeper, he had found that some other poor wretch had made a place for himself behind the empty wooden crates, caching meagre possessions there. James had crouched down and was going through them, pocketing a nickel caught in a crack in the floorboards, a pair of much-darned socks, and was considering what the moths had left of a thin blanket, when his shoulder had been gripped and his arm twisted ruthlessly behind his back. He had felt the pressure of steel under his ear, and had been pulled to his feet while incomprehensible threats were growled into his ear. He had submitted without protest, waiting until the pressure eased, and then twisted away, slamming his foot viciously into the ankle of his attacker, and thanked Jacko's spirit for a sound and thorough education. He had banged his assailant's hand hard against the brick wall, but somehow the man had managed to hold on to the knife, swearing and slashing wildly at James, cutting through the worn seaman's jacket he had stolen some weeks ago to pierce his shoulder. James had yelped in pain, and that second's hesitation had cost him the advantage. A moment later he found himself flat on his back with the man's boot on his throat and the knife hovering just above his eye.

'Assez?' the man hissed, and when James made no further move, had added: *'Eh bien.'* Emaciated and dirty James must have looked less than his eighteen years for the man's expression had lightened. *'Un enfant!'* he remarked, looking down at him. He withdrew his foot but still stood astride him, the knife poised – then he reached down and pulled him to his feet, gesturing towards the pilfered possessions, and asked a question. James shrugged and the man peered at him. 'Polske? English?'

'English.' Close enough.

'So. What did you take?' James produced the nickel and the socks. The man had looked at them, then quizzically back at James, and gave a sudden laugh. He put away the knife and dug into his own pocket, bringing out a handful of nickels, dimes, and quarters; and opened his other hand to reveal a gold pocket watch. 'I did better. No?' he said. James had given a wary half-smile, flinching as the man reached towards him, but he had simply pulled aside the rent in his jacket, briefly examined the wound he had inflicted, and dismissed it.

'Come on,' he said, pushing James out of the cold store in front of him.

He had led him back onto the grey streets where snow lay in dirty heaps three feet high, where telegraph poles leant at drunken angles, their web of cables looping low, sheathed by ice. During the day wagons had reduced the carriageway to a track of muddy slush which had refrozen as night fell, leaving surfaces sharp and treacherous. Grey figures shuffled past them, wrapped up to the ears, clouded by the mist of their breath, heading doggedly towards whatever served them as home.

The man had pulled James past sagging wooden buildings propped up between brick workshops and stores, then veered down a side alley and in through a battered door, where the heat and the smell of humanity, unwashed and close, had hit them like a blessing. He had turned to James on the threshold, sticking out his hand, and given him a grin which James was to learn was his trademark. 'Louis Valencourt. And you?'

Friendship had been initiated by two bowls of a yellow broth and several glasses of some fiery spirit, and later cemented in a room above the bar where they had shared the favours of two obliging girls who had been drawn to the charismatic French-man with a pocket full of coins. The proceeds from the gold watch had been quickly spent, and James had thought himself in heaven. Since then they had stayed together, thieving or working, drinking and occasionally whoring, always scheming; Louis's fertile brain was never without a plan.

It had been about a year later that Louis had come into the bar room and dragged James into a corner and, in a low excited tone, told him about an island to the north, an island made of *pure silver*. James had scoffed. It was true! Louis insisted, leaning close, dark eyes gleaming, and there were tunnels under the lake which followed veins of the rich ore. Fortunes had already been made— He'd met a man who'd seen it with his own eyes, who'd worked there, and who'd told him where there was a stash of silver which had been brought up and hidden.

'So why doesn't he go and get it?'

'He was thrown off the island for thieving, but he told me where to look.'

For an intelligent man Louis could be unbelievably naïve, but he would not be gainsaid, and so they had got jobs that spring on a steamer carrying coal through the Great Lakes to Port Arthur at the head of Lake Superior. Too late they learned from one of the ship's stokers that Silver Islet was now all but deserted, the mine closed for many years, its tunnels flooded, the profits turned to losses. Louis had gnawed his lip, avoiding James's eye, and they had gone to look for other work.

James watched Louis now with the same affectionate despair. He was sitting at one of the tables and was deep in conversation with Marcel, a half-breed guide who worked with them on the river, his eyes a-glitter with excitement. James knew that look. He picked up his drink and was moving across to join them when the door to the bar room was flung open and Skinner entered, surveying the occupants balefully.

'Might've guessed,' he snorted, when his gaze fell on them, and he spat, hitting a spittoon with deadly accuracy.

'C'mon, Skinner.' Louis was unmoved. 'We did the job, caught some fish, didn't drown anyone. Have a drink, eh?'

Only Louis addressed Skinner in this manner. 'One drink' – the old man said, with a token growl, and the floorboards creaked as he crossed to the bar – 'then back to the lodge. And if you three're headin' off for a week you don't go until everything's ready.' Heading off? This was news . . . but he caught Louis's eye and said nothing. 'I told ya there were women coming with the next lot, and women mean extra work. An' with the amount they're paying, they get whatever they want.' Louis made a gesture with his fist and a crooked elbow which Skinner ignored. 'Whisky then, if Louis's payin'. Make it a large one.'

Chapter 6

Next morning the air was thick again, and sultry. The bunting hung limp from the masthead, and there was a pale, milky quality to the lake water. Larsen, an early riser, had just set aside his rod when Evelyn came up on deck, and he greeted her with a smile. 'Ah, the resilience of youth.' He gave her a peck on the cheek. 'Did you sleep well, my dear?'

'I did, thank you.'

He called for fresh coffee and rolls. 'And an omelette, perhaps? Or a perch pulled fresh from the lake this morning?'

She gestured to the rod. 'By you?' she asked, and he recognised her father's dry smile.

'Of course. But in truth I find the perch is a bony and tasteless creature. The fun is in the catching, not the eating – which must make me as contemptible as our new friend. I recommend the omelette.'

Rupert Dalston had occupied his thoughts as he fished that morning. Last night he had invited the young man to dine with them this evening, on board the *Valkyrie*. He seemed to be travelling quite alone and had accepted the invitation with a grateful alacrity, and this fact, together with the success of last night's dinner, had planted the seed of an idea in his head. But would Ballantyre approve? His friend's relationship with Dalston's aristocratic father went back many years, but it was a complicated one.

He looked across at Evelyn. 'Your papa and young Dalston's father are good friends. Did you know?' he ventured.

'Are they?' she asked, between mouthfuls.

Only the very surest of friends would have continued to bail the man out to the extent that Ballantyre had done, underwriting large debts to the bank long after Larsen would have called them in. 'In fact it was Earl Stanton who introduced your father to me, in those heady days when everyone was investing in railroad stock, and could do no wrong. They were part of the same syndicate, and he was even more obsessed with railways than your father.' Indeed, it had seemed to Larsen that the earl had invested in every high-risk branch line with an enthusiasm which was little short of reckless. Ballantyre had been more cautious and, as it transpired, more shrewd, steadily repaying a hefty loan from Larsen's bank and quietly disentangling himself from the earl's affairs, investing in the gold fields of South Africa instead.

Larsen stared out over the lake, his eyes grave and unfocussed. And now, as railroad companies were leaving the tracks of solvency in a spectacular manner, there was every reason to be concerned. The tone of the earl's letters, sent in response to Larsen's probing, had changed from an initial bluster and unfounded confidence to what lately had amounted to stiff-necked pleading, requesting additional loans and time to get his affairs in order. Earlier in the year Larsen had felt it necessary to alert Ballantyre to this as he was, by then, for all intents and purposes, a silent partner in the bank. Larsen had been intending to refuse the loan and establish a fixed timetable for repayment. It had been a difficult decision—

'Don't do it, Niels. Trust me. *Indulge* me,' Ballantyre had insisted when they discussed the matter. 'I'll stand surety, but don't tell him so, his gratitude would embarrass us both. If it troubles your banking instincts, increase the interest a little to rein him in;

he can afford to pay that, at least. And he can mortgage half the land south of the Tyne if he needs to.'

'I believe he already has.'

Ballantyre had raised his head. 'He *has*?'

'With Jeb Merlin, as I understand.'

Ballantyre had stared at him. Then, 'Good God. If he's in the Wizard's clutches he needs all the help he can get. Give him the money, Niels, and see if he can fight his way out.'

'Amidst this carnage?'

'Let the man try.'

Larsen looked again at Ballantyre's daughter and wondered if he had perhaps stumbled upon the reason for his friend's uncharacteristic recklessness. Was he perhaps considering an alliance with that aristocratic family? Rupert Dalston might be a younger son but he seemed personable enough, and Ballantyre would not be the first to trade his fortune for a titled connection. It hardly seemed in character, though, and Larsen felt a mild disappointment as he entertained the idea.

Evelyn too was thinking about last night as she ate her omelette below a cloud of circling gulls. It had been an agreeable evening, and after the launch had taken their guest back to shore, Clementina had slipped into her cabin and curled up on the bottom of Evelyn's bed, as if settling in for a cosy chat. 'Rupert's charming, don't you think?' she had asked.

'Yes—'

'He always was good company, and has a fund of such amusing stories. I suppose it comes of travelling such a lot.' She paused. 'He's hardly ever at home these days, he gets restless, he says. This time he was away for almost a year, and we rather missed him. Or at least I did – having Rupert around livens things up. He always has some diverting scheme or other—' She picked up the hand mirror to inspect her face. 'George says that he used to be forever in some sort of scrape, quite the despair of his papa. But I expect he's grown out of all that, and he'll be looking to settle down.'

Subtlety was not Clementina's forte. 'Maybe he doesn't want to.' Evelyn removed the string of her mother's pearls from around her neck.

'He'll have to one day, though. George says he'll inherit a nice little property in Yorkshire through his mother's family. He's not sure of the acreage but says it's enough to provide a decent income.'

Evelyn snapped shut the lid of her jewellery box and began brushing her hair. 'We really ought to know, don't you think? I'll ask him myself, shall I, as Papa isn't here.'

Clementina had not stayed long after that. And while Mr Larsen returned to his newspaper, Evelyn finished her breakfast, wondering if this was how it would be in the future. Had her father instructed Clementina to draw up a list of suitable young men, having first established acreage, from which he would choose? And she wondered if he would trouble to consult her.

———

The day continued overcast and humid, and having explored more of the Exposition, Mr Larsen brought them back to the yacht early, drawn by the cooler air on the lake. Evelyn decided that she had seen as much as she wanted to of the Fair and would not be sorry to go.

Clementina annoyed her as they wandered through the exhibits in the Woman's Building, expressing herself well pleased with everything they had seen, but Evelyn had still been oppressed by her morning mood and been rather disappointed.

The central theme of the exhibits seemed to be that it was in the domestic sphere that women found their natural place, and from there they should foster the seeds of civilisation. The much-lauded murals contrasted the lives of Primitive Woman and Civilised Woman, and Evelyn had frowned up at them. 'Primitive woman seems to be having a more interesting time,' she said.

Clementina had looked around in dismay and bid her lower her voice, but Mr Larsen had thrown back his head and laughed.

Dalston and George had not gone with them but had spent part of the day at a performance of Buffalo Bill's Wild West show which had set up on the margins of the Fair, and arrived back, well pleased with their experience. Perhaps she should have gone with them rather than with Clementina—

Dalston threw himself down beside her and pulled something from his pocket. 'Sitting Bull,' he said, handing her a postcard. 'The great Lakota chief. It was his little wooden cabin, you know, yesterday—'

She took the card and examined it. It showed the chief wearing an extraordinary eagle-feathered headdress which cascaded down his back to reach the ground. A beaded band was slung across his chest over a tunic decorated with further beads and quills, and the tails of small creatures formed tassels at the edge of his sleeves. Next to him stood a moustached white man in a heroic pose. 'And that's Buffalo Bill himself. Sitting Bull was once part of his show, you know, and travelled all through Europe with him.'

'Part of his show? Surely not—' She looked up and saw that Mr Larsen was watching her with a quizzical expression.

'He was with them for several years, I believe,' said Dalston, and Mr Larsen nodded confirmation.

Evelyn sat back, finding the matter quite incomprehensible.

Dalston meanwhile had begun describing the staged buffalo hunt. 'Their hooves really did make the ground shake. Extraordinary creatures! Made me wild to get out there before they're all gone— And then came the grand finale where the Indians attacked a wagon train, rounding up the women and children, whooping and caterwauling.'

'Good Heavens! And what happened?' asked Clementina.

'Guess—' drawled her husband.

Dinner had been set out on the aft deck in order to catch a breath of cooling air, and the crew had rigged up strings of paper lanterns overhead which gave the meal a festive appeal. Other parties had had the same idea, and laughter and snatches of music floated across to them from nearby yachts. The *Morgan-le-Fey*, however, remained in darkness.

'And did the Woman's Building meet your expectations?' George asked her once they were settled around the table.

She made a polite reply as they were served chilled champagne and exquisite little canapés, but Mr Larsen shook his head at her. 'That really won't do, my dear. Courtesy at the expense of honesty? No, no. Say what you really thought.'

She took a sip from her glass, choosing her words carefully. 'It was a little trite, perhaps. In places.'

'Trite?' Dalston's eyebrows shot up, and again he seemed amused by her. 'Go on.'

How could she explain? She was not quite sure herself. 'The exhibits were well done, of course, but a bit predictable.' She paused. 'It was as if the women had put on a clever performance, and everyone was patting them on the head.' She had everyone's attention now, and felt her cheeks colouring. 'Like children.'

'But it showed all *sorts* of things that women can do these days!' protested Clementina. 'You can't argue with that surely?'

'No—' she agreed, crumbling a lobster canapé on her plate, and wished that words came more easily.

'Others have said the same,' said Mr Larsen, smiling as he passed her another selection. 'Some were outraged by the fact that their work was presented in a separate building, rather than being integrated into the whole. There was a mighty row about it, and then the suffragists got involved too. Half the women demanding to be heard, the rest determined to silence them.'

Evelyn gave him a grateful smile and allowed her glass to be refilled.

'Well I thought the displays did everyone credit,' said Clementina. 'And it showed how women can have a *civilising* influence, through nurturing their own families but also by all sorts of charitable work. Something I feel sure your father would have applauded.'

Evelyn dropped her eyes to her plate.

'Come and hunt buffalo with me, Miss Ballantyre,' said Dalston, leaning forward in a conspiratorial manner, breaking the sudden silence. 'You could aim to miss 'em, if you preferred, and still have the thrill of the chase.'

'And I do believe she would go with you!' Mr Larsen said. 'But you're quite right to question what you see, my dear, and the Exposition has stirred up a lot of passion! There's been as much controversy amongst the women as there was amongst the Negroes and the Indians—'

'Perhaps they all felt the same,' said Evelyn; the champagne was giving her courage. 'As if they had to *ask* to be included.'

'Very astute, my dear,' said Mr Larsen. 'I see you've inherited your papa's perceptiveness, along with his disdain for the counterfeit.'

———

Throughout the meal, Larsen had been watching Evelyn and thinking that Ballantyre was surely going to have his hands full. The girl had a mind, and ideas, even if she lacked experience and the confidence to express them. She needed a chance to bloom, and maybe she could do it better in his absence; the shadow of Ballantyre's cynicism could be quelling.

By the time the covers were removed he had come to a decision, and when their young guest had gone, he took Lady Melton to one side and put his scheme to her. 'What would her father say, do you imagine? His stateroom is empty, you see, so accommodation is not a problem, but you must advise me on protocol. In America it won't raise an eyebrow if I asked Dalston to join us. You're here as *duenna*, after all, and I am too, by way of a paternal figure, and the families are well acquainted—'

Lady Melton had been enthusiastic. 'I think it's a marvellous idea! Charles would be delighted, I feel sure. Evelyn has had so few chances to meet suitable young men.'

'And is Dalston suitable?' His eyes followed the departing launch as it approached the landing place.

'My dear Mr Larsen! How can you ask?'

Chapter 7

In the forest north of Nipigon the light was fading fast. The tops of the pines were darkening against a crimson sky as James eased the pack off his shoulders and dumped it at the edge of a clearing. He stretched his muscles, then looked up to see a great double V of geese flying south with the sun under their wings.

They had covered a lot of miles these last few days, first by canoe, then on foot, and he was footsore and weary, but at least tomorrow night he would sleep in his bunk back at Skinner's lodge. He went to gather fuel from the forest floor, small stuff, just enough for one night, while Marcel gutted the partridges they had caught earlier, setting them on spits to roast. Bright mosses marked the way to a small spring and he tracked its course then filled the kettle from a pool of clear water. They worked wordlessly as the evening chilled and grew still, then sat in the arc of flickering firelight, their faces lit by the glow, and the darkness closed around them.

They ate quickly, the roast flesh salted by their hunger, and then stretched out their legs, nursing tin mugs of coffee, and they smoked.

And talked.

There was only one topic. How big would the seam prove to be? How deep, how wide, how long? Did it extend for a yard, a mile, ten miles? Did it branch and fissure? Would they need to sink a shaft or could they work a trench along the seam?

'How do we get the metal out of the rock?' asked Marcel.

'There's a process,' Louis replied.

Marcel looked at James, then back at Louis. 'What process?'

'It's not hard.'

Silence. Then: 'You don't know, do you?' Marcel's eyes narrowed, and James laughed.

'We can learn, can't we?' Louis pulled the stopper from a flask and drank deep, rolling his eyes as Marcel relit his pipe.

James smiled into the darkness as he watched his companions, their faces shadowy in the firelight as they continued to bicker. Louis passed him the flask and James took a swig, grimacing as it seared his throat. It was a mystery to him where Louis managed to find such poisonous brew. And for an instant he let himself remember the smooth taste of whisky back home, that sweet amber fire which coursed through a man's lifeblood to reach his soul—

But Ballantyre's was a treacherous nectar, so he'd take Louis's rotgut any day.

'We'll pan in the streams too,' said Louis, taking the flask back from him. 'I expect it'll be outcropping all over.'

Marcel shrugged. 'But we can't claim it all for ourselves. Achak would not agree, you heard what he said. And there are many men in the forest again – prospectors and railway surveyors, and more talk of another railroad line, farther north, above Long Lake and the north shore of Aminipigon. If the gold outcrops there—'

James looked from one to the other, and shook his head. The whole thing was sort of a mad game they had devised and now believed all spawned from that little word: *gold*! It was like a breath of promise, but a promise which drove men to a frenzy, addling their brains, as the lure of Silver Islet had done a year ago.

He leant back and thought over the strange events of the day. They had met Achak, who was not only Marcel's uncle but also an Ojibway chieftain, and talked. He had been an impressive man, and an intelligent one. He understood perfectly his particular

rights which included the unusual circumstances of absolute ownership of his land, and all its mining rights, outside of the terms
of a treaty which had restricted such matters for native peoples.
Marcel had told them that sometime in the past a white Montreal
trader had married a chieftain's daughter and had the foresight to
purchase a significant tract of land to secure it for his descendants.
The official document recording the sale, now yellowed with age,
had been so well drawn up that it was still a barb in the flesh of
surveyors and prospectors and had been passed down the generations with reverence. Until, that is, it had reached Achak's father,
Chief Dan, and it was then that trouble had started. Chief Dan
had been an avaricious man and over the years his greed, and a
growing taste for the white man's whisky, had led him to sell a large
part of the land to small mining enterprises. Too much land, and
too many enterprises, was his son Achak's view as he watched the
old ways disappear.

And then had come rumours of a large outcropping seam of
white quartz, wired and leaved with gold, and Achak had grown
anxious. A year ago he had confided to Marcel his fears that
mineheads would soon blister the cleared forest, and that railroad
tracks would crisscross the old hunting grounds linking shabby
townships with their bars and brothels. He had seen it happen
elsewhere— So Achak's grief at his father's sudden passing had
been tempered by relief when he discovered that none of the land-
sale documents had been signed, nor had the pending claims been
registered. Having established this to his satisfaction, Achak had
withdrawn into the forest to grieve for his loss in the old way, to
take stock and to reflect.

When Marcel had first told them all this Louis's eyes had sparkled, and he had been thoughtful for a couple of days. Somehow
he had persuaded Marcel to take them to find Achak, to try to
establish a claim. Just a small one. One that Achak might agree

to – no claims had yet been registered and the exact location of the seam was known to few. The original prospector had only been an agent, Marcel had told them, acting for another man. So this was the moment to seize, Louis had insisted, before others beat a path to Achak's door.

And last night, incredibly, they had managed to persuade the new chief to agree to the outline of a deal. He had listened to them in silence, surrounded by his dogs and his family, and then had nodded, and after further discussion the business had been done. They could mine on a limited scale over a defined area, dividing their profits with Achak and his followers, and with Achak retaining a measure of control. It was a better outcome than they could have dreamed of, and they would start next season.

Next season, when the geese returned—

James stretched out and rolled himself in his blanket, listening as Louis and Marcel slipped into the patois they used between themselves, and grinned again in the darkness. There was a glorious craziness to it all! Louis was undoubtedly right, it had been a moment to seize, but what did they know about mining? He might shrug off Marcel's questions, mesmerised by the glinting quartz samples, but between them they hadn't a clue—

He folded his arms beneath his head, and lay on his back, breathing deeply the aromatic scent of spruce blended with woodsmoke from their fire, and listened to the vast silence beyond the circle of its light, sensing the mile upon mile of virgin forest, which surrounded them. A great empty wilderness – unimaginable. Somewhere, in the distance, a wolf howled, and its cry was taken up by others, more distant. They would not approach the camp, but even so the three men would take turns through the hours of darkness, keeping the fire alight, a rifle in readiness.

He should sleep now until it was his turn to watch, and he closed his eyes and tried to clear his mind. But sleep eluded him, and after a while, he opened them again and lay staring up at the full moon watching as it lit the fringes of a cloud.

And, uninvited, a memory slipped into his mind – an image of how the moon shone on the bend in the river above Ballantyre House, transforming it into a ribbon of beaten silver. And he found himself thinking back to when he had lain beside another fire, with a different companion, sheltered by a rocky overhang, hidden by roots and brambles, and how they had listened to a different sort of silence. A softer silence—

But they had remained alert, not for fear of wolves but of men who despised them and wished them harm. Worse than wolves, and meaner. And there was an irony that here, in this wild place, James felt safer. He could travel openly, taking food at will, and sleep untroubled under the starlit dome of the heavens. No keepers stalked him, no landowner could charge him with trespass, no magistrate deny him his liberty. No one would accuse him – and as James stared at the night sky it seemed that Jacko's face stared back at him from the stars, weather-wrinkled and homely, split by his vagabond grin. But then the image fractured and he saw the old poacher as he had last seen him, a toothless wreck, half-crazed as he lay bleeding in his arms.

James rolled over onto his side and tried again for sleep. It was the same each year, the onset of autumn seemed to stir these memories.

Autumn had always brought trouble.

He pulled the blankets close, shutting his eyes, but found he was drawn inexorably back to that day, and to that night – a night that divided the before and after. And he heard Melrose's hooves ringing hollow on the wooden footbridge as he fled astride the mare, the leaves falling around him as he sought the old way through the woods, his passage lit by filtered moonlight.

Bad things happened in autumn.

Once it had been harvest and plenty, full hearts and full bellies, and he, at eighteen, had strutted about the stable yard at Ballantyre House like a game cock, complacent and self-satisfied. Then the shooting season had come, and a single shot had shattered the illusion. Blood had spread on Jacko's filthy shirt like the summer's colours draining from the land, leaving him betrayed and bitter. And cast out.

It had been autumn too, years earlier, when his uncle had died in a bleak cottage on the Kelso road, and Jacko had come for him, then a boy of nine, spiriting him away before the parish worthies arrived. 'They'll not starve you with their cold comfort,' he had promised, taking James's small hand in his. 'Your uncle was my friend, and now I'm yours.' And the old poacher had rolled him in his coat that first night, and he had slept curled up like a hedgehog beside him in a frosty ditch under the waning moon.

Winter, when it came, had been mild, softened too by an early spring and then a fruitful summer, but autumn had brought a new disaster. McAllister and his henchmen had caught them taking salmon one clouded night, using lanterns and harpoons. Jacko had put up a tremendous fight, inflaming the keepers' anger and holding them off until James could escape, yelling – 'Run, lad! Don't look back. *Run!*' And James had run, leaving Jacko to his fate, and had spent the winter working as a stable hand in the inn, fed and housed by the friendly landlord, gnawed by guilt as he awaited Jacko's release.

And then, joy of joys, as May blossoms bedecked the hedgerows, Jacko had come for him, lifting him high with a jubilant roar, swinging him round and round until he was dizzy. But it was a harder, angrier Jacko who had come, more ready with his fists and his curses, though not for James, never for him! He gave James only kindness. And they had had a high old time of it, living well off Ballantyre's bounty, taunting McAllister with their impudence through the whole summer and into the glorious autumn: they had stolen washing from the drying green behind the house, vegetables from the walled garden, milk from cows which strayed to the riverbank, and as much game as they had a fancy to catch. And that winter had been a good one too. Jacko had taken up with the blacksmith's widow and James had slept in front of the fire, well fed and content until the spring, when she had grown tired of Jacko's attentions and thrown them out.

James heard a movement and was wide awake at once. A shadow moved on the edge of the darkness, and he sat up. 'Wolf.' Louis spoke softly. 'Been there awhile, in the shadows, watching us. Cubs too, I think. Smelled the partridges.'

So the creatures had found them after all, they too made reckless by hunger. 'I'll watch now,' said James. 'Can't sleep anyway.' Louis passed him the rifle, pulled a blanket over himself, and was soon snoring. And James sat with the gun across his knees, resting his back against a boulder, watching the shifting shadows around the fire while memories poured through his breached defences.

Another year passed and autumn had come again, and Jacko was taken up a second time. James had hidden, cringing in the brambles near the riverbank, listening in horror to the sounds of Jacko taking a beating at McAllister's bidding: Ballantyre's head keeper was a vindictive man. James had remained frozen there, trembling long after they had taken Jacko away, too frightened to move – and that night it had been a fox not a wolf who had come, casting a contemptuous glance towards his fearful presence.

He had been only twelve that autumn, left hungry and wretched to fend for himself. And what a poor job he had made of it – just two weeks later he had run into the keepers as they sheltered in a copse, the smoke from their tobacco blown the other way. McAllister had grabbed him with a roar of triumph and thrown him to the ground, tearing the jacket off his back, pinning him down with a mighty booted foot while he searched his pockets for an incriminating snare. But James had been well taught and he had found nothing.

'Clever lad,' he had growled as he hauled James to his feet, twisting his arm behind him, his mean eyes narrowed, his teeth black and yellow, his breath foul. 'So it's Jacko's little apprentice, is it? Keeping your hand in while the old man's locked up? Mr Ballantyre's been wanting to meet you, my lad,' and they had pulled him wriggling and twisting until subdued by blows, and dragged him out of the forest, along the riverbank and onto the bottom of the manicured lawns which swept up the slope to Ballantyre House.

A low sound came from the edge of the trees and James stiffened, peering into the darkness. Louis was right, there were cubs, two of them, and one of them was growing bolder, making short dashes, scrabbling amongst the partridge feathers and gore for scraps. Somewhere in the shadows the mother gave another soft growl and the cubs returned to her, and as they melted away into the darkness the forest grew silent again.

James got to his feet, easing his cramped muscles, and went to put more wood on the fire. He moved the kettle to reheat the last of the coffee, although he was wide awake now, consumed by the past and the memories, sharp as the wolf cubs' teeth, that gnawed at his consciousness.

And as he stood there, staring down into the embers, it was Ballantyre himself whom he saw amongst the ashes. Ballantyre, as he had seen him that first evening, strolling on the terrace with his cigar and his dogs at his heels, his small daughter skipping beside him. He had looked up as McAllister dragged James across the lawns towards him, and frowned as they approached. But when

McAllister explained whom he had caught, the man had studied James with a disconcerting intensity, taking in his bruised face and torn clothes. Then he had dismissed them, bidding the keeper to secure him for the night, and feed him. They would talk in the morning.

⇢ Ballantyre House, Scottish Borders, Ten Years Earlier ⇠

James crouched in what was the only dry part of the outbuilding. He had been in that same cramped position ever since he had fallen after trying to shin up the wall to reach the small window only to find it nailed shut. He had lost his grip, landing awkwardly, and twisted his ankle. He could feel it swelling and wiped a sleeve across his eyes, mingling dirt and terror with unmanly tears. Blood soaked through the torn knee of his trousers. The rank-smelling horse blanket he had draped around his shoulders gave little warmth and no comfort, but he stayed hunched there in the darkness, cold and sleepless, in dread of the morning.

And of Ballantyre.

Ballantyre was the enemy, all-powerful, heartless, and hard. Because of him they had been hunted all summer and because of him Jacko was in prison again, and James was here now, on his own. Ballantyre owned the universe around them, while they had nothing. He had had Jacko sent down repeatedly over the years, even before the old poacher had taken James under his wing, convicting him variously of vagrancy, thieving, poaching, disturbing the peace – the length of sentence increasing each time as the courts demanded that he reform his ways. But each time Jacko had come out defiant and unbowed. 'Ballantyre wants to redeem me,' he told James, after the last time, 'but I'll not submit to him or to any authority which exists only to serve its own ends. When there're better laws,

I'll respect them. And until then I'll live by my own rules, in my own way. So let's see whose will is strongest – Ballantyre's or mine.' And James had looked up at the old man with worshipful eyes as he hawked and spat into the fire, sealing his defiance. 'God dropped me and Ballantyre here like seeds to grow beside each other on this same bit of land,' he had continued, warming to his theme. 'But Ballantyre was an acorn, see, and he fell on soil manured by money, so his seed grew mighty branches and became a strong and shapely tree, while my wee willow fell beside the riverbank.' His eyes had gleamed in the firelight. 'But it too grew strong there, see? – all secret, sending down deep roots and dipping its branches in the water, making shade for the salmon. Ballantyre's oak built ships for the empire and roofs for great houses while my willow was only fit for making baskets, or hiding the dabchick and the otter.' James laughed, but Jacko had raised a finger to halt him. 'And yet when the oak is felled all that remains is the stump, a feast for ants and beetles, but what happens if you cut down the willow?' James shook his head, as was expected of him. 'It sends out new shoots, my lad, low and wide along the riverbank, for the willow is a wily one—'

The door of the outbuilding was suddenly thrown open. Sunlight spiked James's reddened eyes, and Jacko's defiant image vanished. 'Out with you.' It was one of the keepers who had taken him up the evening before. 'And wash the stink off yourself.' He was shown the privy, and then the pump in the centre of the courtyard where he was told to strip off his shirt and wash while McAllister stood over him, arms folded, and other members of the household came to stare. He washed quickly, conscious of his puny white chest and thin arms, drying himself with his shirt as best he could, before pulling it back over his head, shivering all the while. When he was done, McAllister gripped his arm and marched him, limping, towards the back door of the house. They went through a wash house, draped with laundry, past stores and pantries, a scullery, the kitchen with its tormenting smells, and finally through a green baize door to emerge from the servants' passage into the hush of another world.

The silence there was reverential.

He gawped as McAllister propelled him along wood-panelled corridors hung with paintings and lined with polished chests, through an aura of order and stability where the heady scent of cut flowers mingled with beeswax and lavender. Silken hangings framed long windows, skirting the floors, and James gaped in wonder, swallowing a rising panic as he thought of the man who could command these riches.

Thick patterned rugs cushioned his footsteps as they crossed a galleried hall, and from above the fireplace a stag's head looked down on his impudence, while a retriever lay dozing, soothed by the tick of a longcase clock. It lifted its ears as they passed, its tail thumping a greeting, and it sniffed, intrigued by the cocktail of smells that James trailed behind him. Then a movement overhead caught James's attention and he looked up to see a child staring down at him through the bars of the galleried landing. He recognised the little girl who had been on the terrace yesterday, Ballantyre's daughter, and she gave him a sort of smile, half-lifting a hand. McAllister looked up, and then pushed him on ahead, stopping at last at a closed door and raising his hand to knock.

A quiet voice bade them enter.

The master of Ballantyre House stood at one of the long windows with his back to them, a tall man, erect and handsome, the embodiment of unassailable authority. The window overlooked the garden borders and beyond to lawns which stretched to the river, and beyond the river to the woods that were James's home. The man turned as they entered and James clamped his jaws shut to stop them from trembling and lifted his chin. *Let's see whose will is strongest – Ballantyre's or mine.*

The man gave him a piercing look, as if he had heard the challenge. It was a look which seemed to prise open James's mind, seeing every grouse snared, every salmon speared, every farthing stolen – and saw through his fragile defiance to base wretchedness. Courage curdled to despair – there was, after all, no contest. Ballantyre's will would prevail and it would take James to one of two places: Rothmere Hall, or the reformatory in Kelso. Or was he old enough now for prison? Jacko would have known—

'Has he eaten?' Ballantyre's first words startled him.

'I gave him food, sir.' Food? A stale piece of bread thrown into the outhouse last night as the door was shut and bolted.

Ballantyre glanced down at him, and seemed to read that thought too. 'This morning?' he asked.

'No, sir.'

Ballantyre frowned. 'Then have the kitchen send something here. Something hot – a bowl of porridge, I think. And eggs. Warm milk too.' James saw outrage on the keeper's face that he should be sent on such a mission and allowed himself a smirk.

As the door closed behind him, Ballantyre turned back to consider James. 'So,' he said. 'Poaching, my lad—'

The smirk vanished. 'You c'n only get me for trespass. He found nothing on me—'

Nervousness made him reckless, and Ballantyre raised his eyebrows. 'Are you teaching me the law, young man?' The tone silenced him. 'I need hardly ask where you learned such subtleties; Jack McDonald fancied himself as something of an expert.' James looked away and began studying the painting above the fireplace. 'How old are you?'

'Thirteen.' Was it better to be young or old? 'Nearly—'

'Well, thirteen nearly is very early to have embarked on a life of crime.' James continued his scrutiny of the painting; it was of an odd crested bird, black in colour with a strange beak. 'It's no sort of life, you know.' James made no response. 'Do you hear me—?' The man had not raised his voice but James jumped, and nodded before looking away again. 'Your patron got six months this time, I recall, and it'll be a year if he transgresses again. *Look* at me, if you will, young man! What's your name?' James told him, and the man nodded, as if this accorded with his information. 'So if you weren't poaching, James Douglas, what were you doing in my woods?' It was a simple question, but James had no answer, so he looked back at the strange bird instead, and stayed silent. It wasn't plain black, in fact, but a bluish-black, glossy like a raven.

'It's a macaw,' said Ballantyre unexpectedly. 'From South America. My uncle brought it back from his travels and it lived for many years.' James looked at Ballantyre again and nodded cautiously, for want of what to say. 'I don't suppose you know where South America is, do you?' James stayed silent. Why would he? 'Do you know your letters?'

'Some—' Jacko had taught him to write his name and to read a little, but he was not sure whether or not to admit to that.

Ballantyre came out from behind the desk and sat on the corner of it, one leg crooked across the other, and looked intently at James. 'But we've met before, James Douglas! Last spring, I think. Yes— I wish I'd known then who you were, we could have prevented this. You minded Zeus for me, held the reins while I went into the manse, and we talked.'

James remembered the occasion well, remembered the shine on the stallion's coat and the gleam of its rider's boots. He had dared to ask if the horse was of Irish stock, and Ballantyre had answered him and then stood beside him, discussing the horse's finer points with him, man to man, before giving him a florin – riches beyond a dream. And for a moment that day he had forgotten that Ballantyre was the enemy, the despised autocrat, and had felt almost shamefaced when he handed the coin to Jacko that evening.

But the old poacher had roared with laughter, flicking it into the air, snatching it back as it fell.

'Knew a bit about horses, as I remember,' Ballantyre remarked, still watching him closely.

James stayed silent and dropped his eyes to the fireplace; there were more curious animals there, brass dragon-like creatures which curled over the fireguard, their eyes catching the flames. It was during his lonely winter at the inn stables, waiting for Jacko's release, that he had learned about horseflesh from an Irish ostler there.

'And doubtless the tip I gave you that day just put beer down the old reprobate's throat.' Was there nothing the man didn't know? James was spared a response by a tap on the door and the arrival of a miraculous breakfast; Ballantyre indicated a small table by the fire. 'Sit down and eat. Then we'll talk.' He dismissed the girl who had brought it and went to sit behind his desk, giving his attention to some papers there, allowing James the privacy of his feast. He gulped down the porridge, scalding the roof of his mouth, and watched Ballantyre with a puzzled wariness. He took a drink of the creamy milk, feeling its warmth coursing through him, and then tentatively he lifted a metal cover and found eggs, light and fluffy, steaming beneath it. He glanced again at Ballantyre but he was still intent on his papers, so he ate quickly, wiping up the last morsel with a slice of bread, and then looked up to find that he was being observed.

'Better?'

His stomach fairly ached with the food. He mumbled his thanks and shuffled to the edge of his seat, unsure whether he should stand again or not, but Ballantyre gestured him to remain where he was and came over to take the armchair opposite him beside the fire.

'Is Jacko your kin?' he asked, and James shook his head. 'Have you any family?' He shook his head again but his heart sank. Orphans went to Rothmere Hall, a cold grim place on the edge of the village. He had seen the children from there paraded weekly down the cobbles towards the church, seen their thin, pinched faces, their eyes dulled by mistreatment and neglect. Could he invent kin? But to what end – he had nowhere to go.

The food had given him courage, though, and his eyes drifted over to the windows, and to the mechanism for locking them.

Ballantyre followed his gaze. 'So you're an orphan and a vagrant, James Douglas,' he said, 'and if Mr McAllister is right you're also a poacher and a thief.' James's eyes fell again and then slid across the floor to the door. Could he reach it before Ballantyre grabbed him? Unlikely – and he'd never find his way out of the house before someone stopped him. 'But if I send you to Kelso you'll end up in a reformatory where all you'll learn is tricks which will set you on the road to ruin. While if I send you to Rothmere Hall you'll bolt at the first opportunity and we'll have to catch you all over again.' He took a cigar from the box beside him and began tapping it on the lid. 'So – what to do with you, James Douglas?'

They sat in silence. Ballantyre studied the cigar, trimming the end before lighting it while James secured an errant piece of egg from under the plate and lifted it to his mouth. He glanced again at the window lock, the food now gurgling madly in his stomach.

'Good with horses—' Ballantyre repeated softly, and James's eyes went back to him. 'You won't find escape through that window, my lad. Not of a lasting type, and besides, it'll soon be winter. What then?' He sat forward again, considering James and demanding his attention. 'So let us discuss another arrangement, shall we? For the offence of trespass, to which you have already confessed' – he paused, seeking confirmation, and James nodded, wary again – 'you are in trouble with me, quite regardless of the unsubstantiated charge of poaching.' Big words, but James got their drift. 'So if you wish to settle the matter out of court, as I do, you must work in my stables for four weeks. I'll pay you thruppence a week all found, which means you'll be fed, housed, decently clothed' – he glanced down at James's feet where his dirty toes protruded between sole and upper – 'and booted. And at the end of four weeks, if I hear good reports of you, I'll find you further work and pay you a proper wage.' He paused, then added, 'You'll be well treated, James Douglas, but if you run off I'll have you caught and sent to Kelso, where you will doubtless be thrashed and driven far beyond redemption.' He then sat back and drew on his cigar, narrowing his eyes against the smoke. 'What do you say?'

James felt his face flush with astonishment. 'Why—?'

'Those are my terms.' Ballantyre dismissed the unformed question. 'Accept them or you're on your way to Rothmere Hall.'

James stared back at him, and when the man made an impatient gesture he heard himself stammer an acceptance. Ballantyre nodded his satisfaction and got to his feet. 'Well done,' he said and went back behind his desk where he unlocked the top drawer and lifted out a green metal cash box. Another key opened it and he took out a coin, and held it up. It was a silver threepenny bit. 'Your first honest earnings, James Douglas, paid in advance as a token of goodwill. Trust me, young man, and you'll find me a better friend than Jack McDonald ever was.'

Chapter 8

→ *Through the Great Lakes, 1893* ←

The *Valkyrie* swung in a wide circle away from its moorings, and smoke from its twin funnels blew back across the curved wake. 'And so we bid adieu to the White City,' Larsen called from the helm as his guests joined him on the stern. 'Did it come up to expectations?'

'Marvellous!' cried Clementina.

'Quite extraordinary,' Evelyn agreed.

'Expectations far exceeded, sir.' Rupert Dalston made a small bow towards Larsen.

The young man was socially adroit alright, Larsen thought as he relinquished the helm to the waiting skipper and stood for a moment watching the roofscape of the White City fade down the line of their wake. A thin fog hung low along the shore, adding to the unreality of the scene. If they had wind tomorrow they could put up the sails but for now they would take advantage of the calm to make progress under steam. They had some way to go. 'So!' he said. 'Go, my friends, relax and enjoy yourselves.'

He directed Dalston to where deck quoits were stored in a locker on the port deck, then retired to the shade of the awning, resisting suggestions that he would join them in the game. He pulled his panama hat low across his eyes, declaring that he would sit by and ensure fair play, and watched them from under the rim. Dalston was displaying excellent manners which seemed to come naturally to Englishmen of his class, and Evelyn seemed pleased with his company. With her father's possible disapproval in mind, Larsen had only extended the invitation to accompany them as far as Port Arthur, from where Dalston could catch a train out west and resume his own plans. It would take them a week, give or take, to cover the distance between Chicago and Port Arthur, longer if the weather played them false, and that would be ample time to see how things developed, and if all went well then perhaps the young man had a taste for fishing—? But that decision would be Ballantyre's when they met him in Port Arthur, and in the meantime – he tipped his hat forward to cover his nose – he need only to be watchful.

He dozed until the game ended noisily with claims of sharp practice from both teams, and Evelyn came and dropped into a deck chair beside him, flushed and breathless. 'The men simply won't admit themselves beaten, Mr Larsen.'

'Ah, male pride! You must understand, my dear—'

'*Beaten*, Miss Ballantyre?' objected Dalston as he collected the quoits. 'We allowed you to step a good foot closer than we allowed ourselves. So how—'

'Yes! But you set the terms at the outset and we beat you *within* those terms. So like it or not, you were beaten.'

The spark of animation became her, and Larsen raised a warning finger to Dalston. 'Take heed, Dalston, a Daniel is come to judgement!' He chuckled and patted Evelyn's hand. 'Some chilled lemonade, I think, to take the heat out of the debate.'

———

After lunch Evelyn stood leaning against the port rail and watched the rocky cliffs and sandy shoreline pass by, the wind snatching at her hair. Ripples fanned out over the lake as the yacht's elegant prow cleaved the lake water. She looked back to where the others were relaxing under the awning, reading or chatting in a desultory fashion, sipping cool drinks, content to let the afternoon pass. It felt strange to be marooned here on this little ship, leaving civilisation behind; the classical beauty of the White City already seemed like a faraway dream. But then that was what it was, after all: a lovely dream, insubstantial and full of strange contradictions. They had seen little other lake traffic, only the occasional pleasure boat or freighter trailing plumes of black smoke, and fewer even of those this afternoon. Mr Larsen said that they would make only one or two brief stops to take on coal and provisions but would otherwise press on northwards to where Lake Michigan met Lake Superior. There was little to stop for anyway, he had said, and indeed lakeside settlements had become more sporadic as they travelled through the afternoon with longer stretches of unbroken forest in between. It would take them another day or two to reach the head of Lake Michigan, and there would be time to go ashore there, if they wished, while the yacht passed through the lock system. And from there they would continue on to Port Arthur, their destination at the head of Lake Superior, and meet her father.

What a vast country this was—

'So, Miss Ballantyre.' She turned her head to find that Rupert Dalston had come up beside her, glass in hand. 'Still gloating over your spurious triumph?' he asked, leaning back against the rail, and facing her.

His hair too was being blown about by the wind, and his boyish smile was hard to resist. 'Of course.' She looked out towards the shore again, shy suddenly. But the informality on board was delightful, and such a contrast to the starchiness at home where a simple friendship had been so completely misunderstood—

'This is quite an adventure, don't you think?' he added. 'Much more fun than going on the dreary railway. It's like being at sea—'

'It's hard to believe this is just a lake.'

'It'll take us about a week, I hear, maybe more.'

'Yes.'

A little silence fell. Then: 'I was awfully glad to be asked along, you know,' he said, his eyes still on her as he sipped his drink. 'Time for us to get acquainted, don't you know, thrown together like this—'

Was he flirting? She wasn't sure. 'Lucky you could change your plans,' she replied. He had the most extraordinary blue eyes, clear and piercing, but she found it difficult to hold their gaze, and looked away again. 'Mr Larsen is a generous-hearted man.'

'He most certainly is.' They watched a flock of shrieking gulls swoop onto their wake as leftovers from lunch were thrown out by the galley boy. 'I'd never actually met him before, you know, though both our fathers have banked with him for years. But I expect you and he are well acquainted?'

'He comes quite often to Ballantyre House. He and Papa are good friends.'

Dalston gave a short laugh. 'And having a banker for a friend is rather handy these days.' He looked away. 'Greedy beggars.'

She started at his words, then saw that he was looking at the gulls squabbling over the pickings. He turned back with a bland, half-amused expression, and she blushed. 'Have you visited us too?' she asked, to cover her confusion. 'I wouldn't necessarily have known, you see.'

'Lord yes! Pa's been coming to you to fish and shoot for years. I came too, once or twice.' His eyes teased her again. 'I'm rather cut that you don't remember.'

Flirting, she decided, but found she did not mind. 'If you had been there recently, I'm sure I would have done.'

'That's better. Much kinder.'

She coloured again and turned her head away, wishing she did not feel quite so inept. Clementina flirted with Dalston with a careless grace, but Evelyn had had no chance to develop the art.

Only James Douglas had ever teased her, and she had been a child then and delighted by it—

And that, of course, had been quite different.

'Actually I've been out of the country a good deal recently.' He handed his empty glass to a passing crew member then turned to lean his forearms on the rail and looked out across the lake, his face more serious.

'Yes, Clementina said.'

'Did she? And what else has she said?' He turned his head to look at her. 'Has she warned you that I'm a Bad Man?'

She looked back at him, unsure whether he was joking. 'And are you?'

'Depends on your viewpoint. But I bet she said something.'

'Only that you got into scrapes, when you were younger. Is there more?'

He grinned at her. 'Let's leave it at scrapes, shall we. I don't consider *myself* to be a Bad Man, of course, but Pa does. And his cronies. Pa doesn't know what to do with me, you see, so I travel. Second son and all that.' He did not seem to expect a response and, after a moment, continued. 'I like travelling and since he won't let me get involved with running the estate there's not much for me to do. He doesn't like me hanging around in London either as I'm too expensive and I'm not army material and I'm certainly not cut out for the church, God forbid!'

She laughed at his expression of horror. 'So what will you do?'

'If there was a war the army might have suited me but a peace-time army's a dead bore. I'll inherit a decent little property one day, all being well, and settle down there eventually, I suppose.' But what about income from it? She thought about her chat with Clementina. The amount had not been established. 'Having an older brother who's a paragon doesn't help either. Steady Freddy, with his plump little wife who brought him a *very* plump little estate of her own and then provided him with an heir, equally plump, I daresay, though I have yet to meet the Honourable Infant.' His expression was moody now as he looked out across the lake. 'First of many, I daresay, and it all leaves me rather surplus to requirements.' A frown deepened between his eyes and there was a petulance around his mouth. 'So I travel, you see. And I hunt.'

She recognised a spoiled but neglected child, and felt a sudden empathy. 'That hardly makes you a Bad Man.'

He gave her an odd, unaccountable look then made a mocking bow. 'You're terribly kind.'

She felt out of her depth again so said nothing.

'And what about you, Miss Ballantyre? What do you like to do?'

'I should like to travel too.'

'Should you?' He had moved closer to her on the rail.

'It's tiresome always being at home, with nothing much to do.'

'My sentiments entirely.' He smiled at her and she smiled back, and then, hearing a distant honking, she looked up to see a great double V of geese flying high above them, heading south. So many of them! Travellers too—

When she looked down again she saw that Dalston was studying her. 'Do you ever go to London?' he asked.

'Never.'

'But you might?'

'I doubt it.'

'Edinburgh, then?'

'Sometimes. But I spend most of my time at home.'

'Ballantyre House is such a lovely spot, the envy of the Borders.'

It was, of course. Everyone said so. The old peel-house tower at its core had evolved into a substantial gentleman's residence, surrounded by lawns and borders, and these gave way to parkland with well-placed specimen trees and fine views down to the river. The parkland gave way to fields and woodland, and on the crags on the far side of the river was an ancient stand of Scots pine. Generations had moulded the house into this picturesque landscape and now it stood there against the gentle folds of a hill, settled and complacent, radiating an aura of serene entitlement. Had Rupert Dalston been calculating its worth?

She gave a tight smile. 'And it's always the same—'

'But isn't that part of its charm? What we've been taught to cherish? Solid and unchanging ways.' He paused, but she had nothing to say. 'Actually it is a while since I was there. Must be what, four . . . no, *five* years since.'

Five years—

She looked back up at the geese which were now overhead and began counting them, rather desperately, knowing by some sort of intuition where his next words would lead. 'Not since that ghastly business with the poacher and your father's keeper.' She swallowed, and looked aside, feeling a pulse starting to thud in her temple. 'But you were just a child then, of course.' She gave a slight nod but stayed silent and held on to the rail. 'They never caught that lad, did they?'

'No.'

She made a play of catching her hair and twisting it back into order, and kept her face turned away from him.

Not a word had been heard of James Douglas since that night; he might be dead for all she knew. 'Such a kick in the teeth for your father, after taking the wretch in, and all— But that sort always revert to type, you know, no matter what's done for them.'

That sort.

James Douglas was *that sort*. Dalston was only saying what everyone else had said, but she felt a spurt of anger. *That* sort – little better than vermin, and no better than the old poacher who had been shot. Shot dead. She felt the familiar wave of horror and gripped the rail tight, staring out across the lake. With relief she heard Mr Larsen call to them to join the others on the aft deck for tea.

'Teatime, I imagine,' said Dalson, offering her his arm. 'Shall we go?'

In the shadow of the awning, Evelyn played with a slice of cake while the others marvelled at the speed they were making. As soon as she could she rose and made an excuse: 'I think I'll just lie down for a while before dinner, I've the beginnings of a headache. The wind, I imagine, and the sun—' No, no really she had no need for headache powders, the tea had helped. 'Just half an hour and then I'm sure I'll be fine.'

She smiled briefly, slipped away, and went below. Closing the door of her cabin behind her she threw herself onto the bed and flung an arm across her eyes.

→ Ballantyre House, Five Years Earlier ←

'Come away, miss! You *must*! Come now—' Miss Carstairs pulled her away from the long window on the landing but Evelyn wriggled free and ran downstairs, calling out for her father, with the governess in hot pursuit. She pelted across the hall to reach the study door and flung it open, her breath coming in gulping sobs as she catapulted into the room. 'Papa!'

But he was not alone. He was standing with his back to the fireplace and had a face like thunder. It seemed that he had been addressing an older man who sat smoking in one of the leather armchairs, but he swung round at her sudden entry and then stared at her as if she were a stranger. Her stomach turned over at his expression. 'Papa—?'

'Take her away, Miss Carstairs.'

'*No!* Wait, Papa. They're saying—'

'Now, if you will, Carstairs. *Now!*' He was white-lipped, and this was a tone she had never heard before.

Miss Carstairs gabbled another apology and pulled Evelyn out of the room and back up the stairs in tearful revolt. 'It *wasn't* James. I *know* it wasn't.' But she was told to hush, and her shaking body was bundled into a nightgown and unceremoniously into bed. Warm milk and a biscuit were sent for and Miss Carstairs stayed, as if on guard, until, still gulping fitfully, Evelyn fell asleep.

Some hours later she woke to darkness and a sickening weight of dread. It took a moment for her mind to recall its cause and then the ghastly image she had seen came into focus – the cart with the bundle wrapped in oilcloth, the boots protruding, the uppers curling away from their soles. And then the whispers that had spread through the house like a yellow poison. No— It all snapped back into place and she sat up. *No!* She must find her father . . . and *make* him listen.

She could hear Miss Carstairs snoring through the closed door of the adjoining room so she pulled on her dressing gown and sped barefoot down the dark corridor to her father's room – only to find it empty, his bed not slept in. She was momentarily nonplussed, then became aware of voices below, and laughter, and glanced at the clock on the mantelpiece. It was not yet midnight.

Slowly, soundlessly, she retraced her steps and then slipped down the back stairs and into the passage below, encountering no one, and emerged through the green baize door and stood a moment listening. The sounds were coming from the drawing room, and she remembered the guests who had been arriving in the course of the afternoon. The shooting party—! She had quite forgotten. That was where he would be, of course, with his guests.

And yet how could it be? There was a man lying dead on a cart in the courtyard, a man known to them, and yet people were drinking and laughing, carrying on as if nothing had happened! But even so, she could hardly go to him there, amongst them all – and yet she *must* talk to him. He was *wrong*!

And he had sent the hounds out after James, which was a terrible thing to do.

Then she remembered the look on his face, the white-lipped fury, and felt sick. A shiver went through her.

It *couldn't* have been James. He had loved Jacko, despite everything that had happened, he loved the old man. She knew he did. She hopped from foot to frozen foot, chewing at her lip as she considered her options. Leaving matters as they stood was impossible – but what could she do? Then an idea came to her. Her father often went to his study for a last read of the newspaper, or a final cigar, and there might still be a fire in the grate. She could wait for him there, all night if she had to.

She glided down the corridor, like a small ghost, raising a passing interest from the dog who lifted a lazy eyelid as she crossed the hall to reach the study. At the door she paused and pressed her ear close, anxious to avoid a repetition of her earlier encounter there. No voices. But there was movement— He was in there! Relief flooded through her and she turned the handle, keeping her eye to the crack as she opened the door.

But why was he in the dark—?

The gap widened and she saw him bent over the desk, intent upon something there. '*Papa?*' she whispered, and his head flew up. And then there was a knife in his hand, and the moonlight played along its blade—

A scream caught in her throat, and became a gasp. 'James!'

The silhouetted figure stared back at her in disbelief. Then: 'Go back to bed, Miss Evie,' he said. The blade flashed silver, and her eyes fixed on it in horror. He laid it quickly on the desk, holding up his empty hand for her to see. 'It's alright. But go! Quickly now . . .'

She couldn't. She had turned to stone.

Then she took a step forward, instinctively pulling the door closed behind her, and started trembling again. As her eyes grew accustomed to the pale moonlight, she saw that a saddlebag lay on the desk, coins spilling from it – coins from the green metal cash box which her father kept locked away, occasionally taking it out to produce a penny or tuppence to reward her schoolwork. He kept it in his desk drawer, a drawer which was now wide open, its walnut veneer splintered and broken around the lock. The lid of the cash box had been wrenched off too, and its contents were scattered across the polished surface of the desk. Coppers, silver and gold sovereigns.

James was *robbing* her father—

'Go back to bed, Miss Evie,' he repeated as indignation swelled in her. 'Don't cry out. Don't make a sound. Just go.'

He resumed his task, his eyes not leaving her as he continued filling the bag. He glanced just once at the long window behind him and she saw that it too had been forced, a pane broken to release the lock.

She felt winded, hollowed out, and sick again, as she watched him push another fistful of coins into the bag, his eyes still on her.

If James could rob, could he also kill? She took a step backwards, licking dry lips, her dressing gown bunched in her hand, ready to flee, and looked down at the splinters of wood at his feet, and then back at the leather bag in his hand. And beside it, the knife. 'They're looking for you,' she whispered, uncertain now. 'They say you shot Jacko.'

The cash box emptied, James pulled the strap of the saddlebag through the buckle, his movements quick and angry. 'Is that what your father told you?' He slipped the knife into his belt.

She shook her head. Not her father, no, he had sent her away, his face a mask of unfathomable fury, but it was what she had heard whispered through the household. 'You were at the river, helping Jacko set his nets, and you quarrelled . . .'

Moonlight lit an ugly expression on his face. 'So that's the story, is it?' The light also revealed a dark stain on his shirt front and sleeve, and she stared at it, her tongue cleaved to the roof of her mouth. James moved so that he was in shadow again. 'He died in my arms, Evie,' he spoke quietly, 'but not by my hand. I swear it.'

'Then why—?'

He hitched the bag up onto his shoulder, and took a step towards the window. 'Because a bloodstained shirt and your father's lies will be enough to hang me, don't you think?' He looked down at his discoloured sleeve. 'Then he'll have *my* blood on his conscience as well—'

They both started as the stable clock began to strike midnight and James swore. The sound was followed by a great whooshing noise and then a succession of loud bangs as the first of the fireworks lit the sky. Evelyn squeezed her eyes closed to shut out the terrible sound, and the even more terrible words. Cries of appreciation and laughter reached them from the terrace where the guests had gathered to watch the display, and Evelyn opened her eyes again. 'You're lying—' she said, but James already had one leg astride the windowsill, and was pulling the bag after him. She flew to the window and grabbed at his sleeve. 'You're lying, James Douglas. Tell me what happened!'

He detached her fingers impatiently. 'Ask your father,' he replied, and with that he slid over the edge of the sill and was gone.

Evelyn began to shake. 'He wouldn't have—' she whispered into the darkness. Another burst of stars punctured the night sky, and the smell of cordite became the smell of nightmare.

Chapter 9

'There, see it! That line of smoke on the horizon? Port Arthur.' Mr Larsen had ordered the yacht's engine to be cut, and they were scudding across the water, like a great white bird. It was all quite lovely! 'Canada's little Chicago of the North; from tents to boom town in the blink of an eye.' Evelyn felt a surge of excitement, looking up at the swelling expanse of white sail, listening to the creak of the rigging and rejoicing that the thrumming of the engine at last had stopped. They had been steaming well into the night these last few days, and she had begun to crave silence. She smiled at Mr Larsen's enthusiasm, and he patted her arm. 'You'll soon see, my dear. Hotels, depots, stores, and even an electric streetcar. Port Arthur will still be growing long after the White City is forgotten.'

Dalston joined them, invigorated after a spell at the helm, and stood beside her at the bow. Quite close. 'But there's nothing up here but trees!' he said, and it was true. They had stopped once or twice en route but there had been little to see except haphazard settlements spilling down to the shoreline, their jetties and wharves reaching out into the lake. They had passed islands, some little more than bare rocks, none of them inhabited, with only the roots of shapely pine trees clinging to them. Occasionally they saw a puff of smoke rising above what seemed like unbroken forest; Mr Larsen said they were probably native settlements. 'So what's making the place boom?' he asked.

'Furs, then silver, and now it's the railways bringing wheat from the west.' He handed Dalston a telescope. 'See those big high buildings? Grain silos. Canadian grain will soon be feeding Europe, my friend.'

Evelyn stood between Mr Larsen and Rupert, only half-listening as she lifted her chin, turning her cheeks to savour the wind fresh on her face, careless of her hair streaming behind her.

George came up behind her. 'You have a new figurehead, Mr Larsen,' he said, with a smile.

Mr Larsen turned to see. 'And a very fine one too, though not for this ship. I can't imagine Evelyn as a Valkyrie.'

'What *are* Valkyries?' asked Clementina, tucking her hand into the crook of her husband's arm.

'Beautiful harbingers of death, dear lady. They choose which warriors live and which must die, and then bring the chosen ones to Valhalla to prepare for the final battle.'

'An interesting choice of name, then—' George remarked.

'Not if its owner's a banker.' Rupert spoke softly, his head turned towards George but forgetful of the wind which blew his words back.

Mr Larsen chuckled: 'And not if that banker was raised on Norse myths, and is a devotee of Wagner.' Evelyn felt mortified on Rupert's behalf, but their host was continuing, apparently unoffended. 'Do you see that island?' He pointed ahead of them to a long low island. 'From the town it looks like a sleeping giant guarding the entrance to Thunder Bay. Legend has it that he was turned to stone because of man's lust for riches. His name—' He broke off as one of the stewards came up to suggest that they take tea inside. The wind had shifted, he said, and was freshening, and they would have to tack; the skipper thought that a squall was on its way.

Evelyn followed the others inside, reluctant to leave the exhilaration she had felt on deck, but the waves were now flecked with white and the bow had begun plunging deeper.

Mr Larsen continued his story as they went below: 'His name is Nanabijou, the spirit of the deep seawater. He guarded a rich seam of silver which ran below the lake. Only his people knew about it, but the white man's firewater loosened tongues and the secret got out, so Nanabijou was turned to stone. He pays the price of betrayal in eternal sleep.' He reached for his cup and smiled at them. 'But as the white man has known of the silver vein for less than half a century, I think some of the legend is of recent crafting.'

'So there *is* such a mine?' demanded Dalston.

'Oh yes. It produced two and a half million ounces of high-grade silver, averaging one dollar and twenty-six cents an ounce.' Larsen refilled Evelyn's cup, then offered more to Clementina. 'And when the shafts flooded a few years back the Ojibway claimed Nanabijou was taking his revenge.'

'But he didn't waken?' said Evelyn, as she tried to focus on the story, finding the motion of the ship unsettling now that they were inside.

'Ah! No, my dear. And only when he wakes will his revenge be complete.' Mr Larsen turned and pulled a bell-pull to summon a steward, and as he did Evelyn saw Rupert take a hip-flask from his pocket and dash some of its contents into his teacup.

'But why weren't the shafts pumped out again, if the lode is so pure?' he asked, deftly returning the flask to his pocket and raising the cup to his lips.

'Some fresh tea, I think,' Larsen addressed the steward, adding blandly, 'unless the gentlemen prefer something stronger?' He passed Evelyn one of the sugared pastries, and she took it without thinking. 'Getting the water out was one thing, but rebuilding the crib to *keep* it out was another. We had to accept it was no longer worthwhile.'

'We?' Dalston looked up. 'You were involved, sir?'

'One of many.'

'But if there's still silver down there, then surely with the right equipment . . .' he persisted.

'Don't imagine you're the first to think of it.'

Conversation halted as the yacht altered course, swinging round to approach the entrance to Thunder Bay, and they now rode with the swells, the hull rising and falling in a slow mesmeric rhythm. The sails were lowered, the engines restarted, and the smell of oil and soot was blown into the cabin; Evelyn regretted the sugared pastry after the first bite and felt a sudden need to be back on deck.

She excused herself and staggered across to the rail, gripped it tightly, and took in great gulps of air. The wind had risen and the sky was darkening, the clouds were shredded to rags across its wide expanse, and every now and then, far in the distance, flashes of sheet lightning split the charcoal skies.

'Alright, old thing?' Rupert appeared beside her, pulling off his jacket and draping it over her shoulders, resting his hands there a moment. 'You've gone a very pretty shade of green. Mr Larsen has sent for a remedy and said I was to bring you in before you froze. Clemmy's gone below.'

'I'll come in a minute. The air helps.'

He chafed her back vigorously, and then rested his hand on the small of her back. 'It's a rotten feeling . . .' She gave him a tight smile and breathed deeply, closing her eyes. It was nice of him to come out to her, but if she was going to be sick she would rather be alone. A rumble of distant thunder reached them above the noise of the engines, and the wind blew in sharp gusts, spots of rain pitting her cheeks. 'Poor old girl.' At the touch of his fingers on her cheek she opened her eyes again. 'Such a rotten feeling . . .' he murmured. His face was only inches from hers, and she smelled brandy on his breath.

She drew aside, nausea replaced by a sudden startled apprehension that he was about to kiss her. 'I'll go in now. I'm feeling so much—'

'— better?' He gave a crooked smile and straightened. 'Good girl. Come along then, but hang on to me, the deck is slippery.' And tucking her arm into his, he led her back to the saloon.

———

In the end the yacht had to spend the night sheltering behind the solid presence of the sleeping Nanabijou, but by morning the weather had cleared enough to allow them to steam the last short distance across the bay. Long wooden wharves stretched out from the town, and a complex smell of pitch and coal drifted towards them, mingled with woodsmoke and an evil aroma from what George said was probably a tannery.

'The reek of commerce,' said Mr Larsen as he joined them at the rail. 'Gracious me! Half those buildings weren't there last time I came.' Old wooden structures, silver-grey with age, stood gable end to the shore, while new ones of brick, large and built to impress, loomed over them. Beyond them was the railway track and beyond that a large square structure with ornate ironwork balconies. 'That's the Northern, the best hotel between Winnipeg and Toronto, and that's where your papa is waiting for us. We'll stay for a couple of nights there to get over the journey and visit the outfitters. You'll like it, I'm sure.'

The Northern had been built on a surge of confidence which had come with the railway, he said, along with dozens of smaller hotels and boardinghouses needed to accommodate a tidal wave of entrepreneurs, prospectors, and rogues who came to the head of the lake seeking their fortune. His enthusiasm for the place was infectious, and Evelyn, now fully recovered from her seasickness, studied the scene with interest. An old side-wheeler was churning the water beside them and from somewhere close by came the regular clang of a steam hammer, interspersed with the sound of men shouting and the whistle of a distant locomotive. There was a vibrancy to the place, and a sense of purpose, and she smiled at a pair of small dark-skinned boys who stood fishing on the end of an abandoned jetty, their mouths agape as the yacht drew close.

She had half-expected her father to be on the wharf to meet them, but he was not, and Mr Larsen had despatched a member of the crew to the hotel to tell him of their arrival. She turned to go below.

'The Chicago of the North, eh?' Dalston appeared behind her, blocking her way. 'Some little way to go, I think. Are you feeling better?' She was, she said, and thanked him then tried to slip by. 'Wait. Don't go,' he said, and reached out to take her arm.

'Papa will be here directly, I need to—'

But he pulled her back towards the deck rail, holding on to her arm. 'I feel a chill, Miss Ballantyre' – he mocked her gently with his smile – 'and believe I have offended?' Evelyn remained silent, not knowing how to respond. Had he really considered kissing her yesterday when she felt so ghastly? Surely not. But he confused her. 'The truth is, I was feeling the motion myself and took refuge in rather too much brandy. Works at the time, but devilish afterwards.'

It was difficult to sustain a coolness in the face of such candour, so she smiled and murmured that she was not offended. 'I should hate to think you were,' he continued, looking at her with those intense blue eyes, 'because, you see, our good Mr Larsen has hinted I might join your fishing expedition, and I wouldn't want a black mark against my name.' She looked aside to where floating rubbish trapped between the yacht's hull and the wharf was lifting and falling on the oily swell, and considered whether this news was welcome or not. 'Blame the spirit of the deep seawater, if you like, for roughening the waves.' She laughed a little, and his eyes gleamed. 'That's better. Will your papa mind if I join you, do you think?'

She looked again towards the waterfront, scanning it for signs of him, but saw instead that Mr Larsen's man was crossing the tracks and approaching the jetty. He was carrying an envelope in his hand, and Dalston's question was forgotten.

> . . . more or less a waste of time, I'm afraid. I've managed to miss Kershaw on two occasions and now he's gone back out into the bush, still looking. He left me a message saying that at this time of year the man is likely to be out hunting in the Lake Nipigon area, so he's gone that way. That being the case I might as well go on ahead and see what I can learn from your Mr Skinner. There are lots of prospectors in town and wild talk of big strikes to the north, so the sooner we can resolve matters the better.
>
> Your rooms are reserved at the Northern, I confirmed them before I left. Catch your breath for a day or so as I'll be quite content fishing at Skinner's lodge until you come. Just send me word when you're ready and I'll meet the train. Give my regards to the Meltons and my love to Evelyn.

Larsen folded the letter and put it back in the envelope. His old friend was unstoppable, but this news would not please his daughter. He sat a moment, running his fingers along the fold, perplexed again by the man; this gold-mining venture was not essential for the bank, he had surely made that clear! Money was still flowing freely from South Africa, although he knew the unrest out there was making investors uneasy. But he also knew that Ballantyre did not like being thwarted.

Evelyn appeared at the door of the saloon, her hand on the jamb. 'What has happened?' she asked.

'I was just coming to find you, my dear,' he said, beckoning her in and waving the letter at her. 'This is from your father. He's gone on ahead and—'

'He didn't wait?'

Larsen registered her tone and added quickly: 'His business took him in that direction, you see, so it made no sense for him to come back here. We'll have a day or two to assemble ourselves, and then join him.'

When she had gone Larsen went and stood, looking out of the window, chewing the edge of his moustache. Evelyn's face had assumed that rigid look again, so like her father's, and now *he* was in a hole himself. Damned awkward— He had depended on Ballantyre being here to either confirm or scotch the idea of Dalston continuing as part of the party. The current confusion was George Melton's doing, although all done unconsciously. During conversation over cigars and brandies last night he had simply assumed that Dalston would be coming along to the fishing camp. Dalston had not corrected the mistake, and he had the look of a man who hoped that he *would* be included. Larsen had hinted that he would not wish to delay Dalston's journey out west any longer, and then Melton had compounded the misunderstanding by imagining that Dalston was simply undecided, and had pressed him to come. Larsen had managed to prevaricate, intending to discuss the matter with Ballantyre today, but now, of course, that was not to be.

He turned away from the window, remembering that he needed to ensure that the steward had correctly interpreted his wishes regarding the luggage. Dalston seemed to have fitted in very well, his wit a little sharp at times perhaps, but he had been kindly solicitous of poor Evelyn's *mal de mer* yesterday, and the child did seem to enjoy his company, and Clementina had raised no concerns. But, even so, he thought as he pushed open his cabin door, if Ballantyre did disapprove it might prove rather awkward.

Chapter 10

Drips fell from their paddles like diamonds, catching darts of sunlight, as the canoe carrying James and Louis cut its way through the water in the lower reaches of the Nipigon River. Nearly home. Their strokes had fallen into a well-worn rhythm as they made their way across Lake Helen, aiming for the rocky headland beyond which lay the final stretch to Skinner's lodge. Marcel had left them yesterday at the place where they had hidden the canoe on their way north, giving no reason for his departure, saying only that he would join them in a day's time; Louis had stood and watched him go, and then shrugged. 'Maybe he has a woman somewhere—'

James stopped paddling to slap the back of his neck, wiping away the smear of blood and mosquito, then he rested his paddle for a moment, moving his shoulders to ease their stiffness, and let the current carry them forward, glad of an easy ride. 'Fresh meat,' Louis had mocked when James's face had swollen like a turnip on the first trip of the summer. Marcel had offered him an obnoxious concoction of bear grease, pounded roots, and God-knows-what until gradually his body had adapted to the daily dose of venom. There were fewer bugs now as it grew colder, and before heading north this time he had dared to shave again.

He flexed his shoulders, then relaxed. It had been a gruelling few days, but what could be lovelier now than to drift across the lake where autumn colours lit the shoreline like a ring of flame. And he marvelled again at the strangeness of it all, of meeting

Achak at his hunting camp, circled by his dogs and watched by his dark-eyed sons while he considered their proposal.

A pair of ducks lifted from the surface of the lake to make dark silhouettes against the low sun, and a distant honking floated down to them on the breeze. More geese— The sound was eloquent of the changing season, and James found himself wondering where spring would find him. Back here with Skinner? Or with Louis, knee-deep in gold—

Fool's gold.

Knee-deep in muskeg, more like—

'Am I doing all the work, eh?' Louis called from behind.

James laughed and took up his paddle again. And in two days they would be heading back upstream with this last group of anglers, portaging tents, tarpaulins, blankets, cook pots, pails, stores – and God knows what else besides. A bloody washstand, Skinner had said.

Skinner's lodge came into sight as they rounded the headland and Louis angled his paddle to bring them closer to the shore. They could see Skinner himself on the jetty, talking to another man, a stranger in city clothes. An early arrival? At a gesture from Skinner the man turned to watch them approach.

James lifted his paddle.

And then held it, suspended in midair.

An odd thudding had started in his head, for no reason except that there was something about the set of the man's shoulders that had made his guts twist. And his stance— Impossible, of course. A trick of the eye, a spectre conjured by his restless mind.

Then his stomach lurched as they came closer, and his brain froze. The man on the jetty was looking back at him, rigid and intent, while the distance between them shrank. And then a live charge seemed to zigzag across the water to fuse his senses.

Instinctively he dug his paddle deep into the water, driving the canoe away from the jetty, back into the flow of the current, away from the figure who stood there.

'*Jackass!*' Louis countered quickly and brought the canoe back on course, seized the jetty's end post, and clung on while Skinner stepped forward and grabbed the side of the canoe, hissing his scorn at them.

But nothing registered with James. Blood was pounding in his ears and he sat, staring in front of him, his paddle lifted clear of the water, paralysed by the presence of the figure who stood at the other end of the jetty, a cigar held loosely between his fingers.

And his incredulity became an active force, pulling the man towards him, his footsteps sounding hollow on the wooden jetty. Louis jumped ashore, gesturing to James to pass up their packs, and in a sick daze James obeyed. He was eye-level now with the well-shod feet above him on the jetty, thinking madly that if he had not shaved he might have had a chance, but a three-day stubble offered no protection.

The feet had stopped just in front of him, but James kept his eyes low, knowing that if he lifted them he would meet with recognition as surely as he had done that day in Ballantyre's study ten years ago after a night spent in the outbuilding.

Skinner introduced his guest, dispelling any last shred of doubt. 'Mister Ballantyre has come on ahead,' he was saying. 'These are two of the river boys, sir. Louis Valencourt, one of the best.' Louis wiped his palm on his thigh and shook Ballantyre's hand. 'And this is James MacDonald, who, puttin' aside that odd little stunt, *had* been shaping just fine . . .' Skinner glowered as James heaved himself up onto the jetty, saying nothing, waiting for the words which would unmask him.

Should he run? But where to this time—? He glanced towards the forest but Ballantyre's figure blocked his path. 'MacDonald, you said?' Those familiar tones, smooth and mannerly. And so damned assured. 'A fellow Scot, perhaps?' James straightened to find Ballantyre's hand outstretched towards him.

The mild tone and the words unbalanced him and he looked up, meeting a look of polite interest. Nothing more— He grunted assent, briefly touched the proffered hand, and looked aside. 'And where do you hail from, James MacDonald?' Ballantyre asked.

What game was this?

'Kelso,' he replied.

Ballantyre turned back to Skinner with raised eyebrows. 'Well. How extraordinary! Kelso is not twenty miles from my own house.' Skinner was not interested and continued to eye James sourly, ordering him to take the packs to the lodge, but Ballantyre still blocked the way. 'We must talk, James MacDonald, and you can tell me how you come to be so far from home. There must be quite a tale to tell.' James looked back at him, schooling his face to blankness, and this time he encountered a message, a warning. And something else, swiftly gone. Skinner repeated his order and James bent to pick up the packs. Ballantyre moved away, walking slowly beside Skinner, and his words drifted back. 'Canada provides a sanctuary for many of my countrymen, you know—' Then James became conscious of Louis, holding the paddles and watching him, so he scooped up the packs and headed blindly for the bunkhouse.

Louis followed him in, letting the screen door slam behind him, whistling through his teeth and glancing across to where James stood beside his bunk, distracted and thinking furiously. *Ballantyre!* Here— It could not be! Louis had begun to say something when the door was flung open again and Skinner strode in. 'Where the hell is Marcel?'

'He'll be here by tomorrow, with the others, like he agreed,' replied Louis, unfastening the leather thongs on his pack.

'And, you, what happened down there?' Skinner flung at James. 'You gone crazy or something? A stunt like that at Pine Rapids and we'll be pickin' corpses out of the river.' James shrugged, but Skinner continued in the same vein until his patience snapped.

'Leave it, Skinner.'

The old man snorted. 'Yeah? So who runs this outfit?' James shrugged again, turning a dismissive shoulder, and Skinner swore. 'Anyway, the gentleman wants to go fishing this evening, and he wants you along to show him where. So take him down the trail to the rocks; maybe get some walleye.'

'Why not Louis?'

''Cause he asked for you, that's why, and he's paying. Be ready in half an hour.' Skinner left, letting the door slam behind him. A woodpecker began hammering at a dead tree outside the window.

James started turning out his pack, ignoring Louis. Not even Louis knew his story.

The silence stretched out. Then: '*Ça va?*'

'Yeah, fine.'

'So?'

'Just dead beat, I need some sleep.' And he threw himself down on his bunk and turned on his side.

Half an hour later he sat waiting on the bottom of the lodge steps, picking at the splintered wood of the treads, his mind still racing. His first instinct had been to flee, but now that the initial shock was receding, he knew that would not be an answer.

He was no longer eighteen, running scared.

A moment later the screen door creaked open and Ballantyre came out onto the wooden veranda, Skinner behind him. James rose and looked up at them. Ballantyre blandly returned the look as Skinner described the place where they might cast a line. 'Jest along the trail a ways, out on that little headland. See it? It's a good spot. James knows where I mean, he'll look after you.'

Or maybe he'll drown you there. Their eyes briefly met, and Ballantyre's showed a fleeting gleam as if he had read his mind. That old trick—

'Excellent. I'm at your disposal, young man.'

'Give 'im yer gear, mister, that's what he's paid for.'

Silently James took the rod and fishing basket from Ballantyre and led him towards a break in the trees which marked the beginning of the trail. He did not look round, but he knew that Ballantyre was following right behind.

It simply was not possible—

Neither spoke. How had the man tracked him down? He had surely left no trail. But *why* had he come? And why now – after five years? A dead tree had fallen across the track since James had last come this way and he climbed over it, leaving Ballantyre to fend for himself. He looked fit enough, almost unchanged by those years, still tall and erect, as lean as before, leaner perhaps. Or was it simply that his face was thinner, his features more defined, making his eyes appear more deep-set, more hooded, and there were lines now at their corners, white threads amongst his dark hair.

The trail forked, and James took the path down to the lake. It was all he could do not to stop and confront the man, but he had to be well out of earshot for the things that needed to be said. The trail narrowed, then opened up onto a rocky headland, and they went out onto it. James set down the gear, and only then did he turn to face Ballantyre.

'Prepare the rod as you'd normally do, James.' Ballantyre forestalled him with a staggering coolness. 'I imagine we can be seen from the lodge.' James looked over his shoulder. He was right, curse him, the headland was clearly visible from the porch where Skinner had his rocking chair and kept a pair of field glasses. He bent and picked up the rod.

'You look well.' Ballantyre was examining him in a sort of wonder as James began fixing split-shot sinkers to the line. He made no reply. 'Very well, in fact— Tell me. How long have you been over here?'

James speared a fat dew worm with the hook and held the rod out to Ballantyre, glancing again in the direction of the lodge. 'Five years.'

'Five years! So you came over straight away?'

A new start. A safe haven— 'How did you find me?'

Ballantyre looked taken aback. 'Find you? I'd no idea you were here; I'm as surprised by this encounter as you are.' James said nothing, not believing him. 'You appear to have thrived, though.' *Thrived?* Rage boiled in him at the man's composure. 'You're travelling on false papers, I gather, with an assumed name?'

'You ask a lot of questions, Mr Ballantyre.' James straightened, his arms stiff by his sides, ready again to confront him, but Ballantyre went past him, taking the rod to the water's edge. He essayed a cast, then looked back over his shoulder.

'And you've a few yourself. I know.' He gave his attention back to his rod and sent the line arching faultlessly over the surface, as unconcerned as if he were standing on the banks of his own river, three thousand miles away. A series of concentric ripples spread from where the baited hook landed, disturbing the surface of calm. 'They'll all be answered in due course, I promise you.'

'Then start with this one. Who killed Jacko?'

Ballantyre focused on his rod a moment, and then began reeling in. 'Arrogance killed him, my friend. Arrogance and folly.'

'That's not an answer.'

'No? It's the truth, though, pure and simple. His killer thought him worthless. Fair game.'

And James saw again the two men in sporting tweeds on the riverbank, the gleaming gun barrel pointing across the current at him. God's chosen ones, born to rule. And Ballantyre was no different— 'And so you covered for him. You closed ranks, and put the killing onto me.'

Ballantyre looked back at him, his face unreadable, but grave. 'They'd have hanged you, James, whatever I said.'

Bile rose from the pit of his stomach, and he almost choked on it. 'And that's it? That's *all*?'

'Of course not. But it's the truth. You did well to run.'

When last he had seen Ballantyre, James had been a youth, inches shorter than his master, but now their eyes were on a level. 'So who killed him?'

The question crackled in the air, and then Ballantyre turned aside and cast again. 'You saw the man.'

'I saw two men, from across the river, with the low sun behind them. Your guests – one killed Jacko and then fired at me. And you were standing there, standing right beside him.'

Why should he tell Ballantyre that he had seen the killer again that evening? That he had looked down on him from where he was hidden and had studied his features so that he would know him again. It was Jacko who had once shown him where the branch of an oak reached out over the upper reaches of the river, and told him how a hunted man could leave the water and swing up onto it, leaving no tracks and confounding any following hounds, who would lose the scent. And James had remembered the branch that night as he fled splashing through the shallows, sending a moorhen piping into the bullrushes, his breath coming in brittle gasps, in disbelief that Ballantyre had loosed the pack on him. He had scrambled up into the oak's spreading canopy and had lain close against the trunk in dread of discovery, listening as the baying drew close, then watched the dogs working their way along the riverbank, seeking the place where he had left the water. And he had looked down on the man who was following them, recognising him for the one he had seen across the river, his gun raised to shoot. He had stopped below James's tree, calling back to McAllister, waiting for the keeper to come to him; and he had heard what was said—

He scowled again at Ballantyre. 'And then you loosed the hounds.'

Ballantyre shook his head. 'McAllister did.'

'On your orders.'

'No.'

It hardly mattered. 'So who *was* Jacko's killer?'

Ballantyre regarded him evenly for a moment. Then: 'It was generally assumed to have been the same man who killed Mc-Allister.' He reeled in the last few feet of line, calmly picking the trailing weeds off his hook, and inspected the bait. Then he lifted his gaze again and looked steadily at James.

'McAllister . . . ?'

'He was found dead in the shrubbery later that night.'

Jesus! Then Ballantyre's odd phrasing struck him, like steel in the gut. The same man— 'And so that was pinned on me too?' Horror rose to match his fury, and he took a step forward.

But Ballantyre simply turned aside and cast again. 'Throttling me will hardly improve your position, James.' The line went farther this time. 'You had every reason to hate McAllister.' James's mind was paralysed by this new accusation, and his eyes became fixed on the wake of ripples which followed Ballantyre's line as he reeled in again, his rod now bending. 'Perhaps you encountered him as you left through my study window—?' He glanced back at James. 'Al-though attacking a man from behind didn't seem to be quite your style.' James's legs felt suddenly weak and he put a hand against a silver birch for support, staring down at the shadow it cast on the water. 'In a fight, maybe, but not in cold blood.'

Ballantyre carefully unhooked an undersized fish, still watching James, and tossed it back into the water, where it hung a moment, before darting away into the darkness. 'But after McAllister's body was found, things went from bad to dangerous very quickly. You were much safer away.'

Silver minnows flickered in and out of the reeds at the edge of the rocks where sunlight penetrated the depth of clear water, and James knew that he was right. Shooting Jacko, a worthless vagrant, a known felon, caught with the incriminating net in his hands, was one thing; killing Ballantyre's head keeper, within the grounds of Ballantyre House, was quite another.

He had known nothing of this, thank God, as he pounded along the byways astride a stolen horse with Ballantyre's sovereigns in his saddlebag, while news of the double murder travelled like wildfire through the countryside.

He looked up to see that Ballantyre's expression had lightened. 'Do you believe in fate, James? In destiny—? I never did. Until now.' A smile twisted his mouth. 'You always were an enterprising lad, and it took guts to do what you did that night, real nerve. And it gave me great satisfaction to think of you in my study, coolly emptying my cash box, while the keepers were beating the hedgerows – then riding off on Melrose. I began to believe that you'd get away, and survive.'

James stared at him. 'And yet you thought I'd killed McAllister.'

'It seemed unlikely.'

A heron rose from the shore a few yards away and flew off, carrying the low evening light on its back as it flapped calmly across the lake, legs a-dangling. James watched it for a while then turned back to Ballantyre. 'You haven't told me who killed Jacko.'

Ballantyre's eyes too were following the heron's flight. 'McAllister appeared on the riverbank just as you bolted. He'd seen who killed Jacko and who fired at you, so if it wasn't you who killed McAllister then it was that same man. McAllister must have been trying a little blackmail. He was fool enough.'

'Just a name, Ballantyre.'

But Ballantyre shook his head and his expression hardened. 'Not yet. It's better that you don't know. Retribution will come, I promise you. It was only my word against theirs then, and nothing has changed.'

Anger hit him then, red hot behind the eyes. 'The biggest land-owner in the county, a magistrate, a well-respected figure. Your *word* would have carried—'

'— no weight at all against that of the other.' Ballantyre had not raised his voice, but James was silenced. 'Believe me.'

James looked away, and the silence stretched out between them. Then he said what he had long suspected. 'So it was some titled wastrel.'

'Precisely.'

Contempt almost choked him. 'And if I took the drop then a nasty scandal could be avoided. And you, with your courtrooms and your justice and your fine reputation – *you* went along with it all!' He knew it to be so, ever since he had overheard McAllister say: *And Ballantyre's agreed to that?* and the other man had nodded.

Ballantyre's expression darkened. 'Trust me, there was more—'

Trust me. James got to his feet and went to the edge of the rocks, sick with disgust. For five years he had tried to put behind him the sight of Jacko's bloody corpse, but coming to terms with Ballantyre's baseness would take a lifetime. He leant against a lone spruce which had found soil enough for its roots to cling to, arms folded, and looked down into the lake seeing the low sun filtered through the still water to shimmer on the sand beneath. *Trust me.* And he was back in Ballantyre's study that first morning, wood crackling in the hearth, the firelight flickering over gilded letter-ing on the leather-bound books. A thin child, shivering with fear, telling himself it was only the cold that made him tremble. And he had raised his eyes to the godlike figure before him and seen a warmth in his expression, and a hand held out. *Trust me—* In taking the hand, he had stepped into a world of order and plenty, where he had learned a sense of purpose and the distinction between right and wrong. And always, after that day, he had known he was under the watchful eye of a benevolent master.

The same man was watching him now. 'The matter *will* be resolved, James. I promise you.'

And despite everything, despite the shock of murder and the corroding bitterness which had followed, the child at the core of him wanted to believe—

But he didn't. 'After *five* years?'

'It's taken that long.'

'Horseshit.'

'When all is resolved I will explain matters to you, and hope that you will understand.' Then Ballantyre's line tautened and his rod bent and he turned his attention back to the water. 'But for now there is one thing you must know,' he said, keeping tension on the line, his tone suddenly authoritative as of old. 'My daughter is travelling with the rest of the party, and when she arrives, she'll recognise you.' Miss Evie? Ballantyre paused and glanced over his shoulder, taking in James's astonishment. 'I'll contrive to have time alone with her before she sees you, and explain the situation, but neither of you must in any way indicate that you know each other. You are strangers. Understand? The others pose no problem, but Melton is a magistrate, and I don't want him to discover who you are. It would complicate matters.'

James stood watching as Ballantyre calmly reeled in his line, but in his mind's eye he was seeing Miss Evie as he had last seen her, eyes wide as dinner plates, clutching her dressing gown to her thin frame, shaking with cold, or shock, with her hand pressed across her mouth. Had she told her father she had seen him that night?

A large dorsal fin broke the surface of the water as Ballantyre drew in his catch. He gestured to the landing net and James stepped forward, scooping it under the fish's arching body as he had so often done before, when Ballantyre had taken him with him to the river – when James had gone with glee, flattered by the master's attention.

Once he had worshipped the man.

'Walleye?' asked Ballantyre, examining his catch.

'Yes.'

'Good eating?'

'Yes.'

Ballantyre disentangled the fish from the net, studied it a moment, then deftly removed the hook from its mouth and went to crouch at the edge of the lake, holding it between his hands. 'But I came for brook trout. So! A reprieve, my friend,' he murmured and opened his hands. The fish stayed motionless a moment, as if in disbelief, and then, with a powerful twist of its body, it was gone.

———

James could get no more from Ballantyre, who had carried on fishing with a cool disregard for James's fury until, eventually, he had reeled in and they had set off back to the lodge. Louis was waiting for them on the steps of the lodge as they emerged out of the woods, and he rose when he saw them, batting away a cloud of mosquitoes as he came towards them. He held out a telegram. 'This was just sent over from the station,' he said and gestured to where a canoe was pulling away from the jetty. 'Only bugs biting tonight?' he enquired, glancing at James.

'Walleye, I am told, but we were merciful and let them go,' Ballantyre replied. 'I came for brook trout,' he repeated as he tore open the telegram, mounting the steps to the porch. 'But it will be a different matter upriver.'

James watched him. Telegrams meant contact.

Ballantyre glanced at the paper then turned and handed it down to James with a quizzical look. 'Read it to me, will you?' he said. 'I begin to think I need spectacles.'

James passed it back. 'Their train arrives at two tomorrow.'

'Thank you. So that, at least, is clear.'

Louis looked from one to another. 'We eat together tonight, and the food is ready.' Louis held open the door, still watching James as he entered. He had little appetite but no reason to refuse, so he propped the rod up against the wall of the lodge and followed Ballantyre in.

———

Skinner's lodge had started life as a bunkhouse for railway workers many years ago, the old man informed Ballantyre as he poured him a generous shot of whisky. Before then he had worked in the Hudson Bay Company stores at Red Rock House, married a half-breed girl, and raised a family. 'But she died, and our boys were grown and gone, so I built this place to get me some company.' A native girl brought a steaming pot to the table and began ladling a meaty stew onto their plates while Skinner poured two much shorter measures for Louis and James, waving them towards two stools. 'Got more company than I'd bargained for. When the footings for the railroad bridge went in, I'd men packed in here like sardines. Close on forty to fifty of 'em some nights . . .' As the old stories came out again James sat back and contemplated Ballantyre. How was it possible that he sat opposite the man, breaking bread with him and not choking the life out of him—? His old master had changed, though his face was more finely chiselled, but it was more than a physical change. Something deeper— The warmth in his eye which had drawn James to him had gone, replaced by something sharper, a glint, cold as steel. Then James became conscious of Louis's scrutiny and gave his attention to his plate instead. '. . . places filled up as soon as they emptied. Folk think it was the terrain that held up construction north of Superior, but no, sir, the gang bosses complained the men strung the work out in order to stay on at Skinner's place,' and he cackled at his well-worn joke.

Ballantyre laughed obligingly, then added: 'As someone who has shares in the company, Mr Skinner, I'm not sure I want to hear this.'

Skinner's face fell ludicrously. 'Well, I mean to say . . .' So Ballantyre had business interests here, did he? James watched him as he ate. Railways had always been his passion. Many times he had been sent in the trap to collect the master from the little Borders branch-line station when he had been in Edinburgh, and on the way back Ballantyre would regale him with the wonders of new railways crisscrossing vast continents.

'Tell me, Mr Skinner,' Ballantyre continued, pulling a flask from his pocket. 'Are there many prospectors around these days?' He poured generous measures from it into all four glasses.

'More'n ever, now the railroad's opened things up. And there're rumours of big gold strikes up north.' Louis and James exchanged covert glances. 'Diamonds too, I'm told.'

James raised his glass, and his lips met with the sweet taste of home. Ballantyre, it appeared, had brought his own supplies. The taste transported him back to Christmas or to occasions when Ballantyre's horse had won at Kelso races and bottles appeared in the stables. He watched Louis take a drink, pause, his eyes widening, and then take another sip, almost reverently, raising his eyebrows at James. Distracted by the taste, Ballantyre's next question took them by surprise.

'Did either of you hear tell of an Indian by the name of Achak in these parts?'

James had taken a mouthful of food and continued to chew, making this an excuse for not replying. Louis paused, his glass halfway to his lips, but he recovered fast. 'Everyone knows of Achak. He had lands here.'

'And do you know where he is to be found?'

Louis shrugged. 'He could be anywhere. Hunting—'

'Like I told you, mister,' said Skinner, taking a drink and smacking his lips in appreciation. 'My oh my . . . You won't get stuff like this round here. No, sir. It's all cheap rotgut, even in the bars. And back then they didn't allow any sort of drink for those railroad gangs, but I used to turn a blind eye to the stills they set up in the forest. Provided they behaved themselves—'

'Do they know of Achak in Scotland, Mr Ballantyre?' asked Louis, wide-eyed and incredulous, then slanted a narrow look at James.

'— those boys needed a little comfort after a day's work, no harm in it—'

'No. But I'm interested to meet him.' Ballantyre stretched an arm across the table and topped up their glasses, his eyes flicking between them.

'— no women, though. Women are more trouble than drink, and if the men wanted that sort of comfort they'd—'

'He could be anywhere, his lands stretch for miles.' The light from the guttering lantern highlighted the sharpness in Louis's eyes, leaving the rest of his face in shadow.

'But someone must know where to look,' Ballantyre persisted.

Skinner had long since ceased to expect an attentive audience and his story was continuing along its well-worn tracks: '— but if anyone tried to sneak a whore over the threshold they got kicked down the steps to sprawl in the mud—'

'The old chief has died recently, his people are grieving in the traditional way.'

'So I'm told.'

'— I was more respectful to the women, of course, whores or

no, but they still had to leave. They knew the rules, and having women here was agin' them.'

'Then we're fortunate you're willing to make an exception for my daughter and Lady Melton.' Ballantyre's gravity was belied by a gleam in his eye which James caught but Skinner missed. The old man dissembled rapidly, covering his confusion by describing the comforts he had in mind for the ladies, before veering off to the safer topic of the number of anglers who now came to the Nipigon, drawn by the river's reputation. 'Near on a hundred permits issued last year, but most stay below the viaduct where you can haul out fish for as long as you wanna stay there and haul. But those like you who want more—' He broke off as figures passed the window, and his tone hardened. 'So Marcel's back, is he.' Louis looked up, glancing quickly towards James. 'And he's brought Tala and Machk, has he? Couple more too, I hope,' he muttered, 'with all the gear we got.' Louis rapidly finished his food and excused himself, saying that he would go and find out. And James saw that he avoided his eye as he left, letting the lodge door slam closed behind him.

Chapter 11

Mr Larsen ushered his party onto the train in Port Arthur, out of breath from having seen the luggage safely stowed. 'I've just sent your papa another telegram telling him that we are bringing Dalston with us,' he told Evelyn as she settled onto the worn plush seat in what passed for the first-class carriage. 'He'll have the one I sent him yesterday about our arrival, so Papa'll be there, my dear, waiting at Nipigon station. Never fear.'

Papa could hardly do otherwise, she thought, and smiled at Mr Larsen in acknowledgement. Even Papa—

As the train began to move, she watched the brick stores and station buildings slipping away, and had a final glimpse of the Northern Hotel and of the lake frontage with its wharves and warehouses, and of *Valkyrie*, which would remain there awaiting their return. The speed quickened and the sprawl of low wooden buildings petered out into a ribbon of shacks and tents pitched along the line of the track. Evelyn sat forward, seeing Indian wigwams amongst them, but soon they too vanished and the train was engulfed by the forest. Just a single track taking them into the vast wilderness—

'Rupert's awfully pleased to be coming along, you know.' Clementina leant close and squeezed her arm. 'And *not* because of the fish.' Evelyn smiled, as was expected of her, and turned back to the window.

Rupert Dalston had certainly been making every effort to be agreeable, and putting aside a residual annoyance with her father, she had very much enjoyed the two days they had spent exploring Port Arthur. It had a raw energy, which she found exciting, and Rupert had been a lively companion. They had stood together watching a group of Chinamen squatting on a street corner throwing dice, and she had studied their wide hats and odd garb until he had tugged at her sleeve and drawn her attention to an Indian woman driving a pig down the street, pursued by dogs and laughing children. The streets themselves were no more than beaten earth tracks, muddy after last night's rain, with deep grooves left by the wagons that drove up and down. Wooden boardwalks served as pavements.

The main street, however, was being paved. 'Behold! Progress,' Rupert had remarked, gesturing to the labourers, some of whom were dark-skinned. 'Civilisation—' Then a group of tipsy young men had jostled past them speaking loudly in what he told her was Italian. 'Better than the Midway Plaisance,' he said, pulling her aside and shielding her from them.

Much better, she thought, for here the exotic was real and these people were not exhibits to be stared at but had a purpose. She walked with the others along the boardwalk, past shops which sold everything from shovels to bonnets, past a land sales registry, an assay office, a livery stable, and several bars. She was attracted by the swagger and the brash confidence of the place, the billboards with their bold advertising, and the noise and the bustle, and she watched unescorted women striding along the wooden walkways, resolute and confident with their skirts swinging above their ankles. No one gave them a second glance— Some women ran boardinghouses and stores, Mr Larsen had told her, and one even owned a lumber yard. 'So much for the murals in the Woman's Building,' she had replied, 'with their sanctioned spheres of womanhood.' And he had smiled.

While Rupert's company was entertaining, he occasionally displayed a rather patronising attitude, adopting a superior tone which she disliked. 'It's a new town, for goodness' sake,' she had countered to one of his remarks. 'They're still hacking it out of the forest. And look! There's the electric streetcar coming! Not even Edinburgh has one of those.' Rupert had laughed at her indignation, and Mr Larsen had insisted that they ride on it.

'Not as exciting as the Ferris wheel, perhaps,' he said as they clung to their seats, looking out to where men were surveying lots along newly laid-out streets which were filling the gap between Port Arthur and the old trading post at Fort William. 'There are more shops at the terminus as well as hotels and bars, and it's there, I regret, that I must leave you for an hour or so while I meet a business associate. Perhaps you might try one of the new ice cream parlours I've been told about.' The streetcar screeched to a halt, and he had raised his hat and left them, strolling off towards a square brick building beside the railway sidings.

'*One* of the ice cream parlours? I thought he was teasing!' Evelyn said as Dalston propelled her through a swinging door. 'How *can* there be ice cream, here in the back of beyond?' He had laughed as she and Clementina hung over the selection of flavours, and she had chosen three different ones. They had eaten them at a small round table, and Rupert had leant forward to dab an errant blob of Lime Delight from her chin with his handkerchief saying, 'What a greedy child it is, to be sure.'

———

Larsen, sitting across the carriageway from Evelyn, was thinking that it would be a relief to hand her back to her father. His hand had been forced in regard to young Dalston, with George Melton persuading him to postpone his buffalo hunting, and Dalston thanking his host so profusely. It had been difficult to do anything other than extend the invitation, but better, perhaps, than provoking an awkwardness between well-acquainted families, and he was confident that Ballantyre would be able to handle the matter. He turned his head and caught part of the conversation from across the carriage where Dalston was regaling Melton with his exploits at the card table late into the night. A gambler, was he? His father had certainly been playing for high stakes—

And losing. The train swayed as it rounded a bend and the rhythm of the wheels changed tone. From the window he had a brief glimpse of the lake and derelict buildings on the tiny Silver Islet just offshore, little enough to show for the frenzied activity there had once been there, and he mused a moment on how rapidly fortunes were made and lost. The train jolted again and his thoughts went back to the worrying news he had heard in Fort William. The newly completed Port Arthur, Duluth and Western railway, which had opened to a jubilant fanfare only a few months ago, was already losing money. Worse still, there were rumours that the corresponding American section would never be built; the mines it had been intended to serve were not proving profitable. He glanced again at Dalston; while both Ballantyre and himself had long since sold their railway stock, Dalston's father had not and had invested heavily in the PAD & W. That investment, like so many others, had been quietly underwritten by Ballantyre, and if the rumours proved accurate, it could be disastrous for the earl – and any loss now would be the bank's loss, and Ballantyre's problem.

He took a deep breath and let it out slowly. He could only hope that having Dalston along would not prove to be an embarrassment for Ballantyre. He watched as Evelyn addressed the young man over her shoulder, laughing at his response as he leant forward, eyes a-glint, and Larsen wondered what forces he might have unleashed.

———

James had been up early, helping the others to lower the big transport canoes into the water in readiness to go and meet the train at Nipigon station. The lake was like glass this morning, but there was the sharpness of autumn in the air—

Ballantyre had accompanied Skinner down to the water's edge and James had heard him trying to engineer it so that James remained at the lodge, telling Skinner that he would take his place in Louis's canoe. It would give everyone more space, he had pointed out, as well as impress his daughter with his prowess with a paddle. Skinner had laughed but shaken his head, insisting they needed extra hands for all the luggage and stores, and Ballantyre had not pressed the point. But he had found an opportunity to draw James aside. 'Keep your distance until I've had a chance to talk to my daughter,' he said, 'she'll give you away otherwise.' The words, spoken in his old stable-yard tone, had deepened James's resentment.

Last night he had lain sleepless in the dark, asking himself how he could even think of trusting the man again. And as dawn's light filtered through the shutters he had risen, haggard and hollow-eyed, convinced that he was walking straight into a trap, and that there would be constables waiting for him on the jetty. He was half-tempted to confide in Louis but needed more time to think. Things were happening too fast, and yet he had buried the past so deeply that digging it up did not come easy. But Louis was no fool and had been giving James puzzled, slant-eyed glances. A silence had fallen when James had walked into their cabin last night, and the air had been heavy with suspicion. Louis must have said something to Marcel – neither had questioned him, though, deterred perhaps by the presence of the other guides. But it was only a matter of time before they cornered him and he would have to tell them something.

Ballantyre had shown such a keen interest in the whereabouts of Achak! No wonder Louis was suspicious! And James had been completely thrown by that twist. Somehow rumours of the gold strike must have reached Ballantyre's ears; card-table talk in Port Arthur, probably, there was always plenty of that. But, if so, then Ballantyre had come too late— James placed the paddles in the two canoes in readiness, conscious of a grim satisfaction at having stolen a march on the man.

———

He felt Ballantyre's presence behind him was like a goad as they paddled across Lake Helen, and James felt himself tensing as they passed under the railway viaducts and rounded the wooded island beyond. The town wharf came into view. It had been built years back when there had been expectations that Nipigon would become the railhead and a great port, but the railroad had pushed on to the head of the lake instead, and the track had been laid almost half a mile inland, taking the emerging town of Nipigon with it. So the wharf now served no greater traffic than the occasional side-wheeler and a growing number of commercial fishing boats.

James felt the anxiety twisting in him as the canoe bumped against it a moment later, and the second canoe slid in behind them. He looked up as he saw a figure striding purposefully down the track, but it was only Stewart from the station office. He came out onto the wharf and reached down to steady the canoe. 'You Mister Ballantyre?' he asked, and held out another pink telegram envelope. 'This came, and we'd no one to send with it.'

Ballantyre took it, frowning slightly as he did, and turned away, ripping the envelope open. James was instantly suspicious. He kept his eyes on him and saw him stop and stare down at the paper for a lot longer than it took to read it— Then he stuffed it into his pocket and walked on to the end of the wharf and stood there staring out across the river. It was all that James could do not to go after him—

'Oi! You just going to stand there?' Louis called out sharply and James turned. Above them two gulls dived, screeching as they fought over a scrap plundered from the riverbank, and he saw that the station wagon was approaching. 'Ten minutes, sir,' Louis called down the wharf, glancing again at James. Ballantyre did not move and Louis called again. 'Mr Ballantyre! Ten minutes.'

Ballantyre spun round. 'What?'

'The train, sir, it'll be here in ten minutes.'

Ballantyre's face was a stony mask as he strode back down the wharf and past them, and he jumped up beside the waggoner without a word. The four guides climbed in behind him, and James sat there staring at his rigid back, anger battling fear.

What the hell was going on—?

A few minutes later the wagon pulled up outside the station and the men climbed out. 'Just keep your distance,' Ballantyre repeated in a low voice as he shouldered past James and out onto the platform.

James went to sit on an upturned barrel against a snow fence, leaving Louis and the other guides to lounge beside the wagon, smoking or chewing. He had chosen his position carefully; from here, he had a clear view down the platform, and if he had to run, the train would serve to mask his escape. He could slip round the engine, cross over the tracks, and vanish into the dense scrub beyond.

What *had* that telegram said?

A distant rumble heralded the train's approach. He wiped his palms on his thighs and pulled out his knife to have it handy, and began whittling the end of a twig, every muscle and nerve alert for trouble.

Whatever it was it had unsettled Ballantyre.

A cloud of steam and smoke appeared above the treetops and a moment later the engine broke cover with a series of mournful wails, and the brakes screeched like souls in agony as it slowed. The carriages came to a standstill directly in front of where Ballantyre was standing.

James kept his eyes fixed on him—

Almost at once the first carriage door opened and James watched Ballantyre step forward to greet a stout gentleman who descended to the platform. He was the usual type of wealthy sports fisherman, too much time and money to spare. Neither he nor Ballantyre looked towards James— Then a younger man emerged and turned back to hand down a slim, light-footed woman, and they too were greeted by Ballantyre: a handshake for the man and a kiss for the lady. Familiar types, well dressed and with that air of God-given assurance, the sort who used to come to Ballantyre House. James pulled at a loose piece of wood on the barrel and cursed as he drove a splinter into his thumb, and when he looked up again Ballantyre was handing down another young woman.

Good God! Miss Evie – all grown up.

He stared at her. Had he been away that long? She was a little taller, perhaps, but unmistakable. Hair worn up now, lighter in colour than he remembered, a neat trim little figure— But would he have known her if they passed on the street? Probably not. Then he saw her glance up and down the platform in her quick way, and dropped his head. But she was lovely—! And he thought of the thin terrified child, eyes wide with horror as they fixed on the knife blade in his hand. He spat to rid himself of the thought, and risked another glance.

Ballantyre had greeted her with a kiss and now had a hand on her elbow, keeping her beside him as he shook hands with another figure who had emerged from the railway carriage. James stiffened. Skinner had said a party of five— The figures on the platform moved and James saw that it was another man, a young man, well dressed, same type – but not a lawman, by the looks of him. James remained still, waiting to see who else would leave the train, but the rest were second- or third-class passengers, locals for the most part, some he knew by sight, the others probably anglers.

And then he saw that Ballantyre was leading his daughter away, down the platform, his hand still under her elbow, his head bent to her as he spoke.

Meanwhile the luggage had been unloaded and the wagon was being brought forward. Louis whistled at James, gesturing at the pile of bags, and James got to his feet, taking his time, stretching elaborately, his eyes not leaving the couple at the end of the platform.

As he put his knife away.

He reached the pile of luggage as Ballantyre turned around and led his daughter back down the platform towards them. She walked stiffly, holding on to her father, her head averted as they approached him. James bent to pick up a leather valise.

'Have a care, will you,' a voice drawled beside him, 'there's breakables in it.'

James looked up, and into a pair of startlingly clear blue eyes—

It was all he could do to hang on to the straps of the valise. A pulse leapt in his throat, his breathing faltered, and he turned away, then heaved the bag onto the wagon in a blur of panic and rage. So it *was* a trap!

'I said have a care, man!' the voice snapped, but James was making for Ballantyre.

Ballantyre saw him coming. He met his eyes with an expression of shock – horror almost – and stepped swiftly into his path, grabbing another bag which he thrust at him, winding him and stopping him in his tracks. 'Keep your head, James,' he said, then more loudly, 'There's only clothes in that one, I expect,' and he brushed past James, propelling his daughter towards the wagon and swinging her up to sit beside the other woman, who was laughing, oblivious to the sudden tension, leaving James where he stood, clutching the bag to him, staring at the retreating train.

Louis said something; he was not sure what. Then he came

forward, took the bag from James, threw it up with the rest, and gave a shout to the driver. The old horse strained a little as it turned the wagon, churning up the dust, and set off back towards the landing. The guides walked alongside, but James still stood, stock still, watching it go.

Louis dropped back. 'What's wrong?'

He clicked back into the moment. 'What? Nothing.'

'Like hell.' But James shook his head and strode off after the wagon, leaving Louis to follow.

———

Somehow they got the guests and their luggage stowed aboard the canoes and passed down the stores, somehow they cast off from the wharf. Ballantyre had gripped his arm briefly, murmuring: 'We must talk,' and then he had stayed close to James, arranging things so that he, the stout man, and Miss Evie were put in the same canoe, together with Louis and James – the rest, including the blue-eyed man, in the other.

They pushed off from the wharf, and James paddled blindly.

The great railway viaduct cast a chill shadow as they slid past the great stanchions where the brook trout spawned. They emerged from beneath it, and James straightened his back, marshalling his disordered thoughts. *Do you believe in destiny*, Ballantyre had asked him yesterday and he had scoffed— But now he knew that Ballantyre had contrived all this for his own purpose, and yet in so doing had provided James with a God-given opportunity, for beyond the viaduct was Lake Helen, and beyond the lake was the Nipigon River— And James knew its ways. It was a wild river, and it would take them north through gorges and white water, away from the constraints of civilisation to where there was space enough to settle scores.

Chapter 12

'Yes, I see it.' Evelyn gave a perfunctory glance in the direction that her father was pointing. A large black and white bird was swimming low in the water, moving fast away from them. It dived and she turned her face forward again to stare in disbelief at James Douglas's back.

He had a scarf knotted around his neck and wore a sort of shabby waistcoat over a shirt of some coarse material, dirty white, with sweat patches staining the underarms. His sleeves were rolled up to the elbow, revealing sunburned forearms, and she saw the strength in them.

James.

He looked so very different – and yet the same.

Unconsciously she rubbed her own arm, feeling a bruise where her father had gripped it at the station. 'Walk with me a moment, my dear,' he had said, in a smooth but uncompromising tone, and had led her down the platform. 'And don't look back.' She had looked at him and seen the muscles in his jaw clenched tight, and realised that he was in the grip of some powerful emotion. Instinctively she had half-turned her head, but he had tightened his clasp. '*Don't* look back, I said.'

Then he had explained.

And as he spoke the world seemed to spin as the nightmare escaped its bonds and reared up in front of her, like an evil smoke. And she was a child again, leaning out of the study window, shaking with fear.

'*Here?* But how is he here?'

'He's calling himself MacDonald—'

'Did you *know* he was here?'

'How would I?' He had stared at her. 'You're trembling, my dear—? But listen! You *mustn't* show that you know him. Not in any way. Do you understand?'

She had looked up to meet his eyes, intent and very dark.

'Why not?'

But he had shaken his head and the old terror consumed her. She had tried to pull away, but he had held firm, his grip tightening painfully. 'Listen! I will explain everything to you, when I can – every damn thing – but for now just do as I say. Discuss this with no one. Understand? No one! Not Clementina or Melton, not even Larsen, and not . . . Dalston. Don't talk to James. Treat him as you do the other guides, like a stranger. He won't address you.'

'But I *need*—'

'Enough! Not a word. Not a glance. Ready?' And he had led her back down the platform towards the others, his hand still gripping her elbow.

In the other boat Clementina gave a peal of laughter at something Rupert had said, and Evelyn looked across at them. 'Alright, my dear?' her father asked softly. She made no reply and turned back, her eyes fixed again on James's waistcoat, at a patch carelessly applied, stitched in a thick black thread, probably his own work. The diving bird rose a little way in front of them and let out a weird trembling call, and a response echoed from somewhere across the lake. A sudden gust blew the drips from James's paddle onto her skirts and he half-turned, grunting an apology over his shoulder, and she saw that his neck was dirty and there was stubble on his chin. At home he had always been well dressed in accordance with the high standards her father demanded, handsome in his groom's livery when he drove them to visit neighbours. She would study his back then too, ridiculously proud of him. She knew every detail of him, the set of his shoulders, how his hair grew over his collar, and remembered how he would smile at her, a conspirator's smile, as he assisted her from the carriage.

But there had been murder in his eyes just now, when he had come towards them on the platform—

———

That evening James ate with the other guides in their own cabin which was set back a little from the lodge. He ate quickly, not join-ing in the usual discussion of the newly arrived guests, the amount of baggage they had brought, or of the physical merits of the two women – and the food stuck in his throat. When they had finished eating Louis pulled out a pack of greasy cards and began dealing them onto the top of an upturned barrel which served them as a table.

James pushed back his stool and got to his feet. 'I need to check that patch.'

Louis continued to deal, glancing up at him. 'It's fine. I looked.'

'It was leaking on the way back.' A lie, but never mind. He picked up his jacket and left before Louis could protest further.

Letting the door slam behind him he went down to where the smaller canoes were assembled, ready for the morning, slowing as he passed in front of the lodge window where the guests should now have finished eating. He glanced that way just once and then went down to the shore.

He pulled out his knife and slid the blade along the seam he had repaired so carefully the evening before, opening it again, just a small tear but enough to provide an excuse to be there— And he could spin the job out for as long as it took, certain that Ballantyre would come to him. He crouched down and lit a small fire in the fireplace built for the purpose, and began heating a tin of spruce gum, pulling a length of sinew from his backpocket to resew the tear. And, if necessary, he could tip the nearest canoe into the lake and he would be gone, letting the current take him.

He did not have long to wait. A few moments later the door of the lodge opened and Ballantyre came out onto the porch and stood looking across the lake with a studied nonchalance. Distracted by his appearance, James let hot spruce gum drip onto his hand and swore, and when he looked up again Ballantyre was strolling slowly towards the jetty. James bent again to his task, the burn heightening his anger, and he moved his knife closer, covering it with a strip of birch bark.

He straightened as Ballantyre approached. 'What game is this—?'

'You said you didn't know him.'

'I had a face, no name. Who is he?'

There was a tiny pause. 'Rupert Dalston. Earl Stanton's younger son.'

'So now I have both.'

'He doesn't know you, though, does he?'

'He soon will.'

Ballantyre frowned. 'James – if you take matters into your own hands . . .'

'I'll not play your games, Ballantyre. Why did you bring him here?'

Ballantyre shook his head. 'I didn't. I'd no idea he was coming until I got that telegram, this morning, on the jetty.'

'You lie. You knew.' And he bent to spread the dark pitch over the resewn seam, seeing a blister rising over the burn on his hand.

Ballantyre shook his head. 'No. They met him in Chicago. Believe me or not, as you will, but this changes things. It's too risky. You must go back to Port Arthur and wait for me there, at the Northern. I'll give you some money and I'll come to you after—'

'No.'

Ballantyre considered him, then pulled his cigar case from his pocket, took one out, and tapped it on the case. 'James, listen to me—'

'No, you listen. I want answers. And then I've scores to settle, first with him, and then with you.'

Ballantyre continued to contemplate him. 'You'd more sense at thirteen—' He took out a silver penknife and began trimming the cigar, then lit it, blowing the smoke at the mosquitoes which were dancing in the air around them. 'So what will you do, James, murder us both?' He put away the penknife. 'If you take matters into your own hands you're sunk, and there'll be nothing I can do for you.' James threaded the length of sinew through holes punctured in the birch bark, his hair falling forward, his hand shaking with suppressed fury.

The silence stretched out. Then: 'How is it that you *did* know him?' asked Ballantyre.

He would have known the man anywhere. That perfect sculptured face, those cold blue eyes scanning the riverbank, his well-dressed figure surrounded by the hounds, frantic as they sought the lost scent. James had looked down from the cleft in the oak tree trunk, watching as McAllister joined the man, servile and fawning, knowing that the hunt was a sham. Once they had looked up into the branches, and James had lain close, his face pressed hard against the bark, not daring to breathe.

Briefly he told Ballantyre.

'So. Jacko schooled you well,' was his only comment, then he swung round as the screen door banged again. Skinner and the stout gentleman had emerged from the lodge and started down the steps towards them. Ballantyre pulled on his cigar and spoke quickly. 'So he'll not know you then, and I've told my daughter to ignore you. She knows nothing of this, or of him— And if you insist on staying, for God's sake keep a hold of your temper and let this play out.'

'That's not good enough.'

'No? Well, make it so.' Ballantyre turned to greet the two men as they approached. 'Eh, Mr Skinner? Make it good and tight for those rapids you told us about. Preparation and planning, that's what's needed – and then a cool head in fast water.' And he led the stout man away, leaving James to answer Skinner's incensed enquiry as to what he was doing leaving repairs until now.

And as he looked over Skinner's shoulder, back towards the lodge, he saw that Louis had come out of the river guides' cabin and was standing, arms folded, leaning against the doorjamb, looking back at him.

———

Evelyn too had been watching the exchange down by the landing from her room in the lodge. Whatever were they saying—? James had had his back turned to her, and her father was calmly smoking, giving nothing away. She was tempted to go down to them, now, and demand answers, and be done with it all.

But which did she fear the most – the truth, or the lies they might tell her?

She had never known her father to look anything but entirely in control, yet all through the meal that evening she had sensed the tension in him. It had been cramped in the little room where they ate, and the hurricane lamps set on the window ledges had created shadows, darkening the corners and illuminating the dusty rafters. In one corner a pot-bellied stove took the chill off the autumn evening, and a pair of thick candles lit the centre of a table. In any other circumstances she would have been enchanted.

A dark-eyed Indian girl had served their food, padding across the floor in dirty moccasins, bringing plates to each guest while Mr

Skinner outlined his plans for them, describing the route upriver, and telling them to keep their belongings to a minimum. Rough clothes, he had said, just a change or two in case things got wet, something warm, long sleeves to keep the bugs at bay. 'Although I've got a concoction which I swear—' She was only half-listening, letting Clementina ask the questions, remembering to smile occasionally when the others laughed. The Indian girl had retreated into the shadows and Evelyn wished she could join her there, and be swallowed up by the darkness. At one point Clementina had leant across and asked if she were quite well, and her father had switched his attention to her, his eyes searching her face. Under his steady stare she had dissembled, confessing to just a little fatigue, and made a greater effort to appear engaged.

'So there's gold and silver *here* too?' Rupert was asking.

'Gold, silver, copper, iron, nickel . . . you name it, we got it somewhere,' Mr Skinner replied. 'Diamonds too.'

'Diamonds!'

'Yes, ma'am, as big as yer fist. A prospector dug up some old Indian and found a band of pure copper round his neck with a diamond the size of a chicken egg strung on it. Sold it fer a thousand dollars.'

'And since then?' persisted Rupert.

''Nother Indian came into town with his family.' Skinner spoke between mouthfuls. 'Kid was playing with a rattle thing, rock crystals and stuff tied to it. 'Cept one wasn't rock crystal.'

'And no one knows where they're from?' Skinner had shaken his head, and Rupert had turned to her father. 'You'd know where to look though, wouldn't you, sir? With your South African connections. What sort of terrain—?'

'My dear Dalston! I've no knowledge of diamond mining.'

'No? But I understood—'

He had stopped, discouraged perhaps by her father's sardonic expression. 'Dreaming of another Kimberley, are you?' he had asked.

'If Port Arthur can dream of becoming Chicago' – Rupert grinned at Mr Larsen – 'why not?'

Her father had sat back in his chair, and given him an appraising look. 'Was it the idea of doing some prospecting that brought you over here?' he asked, after a moment.

Rupert had flicked his fingers at the Indian girl and gestured to his empty glass, waiting until she refilled it before replying. 'Big game hunting, actually. I was going out west to hunt buffalo, until I chanced upon your party. But if I thought there was the prospect of gold I might linger—' Evelyn saw that his gaze was following the girl as she moved around the table.

'So the Exposition was by way of a diversion?'

'Sort of. I came over with my father, you see. He was here on railway business.'

'Ah.'

A shadow had crossed Dalston's face as he took a long drink and he had fallen silent, staring at his plate. During the voyage through the lakes he had confided to Evelyn his exasperation that his father had continued to invest in railways long after they had ceased to be profitable. It had been a bad year, he had told her. Worrying.

'Tricky things, railways.' Her father continued to look at him.

'Yes, but in the long run they're *bound* to be profitable—' He glanced hopefully between her father and Mr Larsen.

'And is your father still over here?'

'No. He returned home a couple of weeks ago.'

'What a shame.' Ballantyre held up his glass to the girl as she made her way around the table with her jug, carrying it carefully in two hands, her plait dark against the shoulder of her cotton blouse, and nodded his thanks. 'He could have seen that stretch of track you travelled on today. Just a rackety ride now, but probably the costliest you'll ever see.'

'Yessir,' said Mr Skinner, and drew their attention to a series of notches cut into the doorjamb. 'See that? One notch for each five miles. But no one kept score of the dead men, what with rockfalls, accidents and disease—'

'Not to mention fortunes lost and reputations ruined.'

'Worst stretch of the whole goddammed railroad.'

Larsen had retired to pack. He had watched his friend across the dinner table, and seen that the strain was back behind his eyes. He had assumed it was concern over the unresolved gold claim, but when Ballantyre told him that he had failed to make contact with either the young chief Achak or his own agent he had simply dismissed the matter with a shrug. And yet he had seemed distracted, remote— Whatever was eating the man? Not the bank's business, it was as sound as a bell – that much he did know. This fishing trip had been planned initially as a celebration, an opportunity to reflect on their successes at this watershed moment. Accommodating Evelyn and her friends had changed things, of course, but something else was troubling his old partner. Was it his inclusion of Dalston in the party? That, it seemed, had been a mistake, after all. At the station Ballantyre had greeted the young man affably enough, but Larsen had not been convinced. He paused, a pair of socks in both hands, and recalled the odd business which had followed, taking Evelyn off down the platform. It could only have been to warn her off Dalston, and since then the poor girl had disappeared back inside herself, eyes troubled and silent, and he cursed himself for bringing him. After dinner he had tried to apologise for his blunder, and to explain, but Ballantyre had simply clapped him on the back with a smile saying that coincidences never failed to astound him.

'Destiny, my friend. It's a potent force, and we're helpless in its hands. Do you ever feel that way?' It had seemed a curious response, and Ballantyre's eyes had belied the smile on his lips. There had been something deep within them, a shadow, and at the shadow's core – a spark. 'Frankly I'm astonished that young Dalston wished to join us,' he had continued, 'but his presence will undoubtedly add to the interest, so let us see what transpires, shall we?' Larsen rolled up a couple of shirts, discarding the others, and admitted himself a coward, not having had the courage to offer his opinion that Evelyn was probably the reason why Dalston had accepted the invitation.

Chapter 13

They reached the first campsite by late afternoon the next day to find four tents already pitched on the little headland. The low sun was slanting onto the bleached canvas and it lit a backdrop of aspen and birch resplendent with autumn colour— Two half-built wigwams, scruffy but picturesque, stood to one side, and the whole headland was bathed in a vivid, almost theatrical, glow.

'Oh look, George!' Clementina cried out as the canoes rounded the headland, and she clasped her hands in delight as they approached the shore. 'How perfect!'

Mr Skinner looked relieved as he handed them out of the canoes. This was a popular first campsite, he explained as they headed up the slope, and he had sent his men on ahead to secure it. He hoped they would find it comfortable, the best as he could do. 'Some folks just hunker down here and stay if the fishing's good, else they just go a mile or so upstream to Cameron Rapids. You can pull out two- or three-pounders from there easy as spit.'

Low bushy plants and young trees had grown on the edges of the clearing, taking advantage of the open canopy, and they too were aflame with autumn colour; and there were still wild raspberries to be had, ripe and sweet. The whole thing looked almost staged, Evelyn thought as she followed the others up the slope, like a tableau, or an exhibit on the Columbian Exposition's Wooded Isle. Perhaps it should be labelled, just as Sitting Bull's cabin had been – A WILDERNESS CAMP – but with every comfort provided for a well-fed elite. Or were they exhibits too?

'Awfully jolly,' remarked Dalston, stopping behind her to light a cigarette. Evelyn gave him a quick smile and looked back to the canoes, where James was unloading the gear, heaving boxes of provisions ashore. He seemed to sense her gaze upon him and glanced up at her, then quickly away.

Beside the tents a square canvas awning had been strung between four pines to cover an eating area complete with a folding table and chairs; Mr Skinner showed them how sheets of fine mesh would drop down to keep out the flies. 'Got to have you comfortable.' He repeated the phrase like a mantra, and with a growing confidence.

The largest tent, he explained, was for the ladies, and it had been set up between two others: Rupert and George sharing one, her father and Mr Larsen the other. 'The women flanked by their menfolk,' Evelyn remarked softly to Clementina.

'And very glad I am too!' she replied.

The fourth tent, Mr Skinner's own, was smaller and had been pitched close to the wigwams, at a little distance from the guests' tents, where a separate small fireplace had been built. Would they continue to eat separately? she wondered. 'If anyone wants to go fishing while we finish setting up, some of the boys'll take you,' he said. 'It ain't too late.' The men agreed with enthusiasm, but she and Clementina opted to stay and get settled.

There was not enough room in the tent for both of them to move at the same time, so Evelyn sat on her low cot and drew in her feet in order to give Clementina space to unpack.

'Gosh. Do you think we'll manage?' said Clementina. 'It's all rather primitive.'

'Not so – look!' Evelyn gestured to where, at the head end of the two cots, there was a narrow wooden stand which provided a surface for a small enamel jug and washbasin. A thin bleached towel hung at each side, and at the back of the contrivance was a hinged mirror of polished metal which reflected a rather foggy image. 'Every convenience provided.'

'How many nights did your father say we would be camping?' Clementina asked, fingering the towel dubiously. She then examined the cots and found that they had been provided with coarse cotton sheets sewn along the long seams to form a sack or bag which was then covered with blankets and furs. 'Is that where the smell is coming from?'

'Probably,' Evelyn replied, leaning over to sniff. 'But I bet they're lovely and warm.'

A rougher, rather matted, brown fur had been spread on the ground between the cots. 'How cold do you think it will get at night?' Clementina asked, and Evelyn shrugged, and looked up to the ridge pole where an unlit hurricane lantern had been hung. Clementina followed her gaze. 'George said to remember to undress in the dark or in bed because when the lantern's lit we can be clearly seen.'

'Gosh!'

'And he said to keep things in the bags because of the damp. I expect we'll soon look like frights, but at least we have a mirror, of sorts, and can keep clean.'

'And we have no audience of admirers to impress.'

How little one really needed, she mused, as she went through her bag, thinking how absurd it was to have brought her slippers. They belonged to the opulence of a New York hotel room or to the trim luxury of the *Valkyrie*, not to the rough hewn simplicity of Skinner's lodge, or a tent. She stuffed them down into the bottom of her bag, and then crawled to the end of her cot to pull open the flap and watch the men preparing to go back out onto the water, assembling rods and landing nets.

'And Rupert already knows you're pretty,' Clementina said.

Evelyn made no response, but continued to watch as the men climbed back into the canoes. Her father and Mr Larsen were with James in one, the others going with the man they called Louis. Her father had probably arranged it so; little he did was by accident.

Somehow she must contrive to speak to James alone—

She let the flap fall and turned back, and observed that Clementina had brought twice as many clothes as she had and was now wondering where to put them.

'Do *you* like Rupert Dalston?' she asked, on a sudden impulse.

Clementina looked up in surprise. ' Of course I do! Don't you?'

'I think so—'

'Well, he likes you very much— He was a little worried, though, that your father might think he had rather inveigled himself into our party, but he doesn't, does he? I'd told Rupert it would be alright, and they founds lots to talk about at supper.' So Rupert confided in Clementina, did he? And she wondered what else they discussed. Suddenly she felt the need for more space, and pulled over her bag to find her sketchbook and pencils to use them as an excuse. 'I'll leave you to unpack, Clemmy. Stuff things under my cot if you want to. I'm going to go and explore.'

But once out of the tent, she found she was alone with only the native guides, and she felt conspicuous and somehow rather foolish. She stood there, uncertain, and the men looked back at her, openly studying her. Perhaps they were finding it strange as well. And then one of them gestured to the table and chairs, so she nodded her thanks and went to sit down. She looked around for Mr Skinner, but he too had disappeared somewhere.

'You want coffee?' the man asked.

'No. Thank you.'

'You want—' He gestured with his head to where a canvas screen had been erected set back in the forest, and she studied it for a moment before realising its purpose and felt her colour rise. She shook her head, and wondered privately what Clementina would make of the arrangement.

After that the natives ignored her but continued with their tasks, speaking in low voices in their own language. She let a few minutes elapse and then covertly began studying them in return. They were quite dark-skinned or deeply tanned, with unfamiliar features, and were dressed in an eclectic mixture of native and European clothes, some with their hair worn loose and long, some with it braided. But they were different in every way from those disconsolate figures she had seen at the Exposition. Like the people in Port Arthur, these men were not exhibits but went about their tasks with a quiet purpose. She watched with interest as they finished putting skins over their simple shelters, dragging in spruce branches for flooring, then one set an iron cooking pot on a cross pole over the fire, pouring in water collected in a leather pail. All was executed with a calm efficiency. And yet – there *was* a false note here too, she thought with a frown, for all this activity was simply for the comfort of their party, who had come here to play; and who had no doubt paid handsomely for the experience. The men would be rewarded for their work, of course, but what would they have been doing otherwise? What would their fathers have done? Or their grandfathers—

The one who had offered her coffee was called Tala, she had been told, and he seemed friendly enough, but the other one, Machk, never seemed to smile. His lean face was weather-beaten and dark, and his high cheekbones and hooked nose gave him a striking profile. Tala's face was quite different, rather broad and flat. She would like to try to sketch them but dared not. Another man she had heard James call Marcel; Skinner had said that he was a half-breed, half French, half native, but he looked no different from the others. He was small and wiry and had a ferocious scowl, and she sensed that everyone, even Mr Skinner, treated him differently. And then there were two others who had not been introduced, hardly more than boys, who went about their business talking to each other in low voices, occasionally laughing.

If you counted Mr Skinner, Louis, and James, there were eight of them in all, to look after a party of six!

She began to feel more self-conscious, just sitting there idly while they worked, so she went down to the shore and sat on a boulder to watch the sun as it began to sink behind the pine trees. Out on the water she could see the canoes some distance away, no more than dark shapes on a plane of silver. There was not a breath of wind and the far shoreline was mirrored perfectly in the still water, the top of each jagged pine reflected there, like the ink stains in the fold of an exercise book she used to make as a child. And looking back down the river, the way they had come, the two banks converged in flawless symmetry, perfectly bonded with their reflections, while upstream she could see swirls of current, deep and powerful. There was a majestic beauty to the place, unchanged since time began— She opened her sketchbook, but doubted that she had the skill to capture it, and after a while she simply sat there, her arms clasped about her knees, and watched as evening fell.

It grew chilly. Little zephyrs sped across the surface of the water, shattering the still reflection, and the darkening forest sighed in the sudden breeze. Night fell quickly here.

She looked back at the camp which, now drained of light, had lost its theatrical quality and become solid and real. And exposed— She would be glad now if the men came back. There was no other light in the forest, and they might be quite alone in the world. One or two other boats had passed them in the course of the day, but as they travelled upstream there had been fewer, and now there were none. She stood and went down to the water's edge, looking across the river, and then to each side. There were wolves and bears out there, Mr Skinner had said – and always eyes in the forest. And when night came there would be nothing but thin canvas between them and the wilderness.

Yet this was the life that James now lived—

Once, years ago, he had described to her the delight of sleeping outdoors on a bed of heather and bracken, with only the scuffling sounds of nocturnal creatures for company, and she had schemed, hopelessly, to contrive it, for just one night, and he had laughed at her. But the woodland at home was familiar and benign, bordered by tracks or gently rolling fields, with nothing more savage than a hedgehog or a fox roaming the hedgerows, while here the forest seemed to stretch forever. A man could soon lose himself, Mr Skinner had said—

The breeze shifted and blew the smoke from the campfire towards her, and she felt absurdly comforted by the familiar smell. It reminded her of the bonfires which the gardeners would light in the autumn when the leaves had been raked into heaps and then wheel-barrowed off the lawns to be burned down near the greenhouses. One day she and James had come across one bonfire which was still smouldering, unattended, and James had dismounted and crouched down, blowing the embers back into life so that she could warm her hands. And she had slipped from her saddle and gathered twigs and pine cones to throw on it, delighted as they crackled and spat. But there had been trouble later when she had returned home reeking of woodsmoke, and she had hid her dirty hands behind her.

When she looked up again she saw that the canoes were returning, and felt both relief and a renewal of tension. If she did somehow contrive to get James alone, what would he say? The thought provoked another flutter of panic. Would it be easier to hear the truth or lies—?

So far he had steadfastly ignored her; only once, as they assembled that morning at Skinner's jetty, had she looked up to find him watching her, but he had turned aside and taken his place in front of the canoe, leaving Mr Skinner to help her aboard.

And yet, not so very long ago, she had thought of him as her friend.

Ballantyre House, Five Years Earlier

Evelyn stepped quickly into the courtyard, escaping from Miss Carstairs's protests which had followed her all the way from her bedroom. 'I shall speak to your father when he returns. I'm not sure it's right anymore, not now you're older.'

'If you could ride you could come too.' No danger there, old Carstairs was terrified of horses.

'Let us go out in the trap instead, my dear, it's a lovely day.'

'Where's the exercise in that?' She could see James waiting for her beside the pump holding Bella's reins in one hand, Melrose's in the other, studiously not listening.

'Then we could go for a longer walk—'

'Papa wants me to *ride* each day. You heard him say so.' That usually did the trick. 'Good morning, James.'

'Good morning, Miss Evelyn. Lovely morning, Miss Carstairs.'

Evelyn heard Carstairs sniff. 'Don't you take her so far today. I was ready to send someone after you last time. Miss Evelyn was late for tea.'

'Oh, good heavens,' Evelyn muttered as James led Bella to the mounting block and offered his hand. '*Tea.*'

'Right you are, Miss Carstairs,' said James, his eyes flashing Evelyn a smile as he checked the stirrups. Then he swung himself into Melrose's saddle, gave a small salute to the much-tried woman, and urged the horses forward.

'And stay on the paths.'

Neither of them troubled to answer but left the governess standing on the cobbles, lips pursed and arms folded, watching them go.

'Same thing, every day! *It's not right*,' Evelyn mimicked, over her shoulder to James. *'At fourteen you're almost a young lady.'*

'Nothing like,' he replied, and she giggled.

They rode down the drive which led from the house and turned onto one of the leafy rides. As soon as they were out of sight of the house she dropped back to ride beside him.

'How much longer will Papa insist I put up with her? Between Miss Carstairs and Mr Jenkins prosing on about Roman gods, you've no *idea* how tedious life is. And everything I do now is *unladylike* or *unbecoming*. It makes me want to scream. Yesterday, just imagine, I went down into the kitchen and Maud gave me two scones. I ate one there and put the other in my pocket, and then I forgot about it and left it on my dressing table. *She* found it at bedtime and was outraged, telling me if I was hungry I should ring for someone to bring me a tray, not go down to the kitchen and help myself as if I were a child.'

He gave her an odd sort of smile. 'It's a terrible life you have.'

'*You* can go into the kitchen whenever you like.'

'Aye, but they throw me out.'

'That's not what I hear,' she said, giving him a glancing look and a smirk.

He raised his eyebrows. 'Nothing of the lady about you at all. Look out for that branch, and sit up straight. You're like a sack of flour.'

She ducked to avoid the low beech branch and felt herself relaxing, the frustrations sloughing off her as they proceeded down the leafy bridle way. James was so companionable— She took a deep restorative breath and looked about her. Everything smelled so fresh and clean after last night's rain, the cow parsley had grown quickly this year, it almost reached her knees already, nettles too, and every now and then the horses' hooves trampled patches of wild garlic and released the sharp sour odour. How fast spring came once the frosts were over! And she could feel it frothing up inside her, bringing a strange restlessness, as the tiny may blossom flowers spread like snow along the hedgerows, and primroses unfurled amongst the roots. The dawn chorus woke her earlier each morning.

'I should love to sleep outdoors, like you used to do,' she said. He made no reply. 'It must be splendid.'

Sometimes he would talk about his past life, sometimes not, and she had yet to judge his mood today. She had taken a proprietary interest in him ever since that first evening when the keepers had dragged him across the lawn, a ragged dark-eyed boy, and she used to ask Papa about him. Did James Douglas like working in the stables? Hopefully, he would answer. Did he have new boots? Of course— And was he not hungry anymore? No, not hungry— And her father would tell her how Sinclair was teaching James his letters, and how skilled he was with the horses. Then later had come the delight of riding lessons, with James holding the leading reins, grinning at her, whispering encouragement to counter her father's exacting criticisms delivered from Zeus's lofty height. And now their daily rides through the estate were what she lived for. She could shed her frustrations along the dappled tracks, and in forbidden canters across the fields, out of sight of the house. From James she had learned where the moorhen had her nest in the reeds along the riverbank, and where tadpoles could be found. They had caught some a couple of weeks ago and he had put them in a basin stolen from the kitchen for her, and then secreted them behind the stable. Whenever she could she would escape from Miss Carstairs and watch them grow. Some of them already had legs; she must tell him—

'Do you miss it, sleeping outdoors?' she coaxed.

'Aye. Mostly in November after a good hoar frost.'

She frowned at him. 'I meant *now*, of course. In spring.'

'Still cold at night.'

'I suppose so. But if you had a little shelter, or a cave. And lots of clothes on, and blankets. And a fire. And soup.' He smiled but said nothing. She tried another tack. 'Shall we go down to the river again today?'

'No. McAllister has his men patrolling the banks; there's talk of poachers again.' His voice had hardened. She glanced at his profile but it gave nothing away. Was Jacko back? She dared not ask— She had stopped believing that James would one day run away again and rejoin his old companion, but whenever there were rumours that Jacko was in the district she grew uneasy.

'Taking the salmon?' she ventured.

'No. Tadpoles.'

She grinned back at him. 'Ours have grown legs now, some of them.'

'Aye? They're clever like that.'

She smiled again and took advantage of this shift in mood. 'Then let's go up to the hazel wood and you can show me how to set a snare. You said you would! And we can come back tomorrow and see what we've caught. And maybe even cook it?'

'I never said we'd do *that*.'

'You said we'd set a snare, though. You promised.'

'I don't make promises.' He looked across at her and she could see the beginnings of a smile. 'I've no twine, anyway.'

'I have.' She had been carrying it in her pocket for days, awaiting her chance, and pulled it out to show him.

At that he laughed. 'In that case, little Miss Poacher— First lesson. Go somewhere where you won't get caught.' He leant forward in his saddle, his eyes glinting in the way that Evelyn loved, and gave Bella a hearty smack on her rump. She shrieked as the startled mare shot forward.

———

They had not been caught, not that time anyway. But having shown her how a snare was set he had kicked it away again, gathering up the twine, declaring that he would not set the keepers' noses a-quivering. And as the soft summer stretched out he had shown her many things, plunging into the hedgerows to pick the berries of the deadly nightshade so that she would know them, and then gathering blackberries instead. They had feasted on them, washing away the telltale stains from her fingers in the river.

It was on that occasion, just as he helped her back into the saddle, that McAllister had stepped out of the undergrowth to confront them. 'Having trouble, Miss Evelyn?' he had asked, his eyes darting from one to the other. James had swung round to face him. During their rides she was not supposed to dismount.

'We're fine.'

'I asked Miss Ballantyre.'

'The saddle was slipping,' she had said quickly, knowing that some excuse was needed.

'Careless—' McAllister elbowed James aside to check the girth strap.

'She must have blown out her stomach when it was put on,' Evelyn added, by way of defence.

'That old trick—' He looked scornfully at James. 'Didn't you check?' James made no response, and turned to remount Melrose. McAllister moved to block his path. 'I'll take Miss Evelyn home.'

'No need. The saddle's secure now.' James made to go round him.

McAllister sidestepped, and they were chest to chest. 'I said I'll take her. You walk.'

On impulse Evelyn had pulled on her reins and turned Bella's head, forcing McAllister to step aside. '*James* will take me back. Why wouldn't he?' James had gone past him then and thrown himself over Melrose's back.

'Obliged, just the same,' he said and smirked down at McAllister, then urged the horses forward.

They had laughed once they were out of earshot, but the next day it was Sinclair, the stable master, who awaited her on the cobbles with the horses, and for the days that followed. She glimpsed James only once, but it was enough to see that his face was swollen and his eye an ugly purple. She had been deeply shocked, and then boiled with impotent rage.

At the end of the week her father returned and she had wanted to tell him, to explain what had happened, but she had glimpsed undercurrents at play that were beyond her understanding. Perhaps she would make things worse for James— The following day, however, she went down to the courtyard to find that James was there holding not only the reins of Bella and Melrose but of Zeus too. Then her father had appeared, with Sinclair walking beside him, and he had tossed her into the saddle without a word, signalling to James to mount and follow them.

After half a mile of silence her father had bidden her to ride on ahead and dropped back beside James. Whatever was said she had never learned, but a moment later her father had trotted past her, commending her on her posture, and left her to finish her ride with James as escort. James shook his head when she asked him to tell her what had been said, but after that their rides resumed as before, and as James's bruises faded they slipped back into the old easy companionship, a little more circumspect perhaps, but only for a while.

She looked up to see the canoes approaching the landing, James paddling in the stern of the leading one. Her father and Mr Larsen were still trailing their lines on either side, and she heard the low murmur of voices.

It was much later that she came to understand the message that her father had intended to convey to his household that day. James Douglas, the feral poacher's boy, was now a member of that household and was trusted with the master's most precious charge— But she also came to realise that although James would never lead her into danger, there was in him a sort of joyous defiance at breaking the rules which confined him.

And, like any other boy, he had liked an audience.

The canoes drew closer. He had been little more than a boy then, younger than she was now. But it was a man who paddled towards her now as darkness crept across the lake, and a very different James, broader and harder, his features more sharply angled, unsmiling as he went about his tasks.

And the looks he gave her father set her heart thudding with fear.

'Evelyn, are you alright down there?' Clementina called to her. 'Come up again. Mr Skinner is making us some tea.'

Tea.

'I'm coming.' She climbed back up to the plateau of the campsite and accepted a tin mug and drank a thick brown tea, and thanked Mr Skinner for all the trouble that he had taken. And as the sun finally disappeared behind the trees, the tops of the trees were backlit with a golden brilliance.

'This is what we came for! Look!' She and Clementina had gone down to the strip of stony beach to meet the canoes, and George held up his trophy for them to admire. 'What a beauty, eh? Must be sixteen inches, and the girth is easily eight. Who has the scales?'

'I hooked a much larger one, but it got away,' Rupert told them as he dismantled his rod.

'Fibber,' said Clementina.

'It's true.' He laughed. 'Ask George.'

'We'll eat 'em tonight, if you want,' said Skinner.

———

The trout tasted good, cooked in some sort of skillet and served with bannock, washed down with another brew of strong tea, and eaten by the light of lanterns hung in the trees. Evelyn felt better, now that the men had returned, and the firelight strengthened her spirits. Somehow she would get James on his own.

She watched him as he took his food and went to eat with the natives in the shadow of the two wigwams. Mr Skinner and Louis, however, remained with the guests, and between mouthfuls, they described the river upstream, and the places where good fishing was to be had.

'Wet or dry flies?' asked George, and Mr Skinner chuckled.

'They'll all be wet, mister, soon as they touch white water. But there're quiet pools higher up if you're looking for something fancier.'

James sat with his back to the party, just a dark form. Earlier she had seen that he was wearing the same patched shirt he had worn the day before, the same red scarf knotted at his throat, sleeves rolled up above his elbows. Where did he live when he was not on the river? she wondered.

'You can use bait too, minnows or cock-a-doosh. Ol' broad-tail don't care a bit. But you'd as like to hook a pike—'

'Pike!' said her father. 'Not worth the powder.'

It was another measure of the strangeness of it all that James sat apart. At home he would have been at the centre of things, always with something to say and with views of his own. He had been a favourite with the maids, and she would hear them discussing him, eyes aglow, and watch as they waylaid him in the stable courtyard, and if she learned that he was showing a preference for one or another she found herself filled with an unfamiliar, unreasoning fury— Sometimes she would find him in the kitchen when he brought vegetables in from the walled garden and watch him teasing food from the cooks, and he would slip her a biscuit, and then laugh when he was caught. A favourite with them all, except, of course, the keepers.

She had asked Alice, the little housemaid, why they still showed him such hostility, and Alice had paused in her tidying. 'They say that they got the old dog locked up but the whelp's been made the master's pet.'

At the time it had seemed quite normal that Papa had chosen James to assist with her riding lessons, and to escort her daily rides. It was only later that she realised that he had been singled out for this task. And her father would sometimes take James down to the river when he went fishing, and sometimes she went too, leaving Miss Carstairs behind, and she had watched him teach James to tie flies the way he liked them, using the feathers from a long dead macaw. 'My talisman,' he used to say. 'Never fails me.' A picture of the bird hung in the study and it had lived for years, he told them, producing a steady supply of blue-black tail feathers. When it died he had had it plucked, and he had apologised gravely when she had expressed her horror at this, and James had laughed.

Those were the best of days. But some nights she used to lie abed and worry in case Jacko returned and whistled for James, as he said he used to do. Would he go if he did? Once she had over-heard talk that Jacko had been released again after another spell in prison, and on their ride next morning she could not resist asking James if he knew.

"Course, I know.'

She had digested that, and another question had bubbled up. 'How do you know?'

'I just do.'

'Have you seen him?'

'Nosey little thing, aren't you?'

'Tell me.'

'Alright. I saw him.'

Her heart lurched. 'You did? Where?'

'You wouldn't know the place.'

'Did he want you to go off poaching with him again?' He had given her a scornful look. 'Would you go, if he'd asked?' He urged the horses on to where the path narrowed and dropped behind her. 'Did he ask you?' she had persisted over her shoulder. 'You must refuse if he does, you know— Did you refuse?'

But the question was never answered.

———

From the corner of her eye she watched him now as he went with the others back down to the canoes, a dark silhouette against the silver water, and she saw them heave the boats onto the land, away from the shore, then turn them onto their sides. James took his pack over to one, unrolling a blanket under the shelter of its up-turned hull. Would he sleep there? Surely not—

'It'll be a fine night,' Louis said, regarding her with a fixed expression.

'But cold, surely?'

'We warm each other,' he said softly, and gave a wolfish smile which seemed intended to discomfort her, and she looked away again, annoyed that it had.

Clementina got to her feet. 'I don't know about you, Evelyn,' she said, stifling a yawn, 'but I shall turn in for the night. Come too and give me courage?'

'Good night, my dear,' said her father as she passed him.

Chapter 14

'Sports fishermen like yerselves just keep on coming! More every year—' Skinner smacked a mosquito which had settled on his arm, then wiped his hand on his knee. "Specially after some magazine wrote that the Nipigon was the finest brook trout stream in the world; there's bin no stoppin' 'em.' He sat back, released a satisfying belch, then remembered his company and excused himself. Out on the lake, Larsen watched a laden canoe appear like a ghost through the light morning mist, heading silently downstream. He raised a hand in response to their greeting. 'Most folks are packin' up for the season now, though,' Skinner added, nodding towards them. 'So you'll have the place to yerselves.'

'I used to fish in the Adirondacks twenty years ago,' Larsen remarked as the canoe disappeared round a bend in the river, taken quickly by the current. 'But then the hotels came, and then the resorts and the cabins—' He drained his coffee and set down the mug. 'It seems we crave the wilderness, and then in finding it, we destroy it.' He had noted with consternation the number of boats they had seen on Lake Helen the day they left, even this late in the season, and they had seen the glow of one or two other campfires. Twenty years ago there would have been none.

How many more trips would he be able to make here? he wondered; the years were beginning to hang heavy. But soon he would have more time to take his pleasures, and to savour them, knowing that the bank he had built up from nothing would be in safe hands.

He could think of no more worthy successor than Charles Ballantyre, nor a man of greater integrity.

He glanced across at him now. Last night out on the lake his friend had seemed at last able to shed his worries and focus on the matter at hand, the glint of battle alight in his eye as he played his line. He still looked relaxed and was giving courteous attention to another of Skinner's rambling anecdotes, but perhaps only a part of his attention, as Larsen saw that he was also listening to a conversation between Dalston and Louis.

'Bears, black and brown, moose, of course,' Louis was saying. 'Hunters have their own preference. But this is Indian land and—'

'What about big cats? Cougar? Lynx or—?'

'We've come to *fish*, Rupert.' Melton yawned beside him. 'Keep your shots for the poor buffalo.' And then Dalston seemed to become aware of Ballantyre's bland scrutiny and took refuge in his hip flask.

'And what is it the Indians themselves are hunting now?' asked Ballantyre, taking advantage of a gap in Skinner's story and offering his own flask to Louis.

'Anything to get them through the winter,' he replied, taking a swig. 'That is *very* good, sir,' he said, licking his lips and taking another. 'And they need food for their dogs too.'

'So this chief Achak,' Ballantyre continued, 'what will he be hunting for?'

Louis seemed to pause, then took a third swig before returning the flask. 'Same things. Moose, deer—'

'And they can be found anywhere?' Louis nodded. 'No favourite hunting grounds or fishing places?' Ballantyre was like a dog with a bone, Larsen thought, he simply could not let the matter go.

'I wouldn't know.'

'But your friends might?' Ballantyre lit a cigar, gesturing in the direction of the guides down by the water's edge.

'Perhaps.'

'If it's Indians you want to find, mister,' offered Skinner, 'we'll likely meet up with some of them camping higher up the river. There ain't much to see, though, just more shelters like those over there, and a bunch of dogs, women, children. Families mostly—'

'But they might know where Achak was camping?' Ballantyre looked across at Larsen and raised his eyebrows just a shade. Persistence had ever been his friend's driving force – if the man was out there Ballantyre would find him!

'Maybe.' Louis shrugged, then a moment later got to his feet and strolled over to where Marcel was chopping wood, and he stood there pouring away the rest of his coffee as they talked.

James too had been listening to the conversation while he fixed a fault with Larsen's reel, and had watched Louis go over to Marcel. He had seen Marcel nod and lay down his axe, so he was more or less prepared for what came next.

'Hey,' Louis called over to him. 'Let's put that big canoe back in water, shall we? Either that same seam's leaking, or it's another one. Marcel and I'll paddle while you—'

'*Leaking?*' Skinner hollered. 'You told me—'

Louis went past him with barely a glance. 'Don't want problems later.'

James put aside the reel and followed them down to the shore, while Skinner continued to rant. It was inevitable, he supposed, given Ballantyre's persistent questions, and he had been watching Louis's face, seen him trying to work it all out, looking for connections, and struggling to make sense of it all.

God knows he had been doing the same himself.

They paddled swiftly away from the camp, cutting across the current with big powerful strokes until they reached the far side of a rocky headland, then turned towards the shore. They were hidden there, out of sight of the camp, where questions could be asked. He had recognised the expression on Louis's face as they lifted the canoe onto the water, having encountered it first when Louis had his foot on his throat in the freezing warehouse in Montreal. And he had seen it subsequently, usually as a prelude to a fight.

He felt a fierce stab of resentment, but not at Louis—

The bow scraped on a patch of shingle, and Marcel leapt into the shallows and pulled the canoe higher up the shore. Then Louis climbed out and stood looking down at him.

'No leaks,' said James, returning the look evenly.

'No.'

Louis gestured with his head for James to get out, and so he did, keeping the canoe between them. He had been thinking hard, still undecided as to how much he should tell them. Not quite everything, he resolved. The arrival of Dalston on the scene had altered things, and Dalston he would handle alone.

Louis went and sat on an old log long stripped of its bark, bleached bone-white by the sun, and pulled out his pipe. 'You are anxious, my friend,' he said, squinting up at James as he stretched out his legs. 'These guests, they're not strangers to you.' Marcel went and slouched against a nearby tree.

James came slowly up the beach, and then no farther. 'Not all of them.'

'Yet you pretend, you and this Ballantyre. His daughter too. Why is this?'

'There're reasons.'

'*Bien sûr*. What reasons?'

'I knew them, back in Scotland.' James's resentment blazed to anger. Damn Ballantyre, sowing these seeds of mistrust – and damn Louis too, with his interrogation. 'It's an old story.'

Louis gave James a wide smile which failed to reach his eyes. 'We like stories. So, tell!'

James glanced from one to the other, then went over to a boulder worn smooth by ice and water and sat, staring down for a moment at a wiry plant which had struggled up through the shingle to find the sun. Then he ran his hands through his hair. What the hell!

And so he told them. Briefly. Just the bare facts, omitting any reference to Dalston. Or Evelyn. When he had finished Louis looked puzzled.

'But you *didn't* kill these men?'

'No.'

'And he knows that?'

'Yes.'

'Then why the pretence?'

'Sir George Melton is a justice, a law man, and I'm still wanted for murder.'

'So why doesn't Ballantyre just tell him the truth?'

Why indeed.

'He talks of clearing my name, now he has found me, but that Melton is a risk—' It sounded weak, even to his own ears, and he watched Louis and Marcel exchange glances, perhaps guessing that they had been told half a story. But how far would they push him?

'And the girl?' Marcel had taken out his knife and was whittling the bark from a sapling. 'Her eyes follow you.'

'And her friend asks her what is wrong. Why so quiet? Are you *quite* well?' Louis mimicked Lady Melton's well-bred voice but his eyes stayed hard.

James got to his feet. He'd had enough. 'She was only a child when it happened. So just forget her, eh?'

But Louis leant back on his elbow, still watching him, and pulled on his pipe. 'And your Mr Ballantyre is so keen to find Achak. Why is that, do you think?'

'Maybe he heard something—'

'Maybe he did.'

Silence. And from Louis, a steady stare.

'Not from me.' James spoke through clenched teeth.

So quickly was trust lost! That much he knew.

'What have you told him about Achak?'

'*Christ*, Louis!' They would be watching him now, suspicious of his every move, his every glance. And this too went on Ballantyre's account. 'I've told him nothing. Why would I?'

Louis continued to look at him, long and hard, then muttered something in French to Marcel and got to his feet. Marcel straightened and went back down to the water's edge.

'You have friends, *mon ami*. Partners. Remember?' He pushed the canoe back into the shallows, signalling James to get in. 'And we are here, beside you.' Watching you— The words were unspoken, and yet they hung there, though James sensed that, for now, the crisis was passing. 'And in the meantime we'll be dumb mules and know nothing of Achak's whereabouts. Yes? And we won't notice that you watch the man like an angry wolverine, or that his daughter's eyes never leave you.'

———

Next morning Evelyn woke to find that dawn was lightening the walls of the tent, and she lay there, watching the shadows cast by pine branches as they stirred with the breeze, feeling the chill morning air on her face.

She had not expected to sleep, but she had, and it had been a deep and unbroken sleep. Last night Clementina had declared that she would not dare to close her eyes for fear of bears, but her breathing had soon deepened and she slept still, only the very top of her head visible. The furs did smell, a strong animal aroma, strange though not unpleasant, but they had kept her warm through the night. She snuggled back down beneath them and lay there, watching as the light grew stronger. How had James fared, she wondered, rolled up in a blanket under the canoes. Had he slept? Or had he lain there, watching the stars, and seen the moon-light across the river?

And she remembered how she had once plagued him to ex-plain how to find the Pole star, and he had done his best, using a stick to draw the stars in the dust. Then, on the next clear night, he had come and thrown gravel up at her bedroom window and she had risen and peered down at him, pushing up the sash in response to his gesture. And he had pointed up into the sky, and she had seen the plough, just as he had drawn it, and he had directed her to the dim flicker of the Pole star. That he had remembered her question and come to show her had delighted her beyond reason.

She sniffed, smelling woodsmoke and something cooking which must be breakfast. Low voices grew louder and more distinct, and she could hear Mr Skinner giving instructions and then the metallic sound of water being poured into a tin kettle. He had said that he would wake them early, as something called the Long Portage lay ahead. Beside her Clementina stirred. She heard Mr Larsen's voice too, then her father's just outside knocking on the canvas asking how they had slept. She sat up and reached for her clothes as Clem-entina opened her eyes.

Breakfast consisted of a thick sort of porridge and coffee. Ev-elyn took hers over to a tree stump, the table and chairs having already been packed away, and sat there eating and watching as the men began to strike camp. They worked with the same swift efficiency, emptying the tents and stowing their contents. Bedding was pushed into oiled dunnage bags, the cots taken apart and the washstand folded up, and then all was taken down to the shore and packed into the canoes. The same performance was repeated with the gentlemen's tents, the cooking awning, and the folding chairs.

All that for six guests, while the guides themselves had managed perfectly well sleeping in their clothes under upturned boats or in simple shelters.

Once back on the river they made slow but steady progress upstream. James had not so much as glanced at her as he saw her settled into the canoe beside her father, nor did he look at her when he helped her ashore some hours later when they arrived at a small, half-broken jetty. This, Skinner told them, was the beginning of the Long Portage, which would take them around a series of rapids and shallows that stretched for almost three miles. The men would continue a little farther, he explained, poling the lightened canoes through the rocks for a while; it was easier than portage.

She stood between her father and Rupert and watched as James, together with Louis and Marcel, climbed back into the boats and then, stripped to the waist, began the strenuous business of poling the canoes up through the rocks while Machk and Tala walked on ahead, dragging on ropes secured to the front. She could hear them shouting to each other across the noise of the river.

'Backbreaking work,' remarked George.

'They're young,' said Mr Skinner, "nd fit.' And he turned away to oversee the remaining guides who shouldered the off-loaded packs and started up the trail. The rest of the party followed at a more sedate pace.

It was a well-worn track which climbed steadily uphill through the forest. At first it was wide enough for them to walk two abreast and every now and then they had a glimpse down through the trees to the sparkling river where the canoes were making their laborious progress upriver. 'How long will they keep that up?' she heard her father ask.

'Half a mile, maybe more if they're lucky, the river's high since the rain. They'll come ashore when it shallows, and then pull 'em out.'

'But do they carry the *boats* as well?' asked Clementina.

'Yes, ma'am. But empty they're light; it's the tents and gear that weighs heavy.'

And the folding chairs and the table and the awning, Evelyn bit her lip, and the cots, and the wretched washstand. Did their party really require so much cosseting? Or was it because she and Clementina were there? Why was it always thought that women required more! She used to complain to James that she would ride so much better if she was allowed to wear trousers and sit astride, and he had laughed at her. 'Get yourself breeks then, and shock old Carstairs.'

'In India we had a string of bearers a mile long when we went out hunting.' Rupert dropped behind to walk beside her. 'They'd have carried us too, if we'd asked them.'

'And did you?'

He glanced at her, an eyebrow raised at her tone. 'Hardly.' The trail narrowed and they were forced to walk single file awhile, and he dropped behind again. He seemed entirely untroubled by the exertions that were being made on their behalf, and she had heard him complaining to George about the food last night. A little way farther up and the path widened. 'Anyway, they were glad of the work,' he said, drawing level with her again.

'Who were?'

'The native bearers. Same here, I expect, these chaps. It gives them a livelihood.'

'But they had a livelihood before.' How must they feel, fetching and carrying for white men and women, the very people who had taken it from them. 'I don't suppose this is what they'd choose to do.'

'No, probably not. But it was the same in Africa. It takes a generation or two to adapt to civilised ways. Bound to, of course.' And she thought of the Indian who had been sitting at the door of Sitting Bull's cabin, a human exhibit scratching in the dirt, and these men now, earning their living by carrying the pointless trappings of those civilised ways on their backs. Adapting, as Rupert would have it. She had begun to refute his position when she heard the sound of rustling in the woods and the thump of footsteps behind them. 'Step back, miss, and let them pass,' said Mr Skinner, and the first of the canoes came into sight along the trail, carried shoulder high by James and Louis, moving fast.

'Good heavens,' exclaimed Clementina as she caught up with Evelyn and Rupert a moment later. George had dropped behind to walk with her as her boots, she said, were pinching.

The men had been sweating and breathing heavily, the canoe itself still packed with gear, but they hardly paused, except to wipe their forearms across their brows and confirm with Skinner that they would send the others back for what remained at the landing. As they disappeared along the trail, the second canoe appeared, and passed them.

'This is the longest portage we have to do,' said Mr Skinner as that too disappeared ahead of them. 'The others 'r soon passed. On the way back downstream, if you like a thrill and don't mind a wettin', some of you might want to stay with 'em and go through the fast water.'

A little farther along, they met Tala and Machk returning to collect the last canoe, and after another mile they reached the end of the portage to find the first two canoes were already in the water, half-stowed with equipment, and the men stretched out on the rocks smoking, or sleeping under the shade. Louis had his neckerchief spread over his face and it rose and fell with his snores.

James, she saw, was sat on a rock down by the water tossing pebbles at a half-sunken branch, and he looked up as they appeared out of the woods. Mr Skinner gestured to the small fire they had lit. 'How about some coffee? Is that can hot?' he asked, and James rose to obey.

Her father had picked up one of the poles and was examining

the iron tip. 'That was an impressive performance,' he said as James passed, but he was ignored.

'Ach, they're fit,' Mr Skinner repeated, dismissively. 'The others'll be here with the rest of the gear in half an hour, and then we can get going again.'

And then, thought Evelyn, these men must paddle the laden canoes upstream against the current, and pitch camp again, arrange the wretched washstand and cots, draw water and cook supper before they could even think of sleeping.

She went down to the river to rinse out her own cup.

'This new railway line that's spoken of. What route will it take?' she heard her father ask as she rejoined them.

'Other side of the river, with a whistle-stop at the lake a few miles to the north. So then we'll have fishermen coming downriver as well as up.'

'And one day perhaps a very different river.' Her father looked out across the water to where the current was strong. 'If what we learned at the Exposition is anything to go by.'

The old man looked puzzled. 'Meanin' what?'

'Meaning dams, sluices, and turbines, Mr Skinner. Water-power.'

'On *this* river?'

'I imagine someone is considering it.'

Mr Skinner looked aghast.

'Are you investing in the electricity companies too, Mr Ballantyre?' asked Rupert. 'I understood these new long-distance currents can be lethal.'

'They will be,' he replied. 'For the Nipigon as Mr Skinner knows it.'

Evelyn looked about her to where the sun lit the bright autumn colours along the riverbank, watching the poplar leaves tremble in the breeze before spiralling down to join the current, dropping like so many gold coins to the water. So the modern world would encroach here too, would it? Where the canoes resting on the shingle and their tiny fire were the only signs of human life—

'Ah! What took you?' Skinner's shout broke into her thoughts. Tala and Machk appeared from the woods, panting, weighed down by the last canoe. 'C'mon, get moving,' and he gave Louis's recumbent form a quick kick. 'We ain't done yet.'

Chapter 15

The second campsite was at a bend in the river.

Evelyn stood on the shore and watched the men begin to unload the gear again, then carry it piece by piece from the boats up to the cleared area where, wordlessly and efficiently, they re-created the camp. The new site was on a little knoll where the land fell away on both sides, and was reached by a short wooded trail. Once up on the knoll the rushing sound of the river surrounded them, absorbing the softer tone of the wind passing through the trees.

Bedrock had been exposed over much of the site and so tent ropes were secured to rusting iron hoops, or were slung between trees and tied to branches. The tents themselves were arranged as before with the three for the guests on the flattened area, separated by Skinner's tent from the Indian shelters set slightly to one side. Two worlds, divided—

And would James and Louis sleep under the canoes again? It would be hard and cold down on the rocks by the river.

In what seemed like no time at all fires were lit and a meal prepared, and again the party divided to eat around two separate fires. The guides looked dog tired by then, as well they might, and even Mr Skinner was less garrulous than usual, content to suck on his pipe. There was good fishing here, he told them, so they would stay at this camp for two nights.

At least the men could rest a little, Evelyn thought, and she

165

sensed them waiting with ill-concealed impatience for their charges to retire.

But the gentlemen seemed content to sit beside the crackling fire and talk on into the fading evening. Her father and Mr Larsen sat on one side, smoking their cigars, and Mr Larsen addressed occasional remarks to Mr Skinner. Her father, she saw, was staring fixedly into the fire, absorbed by his own thoughts. Whatever they might be—

She had not seen him speak to James at all today.

Rupert, flask in hand, leant across her to talk to George, who sat on her other side with Clementina's head resting on his shoulder.

'Like I said before, now's the time. Before word spreads . . .' he said.

'Word about what?' she asked.

'Rupert's going to make his fortune in diamonds,' George replied, with a smile.

'Scoff, George, by all means! But there was plenty of talk around the tables in Port Arthur, I tell you. Mostly about some big gold strike, but of diamonds too—' Rupert paused as Marcel came over to collect the tin plates, and his eyes followed him until the half-breed was out of earshot. 'I'll bet these fellows know a thing or two, but getting them to tell you anything is another matter.'

'You can hardly blame them, if there *are* fortunes to be made,' murmured Clementina.

Rupert appeared not to hear her, and his face adopted a mulish expression. 'A gold mine would come in pretty handy just at the moment,' he said, and began tossing pine cones into the fire.

'Just the one?' asked George, with a wry smile at Evelyn.

Money mattered to Rupert, it seemed, and mattered a great deal. But was it a natural avarice, or debts? He had told her that his father's investment had been badly buffeted by The Panic that had so concerned Papa and Mr Larsen.

'You know,' he continued a moment later. 'I've half a mind to go back to Port Arthur after this trip and see what I can discover. Maybe get some backers—' He glanced towards Mr Larsen and her father, and then murmured to her, 'Your papa has connections here, doesn't he? And Larsen too?'

'I really don't know,' she replied.

Mr Skinner called out to James to build up their fire and she watched him rise from the other group to obey. Conversation died again as he brought more logs over to them and raked the fire's dying embers into a heap.

Rupert watched him, wordlessly, then: 'Have *you* heard about some big gold strike just north of here?' he asked.

James did not immediately answer but shrugged, his face half in shadow. 'Gold this year, diamonds last year, there's always something.'

He made as if to withdraw but George addressed him. 'You hail from Kelso, I understand?' Evelyn stiffened. James grunted a brief assent but she was unable to see his expression. 'I know the place well,' George continued, 'or the racecourse anyway, and certain beats along the Tweed.' James made another noncommittal sound as he bent again to the fire. 'You must have known the Ballantyre estate then?'

She sensed her father switch his attention to them.

James straightened and looked steadily back at George. 'Of it, yes.'

'And what was it that brought you over here?' Clementina asked, in a social tone that managed to sound patronising. 'A chance to see more of the world?'

Evelyn sensed another tiny pause. 'Something like that,' he replied.

'And have you found it was an advantageous move?' Rupert asked, looking around the camp, his gaze lingering on the scruffy shelters. His tone was condescending too, and she saw a spark in James's eye.

Rupert could not know what he asked—

'Aye, it was.'

James turned to leave them but Rupert held out a pack of cigarettes, offering them to him, and blocking his route with his outstretched arm. 'So what was your work in Kelso? Before you came over.'

James ignored the proffered pack. 'Whatever I could find,' he replied, and as Evelyn searched for a way of deflecting the conversation, she saw that her father was slowly rising to his feet. If James was aware of this he gave no sign but said, 'My master was a corrupt scoundrel, so I came out here.'

Heat burned Evelyn's cheeks, but she felt her father's hand drop onto her shoulder. 'A prudent move, I feel sure.' He pulled over his seat and sat down beside her. 'So you dream of gold, do you, Dalston?' he asked, and she watched James withdraw to the other fire and turn his back to them. 'Worse poison to men's souls, or so the bard would have it.'

'It's all very well for the bard—'

'And what would gold bring to you, do you think? Freedom and benefit, to quote Emerson?'

Dalston gave a short laugh. 'I'd be free from my creditors at any rate.'

'And benefit?' her father persisted, the firelight playing over his features. 'To what purpose would you put your fortune?'

Dalston lit a cigarette and flicked the match into the fire. 'The same as any man, of course. To support myself.'

'Ah.' It was a little word, but it managed to convey contempt. She saw Rupert's expression change, and this time she bridled in his defence. What right had Papa to judge any man? He no longer had the right to judge! He, who presented himself to the world as a generous benefactor, an upright man of principle, and yet by his own actions had . . .

And there her thoughts faltered, at that point where they always stalled. *A corrupt scoundrel* James had called him, and the old sick fear rolled over her as she looked across at him. He had absorbed James's insult without demur, as if accepting that portrayal of himself, and his face was now a mask.

And she recalled that day in Edinburgh when the mask had slipped: *I'm beyond redemption*, he had said.

———

The temperature dropped low that night and she awoke chilled, the furs having slipped off her cot, and her breath was misty as she emerged from her tent. She returned at once for a shawl, warning Clementina that the day was colder, and then returned to stand a moment and watch patches of low cloud drifting across the distant cliff face, hanging like lambs' wool amongst the trees.

Whatever must it be like here in winter—?

'Mist'll burn off in the sun,' Louis told her as he passed. And true enough, as she sat huddled close to the fire eating her breakfast, patches of blue sky appeared between the clouds and the sun's rays filtered through the trees to reach the camp. She moved her chair out of the shadows into a patch of warmth where low-growing plants cushioned her. The green of the leaves was splattered with autumn reds and yellows, and sheltered plum-dark berries, while spreads of moss and bright lichens covered the bare rocks. If they were staying in camp today perhaps she might paint—

The men must have been up for a while. She saw them down by the water's edge where the canoes had been lifted back onto the water, all ready for the day's fishing. James was there too, talking to George, and examining his rod.

'Will you go with them, Evie?' Clementina asked as she emerged from the tent and came to sit beside her.

'No. Will you?'

'Heaven forbid! I shall stay here and try to keep warm.'

So what would they do, the two of them? What would be their *sphere of activity* today, out here in the wild? Their duty was to be a civilising influence, but how should they approach it, when all their needs had been anticipated by these rough men who served them? They had completed all the domestic tasks of the camp well so she and Clementina were entirely without purpose.

'And what will you do?' she asked.

'I'll catch up with my journal,' Clementina replied. 'It's days since I wrote anything.'

So at least their continuing existence would be recorded—

'Why don't you come with us?' Rupert called up to Evelyn.

'Next time, perhaps,' she replied, catching a brief glance from James.

'That's a promise, then,' Rupert called back, and smiled at her as he stepped into one of the canoes.

And so, with nothing else to do, and having tidied themselves up as best they could, the two women settled themselves at the table, Evelyn with her paints and Clementina with her journal. And as the sun rose higher, it burned away the last of the mist, just as Louis had predicted. Tala brought them coffee, but then he and the others stretched out beside the fire, dozing or smoking their pipes, and ignored them – mere women without their men.

Evelyn opened her paint box and surveyed the range of colours. Even with an infinite number of shades she could not begin to capture the scene before her: the dark forest and, beyond it, the solemnity of the cliffs, rosy pink in parts, slate grey in shadow. Such an immense landscape— She would attempt a detail of it, perhaps, so she studied the trees which were growing above the rocks beside the river, seeing how the branches hung from the trunks in ragged half-loops, each one a worthy subject, each one unique. Some were very dark, green-black, while others had a blue-grey hue which made a pleasing contrast to the flame colours of the maple and poplars; so much more vivid than the mellow golds and bronzes of autumn at home. There the woodlands were generally sunny, open places, and the trees were rounded or fan shaped, some standing alone, others in small copses set against a backdrop of hillsides, which had been grazed to a soft felt by generations of sheep. There could be no greater contrast.

She looked across at Clementina, who was writing briskly, absorbed in her task. 'Is this what you had expected when Papa asked you to come?' she asked.

Clementina raised her head and considered. 'I don't really know,' she replied. 'He arranged matters with George, you see, once I'd agreed to come. All George told me was not to expect much comfort, and warned me about the flies, so I wasn't sure *what* I was coming to.' She paused, looking around. 'But I did expect there to be rather more people, other fishing parties. And at least *some* houses.'

Evelyn looked back across the river to the high cliffs. 'We might be the only people in the world.'

Clementina gave a theatrical little shiver. 'It's rather terrifying, don't you think?' But Evelyn knew that as long as George was close by Clementina would simply abdicate responsibility to him in the certainty that he would take care of her. That too fell within the sphere of womanhood.

Then Clementina leant close and spoke in a low tone. 'And I didn't expect to be living in *quite* such close quarters with the natives. I woke last night and swear I could hear them snoring! And have you seen the size of the knives they carry around? Like brigands!'

'So should we feel more safe, or less, I wonder.'

'And they have a rather peculiar smell. Sort of composty—'

'But then they haven't the benefit of a folding washstand.'

'They could wash their clothes more often, though.'

Evelyn looked at her and saw that she was quite serious. She dropped her head to hide a smile and opened her paints and began trying to establish a palette: vivid crimsons, soft umber, so many shades of green— Had Clemmy expected some sort of rustic shooting party with attention given to style and elegance, the natives servile and well groomed, and with the distinctions of class preserved and venerated? Perhaps so—

The divisions were there right enough, and class preserved in the siting of the tents and shelters, and in the two fireplaces.

'But they're very attentive to our needs,' she said.

'Yes, though they do stare so.'

'And not just the natives. I've caught both Louis and James watching you, you know, when you aren't looking.' Evelyn fixed her attention on her paints. Had James really been watching her? 'George won't stand for any nonsense if I mention it to him, and I'm surprised your father has not remarked it. Perhaps I *should* say something.'

'Please don't—'

Clementina frowned. 'You need to become aware of these things, Evie. Your impudent groom would not have . . .' Evelyn raised her head, and Clementina stopped. 'Alright. No more on that, but do maintain a distance. It's very important—'

Was it?

Clementina was looking out to the river where the canoes had now vanished from sight. 'And I'm not sure I like us being left alone with them.'

Evelyn glanced over to the recumbent forms of Tala and Machk, now both sleeping, and then at the two youths, who were squatted down by the water's edge scrubbing the pans from last night's dinner, talking, and quite indifferent to them. Did Clemmy not see that they were entirely dependent on these men she despised and mistrusted? This was no place for mannered condescension.

She picked up a pencil and began blocking out the shapes of the trees against the cliff face, then lightly sketched the course of the river upstream. Unchartered waters—

The men in their party were able to deal with the guides on different terms, of course, and there were fish and rods and reels to talk about. She noted that her father treated them all with an un-failing courtesy, as did Mr Larsen and George, but Rupert seemed to subscribe to Clemmy's view that a distance must be maintained, and so treated them as he might treat servants at home. And yet, she sensed that he was not entirely at ease, and he stuck close to George, as if a little wary of the two older men, while in return Papa seemed to study Rupert with an oddly detached air. Calculat-ing acreage and income, perhaps?

———

The fishing that morning had been good, and the men returned at noon in high spirits. Seven trout were neatly laid out on the rocks for inspection when the two women went down to greet them. Fine specimens, with their hues of purple, gold, and silver.

'What beauties!' said Clementina.

Seven fish. And they had come three thousand miles to catch them— Their colours faded even as Evelyn studied them, and their eyes dulled. The largest had been landed by her father.

'What a brute. I watched you playing him,' remarked George. 'He put up quite a fight.'

'As befits his class,' her father agreed. 'A prince among fish.'

'Must be near on ten pounds,' said Rupert, watching as they suspended the fish from the scales.

'Eight,' her father replied.

'I quite thought you'd lost him once.'

'Perseverance and patience, my dear Dalston, wins the day.' He turned to address Evelyn. 'And you, my dear, how did you spend the morning?'

'Doing nothing very useful,' she said, and moved aside as James passed her carrying rods and paddles.

———

'What is it about fish that corrupts us, do you think?' Mr Larsen remarked as they sat down to eat their midday meal half an hour later. A pan of beans and bacon had been quickly prepared and they had assembled around the table to eat it, together with the inevitable bannock. 'I've known men who, in every other aspect of their lives, are the very souls of probity, but who will shamelessly add two or three pounds to the weight of any fish they'd caught—'

'*After* consuming it,' her father murmured.

Mr Larsen smiled and continued. 'And yet they would not sway from the truth in their other dealings, not by as much as a hair's breadth.'

'Strict accuracy can be overlooked in these matters, surely,' George remarked as he flattened a mosquito on his wrist.

'You make Larsen's point for him, George,' said her father, between mouthfuls. 'I'd have sworn that there was no soul of greater probity than George Melton. Except, it appears, when it comes to fish!'

Everyone laughed and Clementina nodded. 'George's fish grow by an inch every time he talks about them.'

'And there's always the monster that gets away,' said Rupert. 'There was one this morning, I swear. If we'd just stayed another ten minutes—'

'I'm glad you didn't,' said Evelyn. 'We'll be heartily sick of trout by the end of the trip.'

'*Heresy!*'

'Well said, missee,' said Skinner, nodding. 'Some folk just keep on catching 'em to string 'em up fer the camera, and then throw half of them away.'

'Well, we shall eat ours tonight, I assure you,' said Mr Larsen. 'And any others we catch.'

———

When the party broke up after lunch Evelyn overheard Mr Skinner telling James to go and clean the morning's catch and she observed him going down to the shore with a bucket. Her father had disappeared into his tent, and George and Rupert had taken out a pack of cards; Clementina sat beside her husband, watching him deal, and Mr Larsen was asleep.

This was her chance— She glanced over to where the water-closet screen had been re-erected a little distance downwind from the camp. At first Clementina had refused to contemplate using such an arrangement until Evelyn heard George quietly explaining that she had no choice, assuring her that she would not be sharing it with the natives. It would be quite alright, he said, provided that she remembered to display the red rag tied to a stick when behind the screen. Evelyn glanced around the camp again. No one would question her if she headed towards it and, screened from view, she could slip away through the trees to join the short trail to the shore, leaving the rag signal in place. It might buy her some extra time, and later she could claim to have forgotten to move it.

She crossed the camp as unobtrusively as possible, and paused behind the screen. Flies buzzed around the collapsible box arrangement which had been positioned above a shallow pit scratched into the thin soil. She waited just a moment, and then headed down through the woods towards the shore where, at the end of the trail, she stopped. The spreading branches of a larch hid her from view, and she could see James down at the water's edge, rinsing fish guts from his hands.

Would he speak to her?

She stood, twisting her fingers in the sharp needles, and felt a strange new ache swelling deep inside her as she watched him. How much she had missed him! And she remembered how once he had crouched beside another river, and how he had turned to grin at her, an uncomplicated grin, boasting how he could catch trout with his bare hands. She had not believed him, so he had stretched out full length on the riverbank, bidding her be silent, his cheek pressed against the turf as he dangled his arm into the river. Minutes passed, then he had rolled over with a whoop and flung a dart of silver into the bushes behind her. She had clapped her hands in delight and insisted on trying for herself, so he had spread his jacket on the bank, gravely pulling up her sleeve to above the elbow, his eyes smiling down at her.

He turned now, as if alive to her thoughts, and saw her standing there. But he did not smile—

Straightening, he slowly shook his hands dry then wiped them on his trousers, not moving from the water's edge but looking steadily back at her. She took a step forward, then hesitated.

'James—'

He turned away, picked up another fish, and crouched to his task again, and the blade of his knife caught the light of the sun along its length.

She went towards him. 'James. I need to talk to you—'

His hands stilled and he looked up again. All the words, all the questions shrivelled at his expression, and she could only stare back at him.

'Go back to the camp,' he said.

'I have to ask you—'

'I said go back to the camp.'

He glared back at her, a hostile stranger, but she might never get another chance. She had not expected this to be so hard, and so took her courage in her hands. 'Was it true what you said to me that night?'

It came out in a breathless rush, and the glare was replaced by a frown.

'About Papa—'

His frown deepened and then he shook his head, returning his attention to the fish. 'Go back to camp.'

'You told me Papa had Jacko's blood on his conscience—'

'His conscience!' He slit open the fish with a swift clean cut, and the mess of guts slid over the rocks to foul the water. 'Has he one? If so, then yes, Jacko's blood is on it. Now go back to camp.'

Panic swamped her then, driving her pulse hard, but there was no going back. 'So *he* killed Jacko?' – James seemed to freeze – 'and let you take the blame?'

He swung round on his heel with a strange expression on his face. 'No! That is— Yes, at least—'

Then the branches of the larch at the trail's end were pushed brusquely aside and her father appeared. He stopped there, a little breathless, to take in the scene.

'Here you are, my dear,' he said, and came quickly down onto the little beach. 'I wondered where you'd disappeared to.' He joined them at the water's edge and stood there, looking from one to the other. 'Go back to the camp, Evelyn,' he said, with quiet authority. 'And I'll join you directly.'

'No.'

James had straightened and faced him, the knife held loosely in his hand.

'This is neither the time nor place, my dear, so go.'

'James said—'

Her father raised his hand. 'James will do well to remember

what I said to him.' He spoke with a finality that was impossible to counter. 'And neither of you will force my hand. Now do as I say, Evelyn, and go back to camp.' He gripped her shoulders and turned her firmly towards the trail. She took a step, then looked back to where James stood with the knife now gripped in his hand, and her eyes fixed on the bloodied tip.

Her father gave a snort. 'We shall do each other no damage, I promise you. Now *go.*'

'What did she want?' Ballantyre asked as Evelyn disappeared down the track.

James turned back to Ballantyre and regarded him. 'Answers. Same as me.'

'And what did you tell her?'

'Nothing.' He crouched again and resumed his task, shaken by what Evelyn had asked him. Whatever had he said that night that had made her believe such a thing—?

Ballantyre narrowed his eyes. 'Are you sure?'

Should he tell him now what his daughter had asked, what she had believed for five years? He ought to. 'Nothing,' he repeated.

Ballantyre grunted. 'Keep it that way, and leave her out of this.'

James rocked back on his heels, balancing the knife in his hand, and squinted up at the man. For once Ballantyre was looking rattled. 'Did you ever ask yourself what she made of that night's events—?'

'She was a child.'

'— two men dead, and the dogs set on me. How did you square it with her?'

'Leave Evelyn to me,' Ballantyre spoke softly. 'I will tell her everything in due course.'

'But she's asking questions now.' James bent his head to slit open the next fish. She thought *Ballantyre* had killed Jacko. Good God! And somehow *he* had planted that worm in her brain. 'And you need to talk to her.'

Ballantyre went to stand at the edge of the water. Small ripples gurgled over a fallen branch out in the current, and midstream a fish jumped. 'Evelyn is my concern, not yours.'

'And yet she's keeping company with a killer—'

Ballantyre turned back. 'Dalston is a fool and a braggart, but he offers her no threat.'

He paused, contemplating James, then added, 'You and I will go fishing this afternoon, my friend, just the two of us. Out on the far side of the river. A good spot, don't you think—? And in the meantime, be patient or you will throw my plans into disarray. It's taken me too long to reach this point.'

As James lifted his head to retort he saw that Marcel was standing at the end of the trail. He came forward, gesturing to the fish at James's feet. 'Not finished?' James shrugged and Marcel pulled out a knife, crouched beside him, and took up the next fish as Ballantyre turned on his heel and returned to the camp.

Chapter 16

'Alright, old girl?' When Evelyn emerged from the trail, Rupert was sitting alone by the fire, smoking a cigarette. She needed some time to herself and had hoped to find refuge in her tent. She could get used to finding pine needles in her bed, and to the persistent mosquitoes, but it was difficult to get used to the lack of privacy.

James had been so terribly changed – and she was more confused now than ever. What had he meant? No, but yes—

'You look . . . stormy.' Rupert pulled out a seat beside him. 'Sit down, and tell Uncle Rupert all about it. Shall I get you some of that ghastly coffee?' A quick glance around the camp indicated that Clementina was in their tent, probably sleeping. Then Marcel went past, ignoring them, and headed down the trail. So whatever was being said down there would have to be cut short.

Rupert had filled two mugs with coffee and passed her one. 'Pour it away if it's terrible,' he said. She gave him a tight smile and muttered her thanks. 'Now then. You promised me you'd come fishing, you know.'

'Did I?'

'Good as, at any rate. George and I decided there's to be a ladies' fishing competition, and we've been laying wagers. I've put my shirt on you, dear one, so you simply can't pull out. We're going to try from the shore, out on that shingle bar.'

'Are we?' Did he realise that his knee was exerting a steady pressure against her leg? She tried to move but was caught there between him and the table.

Then her father emerged from the trailhead, and his face was grim.

Rupert glanced over his shoulder, following her look, and shifted his seat slightly. 'Aha!' he said softly, turning back to her. 'A tiff with Papa was it?' He pulled on his cigarette, his eyes twinkling at her. 'Poor Evelyn. He terrifies me.'

Her father stood a moment looking across at them and then came over. 'Where are the others?' he asked. His tone was light but Evelyn sensed the tension in him.

'Larsen's reel has been giving more trouble,' Rupert replied, 'so he and George went to test it again. They are out on the cobbles.' He pointed downstream to where the men could just be seen, partly shielded from view by overhanging branches. 'And Clemmy's in her tent having a nap.' He paused. 'If it's alright with you sir, I thought I'd take Evelyn out there later to fish. With George and Clementina too.'

Her father nodded and glanced at her. 'Of course. If she wishes to go. And I shall take to the water again, I think, with one of the guides. But for now, I'll join George and Larsen.'

When he had gone Rupert leant close, his shoulder next to hers. 'So – what's the tiff about?'

'There was no tiff.'

'Was it about me? Your papa disapproves of me, I think.'

She gave a slight smile. 'Because you're a Bad Man?'

'Exactly. Frivolous. Feckless. Pointless. It's what my own father says.' His expression had changed, and his eyes grew distant. She was torn between sympathy and irritation.

'Then why not strive to change people's opinion, if you think they regard you so little,' she said.

He edged closer again. 'Perhaps I need the guidance of a good woman.' She turned her shoulder to him, and he laughed. 'So, it was about me, then? The tiff.'

'There was no tiff.'

'Fibber.'

'You weren't even mentioned.'

'So there *was* a tiff.'

She got to her feet but he caught at her hand, pulling her back. 'No, don't go! Just when it gets interesting—' James and Marcel appeared at the end of the trail, and James looked across at them, then came over and dumped the plate of filleted fish on the table.

———

'Did the gypsies give you a good price for Melrose?' Ballantyre asked as James paddled him out across the river later that afternoon. The sun was hidden behind a cloud and they made for the shadows on the opposite shore where it was dark and cool.

How the devil did Ballantyre know about the gypsies? 'No,' he said.

Larsen had gone out with Louis, in the other canoe, which was well downstream of them, out of earshot. 'I thought not. They tried to sell her at Kelso fair a few weeks later, you see, having dyed her white patch. Selkirk spotted her straight away, and so we got her back. I have her still, my daughter rides her sometimes.'

James nodded briefly. Parting with the mare had been a wrench, but necessary; it was good to think of her back in her old stable. 'They knew she was stolen,' he said and brought the canoe to a place where there were riffles amongst the rocks, places where trout might hide.

'So where did you go? You covered your tracks very well.'

'Glasgow.'

'Good God!' Ballantyre swivelled round to stare at him. 'And I told the constables to look for you there, knowing you to be a country boy. Never dreaming—'

James remembered the men with shifty eyes who had been asking questions in the taverns and hostelries of the Gorbals where he had gone seeking work. So Ballantyre had sent them, had he, expecting him to be skulking in hedgerows.

'And from there to Canada?'

'With the last of your sovereigns.'

Ballantyre gave a short dry laugh. 'Then you used them well.' He assembled his rod, checked the gut and the fly, and then cast. 'One thing has always puzzled me, James,' he continued after a moment. 'Tell me, if you will. What were you doing by the river that day? With Jacko.'

The question was unexpected and James let it hang in the air, remembering the look on Ballantyre's face that day when their eyes had locked across the river. 'You thought I'd thrown in with him again,' he said.

'I thought it unlikely. But I'd like to know.'

James dug his paddle in deep and the canoe jerked forward. Anger rose and stuck in his throat. First McAllister's killing and now this. 'You thought that; even after the other time and the fire—'

'And had you?'

❧

⇢❧ *Ballantyre House, 1888* ❧⇠

James had been just six months under Ballantyre's benevolent roof when Jacko was released. He had waited anxiously for the old poacher to come for him, as he had promised he would, and when he failed to appear, James had experienced the first bitter pain of betrayal. Weeks later, though, he learned from the stable master that the old reprobate had reoffended and been sent down again, for longer this time, and then James had worried about him, and ached for the sight of him. Even then, though, he had to admit to a guilty relief that he would not be forced to choose—

Months had passed, then years, and he heard no more of Jacko, and gradually the memories of those wild times had faded. Life at Ballantyre House was tame in comparison with his old existence, but it was easy. At first he had balked at the regulations imposed on him, but he was well fed and was filling out and growing, he slept each night in a warm bed, and he soon found ways around the rules that did not suit him— And nothing could beat the joy of those crisp mornings when he went out with the other grooms exercising the horses, pounding the fields, intoxicated by the scent of spring. The day he first rode out on Zeus he had felt like a god.

And he was aware of Ballantyre observing him from a distance, always with a word or a nod when they met, and he sensed, and soon sought, his new master's approval.

Then, after almost five years under Ballantyre's roof, one late summer afternoon, when the woodland was in full leaf and alive with birdsong, the old poacher had simply stepped out from behind a tree beside the track as James rode past. Miss Evie was on her pony, out in front, and had not seen him, but Melrose shied.

Jacko glanced after her then dodged back into the shadows. 'Nursemaid now, is it?' he said, smirking. 'Tonight, when you've tucked her into bed come and find me, if you can remember where to look.' And he had vanished, leaving James staring at where the dappled undergrowth had swallowed him.

And so he went to him that night, slipping away after the evening meal, using the old ways, the secret ways, across the river and through the darkening forest, his mind sharp and alert, praying that McAllister's men were not abroad.

Jacko greeted him like a son, and engulfed him in one of his great hugs just as always, except that now his clasp reached only to James's chest. 'By God. Look at you, the *size* of you! A heartbreaker too, I don't doubt. By God— You'll be what . . . twenty . . . is it?'

'Eighteen.'

'I lose track of the years—' James stared back at him, thinking that wherever Jacko had spent those years, they had not been good to him. The old man clutched at James's jacket, his rheumy eyes beseeching. 'I came back before, lad, like I promised, but I heard you'd been taken in, and were being treated well so I left you. Ballantyre's conscience, they call you. Did you know that?' Jacko hawked and spat. 'His guilt offering, more like, to stave off the hell and damnation he deserves. His conscience. Pah!' He pulled a bottle from his pocket and took a drink, not offering it to James. 'But seeing you all set up and cared for, I went away again. You'd a better chance here, see? Until you were grown.'

James looked back at the ragged figure in front of him and felt a keen sorrow. Jacko's clothes were torn and filthy, a front tooth was missing, and there were scars, old and new, across his face – and a deadness in his eyes. He had been doing fine, he told James, not meeting his gaze, just fine, but recently his luck had run out, and so he had come back to find him. 'Because you're a good lad and won't let me down—' James's heart sank. Jacko must have sensed this for he pulled the bottle hastily from his pocket again, and passed it to James. 'Drink! Have a drink, lad. Let's celebrate our reunion! Sit you down, boy.'

They finished the bottle between them, stretched out under the rocks and roots of the overhang, hidden among bracken and brambles like the old days, and Jacko grew garrulous. His life had taken a steady downturn, he admitted, and he lay all his misfortunes at Ballantyre's door. The man had conducted a personal vendetta against him, he claimed, poisoning the world against him. He and his land-owning cronies had sent him down time and again for petty offences, relentless in their persecution, harsh in their judgement, no clemency, no understanding – and Jacko was looking to settle the score.

He ran his tongue over yellowed teeth and drained the bottle, then brought his face close to James, his breath foul, eyes bleary. 'I've got a plan, see? It's a simple plan and a good one. Simple is best. And it'll set me up— There'll be a little fire, see, near the stables.' James stiffened and Jacko put out his hand. 'No, no. Not you, lad. I won't ask that of you. All you do is raise the alarm, see? And we do the rest.'

'Who is *we?*' James demanded. 'And what's the rest?'

Jacko cracked a smile. 'My associates. Let's call them that, shall we? They'll wait until everyone's rushing round with buckets and then pop in and explore the house, see? Ballantyre won't care, so long as his horses don't roast.'

James went cold at the thought. Melrose, and Bella. Zeus—

He refused and they quarrelled, hard words were exchanged, and but for James's refusal to be drawn they would have come to blows. He left the overhang with Jacko's curses ringing round his ears, and returned to the stable block to lie sleepless through the night, sickened by the encounter.

In the morning he went to Ballantyre.

And so he stood once more in front of the great desk in Ballantyre's study, and the master sat and listened to him without comment; the slow tick of the clock on the mantel measured the ensuing silence. James glanced up at the painting of the exotic bird above the fireplace, the source of feathers for Ballantyre's fishing flies, and remembered that other time.

Then: 'He's back, is he? I hoped we'd seen the last of him.' Ballantyre leant back in his chair, contemplating James. 'And you've been meeting him.'

'I came across him in the woods.' Not for anything would he reveal that secret overhang.

Ballantyre said nothing, no doubt scenting an evasion. 'And he told you all this,' he said, at last, 'at a chance meeting on a forest path?'

James's eyes slid away. 'He expected me to join him, you see—'

Ballantyre remained silent, making a pyramid of his fingers, bouncing the tips together as he looked back at him, considering. 'So what will he do now?'

'I told him he was mad. We argued. He'll know I've told you . . .'

And that seemed to be the end of it. Nothing happened, and despite the keepers and the constables searching for him, there were no further sightings of Jacko, or of strangers on the estate who might be his associates. But three nights later, when James was leading Maud, an accommodating laundry maid, behind the stables to where a ladder reached up to a hayloft, he smelled burning and saw flames leaping inside an empty cottage beside the stables, and cursed Jacko. 'Quick! Go back!' He pushed Maud towards the house and then tore round into the courtyard to ring the stable bell, yelling for assistance— And what a night they had of it. The horses had been led out through the smoke, wild-eyed and balking, and Ballantyre had worked beside them, giving orders and encouragement, passing buckets until the fire was contained – while the keepers patrolled the lawns and shrubberies and the household prepared for trouble.

None came. But in the morning the farms and villages were buzzing with the news that a gang of poachers had set nets across the river and hauled out dozens of the salmon which had been making their way upriver to spawn. So many salmon, it was said, that households for miles around were satiated, and fish were found rotting in the hedgerows.

It did not take long for this news to reach Ballantyre House, nor did it take long for McAllister to remark that it was James

Douglas who had first seen the fire, who had raised the alarm, and who had given a false warning—

And that afternoon James found himself brought before a coldly furious Ballantyre.

'Did you know this was planned?'

James looked back at him, stunned that he would think so. 'No.'

'The old cottage isn't visible from the courtyard. How did you come to see it was alight?'

There was Maud to protect so his excuse was weak. Under relentless questioning he admitted to an assignation, but refused to give a name. Ballantyre rose from behind his desk and leant forward, his weight resting on his knuckles.

'Then why should I believe you?'

James gave him look for look.

'Because it's the truth.'

Ballantyre continued to glare at him, eyes narrowed. 'You can save this girl's dubious reputation, or yourself. Your choice.'

'I knew nothing of what was planned. You have my word,' he said, and he refused to say more. Ballantyre considered him a moment longer then called for McAllister and ordered him to lock James in the tack room until he came to his senses. The keeper led him away, threw him to the floor, and administered his own brand of justice with his boot.

James had picked himself up and sat there, staring at the wall, incensed that Ballantyre thought him capable of such betrayal. He could have easily escaped through the roof light but scorned to do so. And where would he go? To find Jacko? A wreck of a man sustained by hatred and dreams of revenge—

Less than an hour later, he heard the sound of the door being unlocked and looked up to see Ballantyre himself standing at the threshold. The master came in and shut the door, then leant against the wall.

'All these years, you've never given me cause to regret taking you in, James, or to mistrust you. You gave me your word, and I refused it, and that's the worst part of this wretched business— I can only ask your pardon.' He put out his hand, and James took it. Someone had seen him that evening with Maud, Ballantyre said, had seen him on other occasions too, with other girls— Amusement flickered in his eyes and was gone. Maud had been questioned, and in a terrified flood of tears had substantiated James's story.

'You'll not dismiss her, will you, sir?' James had asked as they left the tack room together a moment later. 'She's innocent—'

Ballantyre had raised a quizzical eyebrow but agreed that she would stay, recommending that James left the maids alone in the future, or there would be a reckoning.

And so the household had settled down again, while the keepers on neighbouring estates spread out to beat the bracken and join in the search for Jacko.

It was only later, as James went about his chores around the stables, that he had looked up to see a small face at the schoolroom window, and realised that it was the only window which directly overlooked that corner of the hayloft. The face had disappeared but a crown of curls suggested that he was still being watched so he bowed in the direction of the window and blew his saviour a kiss.

———

'I misjudged you then.' Ballantyre's voice recalled him to the moment. 'I was reluctant to do so again.'

'But you did. When you looked across the river that day and saw me with Jacko.' And in that moment, when Jacko lay dying, his fingers clawing at James's arm, urging him to run, Ballantyre had doubted him. And it was that hesitation which had brought them to this place.

Ballantyre made no reply. Then his rod bent and his attention was diverted. James brought the head of the canoe round to assist him and Ballantyre began to play his fish, but as he began to reel it in the line slackened, and the rod straightened. 'Gone. Another misjudgement—' He took in the rest of the line and set his rod aside. 'Yes, I doubted you, to my eternal shame. So, tell me, whatever was the old rogue up to that day, setting a net in broad daylight—?'

———

Jacko had vanished after the night of the fire, but he had returned that autumn, and James had glimpsed him at the inn where, years back, he had spent that lonely winter, but the old poacher had melted away into the shadows. Later James had gone again to the overhang and seen signs of recent occupation, and had returned several times, never seeing him but suspecting that he was close by, maybe even watching from amongst the bracken and brambles – and he had left him food, money from his scant savings, notes urging him to go. And James was torn again by conflicting loyalties— He had seen more of Ballantyre since the fire; there had been talk of him working with his racing bloodstock, taking more responsibilities to relieve the ageing Selkirk. And then the master had very publicly demonstrated his support that time when McAllister had accused him of neglect – or worse – regarding Miss Evelyn. Ballantyre had ridden out with them, noting but ignoring the bruises left by the keeper's fists, bidding his daughter to ride ahead. 'Is there any truth in what McAllister says?' he had asked. 'None at all,' James had replied. 'And she'll never come to harm through me, sir.' Ballantyre had given him a twisted smile. 'No. I'm quite certain of that.'

But even as his regard for Ballantyre grew, concern for Jacko quickened. Fire-raising was an altogether more serious matter than poaching. If he was caught he would hang—

He redoubled his attempts to find the man, and then one day,

James spotted a net, stowed deep in the mossy overhang, and realised, with despair, that Jacko was planning another haul. This time he said nothing to Ballantyre but left a note telling Jacko he was a fool, and begging him to go. 'Take the purse and leave. Go now, while you still can.' And he had left him all the money he had, and food wrapped in a cloth stolen from the kitchen, something for the journey. They were anxious times. Next day the net was gone but the purse, still full, had been tucked into a crack in the rocks, half-hidden by a threadbare blanket. Had Jacko left, scorning the idea of taking James's money? A crust of hard bread and some cheese were still wrapped in the cloth where the ants had found it, and the charred remains of his notes were scattered amongst the ashes of a tiny fire. James had stood outside the overhang, thinking hard, watching the low sun filtering through the trees, smelling the acid trace of burning from the disturbed ashes, and been overwhelmed with grief. That Jacko, the fearless champion of his childhood, had come to this—

And then he had remembered the place where the river narrowed, where the branches dipped low, where once they had speared fish in the moonlight, a place where a net could be slung across, even by one man working alone. And he had set off at a run.

———

Ballantyre's voice again reeled him back into the moment. 'The dogs tracked your scent to a rocky crevice where it seemed the man had been living. A purse of money was identified as yours, a dishcloth from the kitchen, and scraps of paper with your writing on it. Selkirk recognised it, having taught you your letters. You'd been stealing food for Jacko—' He paused, and waited. 'You were innocent of his death, I knew that, but I had reasons to doubt you, you see.' The paddle made a splash as James moved the canoe forward, saying nothing, and a duck flew low along the river, followed a moment later by its mate. The pair landed a little way downstream and settled onto the current. 'For God's sake, man, it makes no difference now,' Ballantyre added, in exasperation. 'I simply want to know.' And James, swamped by a sudden weariness with the whole wretched business, told him, no longer caring whether he was believed or not.

When he had finished, Ballantyre was silent for a long time, staring into the thickness of the forest beyond the riverbank, his rod propped in the front of the canoe, the line reeled in. Then he turned towards James. 'We struggled for your soul, James,' he said. 'And I saw myself as your saviour, but it was the things Jacko taught you which saved your life.'

He looked across to the other side of the river where they could see the rest of the party, and his expression darkened. Dalston appeared to be carrying Evelyn from the shore to the bar midstream, and James heard Ballantyre swear softly.

'Why is that man still free?' James asked as they watched Dalston set her down and then stand behind her, his arms encircling her waist.

'He won't be for much longer,' Ballantyre replied, his face grim. 'But first I mean to settle with his father.'

'It was Dalston who did the killing—'

'His father would have seen you hang.'

'But why do you wait?'

'I need a confession from Dalston.'

James turned to him, staggered. 'Is that *all*! I'll get—'

'One I can use in a court of law,' Ballantyre said. 'So bide just a little longer.' They both looked over again to where Evelyn was now alone on the rocky bar.

'And your daughter? She—'

'Makes him believe his sins are forgiven.'

Out on the bar Evelyn had managed a very creditable cast. But she looked vulnerable there, alone, surrounded by the fast-moving current. 'So she's bait, is she?'

Ballantyre scowled at him. 'No. Not bait—'

'You're very sure of yourself, aren't you, Mr. Ballantyre? But I tell you again, you should talk to her.'

Ballantyre turned and searched his face, but James sat mulishly silent. Let him learn from Evelyn herself what she had believed of him. And may it bring him pain—

There was a flash of colour as a kingfisher dropped like a dart from an overhanging branch beside them, rising a moment later with a silver minnow arching in its beak.

'Take me back across,' said Ballantyre.

Chapter 17

The finer points of the ladies' fishing competition were being fiercely argued as the four younger members of the party made their way along the track to where the water was shallow enough to cross to the cobble and shingle bar. Rupert was now offering ludicrous odds in Evelyn's favour.

'You face ruin, you know,' said George, 'like when Thunderbolt fell at the last rail.'

'I feel rather offended' – Evelyn was making an effort to join in the spirit of the occasion – 'being treated like a racehorse.'

'Oh, men make a competition of everything,' Clementina replied. 'They simply can't help it.'

'And you're going to romp home, Evelyn,' said Rupert, 'and make me a rich man.'

Somewhere along the journey the formality of address had been relaxed, but she was not sure where— She and Clementina sat on a boulder near the shore, while the men crossed over and made a few initial casts. Getting the lay of the land, Rupert explained.

Taking off her hat, Clementina delicately wiped the back of her neck with a handkerchief. 'Oh, these wretched flies!' Mr Skinner had offered them some evil-smelling paste but they both preferred the pungent leaves which Tala gave them, and Clementina had a handful in her pocket. 'I suppose these work like dock leaves,' she remarked, offering some to Evelyn then rubbing them between her palms and carefully behind her ears, 'but as a prevention rather than a cure. I just long to have a bath and get properly clean.' Clementina's complaints were becoming more frequent as camp life began to pall.

Downstream, and in the shadows on the other side, Evelyn observed her father and James in one of the canoes. They appeared to be talking, and she would have given anything to know what was being said.

'Isn't it extraordinary to find someone from home in this wild place?' Clementina said, following Evelyn's gaze.

Extraordinary indeed.

'Rupert's struck!' George called out, and they turned back to see Rupert's rod bending, his line taut. They heard him crowing as he began to play his fish.

'This one's yours, Evelyn,' he said, over his shoulder. 'Come on. You land him and then we can start the bets. Bring her over here, George.'

'Isn't that cheating?'

'Almost certainly,' said George, stepping back over the stones towards them and offering Evelyn his hand.

But even as she rose, they heard Rupert curse. 'Gone! Dammit. And taken a good few yards of line too, I expect.' He reeled in, inspected the broken end, and waded back across to them. 'As well as an excellent fly.' He flung himself down beside her and began flipping through George's fly book, dismissing them one by one. 'Can't lose too many either. I don't expect these natives have a clue how to tie 'em. Except the morose Scotsman, maybe, if he's a Tweed valley man—' Then he straightened and patted his pocket. 'But no! Wait!' He pulled out a waxed paper parcel. 'To the devil with your flies and your posturing, this'll do the job for me.' A brightly coloured jigger fell from the package, red with white spots, fish-shaped and lurid. He had acquired it in one of the dry-goods stores in Port Arthur, to the horror of George. 'My

God, man, have you no principles?' he had said. 'I wouldn't let Ballantyre catch you using that.'

Rupert began attaching the jigger to his line, ignoring George's further condemnations, and addressed Evelyn. 'I expect you were taught to tie a fly rather than embroider a handkerchief, m'dear.' He gave her his slow mocking smile, his hair falling forward. 'I can imagine you sat at Papa's feet, being shown the niceties of the Silver Doctor.'

She found herself smiling back. 'He ties his own.'

'I'll bet he does.'

George joined them on the rocks. 'And isn't there some sort of voodoo or other he believes in? Dead parrot feathers or something?'

Evelyn shook her head at him. 'It's a secret.'

'A *secret* dead parrot?' said Rupert. 'Do tell.'

'He'd never forgive me; I'm surprised that George knows.'

'I had it from one of your keepers, in his cups at the time,' George replied. 'The one who got himself murdered, poor fellow.'

And it was as if a cold hand had closed around her heart and a cloud shut out the sun. She turned her head away, feigning a renewed interest in what was happening downstream.

'Whatever voodoo it is, it's not exerting its magic now,' Clementina remarked, again following her gaze. 'I've only seen your father's rod bend once.'

Rupert glanced across at the canoe on the far bank, and at the rod propped against the side. 'But then, he's not exactly trying—' He watched them a moment longer then got to his feet and put out a hand to Evelyn. 'So let's show him up, shall we? That whopper's still out there, you know, and I've got good money riding on this. No excuses now, up you get. Do your bit.' And Evelyn found herself swept off her feet and lifted across the eddy to the narrow strip of stones and weed where he set her down, ignoring her protests. 'There. Marooned. Now, *fish*, woman!' His hands stayed on her shoulders a moment, then he bent to pick up the rod and stood behind her, his arms sliding round her waist from the back, his hands closing over hers, gripping the rod just as her father used to do when she was a child.

'You chump, Rupert,' Clementina called out quickly, and looked anxiously across the river. 'Evelyn can cast every bit as well as you can.'

'Better, probably,' said Evelyn.

Dalston released her at once. 'Apologies, I'm sure.' He returned to the shore while Evelyn got her bearings and managed a good cast.

'See!'

George applauded, and Evelyn heard Clementina commanding him to carry her across to join Evelyn on the shingle bar. They then fished side by side, watched with amusement by the two men, who sprawled lazily on the rocks. 'An inspiring sight, eh, George? Two intrepid women, braving the wilderness.'

'And if we could dress more sensibly we wouldn't have to be moved about like sacks of potatoes,' said Evelyn. 'Pantaloons and waders are what is required.'

'What a bewitching thought—!'

'Be quiet, Rupert. Was that a bite you had?' Clementina asked as Evelyn's rod bent.

'Weed in the current, I think.'

Evelyn cast again. Once, in another life, she had stood beside a different river, lulled by the gentle cooing of wood pigeons in the copper beeches, watching a cock pheasant scuttle across the path, neck outstretched. And there she would breathe in the heady scent of the wildflowers as she watched her father, quietly patient as he fished, soothed by the placid water, and in a state of contentment she felt she could never recapture.

'I'm really quite hopeless at this,' said Clementina, a moment later, twisting to release her skirt from the hook after a failed cast. 'You do it so beautifully.'

'She was taught by a master,' she heard George say.

A master of evasion—

'Neither of us are even getting a nibble!' his wife protested.

—and deceit.

———

'Your wrist was a little stiff on that last cast, my dear.' Evelyn turned at her father's voice and saw him emerging out of the trees to join them. She had not noticed the canoe's return. 'Never attempt to throw more than you can send out clean and straight. The one before was much better.' He came across the rocks towards them. 'But with the din you're making you're never going to catch anything. I thought I'd taught you better manners.' He smiled dryly at Clementina. 'And you, madam, are just as bad.'

'Worse,' said her husband.

Clementina laughed. 'You men take it all far too seriously.'

'It's a serious business. Eh, Dalston?'

Dalston had gone to the water's edge and cast his line, perhaps in an effort to hide the offending jigger from her father's scrutiny.

'What? Oh, absolutely.'

'Walk back with me, my dear,' her father said, turning to her, 'unless you've a mind to fish a little longer?' There was purpose in his tone. 'No?' He picked up her hat from the rocks and handed it to her. 'Then you'll excuse us, I hope.' He nodded to the others and started back over the rocks. 'Suppleness is everything, my dear,' he continued, 'and then follow through.'

They had reached the edge of the woods when Rupert gave a whoop and his rod bent. Ballantyre stopped, turning to watch as the water a yard or two off the shingle bar roiled and splashed. But though Rupert's rod remained bent, the fight was quickly over and he reeled in as if pulling a piece of waterlogged wood. George made ready with the net and then scooped up the catch and held it high with a crack of laughter. 'Ha! Serves you right.'

The red and white jigger was shamefully exposed along the creature's jaw, its hook embedded in the bony lip of a narrow-bodied and ugly-looking fish.

'Pike,' remarked her father, and then continued up the rocks.

At the top of the bank, instead of going back up towards the camp, he paused and stepped onto a narrow track which led into the bush. 'Let's see where this takes us, shall we?'

Silently she followed him. And they continued in the same silence, single file, he in front pushing aside the low branches of larches and maples which covered the trail, and holding them for her. And in that silence a mixture of fear and anticipation grew inside her. This time *he* had sought her out—

The trail narrowed still further, closing in to form a cool dark tunnel which brought them eventually to a small clearing which overlooked a bend in the river. At one side was a stand of silver birch, and the low sunlight lit the slender trunks with a brilliant starkness, while the yellow leaves trembled and dropped to join their fellows below.

'Let's sit a moment, shall we—' he said, and gestured to the shoulder of an outcropping rock. Then he wasted no more time. 'Tell me, what did James say to you yesterday?'

'Very little. You interrupted us.'

He gave a brief smile. 'But what were you speaking of?'

'Need you ask—'

'No—' From somewhere deep in the forest a song sparrow trilled its sweet melody, in counterpoint to the tension. 'But tell me what he did say.' His tone was perfectly calm, but she found that her breathing had become shallow, and she dug her fingernails into her palms. She had questions of her own.

'James didn't kill Jacko, did he?'

'He told you that?'

'He didn't have to. I've always known.' There, it was out—

His eyes explored her face. 'How so?' he said, at last.

She swallowed and her mind went blank as a sort of numb panic consumed her. 'Because he had told me before.' Something twisted deep inside her and she began to shake. Just a quiver at first— 'Not yesterday. Five years ago. That night—' She saw his eyes widen, then sharpen, and he was very still. 'He told me that Jacko had died in his arms but not by his hand, which was why his shirt was all bloody.' And then her whole body began to tremble.

'His *shirt*—'

She felt suddenly sick and leant forward, putting her hands over her face, but he pulled them away, gripping her wrists, forcing her to sit upright again. 'It was all over the front, and on the sleeves.'

His grip tightened. 'Evelyn. What are you saying—?'

'He told me that he hadn't killed Jacko' – she spoke in a small voice, as if the memory made her a child again – 'but that a blood-stained shirt and your lies would hang him' – she heard his sharp intake of breath – 'and then you'd have *his* blood on your conscience too.'

He released her wrists and stared at her, suspending them both in a silence which seemed to last a lifetime. And when he did speak, it was slowly, and very gently. 'Evelyn, my child. You must tell me the whole.'

Chapter 18

Larsen had asked Louis to bring him back to camp because, although the fishing had been good, he was in the fierce grip of indigestion. He had gone out too soon after eating, no doubt, but such attacks troubled him more frequently these days; and the heavy bannock which seemed part of their staple fare did little to improve matters. Skinner's raw spirit which he had accepted the night before had also been a mistake— He put the back of his hand to his mouth to disguise a belch, and gently massaged his belly. But it was not only the food and the drink; the tension in the air was enough to give anyone the gripes. Ballantyre's face was strained in the way it had been in those South African days when he had gambled everything on a hunch and a prayer. Evelyn had retreated inside herself, the row with her father perhaps not yet played out, and matters were not helped, he feared, by his own misplaced good intentions regarding Dalston. The easy camaraderie of the voyage through the Great Lakes had somehow evaporated amongst the trees and Dalston himself seemed ill at ease: too prone to loud laughter, too fond of his hip flask. Only Melton seemed content, amiably discussing fishing and hunting with Skinner and the guides, knocking back Skinner's evil spirit with the confidence of a man of easy conscience and a sound digestion.

He could just see the four younger members of the party out on the shingle bar, and Ballantyre was still fishing in the shadows across the river. Everyone was occupied. So a moment of calm—

He reached into his pocket and drew out a leather-bound volume, so well worn that the gilded lettering had rubbed away, and set his spectacles on his nose. After years as a banker he fancied himself to be a fair judge of people, but there were crosscurrents here that he did not understand, and they disturbed his tranquillity. He needed to take refuge in Thoreau's sound and simple philosophy, an infallible cure for all woes.

Ballantyre had mocked him earlier when he saw what he was reading. 'Wasn't it Thoreau who claimed he could draw fish to his boat by playing his flute—?' Larsen had said that it was. 'Then New England trout must be a damn sight more cultured than these hard-nosed Nipigon brutes. What a dreamer! But at least he had a healthy contempt for philanthropy.'

'I thought you'd take issue with him on that—'

'Once, maybe.'

He opened the book, but after just a few minutes he sighed and put it aside, the words were simply not going in, so he closed his eyes and put his head back, letting the sounds of the forest soothe him. Somewhere he heard the call of the song sparrow, so sweet on the afternoon breeze, and from deeper in the forest came the hollow drumming of a woodpecker. Whatever problems there were, they were not his problems, he reminded himself, and soon his only concern would be how to fill his time. And besides, matters had a way of resolving themselves.

He dozed for perhaps half an hour and then awoke, and his thoughts returned at once to Ballantyre. Perhaps it *was* the bank's business which had caused the strain to return to his eyes. Cold feet? Surely not, not Ballantyre! He had nerves of steel— But this new mining venture was beginning to obsess the man, quite unnecessarily so, as Larsen had tried to tell him the evening before in their tent.

'You don't *need* to pursue this, you know, Charles,' he had said as they were preparing for the night. 'There's sufficient capital to withstand any number of defaulters in the short, or even medium term.' He paused, then asked bluntly. 'Are you thinking of Earl Stanton?'

Ballantyre had looked up. 'No. Why Stanton?'

'He's stretched pretty thin.' But Ballantyre had simply shrugged, so Larsen had not pressed the matter. 'I really believe that the worst of this crisis is over now, things will stay flat perhaps before they recover, they always do. And anyway, the vein at Der Veen gulch shows no sign of petering out, does it?' Ballantyre agreed that it did not. 'I know it's as well to have another string to your bow, but opportunities will present themselves. You're very well placed.'

Ballantyre had continued to pull off his boots but had looked up and given him a tight smile. 'I know. And I'm not concerned. I'd just like to speak to this Achak myself.' And that was as far as he had been willing to go.

———

'So waddya say, Mister Larsen?' asked Skinner that evening when everyone was back in the camp. Marcel had been out hunting and brought back a young hind which he had hung and drawn, and it was now roasting on a spit over the fire. 'Do we stay here, or head on up past Split Rock Portage?' No one had heard any shots and when asked, Marcel had shown them his bow, and the place in the deer's neck where his arrow had brought the creature down. 'Or we could go on farther up still. Island Portage's no problem, and it's a great spot to fish, both sides of the island. And then Pine Portage—'

'It sounds like a lot of portages,' said Ballantyre.

'Short ones though.'

Larsen looked at his friend. He looked worse than ever this evening, quite alarmingly so. Haggard and drawn, almost as if he were ill. Perhaps he was— If so, then they would be better to stay put. 'It's dramatic country upriver, but the fishing is just as good here.' He had looked forward to showing Ballantyre the gorge with the cliffs on both sides of the river, but it seemed that the farther north they went the more troubled his old friend grew. He glanced around looking for Evelyn, but she must have still been in her tent.

'It would save the men a good deal of trouble,' Ballantyre agreed.

'Don't consider that, mister. The boys are—'

'Fit. Yes, you said.'

Skinner missed the sharpness in Ballantyre's tone and continued undaunted: '— and if we camp at the place I'm thinking, then anyone who wants to can go on all the way, upriver to Lake Nipigon. The boys'll take 'em. Then they c'n come back down through some of the rapids, and that'd be somethin' to remember.'

Evelyn and Clementina now emerged from their tent and came over to the fire. Clementina sat down beside her husband, while Evelyn perched on one of the tree stumps at the edge of the shadows, her eyes fixed on the roasting meat.

'Perhaps we should ask the ladies how they feel.' Ballantyre turned to where his daughter sat, and Skinner rehearsed the options again. 'So, my dear, what do you think?'

She seemed to jerk to attention. 'Who were all these women?' she asked, as if emerging from a dream. 'That the lakes are named for? Helen, Jessie, Marie—'

Skinner shrugged. 'Womenfolk belonging to the mapmakers, I suppose. Wives, sweethearts, daughters, mothers—' She nodded, but said nothing more.

'What about you, my love?' George asked his wife, who gave him a meaningful look which he somehow failed to interpret. 'You're game, eh?'

'You said we might encounter some Indian camps upriver, Mr Skinner,' said Ballantyre, but his eyes were still on his daughter.

'Sure. Bound to.' Skinner spat expertly into the fire. 'And some of the finest scenery in the land. And it's wild country, bear country, moose—'

'*Bear* country!' exclaimed Clementina, looking across at her husband.

Skinner cackled. 'Don't you worry, ma'am, they're full of bugs and berries this time of year. Fat and content. And there's some old Indian rock paintings, high up on the cliff face. Bit of a climb but there's a good trail.'

———

Evelyn ate little and handed her plate back to Tala almost untouched; she had no appetite and she had found the fresh venison tough and fibrous. She had positioned herself on the edge of the group hoping to avoid attention, not meeting James's eye when he brought her a mug of coffee. Had she imagined it or had he paused there a moment, looking down at her? The relief at learning of her father's innocence was now wrestling with guilt that she had believed James had been McAllister's killer, and she had not looked up.

But she was still appalled at her father's duplicity! And more than ever, she needed someone to explain—

Rupert dragged his seat over to be beside her. 'All bets are still on, you know,' he said. 'So we will reconvene tomorrow, at first light.' She responded with a vague smile. 'Best time, you know, and for all that my pike was universally despised, it was the only damned fish we caught.' She parried his teasing as best she could then pleaded tiredness, made her excuses and rose, bidding them all good night. Her father turned his head and put out an arm to delay her.

'Off to bed, Evie?' He rose, pulling her to him, and bent to kiss her forehead. 'Good night – and rest you well, my dear.'

She lifted her eyes to meet his and encountered a look of such profound sadness that she dropped them again, nodded blindly and headed for her tent.

Once inside she undressed quickly and pulled on the cotton shift that she slept in, shivering as she crept under the furs. She burrowed deep, desperate to be able to feign sleep when Clementina appeared, and turned on her side and watched the flickering light playing on the slanting wall of her tent.

Carefully, deliberately, she went back over the conversation she had had with her father. He had demanded that she tell him the whole, and it had all tumbled out in an incoherent babble, like the discharge from a lanced pustule – five years' worth of festering confusion and fear. When she had finished he had stared back at her in horror, then held her tight against his chest, his hand cupping the back of her head until she grew calm, before pulling away. 'Look at me, Evelyn. No, *look* at me. I did not kill the poacher. Nor did James.' And with grim determination, he had made her go back, step by step, over the events of that night: from seeing the body on the cart, to what the servants had said, and then to her desperate quest to find him, and his terrible expression when she encountered him in the study, and finally to finding James in the study – and to the conclusions she had drawn.

He was silent for a long time after that.

'And then, next day, when I heard about Mr McAllister, I thought that must have been James, after he left me in the study—'

'And so,' he said, 'you made killers of us both.' He stared out into the blackness of the forest. 'My poor child.'

'James had a knife—'

He nodded, and the silence again stretched out between them. 'If only you'd come to me,' he had said at last.

'I tried. But there was that man with you—' Above them the trees creaked as the wind passed through them, and for a brief instant she saw that same thunderous look pass across his features. 'And later— I couldn't, not after what James had said.' He remained silent; she thought he would never speak again. 'It made a sort of sense, you see—'

'Yes,' he said, on an indrawn breath. 'I do see, and you were so very young.' He stared up into the swaying trees, at where the tops were lit like torches by the low sun, and remained silent.

'*Did* James kill Mr McAllister?' she asked at last. Now that the central question regarding her father and Jacko's death was resolved, this mattered so much less.

'No.'

She waited for more. None came. 'Then who did?'

'Neither James nor I.'

'But you know who did?'

'Yes.'

'And you know who shot Jacko?'

'Yes.'

Tension coiled tight between them again, and she began to protest, but he raised a hand. 'Don't ask me, my dear, because I shan't tell you. Not yet—'

'Does James know?'

'Leave it, Evelyn, please—'

Indignation had swelled in her. How could she leave it there? 'But you allowed everyone to believe it *was* James. You let them hunt him down, you loosed the dogs—!' Half a story would no longer do, but she had seen his jaw clench and he had shaken his head.

'Not yet,' he had repeated. 'It is still dangerous for James. He's a wanted man with two charges of murder hanging over him, and Melton is a magistrate.'

That was too much. 'But George would never do anything!' she had protested. 'Not if you *explained* things to him.'

He had gripped her arm as tightly as he had at the station. 'I'll deal with this my own way, Evelyn.' There was a look in his eyes which frightened her. 'And then I'll explain everything to you, and to James. When it's safe to do so. Judge me then, if you will. Both of you.' And he had pulled her to him again, holding her close, hard up against the beat of his heart.

But now as she lay there, listening to the sounds of the forest as it settled into the darkness, she felt her newly vanquished demons begin to stir again, and rally. A killer her father was not, perhaps, but for five years he had allowed the world to believe that James Douglas was.

Chapter 19

'You want to see an Indian camp, mister?' Skinner asked Ballantyre as they gathered for breakfast next morning. "Cause a bunch of 'em arrived late last night, and set up camp a little ways downriver.' He gestured to where a blue smoke haze rose above the treetops about a half mile downstream. 'The boys'll take you there if you like.'

'Will they speak English?' James heard Ballantyre asking as they assembled at the shore a little while later. He had observed Marcel go on ahead and had a hunch that, whatever language was spoken, Ballantyre would learn little about Achak's whereabouts should he make enquiries. Then James watched stonily as Dalston first assisted Evelyn into the canoe and settled himself beside her, leaning close to talk, his hand on her arm.

'We could make it an annual event,' he was saying. 'Why don't we? During the salmon run. There's a prime river running through Melton's estate; I've often fished there. And Clemmy says you'll be coming to stay.'

'Yes, maybe.'

'And we're only ten miles away, y'know. You can come and admire Pa's hothouse and his peach trees. He's terribly proud of them, spends hours bullying the gardeners. They taste of nothing but mush, but don't tell him I said so—'

'No. I won't.'

'And if he offers you one you'll know where you stand. Only the favoured few get offered the peaches.' And he used his hat to waft away the flies from above Evelyn's head.

Why, for God's sake, did Ballantyre let her within a mile of the man?

James turned to find that Ballantyre was also watching them and he met James's scowl with a cool look before stepping into the other canoe, leaving him with no option but to take up his paddle and propel them into the current.

He stared at Evelyn's back as they crossed the river, at the knot of hair in the nape of her neck and her slender shoulders, and mar-velled again at the difference five years could make. When he had seen her at the station she had been a stranger; he would have passed her in the street – just another young lady, well dressed and with that indefinable air of superiority. But all that had fallen away as they travelled north and he had recognised again the child he had known, the joyful, rebellious, but essentially lonely, child. He would like to talk more with her, but he wouldn't.

They reached the opposite bank, downstream from their own camp, and were met with a chorus of barking from dogs which lined the riverbank, noses uplifted. A group of native boys ran down to meet them, some dragging the dogs aside while others ran into the water to grab onto the boats and haul them out of the current, before ushering their visitors up the slope to the camp.

James followed.

It was a typical native camp, like any other, with shelters such as those Tala and Machk slept in, except these were more substan-tial, and for real, not show, and were surrounded by the usual chaos of dogs and children. To one side fish and meat drying racks had been set up, and various pelts had been slung from the trees for in-spection. Fishing harpoons propped against the trunks provoked a flash of memory of spearing salmon back home, with Jacko, under a clouded moon.

He had often seen groups camped here before, and through the summer had witnessed a lively trade in native souvenirs with the various anglers, the proceeds from which were spent in the company stores, on food and cheap whisky. A dollar in cash was worth a lot. He recognised the woman who squatted beside the fire, sewing beads onto the toe of a moccasin, and exchanged a nod with her. She had spread examples of her work out on the rocks nearby, a couple of baskets, a purse, a pouch, and a pair of fine white doeskin gloves, too fine to be useful but designed to catch the eye of a passing tourist. The head of the camp was a man in his late forties who came forward to greet them, holding out a bottle and offering them a drink. James watched with malicious pleasure as Ballantyre nodded his acceptance, took a drink, and then paused, his eyes widening as the liquid stripped the lining from his throat. But Ballantyre thanked the man courteously and adroitly avoided the offer of more. Larsen managed to finish his too, though more slowly, as did Melton, while Dalston, less than discreetly, spat his out.

James left them to it and drifted to one side, bestowing a nickel on an urchin who tugged at his trouser leg but refused the tatty muskrat skin on offer. Then he leant his shoulder against a tree and watched with unholy amusement as Ballantyre questioned the man about the possible whereabouts of Achak with Marcel acting as interpreter. This the half-breed did with a convincing urgency, and through him Ballantyre was directed vaguely to the north, and then to the west, as the man held up fingers to suggest that Achak was one, two, maybe three days' journey away in any one of these directions. Eventually Ballantyre gave up and Marcel threw open his arms in sympathetic regret.

It was laughable, and in fact the whole scene was absurd. These visitors, with their well-cut tweeds and twills, the women with their straw hats and button boots, and all of them with that God-given air of condescension—

At the edge of the fire a brown-skinned child was amusing himself by flicking ash out of the fire with a stick, yipping strange little commands at a half-grown puppy until one of the women snapped at him to stop. She dusted the ash from her wares and brought over a woven basket and a little box for Lady Melton to examine, pulling at her sleeve to gain attention. There followed an elaborate mime of questions and answers until Marcel was again called upon to interpret.

As he watched them he had failed to notice that Evelyn had left her friend's side and moved across to him. 'Do you speak their language, James?'

'Enough to get by.' He quickly surveyed the group but no one was paying them any attention. She looked different this morning, less strained. Pretty—

'She does very fine beadwork,' she said, gesturing to the goods laid out on the rocks.

'Buy something then. They need the money.'

'I will. That little box perhaps. What is it made of?'

'Quills from a porcupine. Like a hedgehog, only bigger.'

'Seen something you fancy?' Dalston strolled up, smoking a cigarette. He glanced briefly at James before presenting him with his shoulder and picked up a purse which was heavily beaded, the fastening slightly off-centre, and raised it to his nose. 'Hmm. Sort of smoky boot leather.'

Evelyn went over and took up the doeskin gloves, and slipped one on. 'These are beautiful.' They were gauntlets rather than gloves and her little hand was lost in them; the wide-fringed cuffs reached halfway up her arm. 'Such fine craftsmanship.'

'How much?' Dalston addressed the woman, and she raised three fingers. '*Three* dollars! I'll give you one.' He held up one finger but the woman shook her head, and took back the gloves.

'Wait.' Evelyn turned back to James. 'Is that a fair price?'

It was an outrageous price, but he nodded.

'I'll give you two dollars. *Two dollars*,' Dalston repeated loudly, and held up two fingers, but the woman merely sniffed.

'Papa! Have you three dollars to give this woman?'

Ballantyre turned and looked across at them, glancing at James.

'No, hang on! Here, let me—' Dalston pushed his hand into his pocket, but Ballantyre was there before him and handed the woman the money, nodding his thanks as she gave him the gloves.

'Very pretty, my dear.' Ballantyre passed them to Evelyn and returned to his inspection of the furs.

Dalston glared at James, holding him in some way accountable. 'Perhaps there's something else then?' he said. 'But, you know, these people expect to haggle. It's a sort of game with them—'

'Is it?' Evelyn again addressed James.

'They haggle over the furs they bring in. But it's never a game.'

From the corner of his eye he saw that Ballantyre had turned back to listen, and he called Evelyn over to where he was examining the furs. 'Tell me which you like, my dear. This, perhaps? For a collar, I thought.' And he draped a pelt of silky blackness tipped with silver around her neck. Dalston fired another angry look at James before going down to the water's edge, where he sat beside one of the canoes and lit another cigarette.

James's eyes followed him. There he was: Jacko's killer; yards away from him smoking with an air of bored condescension, displaying the same contempt for their hosts and their ways as he had shown Jacko. And here he was, doing nothing about it.

He would not hold back for much longer, so Ballantyre had better reveal his hand—

When he turned back he saw that the visit was drawing to a close. Ballantyre had bought the silver fox fur, and was handing out cigars to the men, and making their farewells. Evelyn came across to James in her quick impetuous way. 'I'll take the little box too, the one made from quills. Please will you ask her how much it is? And please don't haggle.'

'No? Then I'll see to it you're robbed blind,' he said softly. And a smile lit her eyes.

———

A thin mist was floating just above the river when Evelyn emerged from her tent next morning and she paused a moment to watch patches of it blown across the surface, filtering the sun's rays. She could see James and Louis down at the river edge, stripped to the waist, crouching to wash, and then using their shirts to dry themselves before filling leather buckets with river water which they brought back up to the camp. As he passed, James gave her an almost imperceptible nod.

Breakfast was quickly prepared and eaten, and within the hour they were back on the river, heading north. The men paddled strongly against the current, then glided over the still waters of the next lake, their reflections mirrored in the surface, and a viscous wake spread fanlike behind them.

Lake Marie, Mr Skinner told her.

At the end of the lake they joined the river again and entered a high-sided gorge where rock rose on either side to form a roofless tunnel. The green-black water was lit occasionally by narrow darts of brilliant light where the sun found a gap amongst the rocks, and the men struggled against the current. They were breathing heavily by the time they reached the next portage, their shirts stained with sweat.

'Split Rock Portage,' said Mr Skinner as he helped the guests ashore. 'Jest a short one.'

It was, but it was over rough terrain. Portage boxes were packed again and raised on the men's backs, tumplines stretched across their foreheads causing neck muscles to tauten and teeth to be gritted. And next the canoes themselves were lifted shoulder high and brought across, and it seemed to Evelyn that the men had barely rested before Skinner was getting them back into the canoes. They paddled on for another hour or so. 'Island Portage,' declared Skinner. 'We'll eat here, and rest awhile. From here on up, the river gets wild.'

The rocks where they spread themselves were worn smooth, scoured of lichens by melting floodwaters and scarred by moving ice. Scrubby plants and mosses had found purchase in some of the cracks and crevices, succoured by the fine spray which blew back from the cascading water. They could not see the nearby falls, but their roar was clearly audible. Skinner offered to take the two women to where there was a good view to be had while the men fished from the rocks, and lunch was prepared.

He led them along a narrow trail which rose uphill to a point where they could look down onto the river, and where a wooded island divided the current. On either side the water surged past in a turbulent flood, dashing through a narrow rocky flume and sending spray into their faces.

'I've pulled some big ones from outa there,' Skinner shouted above the roar, and whatever response Clementina made was lost in the din.

Evelyn looked down from the edge of the rocks, mesmerised by the sight before her. Nothing could be further removed from the river at home which flowed sedately past the ordered fields of her father's estate, tinkling over long-smoothed pebbles where the cattle wandered down to drink. Surely they would never dare put the canoes back into the water above such a place!

At the top of the falls, where the river slid over the edge, the mass of it looked like a curved block of clear ice, before it fell to explode into a mass of thundering white water, sweeping all before it with a relentless energy. The rocks vibrated with the force of it.

Then she felt a hand grip her arm and pull her firmly away. 'Don't stare at it.' It was James. 'You'll lose your balance and you'll be in.' He released her arm and turned to tell Mr Skinner that the food was ready.

———

'All that energy, just disappearing into noise and spray,' her father was saying as they returned to the group. Luncheon, once again, was salt pork, bannock, and beans.

'Difficult to harness it up here,' George remarked.

'Maybe one day, though, when the railways have opened things up.'

Evelyn had been watching large ants carrying off crumbs of bannock and thinking that they looked like the men weighed down with their packs. A brightly coloured butterfly came and landed on a plant growing nearby, whose closed bell-flowers reminded her of the heathers back home. 'But it's too beautiful to spoil, surely, with all that ugly, clanking machinery—'

'You rode the streetcar in Port Arthur, did you not? What do you imagine powered that?' her father asked with a smile. 'And the great wheel at the Fair?'

'And all those lovely lights that danced along the White City's rooftops—' Mr Larsen added.

'There is always a cost, Evelyn, a price you have to pay.'

But the White City was now a thing of dreams, a distant memory, a million miles away. The same was true of the *Valkyrie* with its gleaming brass, its striped awnings and lobster canapés. Even the busy wharves of Port Arthur or Nipigon town were civilisation in comparison to where they were now. Life had been stripped bare. Had they really been on the river only four days? Or was it five—?

And then Skinner was on his feet again and the guides began packing up, stamping out the fire and pouring water on the hot ashes. 'Only short portages from now on,' he said as the men settled the packs onto their backs, 'and we'll make camp at the bottom end of Emma Lake.'

And so they rejoined the river, following it north, and it disappeared ahead of them round twists and bends, in and out of shadow and sunlight. The jagged cliffs before them seemed to converge, in some places almost closing in to form a funnel of rock. Large birds wheeled and turned above them. Eagles, James told her, following her gaze— Solitary pines clung to the rocky heights, standing sharp against the skyline; others had fallen, torn from their flimsy hold to be caught halfway down the cliffs, or had tumbled all the way to lay as brittle skeletons beside the river where they made perches for the kingfishers.

No other boats had passed them since one had hailed them late last night, heading downstream past their campsite, and apart from the crude landings which marked the start of the portages, there was now no sign of human civilisation. They had travelled fewer than twenty miles since leaving Skinner's lodge, barely the distance from Ballantyre House to the North Sea coast, but to Evelyn it felt as if only the essentials of life now remained.

Chapter 20

It was late when they set up their third camp. The evening air was sharp by then and the wind blew fitfully through the forest. 'Season's changing,' Louis remarked as Evelyn pulled on her jacket. The cleared area was smaller here, so the tents had to be pitched close together. Skinner's still straddled the divide, sited between the three guest tents and the native shelters, but the separation was now more symbolic than real, and that night they huddled close around a single fire.

'Try not to get downwind of Machk,' Clementina spoke in a low voice, and Evelyn frowned at her.

'So,' Skinner was saying. 'It's up to you. We can stop here now and fish Emma Lake or there's a good spot just below White Chute. Or some of you c'n carry on up the last stretch past Devil Rapids and on towards Virgin Falls. But maybe not the ladies—'

'Why not?' asked Evelyn.

Skinner scratched his chin. 'Kinda tough going, missee.'

'Then we won't attempt it, my dear,' said her father, with a smile but a note of finality in his voice. 'I don't speak for the others, of course.'

'I'm for heading on—' said Rupert.

'Yes, I think you should,' said her father, and Evelyn saw James raise his head. 'Melton? What about you?' George looked quizzically across at Clemmy, who returned him an uncertain look.

'I shall stay here with the Ballantyres,' said Mr Larsen, 'and let the fish come downstream to me.' Evelyn watched as Clementina pulled George to one side, and some earnest conversation ensued. She could imagine what was being said. Clementina's appreciation of the forest had run its course and she was becoming more fearful as they headed north.

In the end, however, it was agreed that both George and Rupert would continue on upriver, leaving early the next morning. They would fish for a day, then pitch camp, and return the following morning. Clementina looked unhappy with this, but George was clearly resolute. Mr Skinner put Louis in charge of the party going north and said that he would take with him Machk, the two Ojibway boys, and James. Marcel, to his evident disgust, was to stay at the camp in charge of the remaining natives to ensure that the older men got some good fishing. Skinner would stay too.

'You will be fine, my dear,' she heard George say.

———

James began gathering up the plates and kept his head down. He did not want to meet Ballantyre's eye in case the man read his mind. If he was going upriver with Dalston, then this would be his chance to settle the matter at last. He would have to take Louis into his confidence, he thought, as he dumped the plates beside the two boys and began sorting through the gear necessary for the expedition. Louis and Machk could hold on to Melton in case he turned nasty, but he would deal with Dalston himself, and by the time they returned Ballantyre would have his confession.

He looked up as Skinner approached. 'Change of plan. Marcel's going. You're staying.'

James paused, a rope length in his hand. 'No. I'm going—'

Skinner snorted. 'You ain't. Mister Ballantyre thinks maybe

the others got more experience, he remembered that first day at the jetty, see?' He raised his hand, deaf to James's protests. 'You've only got yerself to blame. Can't take the risk, once he's said that—'

But James was no longer listening. He threw the rope aside and went back to the campfire, but Ballantyre was not there. He looked around and he saw him, in the fading light, a little way along the riverbank with his back to him, lighting one of his infernal cigars. James made off towards him, stopping only to pick up two of the water pails to give himself a purpose.

Ballantyre was clearly anticipating him and he turned as he heard the crunch of James's boots on the rocks, and viewed him with grim irony. 'There's nothing wrong with your river skills, of course,' he said, in a quiet voice, 'only with your temperament. I can't take that risk. Fill your buckets.' And he turned away, pulling on the cigar and blowing the smoke out over the water.

'If you think—'

'Fill them, man, and stop glowering at me.' James swore softly but bent to the river's edge and threw in the buckets. 'Tomorrow, James. When they've gone, there will be a chance for me to explain. And perhaps then you'll understand.'

―――――

The morning, however, opened with a howl of rage from Skinner followed by a tirade against the two Ojibway boys. It appeared that the canoe most suitable for the trip up north had been badly packed after the last portage, and the blade of an axe had ripped through the birch bark, leaving a gash below the waterline. It would require patching, stitching, and sealing before the party could set off. Skinner unleashed such a deluge of abuse over the two boys that they exchanged glances, then silently gathered their posses- sions and set off into the forest. Skinner roared at them to return but was ignored, and he turned to Marcel, demanding that he go after them and bring them back.

'They wouldn't come, not after what you called them,' Marcel replied and stood, arms folded, and watched them disappear down the trail. 'Why would they?'

'They're your kin, so go find someone else.'

Marcel tossed him a scornful look, and went over to the fire.

This departure left them shorthanded, Skinner explained, looking rather sheepish, with not enough men to take the party upriver, see? They would have to wait for the repair to be done, and see if extra hands could be found. He would send Marcel off to try to make contact with groups hunting in the area, and maybe bring back more men.

James saw Ballantyre glance at him and then speak with a careful nonchalance. 'So today can be a day of leisure for us all. Very welcome, I daresay. I understand that the ladies' fishing trophy is still unclaimed?' He smiled at Lady Melton. 'Perhaps Niels will take on the role of judge for you – while I've a fancy to try my luck at this pool that James was telling me about, if he'll take me up there—' From the corner of his eye James saw Louis stop and look across at him.

'I'll take you myself, sir,' said Skinner, his face brightening. 'James c'n stay here and start fixing that canoe, Louis too. While Marcel c'n get himself downriver a ways and find someone who'll replace those no good sons of—' He stopped himself, and James saw a flicker of annoyance pass over Ballantyre's face. 'I've been fishing Astra's Pool longer than any of these boys, mister, and there's an old monster lurking up there you might do business with. Bin hooked a dozen times but never landed. A real fighter!'

'And I'll join you, Charles, if I may,' said Larsen. 'And we can judge the ladies' fishing derby together when we return.'

There was nothing to be done. James saw Ballantyre nod politely and then gave a half-shrug as he passed him. 'Another time,' he murmured. 'But soon—'

With her father, Mr Larsen, and Mr Skinner all gone up the trail to Astra's Pool, and with the departure of the two Indian boys, the campsite felt empty. Evelyn was not sure why this made her feel uneasy, but it did. Perhaps it was because the forest here seemed darker and more dense, pinning them to the rocky shelf above the river. How was it that one could feel exposed while at the same time claustrophobic and confused? In this wide, expansive land, she felt trapped.

A small creature with a striped tail and bulging eyes appeared suddenly and took her attention; she watched it dart in and steal a crumb from under the table. And as she followed its retreat up a tree she saw scorch marks on the trunk and that lower branches were blackened. Some past campfire out of control, perhaps? 'Lightning fire, more like,' Louis said, in answer to her question. 'Sometimes it just blows straight through, scarring the bark.'

'But doesn't kill the trees?'

He shook his head. 'It clears out the dead wood and lets in the light. And then the forest is stronger.'

She watched as the small creature came back for more. 'But what about the animals?'

'Some die. Others flee before the flames. The quick ones, the healthy ones, the ones you want to survive. And later they return. Same with the people, the forest-dwellers; they run and then return when the fire's blown through. Been that way always.' And he told her that these people had left rock paintings up above the waterfall, done many years ago, centuries perhaps.

'Could we go and see them?'

'*Bien sûr.*'

She went over to Clementina and asked if she wished to come along. 'And George, will you and Rupert?' George agreed, but Rupert said he had no interest in primitive art and would stay in camp; the gun he wanted to take up north with him needed cleaning.

And so the four of them set off along an overgrown trail through the trees where the sounds of the river and its waterfall soon faded away, leaving a cool sort of silence. Evelyn breathed deeply, savouring the damp pine smell of balsam and crushed needles. She was not sorry that Rupert had stayed behind, although she would have been hard-pressed to explain why. Since the visit to the Indian camp he had seemed restless and edgy, sometimes sulky, and she had found his company less congenial than she had on the yacht. Perhaps he was bored, regretting having abandoned his original plan to go buffalo hunting. His wit seemed to have developed a sharp edge, and too often his remarks were condescending towards the natives, showing little concern that they might overhear. Perhaps he resented the new proximity between the servile and the served.

James, she noticed, watched him with ill-disguised hostility.

She stopped on the trail to pin back the hair that had escaped and was falling over her face. Ahead of her Louis also stopped and turned, looking beyond her back down the trail to where Clementina was struggling over a fallen tree trunk. Her skirts had caught on a snag, and George was endeavouring to free her.

'We will wait for them,' Louis said and pulled out a short pipe, cupping his hand around it to light it, and gestured to a recumbent log. 'Rest a moment.'

They were in a small clearing on the slope beside a clutch of low-growing trees which were covered with clusters of small red berries. 'Are these edible?' she asked, picking one and holding it between finger and thumb.

Louis nodded. 'Try it.' She put it in her mouth and bit. A sharp sourness numbed her tongue and taste buds and she spat it out, wiped her mouth and looked up indignantly at Louis. 'The sharpness gives flavour,' he said, without apology. Then he put down his pipe and went to the edge of the clearing and began gathering berries from the bushes there. He came back and dropped a handful into her lap. 'But if it's sweetness you want, then stick to these—' and he picked up his pipe again.

Clementina arrived, breathless from the climb. 'Is it much farther?' George followed, wafting a wide frond over their heads to keep the flies at bay.

'Ten minutes only.'

'Ooh, raspberries! Lovely,' she said, seeing them in Evelyn's lap and taking one. 'Where did you find them?'

'Louis got them. But avoid those.' She pointed to the other berries and frowned at Louis. 'They're horrid.'

Louis looked back at her through the blue smoke from his pipe. 'But now you know, and can choose. Shall we go on?'

Chapter 21

Larsen essayed a cast, taking joy in the whirling sound of the line as it passed overhead. This was how he had imagined it would be, how he had planned it. Just himself and Ballantyre, fishing in a companionable silence, imbibing deeply of the peace, and the quiet. *Simplify, simplify, simplify,* Thoreau urged.

There was no need for words, and perhaps this would be their only chance, away from the restlessness of the younger ones with their laughter and their chatter, their stories and their demands for one's attention. This was what he had craved through those long dark days in his Boston office, bent over columns and figures, determined to leave things in good order. Just a lake with trees reflected in it, a perfect mirror, its surface broken only by the flies, real and counterfeit, which dared the trout to surface. Life simplified—

Skinner had seen them set up with their rods and then wandered off, and Larsen could see him now, on the far side of the pond, settling himself down in the shade for a nap. Almost twenty years had passed since he had first come to Skinner's lodge, and gone upriver with the old trader. How could that be? He had hardly noticed the years pass. The river had been quieter then, fewer people knew of it, and they had been good days. And now Skinner was an old man, wiry and strong still, but ageing. Like himself.

He looked across at his friend as he cast again. Charles Ballantyre, by contrast, was still in his prime, vigorous and energetic, the restlessness of youth tempered now with a wisdom borne of experience, but still with that essential integrity which had first drawn him to the man— He too seemed to be in his element today, shedding his concerns as he cast his line, revelling in the simple delight of fishing with a friend.

Larsen turned back to his own rod and cast, wondering again what had been troubling the man.

'Niels.' Perhaps the thought had reached him, for he turned to see that Ballantyre had reeled in after the last cast and was standing at the water's edge, looking out across the sparkle of the lake. 'Do you remember, I wonder, that a man was shot on my estate some years back?'

Larsen nodded, taken aback, but he remembered something of the sort. 'Your keeper, wasn't it?'

Ballantyre shook his head. 'The keeper was killed the same night; knifed, though, not shot. It was a poacher who was shot, an old man, a reprobate, a veteran offender. Recalcitrant and remorseless—' Ballantyre laid down his rod and went and sat on a boulder a few feet away from Larsen. 'He tried to burn down my stables once, then netted my river when the salmon were running, the wretch – a regular old nuisance. He'd come before me on numerous occasions, each time more defiant than before.'

Larsen cast again, his head half-turned to listen; something told him this was important but that his attention should perhaps be oblique, giving Ballantyre space to confide— A fish rose, causing shallow ripples.

'Once,' Ballantyre continued after a moment, 'after he'd been caught on my neighbour's land, I remonstrated with him for appearing before me again, for exactly the same offence, and he simply threw back his head, and looked me in the eye. He too was my neighbour, he said, my equal, living off the same God-given food taken from the same God-given land. So where was the offence?'

Larsen smiled. 'Ah. A philosopher.'

'Yes. He was.'

Larsen's line tautened and his rod bent. Both men gave it the required attention, but despite their efforts the fish escaped. Then after a moment Ballantyre carried on: 'And when you're out here, in a place like this, you can see his point of view . . . Anyway, he went on to say that he felt well-disposed towards *me*, and asked why I didn't feel the same about *him*. And he asked why he had been taken up for trying to fill his stomach from the estate's land when I regularly invited those who already had full bellies to come onto the same land to shoot and fish.' Ballantyre stretched out his legs. 'And it was a fair point.'

'I suppose it was—'

'All I could say in return was that I was charged by the authority vested in me to bring him to account, and through example and correction to make him repent of his misdoing. I felt like a pompous ass as I said it – and he damn well knew it.'

Larsen smiled, and continued to reel his line slowly in. 'And so?'

'I started to pass sentence but he put his head on one side and raised a hand to stop me, and then proceeded to point out that the penalty was entirely disproportionate for the so-called offence, and instead of charging him, I could choose to make some changes, to bring real justice into the court. By now, of course, everyone was thoroughly enjoying themselves at my expense.' Larsen said he could imagine that was so. 'Part of me wanted to know how far the man would go, so I decided to give him his head. What a mistake that was! The ruffian was eloquent, a born orator! He spoke of natural and unnatural justice, insisting that neither my neighbour nor myself *owned* the salmon as they were only passing through to spawn, and they had come from the sea, where they belonged to no man and to every man. It was, of course, unanswerable.'

'But, even so, you couldn't acquit him—'

'No. But I wanted to! I could only point out that by doing so I would be sending an open invitation to every thief, rogue, and scoundrel to come onto private land and take whatever they felt was owed them, and he had to accept the justice offered by the court. The man countered by saying that what I served up as justice was an organised form of oppression which did not command his respect, and he would be governed only by his conscience. His *conscience*, Niels—' He paused, as if to drive the point home, and then softly repeated the words. 'His conscience—' Ballantyre stared grimly out over the lake. He was silent for so long this time that Larsen thought he would say no more. Then he picked up and tossed a pebble into the water, and followed it with another. Larsen reeled in. So much for fishing— 'He carried on in a similar vein until old Farquarson, my neighbour, could take no more and got to his feet in what he believed to be my defence, pointing to what he called my many benevolent acts.' The bitterness was unmistakable, and Larsen, all at sea, looked at his friend with concern, but Ballantyre was now unstoppable. 'He demolished that argument by claiming, quite rightly, that he gave away a much greater proportion of his wealth than either Farquarson or I, and that he asked for nothing in return. We, he declared, used benevolence to add gloss to our characters and salve to our consciences for having claimed so much for ourselves.' Ballantyre gave a sardonic smile. 'Poor Farquarson was apoplectic by this time and ordered him to be taken away, and as he went the old rogue capped it all by saying that imprisoning him was an unnecessary cost to the nation as he was perfectly able to support himself.' Larsen laughed out loud. 'But he got six months' hard labour just the same, and I, that day, learned the meaning of an unquiet conscience. Began to, anyway,' he added.

Larsen reeled in and came and sat beside him on the rocks, still struggling to understand where this was leading. 'You'd have freed him if you could?'

'Yes, I wish I had. And what might we all then have been spared—' That too was added in a low tone. 'And he was right! It *was* a travesty to imprison him for taking a few salmon, his reasoning was impeccable, and after that, each time I sat in a court, or in some gathering of a philanthropic institution, I would see his mocking smile and hear his contempt – and knew things for the sham that they were.'

A zephyr of wind blew across the pond and the mirrored surface shattered into rippling shards. On the far side Larsen could see that Skinner had risen and was stretching; he would return soon and this conversation would be over, but Larsen felt that it had not yet been played out. 'You operate in a world that is not of your making, my friend, obeying rules which must, however imperfectly, govern the actions of others.' It was the best he could do.

Ballantyre turned to him, with an odd hard look, stripped of his usual urbanity. '*Imperfectly*, you say? That man, that tattered philosopher, was then shot in cold blood on my land, Niels, in an unforgivable act of butchery. Where was justice that day?' He paused. 'And what followed was worse—' This time the silence lasted longer, and Larsen could only wait. 'Jacko will never know, but that day in court he gave me weapons I would soon need, and a resolution that I too would be governed only by *conscience*, not by the self-serving laws of privilege.' Larsen frowned, quite bewildered but distressed by his friend's obvious pain, and searched for a response, but Ballantyre continued. 'He told me that day that if I would only look through his eyes I would see a different universe.' He turned to Larsen with a twisted smile. 'And here, my friend, in this wild place of yours, I believe that I do.'

Larsen recognised that they had reached to the margin of Ballantyre's troubles, and if he would come to the core he must now tread carefully. More of the incident came back to him, the killer had been a stable hand, he recalled, a lad whom Ballantyre had taken under his protection, an orphaned child. Such a gesture had been typical of the man, and that betrayal must have wounded him deeply.

'Did they ever catch the boy who killed him?' he asked, and he saw the muscles tighten in Ballantyre's jaw.

'No.'

Across the pond Larsen could see that Skinner had started back, working his way slowly round the pool towards them, and he cursed the man's timing. Ballantyre had seen him too. 'And now, Niels, I must ask you a favour.' He spoke in a different tone, more briskly. 'Two favours, in fact. The first is that you ask me no questions.' He gave an apologetic smile. 'None at all. And the second is that you take this letter and keep it close, only open it if you have to, and believe me, you will know when that is.' And he took from his inside jacket pocket a crumpled letter. 'It is merely a safeguard. I wrote a letter which was posted for me and it awaits you in Boston. It will explain things that must have puzzled you, and I ask in advance for your forgiveness, as you will not like what I have done—' Ballantyre held out the letter. 'And, I beg you, act upon the contents if you have to.'

With great reluctance, Larsen took it from him. 'My dear fellow—!' He was deeply apprehensive now; there was a look on Ballantyre's face that he disliked exceedingly. 'Whatever this matter is . . . !' he began but the trees beside them rustled, then parted, and Skinner appeared, asking if something was wrong, as neither of them was fishing. Ballantyre swung round to him, his face composed again, and genial.

'Why no! We were simply—'

He stopped abruptly at the sound of a gunshot. Its echo was amplified by the high cliffs, and a cloud covered the sun.

Two more shots followed, then a short gap, and then another, and another. 'What the devil—' But as they continued Skinner seemed to relax, and began chewing again.

'Shootin' targets,' he said, nodding with conviction.

'How can you know that?' Ballantyre's face was bloodless.

'Stands to reason. What else's it gonna be! An Injun massacre?' He gave a high-pitched giggle, but Ballantyre moved past him and disappeared rapidly down the trail.

The other party had arrived at the site of the ancient rock paintings when the shots rang out. Louis had climbed up onto the rock face to pull aside the branches which concealed where, centuries ago, the rock surface had spalled away to create a smooth stone canvas for the native artists. Paintings of animals and monstrous fish, lines and zigzags outlined in black and red ochre, covered the surface. 'See, a hunter with a bow and arrow—'

He broke off as the sound of the first shot reached them, and Evelyn felt her heart lurch. It was followed by a second.

'Shots—!' remarked Melton, unnecessarily, and looked up at Louis. 'Why would—?' Then he too broke off as the shots continued and Louis jumped down, rubbing the grit from his hands.

'I imagine it is milord Dalston,' he said, with studied unconcern, smiling at the two women.

'Why do you say that?' asked Evelyn quickly, then turned to George. 'We must go back—'

'Or Marcel—' Louis continued. 'They were laying bets about marksmanship, I heard them this morning. That's all it is.'

But Evelyn had started down the track. George called to her to wait but she continued downhill apace, seized with a sudden reasonless panic, and she ran, stumbling over roots, grabbing at branches which whipped at her face, and caught at her hair, filled with an awful premonition.

She had not gone far before Louis reached her and caught her by the arm, swinging her round to face him. 'Whoa! I tell you, mamselle, all is well! And as you do not believe it to be so, then you must allow me to go first, eh?' He pressed her down onto a fallen tree trunk. 'So sit there, wait for the others, and then go more slowly.' And he was off, down the trail, and soon out of sight.

———

The argument had sprung from nowhere. James had been crouched down beside the damaged canoe, spreading pitch on the repair, and barely registered that Marcel had returned to the camp bringing two men with him, two strangers. He looked up again and saw that Marcel was examining Dalston's hunting rifle, his dark eye squinting down the sights. He balanced it in his hands a moment, and then put it aside with obvious indifference and began to walk away. Quite what he said, James had not heard, but Dalston retaliated with some remark of his own. James saw Marcel stop and turn, and then shrug, and carry on walking, but Dalston got in front of him and it was clear that a challenge had been laid down. *Jesus!* Of all the damned foolishness—

And then targets were being set up down by the shingle.

He put aside the pitch pot, wiped his hands on his trousers, and straightened. It needed only this. 'If the others hear shots, they'll be concerned,' he said, addressing Marcel. 'Leave it, man. At least until they're back.'

Marcel assumed deafness.

'Step aside, will you,' said Dalston.

'I said leave it until the others get back,' James repeated, keeping his temper in check. It was the first time he had looked directly into Dalston's eyes, and he felt his gore rise.

'And *I* said step aside.' Dalston pushed past him, immediately raised his gun, and fired, hitting one of the targets, barely giving

Marcel time to get clear. The half-breed hissed a curse as he leapt aside and Dalston fired again, hitting the second target. Marcel grabbed the gun from him and took several paces away from the target and fired two shots in rapid succession; both found their targets. Exasperated, James protested again and was again ignored. He stepped aside then, and leant against a tree, his arms folded, and listened to the sound of the shots echoing from the rocky cliffs, and imagined Ballantyre's reaction.

There was no stopping them now. They let off a few more rounds, and having scored evenly Marcel tossed the gun into the bushes and went for his bow and arrow. He set the target up again, shot off two arrows and then, straight-armed, thrust the bow at Dalston. The men that Marcel had brought back came close, all attention, grinning and urging Dalston to take it, to try his hand, their mockery all too evident. James straightened slowly and prepared for trouble.

But then fate, in the shape of a stranger, intervened. The bushes beside him rustled and parted, and there he was, a man in a slouch hat and stained clothes, appearing as if from nowhere. 'Pretty shooting,' he said.

Dalston stopped, bow in hand, and goggled at him. 'Where the devil did you spring from?'

The stranger ignored him and looked towards the empty campsite. He was a tall rangy man and his clothes seemed moulded to him, the battered hat was pulled down low and his boots were laced up his calves as the natives wore them. He had a small bag slung on his shoulder. 'This Skinner's camp?' he asked.

James answered him. 'It is.'

The man continued to look around 'And is Mister Ballantyre here—?' He stopped and turned as Ballantyre himself broke cover, breathless and red in the face. He had evidently been running, but he halted abruptly at the sight of the stranger, and drew a breath.

'Good God! Kershaw.'

At almost the same instant Louis appeared from the opposite direction, and he too halted. Ballantyre's gaze swept the scene, passing over James to Dalston, and then returned to James. 'There were shots—' he said.

The stranger raised his hands in denial. 'Not me, mister. Jest these two and some tomfoolery with targets. That's how I found the camp. Heard the shots.' He pushed his hat to one side of his head and scratched. 'I came looking for you, sir. I got your messages and I got news.' James heard Louis send Tala back up the trail to reassure the ladies, and watched him draw close, his eyes on the stranger. 'Achak's camped jest a few miles away, with his family. I talked to him and now he wants to speak to you, so I said—'

Ballantyre's face had brightened but he cut him off quickly: 'Well done! That is good news. But have we offered you food? Or a drink? Eat first, and then we can talk. Is there coffee in that can?'

James went over to the fire and a moment later Louis joined him, bringing more fuel, and as he bent to mend the fire he looked up at James, and their eyes met.

———

Evelyn and the others returned to the camp to find a stranger sitting beside the fire finishing a piece of bannock and a slice of venison, tearing the meat with his teeth and chewing with his mouth open.

She looked at him a moment then addressed her father. 'There were shots—' she said, but her pulse was steadying. Nothing here seemed to be amiss. Tala had come to meet them but she had only needed to see for herself.

'Target practice, I am told.' Her father smiled at her, but it was a tight little smile. 'Nothing more. Now, allow me to introduce Dan Kershaw, a business associate of mine.'

'A *business* associate?' Clementina laughed. 'Honestly, Mr Ballantyre. Only you—'

'Everything OK?' asked Mr Skinner as he and Mr Larsen emerged from the trail.

'It was just as you said, Mr Skinner,' her father replied. 'But now, if you will excuse us, since Mr Kershaw has taken some trouble on my behalf, I must hear what he has to say. No, no, bring your coffee with you, Dan.' And he led the man down onto the shingle and along the bank, stopping a little distance downstream.

Rupert came over to join them. 'So what's all this?' he asked, raising his eyebrows at Evelyn.

'With Papa, one never knows,' she replied.

———

Louis and James spun out the job of mending the fire as long as they could, glancing occasionally towards the two figures as they stood talking on the shingled shore. 'This man Kershaw has a lot to say,' Louis said in an undertone as they watched.

'And if he's tracked down Achak . . .'

'. . . what has he been told—?'

Keeping an eye on the two men, James sent Tala to fetch water with instructions to listen if he could. Was it his imagination or did Ballantyre keep looking back at them, or was he simply ensuring that no one approached them unseen? What exactly did Ballantyre want with Achak? Same as everyone else, presumably, and would they now find themselves in competition with Ballantyre? God forbid—! He watched Ballantyre draw the man aside as Tala approached with the water buckets, and it seemed to James that sharp questions were being asked. Kershaw kept shrugging, and once he too had looked back at the camp.

Louis stood there, staring across the river, chewing his lip, then gestured to where Marcel was savagely quartering a small deer he had taken. 'And what's eating him?'

James told him, and Louis rolled his eyes. 'So now I go upriver with two mad dogs, tearing at each other's throats.' He glanced downstream again and straightened when he saw that Ballantyre and Kershaw were coming back towards camp, but they passed without a glance, and Ballantyre went to draw Larsen aside.

Kershaw ambled over to the fire and stood there, rubbing his hands together, and looked into the pot where venison was simmering for the evening's meal. 'Sure smells good,' he said, and sat himself down.

'Are you staying to eat?' asked Louis.

'Looks like it.' The man stretched out his legs, let his hat fall over his face, and settled himself down for a nap. Louis studied him for a moment and then went over to Marcel, spoke to him for a few minutes, and beckoned to James.

'Tala didn't overhear much but enough—' He paused.

'For what?'

Louis and Marcel exchanged glances. 'Enough to suggest that your Mister Ballantyre was the man behind that original deal with Achak's father.'

James stared at him. Oh God. But then, of course – it was suddenly obvious! The deal had been done by an agent, they had been told, working for another man. 'And so we've—'

'Cut him out.'

Louis looked gleeful but James's head swam and he looked over to where Ballantyre and Larsen were now in deep discussion. He should have guessed, put two and two together. Ballantyre's interests in the planned railroad, in the potential of the river, in prospecting and mining, and then his determination to find Achak; it had been more than a desire to follow up a rumour. Ballantyre had staked a claim, done a deal, and would not give it up without a fight. And when he discovered who had stolen a march on him, his interest in clearing James's name would surely vanish.

He watched as Ballantyre turned from his discussion with Larsen to raise a hand and summon Skinner with an authoritative gesture. True to form, his old stable-yard manner again. And when he turned back he found Louis was studying him. 'Did you know?' he asked.

Christ! 'No.'

Louis held his look.

'*Eh bien.*' He glanced at Marcel and nodded, as if closing the matter. 'So what now?'

What indeed—?

The others had gathered around the fire, unconcerned by events, the men smoking while Lady Melton showed them the sketches she had started to make of the rock paintings. But Evelyn was looking straight at him.

She rose and came over. 'What's happening?' she asked, addressing him.

He dissembled. 'Miss?'

She gave him a scornful look. 'What is Papa discussing with that man?'

But before he could respond Ballantyre called out to her. 'Evelyn, my dear. A moment, if you will.'

————

He drew her aside. It was just a small change of plans, he said. 'I'll be gone a day at most. Mr Larsen and Mr Skinner will remain in the camp with you, and the guides.' Evelyn recognised the expression on his face, distracted and driven, and she knew that argument was pointless. Even here, in this wilderness of forest and lakes, he would leave her— 'Kershaw's canoe is just a mile upstream, above the falls, and from there he says it's only a short paddle and then a good trail. If we go at first light when the others set off, there's an

even chance we'll be back by nightfall. At worst I'll be away overnight.' He paused and gave her a twisted smile. 'Another sin to lay
at my door, I know. Add it to the pile.'

'And if he's already moved camp, will you follow him?'

He flicked her cheek. 'And so risk your wrath? I'm not sure I
have the stomach for that! No. But he won't move. Kershaw says
he's expecting me, and then the matter won't detain me long.' He
might have been discussing a short train journey, a meeting in another town, leaving her with a house full of servants, not in this
wild place.

'Will James be here?' she asked, abruptly. He returned her a
questioning look, and then a slight frown.

'I believe so. Mr Skinner!' he called across to the old man. 'Who
is to remain here?'

'Tala and Machk. And James. The two new boys will go with
Louis and Marcel and the gentlemen upriver. We'll look after you,
missee, don't you fear.'

If James was here, and Papa was not, then at last there would
be the chance to talk. To talk properly— And now that the essential facts were clear she no longer considered herself bound by her
father's orders. 'Then I'll be just fine,' she said, turning back, and
unconsciously raised her chin.

'Of course,' he agreed, but there was a glint of understanding
in his eye. 'But continue to apply good sense, Evelyn, and then
everyone will stay safe.'

'Mister, don't you fear,' said Skinner. 'Nothing'll happen in a
day.'

———

'This gets interesting, ' Louis muttered as he passed James; and
then later, when they were down by the river, cleaning the cook
pots: 'What powers does Ballantyre have?'

'Powers?'

'Of persuasion, my friend. He seems to me to be a formidable foe— Will he persuade Achak to go back on his agreement?'

James shrugged. 'He can only offer the man money, in one form or another. He's got plenty of that, but his deal was with the old chief—'

Louis scratched his chin, his eyes darkening again. 'But we've no more legal claim than he had. No documents. Nothing registered.' He glanced up at James. 'We can only trust Achak not to renege.'

And trust was a brittle thing.

They were carrying the water between them, back towards camp, when Ballantyre himself appeared at the edge of the wood. And he came down the slope towards them. 'A word, if you will, with you both.' James sensed Louis tensing beside him. 'There was something of a quarrel between Marcel and Dalston, I believe,' he said, addressing Louis.

'Yes – though I wasn't here.'

'But you were?' He switched attention to James.

'It was nothing – temper and bravado, on both parts.'

Ballantyre held his look then turned back to Louis. 'Are you still prepared to go upriver with them?'

'Of course.'

'Good.' Ballantyre considered him. 'Melton certainly made light of the matter, but if you sense trouble you must return at once, and take whatever measures are necessary.' Louis shrugged, but looked puzzled. 'If they wish to quarrel I'd rather they did it out of this camp while I'm away, but I'll tell you now that you can rely on Melton. He's a sound man. Dalston is volatile.'

Volatile ? Dalston was a killer—

And yet still he went free.

Ballantyre reached into his pocket and brought out two cigars which he offered to them. Louis took the nearest. James shook his head, lips tight, and Ballantyre thrust it into his shirt in a sudden spurt of exasperation. 'Keep it for later, then. Or give it to Louis. Skinner and Mr Larsen remain in charge here, of course, but I place the comfort and safety of the ladies in your hands, young man. See that they stay around the camp until I get back, no more junketing off to see paintings or waterfalls. Understood? They stay here.'

———

Perhaps it was the two-day-old venison, or just his general uneasiness, but Larsen's stomach was burning with acid when they gathered around the fire that evening. Somehow, despite the restrictions of the site, the group had splintered again. The guides had arranged themselves on one side, the guests on the other, with Skinner and Kershaw unconsciously straddling the two. But Larsen saw that they were not a companionable group. Looks were being exchanged between Dalston and Marcel which suggested that their quarrel was not yet played out, while Louis's and James's attention seemed fixed with a strange hostility on the laconic Kershaw. There had been no further mention of the prospector's purpose, but the word *gold* seemed to hang in the very woodsmoke— What was it Ballantyre had said? Worse poison to men's souls. And poor dear Evelyn was looking mutinous again, as well she might, unforgiving of her father again, while Clementina sat close to her husband and stared into the fire. It was as if some strange sense of anticipation had crept into the camp, and already that sublime moment at Astra's Pool was just a memory.

Ballantyre, on the other hand, was more animated than he had been for some time, discussing fishing with Skinner in a way that seemed intended to keep the conversation flowing, and on safe ground. Larsen decided to help him along. 'So you think that old reel of mine might just see me through?' he said, addressing James. 'It feels like a betrayal even to consider replacing it.'

'It's done you long service, I think,' the young man replied with that engaging smile he too rarely showed. 'Did it give you trouble today?'

'No, no.' It was Ballantyre who had troubled him. 'It was fine, and I was using a fly of my own devising. The Pale Horseman I call it, but I think it's more effective in a fast-moving current than a pool, being long and slim.' And he described how he put it together.

Louis too was listening. 'But every fly fisherman has his own secret, I think, his own bit of magic, eh? What was it that fool from Buffalo was using?'

'Silk and skunk's tail came into it,' said James.

Larsen laughed. 'With me it's just my old grey nag's mane – I think I only keep her to ensure a supply of the right coloured hair. But what will I do when she dies?'

James shrugged. 'I know a man who once plucked a dead bird for its feathers.'

Larsen smiled, but as he reached for his pipe his hand stayed and his stomach seemed to tighten. A dead bird— He looked at James, long and hard, as an extraordinary idea occurred to him, then he glanced around and saw that Louis had switched his attention to Melton. 'But one day they too will run out, and what then?' he said casually.

The young man's eyes were on Ballantyre, across the campfire, and he shrugged. 'Jackdaw maybe, or raven.'

'But less exotic than the original—' Larsen spoke softly, watching the young man's face, but James was still watching Ballantyre, and merely nodded.

Chapter 22

'Ah, so the whisky jacks have found us!' Larsen remarked with a smile. 'It doesn't take them long.' Two jays squabbled amongst the pine needles for scraps of bannock and he stood watching them as he drained his mug.

The camp had emptied at first light when Louis and his party had set off up the trail, the guides carrying the canoe and the gear, with Melton and Dalston following. Ballantyre and Kershaw had departed soon after. Both women had risen early to breakfast with the others before they departed, and then Larsen had gone down to the river to cast a line or two, and consider, but his reel had jammed again, so he had had to return. Other than that annoyance he was looking forward to a quiet day, and a chance to think further.

He watched absently as Tala lay a trail of crumbs to lure the jays towards the two women, and the birds, nicely reckoning the risk, followed it boldly. He had seen men follow promising investments with that same greedy look, only to be snared by false trails, and drawn to disaster. 'Just stay still, ladies—' The Indian crouched down, held out his palm, and in a blur of smudge-grey feathers the birds snatched the offering and flew off into the trees. And he had seen the money vanish that quickly too.

'Oh, so cheeky,' cried Clementina, looking up at where they now scolded from a low-hanging branch.

'Camp robbers,' said Larsen, with a smile.

'No,' Tala replied. 'The forest was theirs, long before you came—'

And that, of course, was true.

James looked up from where he sat. He had Larsen's reel dismantled before him again but there was little he could do, the moving parts were worn quite smooth and it really ought to be replaced, but perhaps it would last the trip. He smiled slightly as he watched Tala go through his repertoire of tricks with the jays, placing bread on his shoulder, and then on top of his head, grinning at the ladies' astonishment as the birds swooped down to take it. Over the season they had grown bold and wily, and Tala liked nothing better than an appreciative audience. Evelyn was watching with rapt attention, hands clasped, childlike, much as she had once watched in admiration as a half-grown youth had lain along a grassy bank to pull trout from the river. He had spent most of this trip trying to avoid looking at Evelyn, or thinking about her. But he had not been wholly successful in this resolve, and since speaking to her he found it was nigh on impossible to stop looking at her.

He was transported back to a time when the cow parsley was grown tall, and the woodland around Ballantyre House had been strewn with bluebells. She had been a joyous child, away from Ballantyre House, and he had found companionship with her – God knows he'd had little enough himself as a child. And today she appeared just the same, relaxed and at ease, with her hair falling down her back. In fact, she looked lovely.

'They'd come to you too, Miss Ev . . . Miss Ballantyre,' he said, setting aside the reel, drawn by that familiar smile. 'Give her some bread, Tala. Let her try.' He went over to her. 'Lean forward and then put out your hand.' The birds approached with their lopsided hopping walk, their black eyes greedy-bright, but she was too tense, and fidgeted, pulling her hand away with a squeak.

She had been impatient that other time too, catching trout—

'Stay still! And hold your palm flat.' He came closer and crouched beside her, then he took her hand and turned it, her palm pale against his own, tanned and dirty. He heard her soft gasp as the bird's twig-like feet gripped her finger but she stayed still that time, and let the black beak have its reward.

'It took it—' She breathed, looking up at him.

'Aye.' He smiled, then released her hand abruptly, and went back to his reel. It took him a moment to remember what he had been doing with it.

───

His coffee finished, Larsen withdrew to his tent and spent some time subjecting his whiskers to a long overdue trimming, and thought hard, alternatively accepting and dismissing the extraordinary theory that had occurred to him last night. Could it really be so?

When he emerged the two women were still behaving like giddy girls, testing the limits of the jays' boldness, and he stood a moment watching them, drying his hands on the small towel he had brought with him. James, he saw, had left them and sat with his back to them, bent again over Larsen's reel. 'Any progress?' he called over to him.

'Some—' came the quiet reply.

Larsen went over to the fire and sat, listening to the sound of the wind gently stirring the tops of the trees. It was a fine clear morning, but the air sure was colder today with the promise of a winter not far away. He studied the young people again, still rolling his extraordinary idea around in his head, and then, with a stifled sigh, he pulled out his book and began to read.

But once again Thoreau failed to console. Life had become too complex to follow his mantra: *simplify, simplify, simplify.* The letter Ballantyre had given him was burning a hole in his pocket and he thought again of the shots yesterday, and of Ballantyre's extreme reaction. Whatever had he expected? And he looked across at the young Scot, whose accent, and his own remarks, placed him so close to Ballantyre's estate. But how close—? He watched as he put aside the reel, drawn back into the game, and Evelyn, egged on by Tala, was now balancing a piece of bread on the young man's head, ordering him to stay still, and clapping her hands in delight as one of the jays landed and stabbed at the bread. The other bird swooped down beside it and he winced as they squabbled amongst his hair.

Then, without warning, Tala took up his gun and aimed it at James's head. 'Shall I shoot them off?' Evelyn froze, and gave a strangled scream. And the birds flew away.

James stood up quickly. 'He wasn't serious—' he said, reaching his hand towards her. Tala apologised but grinned wickedly at James. 'I would not have missed my shot, you know, and there are many jays in the wood.' But Evelyn looked shaken.

<hr />

Later James cleared away the plates and watched the women go their separate ways – Lady Melton to her tent while Evelyn headed down to the shore with her book, and he thought again of what Ballantyre had said to him just before he left.

'Refuse my cigar, if it gives you pleasure, James,' he had said, pulling him to one side. 'I shan't explain to you just now, but this business with Achak is central to my plans, and to resolving your own situation.' James, uncomprehending, had searched Ballantyre's expression, intense, as he had never seen it, but not hostile. 'I'll explain when I return, and then close the matter— And in the meantime I ask that you keep an eye on Evelyn as you once did before. You've no quarrel with her.' And with that he had turned on his heel, leaving no time for questions, and had joined

Kershaw at the trailhead, raising his hand just once to his daughter, and was gone.

'You have jays in Scotland, I think.' Larsen interrupted his thoughts. 'I remember seeing them in the woods when I stayed with Mr Ballantyre.'

James nodded. 'Aye, but they are larger here, and more impudent.'

'And not just the jays, eh?' James acknowledged the remark with a smile but made no other response. 'But you've got used to different ways here no doubt, after, what was it, five years—?'

'Aye.'

'Will you go back to Scotland, one day, do you think?'

'I've nothing to go back for.'

'No family?'

'None. Shall I pour this tea away, sir? Or will you have another cup?'

So his probing came to naught, and there was little more Larsen could say after that, but he watched James as he went about his tasks, and thought again about that strange business at the station. Other incidents came to mind too, and just now, that expression on Evelyn's face.

And the letter—

By giving him that letter Ballantyre must be covering his back, which meant that there *was* something going on, and that he had reasons to be concerned. Ballantyre clearly wished to keep the matter to himself, but playing a lone hand could sometimes be unwise. During half a lifetime spent in banking, Larsen had learned that it was only with full knowledge that one could act with prudence and purpose, and Ballantyre, for all his caution, might yet need help.

'I think perhaps Lady Melton has the right idea,' he said to James, his mind made up. 'I too shall retire to my tent for a while.

Perhaps you would be good enough to go and see if Miss Ballantyre is alright, and tell her that I will join her shortly.'

———

James stopped at the end of the trail where he was shielded by the low maples, and looked down to where Evelyn sat amongst the rocks, her book open on her lap. She was not reading, though, but sat motionless, watching the river flowing past her, her skirt tucked under her legs and her hair alight with sunshine. A scarf, the colours of the autumn, was wound loosely around her neck, and her hat was on the rocks beside her. She was so still that she had become part of the scene, and he stood there a moment. This morning he had seen the child in her again, enchanted by the jays, but when the bird had landed on her palm and she had turned to him, her face had been that of a woman grown.

She looked up again now and saw him standing there, and her expression lightened with a smile. 'Hello,' she said. 'I hoped you'd come.'

'Mr Larsen sent me to see that you were alright,' he said, more brusquely than he intended. 'He says he'll join you in a moment.'

'Not too soon, I hope. Come and talk to me until he does,' she said, straightening her skirt. 'And I won't torment you with questions.'

'You won't,' he agreed, but the smile drew him down to the river's edge where he stood a little bit away from her, looking out across the water, his hands thrust into his jacket pockets, watching the light playing on the surface. And found he had nothing to say.

'You ask me questions instead,' she said.

He turned and went to sit on a fallen log near the rocks. 'Alright then,' he said, adopting an easy tone. 'Fill me in. What's been happening?' Five years – a lifetime. 'Mr Sinclair's still with you, I gather. I've never forgotten his kindness.' He scooped up some pebbles, distracted for a moment by a large white quartz stone interleaved with dark threads, and wondered what Ballantyre had learned from Achak. He tossed it into the current and forced his mind back to Sinclair. With his belt and his Bible, the old stable master tried to drag him to a state of righteousness, and had protected him from the keepers' abuse with the ferocity of a lioness.

'Yes, he's still there, older and more gaunt, perhaps, but still with his special way with the horses. He . . . he was distraught when you left.'

James tossed another pebble, looked down through the clear water. Stealing Melrose and the man's coat had been a poor reward for all his efforts. Perhaps one day he would be able to explain— He forced a smile, and took the conversation away from dangerous territory. 'And is Maria still with you? And Kirsty?'

'Maria left to marry the blacksmith's son, and has a son of her own. Kirsty is still with us.'

'And Fiona?'

'Why Fiona?'

'Why not?' He answered the gleam in her eye with a bland smile.

'Why not Maud?'

'Alright then, Maud.'

'She got herself in trouble. Papa wouldn't let her stay in the house, but she has a cottage in the village, and takes in sewing.'

'Hardly a surprise. What about Fiona?'

'She ran off with one of the keepers.'

Dear God! Fair Fiona. 'What a waste.'

'She had better taste once.' Her eyes were dancing now, and a smile twitched at her lips.

'They should have bricked up that schoolroom window.'

A pair of ducks flew low along the river and landed, feet splayed, just in front of them, waggling their tail feathers as they settled to drift downstream. Just as their counterparts would be doing on a different river three thousand miles away. He glanced back at her and the shadow behind her eyes told him that their thoughts had brought them to the same place.

'So you never told him?' he spoke softly, driven to ask against his better judgement. 'About that night, in the study—'

'No.'

He weighed another pebble in his hand, then tossed it out into the current. He had forgotten the ducks, and they rose, protesting, scattering droplets which caught the sun. 'It was a hard thing for a child to see.' They circled a couple of times and then came back to the river, settling again on the far side. Then: '*Why* didn't you tell him?'

'I was frightened—' Her voice was small and thin, and he did not press her.

They were silent for a while.

'What did you do, James, after you left?' she asked, and her voice was a woman's voice again.

He started aiming smaller stones at a branch that was floating downstream with the current. She might ask, but he would never tell her— How could he? That day, and that night, still haunted him, the fear as he saddled Melrose in the dark stable, willing her to silence as he lifted Sinclair's coat from a hook behind the door, before leading her across the cobbles in dread of discovery. Then riding through the night, clinging to her neck, tearing up the miles until dawn came. A half-ruined barn had hidden him during the daylight hours, offering little shelter against torrential rain, with only water to kill the hunger. Poor Melrose had had to make do with a handful of old hay until dusk when he had let her graze, his ears alert for sounds of pursuit.

'I made for Glasgow,' he said briefly. And in Glasgow he had paid for his soaking with a fever, just managing to hide his money before delirium overtook him, and he had lain for days sweating, certain that if he lived he would find it gone.

'And then?'

He looked across at her, sitting there in her warm woollen skirt with her neat black boots, her eyes shining with kindly concern, and felt a spurt of the old resentment. Pretty Miss Ballantyre who had never known a moment's deprivation; even the wilderness had been tamed for her. 'I got papers made and bought a passage for Montreal.'

'And then came here.'

He grunted and stared down between his knees at the pebbled ground. By that time he had lost half of Ballantyre's money in a fight, his boots and Sinclair's coat had been taken from him by a pretty whore whose protector had thrown him downstairs with a kick and a curse. He raised his head and watched the ducks gliding serenely with the flow on the far side of the river, remembering that night, when he had been so desperate for comfort, even the sort that had to be paid for. Should he tell her that, perhaps?

'When they found Mr McAllister dead, they said that you'd killed him too – but Papa says you didn't.'

He raised his head at that and frowned at her. 'But you thought I had?' Then he cursed himself for letting her draw him in.

'You had a knife—'

'What else did your father tell you?'

'He wouldn't speak of it to me,' she said, her voice unsteady. 'Not then, nor ever since.'

'But *why* didn't you tell him you'd seen me?'

'I couldn't. Not after what you said.' He scowled, unable to remember what he had said; that moment in the study was lost in a red mist of fear and fury. 'And afterwards he was so changed, James, so distant. I couldn't—' He watched a blotchy stain creep up her neck, flushing her face as she struggled to find the words. 'And everyone said it was because of you – after all he'd done for you.' He swore silently, feeling the anger in his gut again. 'I believed what you told me that night, James, about Jacko, but I'd seen a knife in your hand, and so when Mr McAllister was found—' She faltered. 'And then you said Papa had Jacko's blood on his conscience. I *had* to stay quiet, because I was so frightened, and I became convinced that if I said anything, one of you would hang—' The sun again lit the gold in her hair, but her face was pinched with fear and he saw that she was trembling, her arms crossed in front of her.

He would have liked to have gone to her then—

But he didn't.

So all these years she had been living in a little hell of her own, had she? – with those two maggots lodged in her brain. But it had been a hell of her father's making, not his.

And then there was no time for more. They heard voices and a moment later Larsen appeared, carrying his rod and fishing basket, with Lady Melton following behind.

Chapter 23

A thin veil of grey cloud spread across the sky as the afternoon wore on, it thickened slowly at first and then more rapidly as the sun disappeared behind the cliffs, and the breeze began to lift the pages of Evelyn's book. She was not reading anyway but staring at the pages, going over her conversation with James— A blue dragon-fly looped above the surface of the water and she remembered how once they had stood together watching the damsel flies submerge, then rise again from the surface, their wings heavy with moisture.

'That breeze is getting sharp,' Clementina said, putting away her sketch pad. 'I think I'll go back.' She pulled her jacket close, twisting the toggles to fasten it. 'What about you, Mr Larsen?'

'Just one more cast, perhaps. My reel is performing well now—' He looked up to where the clouds were moving quickly across a darkening sky. 'But the fish are anticipating the weather, I think, and have gone deep.'

'Will it rain?'

'Almost certainly, I'm afraid.'

Evelyn thought of the flimsy tents and wondered what protection the canvas would offer.

By the time she and Clementina reached the camp they found that the guides too were preparing for rain: equipment was being stowed, wood was being wrapped in tarpaulins and placed under the canoes, while guy ropes and tent pegs were being checked and adjusted. 'Don't touch the tent sides once it starts, ' James broke off to explain to them. 'And take a tarpaulin to pull over the blankets. Tala, another rope front and back, I think, just to be sure.' And even as he spoke there was a distant low rumble of thunder and the trees at the edge of the camp bucked in the wind. Evelyn saw him glance up at the skies. 'We should eat at once,' he said. 'Is Mr Larsen still fishing?' Tala went to get him while food was hastily prepared, and by the time they finished eating the temperature was dropping fast and the wind blowing in fitful bursts.

'Kershaw won't head back in this,' Mr Skinner said, taking Evelyn's plate from her. 'We shouldn't look for your pa tonight, missee.'

'But he'll be alright?' she asked. The forest had darkened alarmingly and seemed to be closing in around them, the branches above them swaying wildly. She wished very much that he was here.

'The worst he'll suffer is a wetting, my dear,' Mr Larsen reassured her, but he too was looking up at the treetops.

'But what about George, and Rupert?' asked Clementina.

'Same with them. Eh, Mr Skinner?'

'Storms come fast and furious round here, ma'am, but they soon pass. The boys'll know what to do.'

Another rumble sounded and was echoed back from the cliffs across the river. It was closer now, low and deep with a latent strength, and a moment later a dash of rain set the embers hissing. James rose and gathered the remaining tin plates and forks.

'You should go into your tents. Now. Before it gets going. And expect to stay there until morning. Have you ladies all you need?'

This last question was shouted above the wind as it unleashed its force on the little clearing. Above them branches began knocking together and the leaves fell in a deluge along with the rain. They rushed for the tents as James began turning the iron cooking pots upside down, and the thunder sounded again, closer now, and threatening. He followed them, his collar turned up, shoulders hunched and his hair already plastered to his head as he fastened the tent flaps behind them.

Evelyn turned at the entrance and bent down to him. Their faces were on a level as he crouched to secure the last tie.

'How long will it last?' Her heart was jumping foolishly inside her.

'You'll be alright, you know,' he said, and he smiled. 'It's only rain.'

'Where will you sleep?' she whispered.

'In one of the Indian shelters.' And he reached out suddenly to brush her cheek with the back of his hand. 'Dry as a bone.'

———

It was two hours later that the tree fell. It was not one of those at the edge of the clearing but a tall jack pine which had stood for half a century a little way into the forest, dying slowly, its dangerous condition hidden by the spread of two larches. The withered roots had withstood many storms but had finally succumbed to this onslaught, and it came crashing through the darkness, cleaving the lower canopy to fall its full length across the campsite, the upper nest of dead branches crushing the ladies' tent which lay in its path.

The camp awoke at the crash of its falling. James was first out, and the others followed, blundering in the dark until a flickering sheet of lightning revealed the trunk sprawled across the flattened canvas.

'*Dear God . . .*' breathed Larsen, beside him.

Somehow a hurricane lantern was lit.

Skinner appeared. 'Get them out. *Move . . . !*'

By the next jag of lightning, James saw that one of the larger branches had broken the tree's fall and it now held the trunk a foot or so off the ground. It was a miracle but beneath it the tent lay flattened, a torn tangle of broken twigs and canvas. He bent over the appalling heap and yelled above the wind. 'Can you hear me?'

A small voice came back. 'I can't move . . .'

It was Evelyn. 'Don't try. Stay still.'

Mr Larsen had grabbed at one of the branches and was pulling ineffectually at it, but James moved him firmly aside. 'Leave it, sir. Tala, get an axe.' He called for a lantern and began chopping desperately at the mass of branches while the others used smaller axes and large knives, staying clear of the long sweep of his blows. Restraint was needed, and caution, as somewhere beneath the chaos lay Evelyn—

Larsen stood by, holding the lantern high, oblivious to the slanting rain, and they worked in silence as the storm passed over them. At length James stopped to draw breath. 'Are you still alright, Evie?' he called out.

'I think so,' came the small, tight reply, 'but I'm pinned down.'

'Any bones broken?'

'No.'

'Can you reach Lady Melton?'

'No. Something's holding the tent down between us. But she's not moving or speaking . . .' Her voice was shot through with fear.

'Just hold on.'

Larsen moved closer. 'We'll have you free in no time, my dear,' and then added in a quiet aside, 'You'll never raise that tree—'

'We won't even try.' James wiped the rain from across his brow.

'We'll go in through the sides when we've cleared a way in. But I think it fell between the cots—'

Or right on top of Lady Melton.

It took them almost an hour to free Evelyn. They pulled her out, soaked and trembling, and James handed her to Larsen, who wrapped her in a blanket and held her close. It then took almost as long for him to make a space large enough to crawl under the canvas to reach Lady Melton. By then the rain was easing, and Tala stood holding the lantern above the wreckage to give James light to work by. The weight of the trunk was still being held off them by the broken branch which, it seemed, had also caught the side of Lady Melton's cot and tipped it, pinioning her against the trunk – and done God knows what damage.

'Get me a knife, Tala.' James spoke from under the canvas. 'I'll slit the base of the cot and get her out that way. Quick, man!'

'But is she alright?' Evelyn clung to Larsen, her hair plastered to her head, shivering beneath the blanket, and refusing to take shelter.

'I have her arm now . . .' James replied, groping in the dark amongst the tangle and finding her. '. . . And there's a good strong pulse. Come on, Tala, give me a hand, and we'll have her free.'

After what seemed like a lifetime they managed to cut away the tent and cot, and between them he and Tala carried her, drenched and unconscious, to where a bed had been made for her in Larsen's tent. Her arm hung limp, and he saw blood congealed on her forehead and matted through her hair.

God, she was pale. And so still.

Evelyn peered through the door of the tent. 'Is she alright?'

'She's alive. And that's what matters,' James replied. She came farther in, there was barely room to move, and he saw that she was shuddering now with delayed shock, and there was an ugly bruise on her temple. Silently, he passed her a flask of Louis's spirit. 'Drink some.'

Her hand shook as she obeyed.

'I'll sit up with Lady Melton,' Larsen said to him.

'Miss Ballantyre can have my tent,' said Skinner. 'It's pretty dry in there. Get yourself wrapped up in those blankets and furs, missee, and you'll be just fine. Storm's passing. I'll bed down with the boys.'

Larsen looked down at Evelyn. 'That's a good idea. Off you go, my dear.'

'No. I must stay with Clemmy . . .'

He shook his head and pushed her towards the door. 'I'll wake you if I need you.'

James propelled her out into the darkness, tucking the trailing blanket around her shoulders and steering her across to Skinner's tent. 'Once you're inside, take off your wet things, and get between the blankets. Go on! Don't just stand there.' He opened the flap and steered her in.

'Come back, though? And tell me how Clemmy is— You will? You must? Promise?'

'I promise. Now get warm.'

He tied the tent flaps behind her and went back to Larsen's tent. Tala was gone but Skinner remained. 'What do you think?' Larsen was asking him, and James looked down at the still figure and thought of the alabaster effigies of Ballantyre's forebears in the church back home.

'Pulse's still strong, but we'll see in the morning. It jest looks bad with all that blood on her face.' Skinner shook his head. 'But if it'd fallen jest a few inches either way—'

'I know.' Larsen's face was pale in the lantern light. 'Will they be alright upriver?' he asked.

Skinner nodded. 'Louis and Marcel know what they're doing.'

Tala appeared at the door of the tent and Skinner went out to him.

'And Kershaw seemed to be a man of good sense,' Larsen muttered, accepting an offer of James's flask. Then: 'You did well tonight, James.'

'We did what we had to.' He banged the stopper back in the flask, and picked up the other lantern. 'Just keep her warm, and call me if you need help. I'll be in one of the shelters.'

James left Larsen's tent and held the lantern high, and for the first time he was able to take in the utter devastation that the storm had wrought upon the camp. It was as if a tornado had passed through— The tree lay like a felled giant across the campsite, littering it with torn branches, and rain dripped from the surrounding trees onto the sorry mess. If it had fallen the night before it would have flattened the gentlemen's tent too, he thought, and so denied him any hope of settling scores with Dalston. But as it was, having destroyed the ladies' tent, it had fallen across the fireplace, crushing the table and chairs, but left Skinner's tent and the shelters miraculously untouched. And it had also fallen well short of the canoes, which were pulled up on the rocks; their loss would have been a blow indeed— They would have to wait until morning to see the full extent of the damage, and for now he should try to get some sleep.

Holding the lantern before him he crossed the campsite, stepping over the debris and headed for the shelters. Then he remembered his promise and veered off towards Skinner's tent.

'You alright now?' he asked in a low voice, through the canvas.

There was no reply other than a scuffling sound like that of a desperate animal, then a pale arm stretched out of the tent to him. 'James? Come in to me. Please . . .' He looked back across the dark campsite towards Larsen's tent where he could see the diffused light of the other lantern glowing through the canvas, but all was quiet. Evelyn's voice held a rising note of hysteria. *'Please.'*

He crouched down and quickly untied the flaps. 'Take the lantern then and move back.' Skinner's tent was not designed for two. 'It's alright. Storm's passed.' He crawled in beside her, put out a hand and found her shoulder, and felt her whole frame shaking beneath his touch, icy cold, still in shock— He gathered up an almost dry blanket and draped it around her shoulders, pulling her to him, chafing her shoulders. 'It's over.'

'Will she die?'

'Of course not.'

'Are you sure?' He could hear her teeth chattering. 'It was terrible . . .'

'Yes. But it's over—'

'. . . and I was pinned down. Clemmy wasn't moving . . .' He held her head against his chest. 'We could *both* have been killed . . .'

'But you weren't.' His hand found the thick plait of her hair which felt like cold rope so he slid his palm beneath it, lifting it away from her neck, and pulled the blanket up between them to shield her from his own wet shirt. Then he held her again— She felt no bigger than a child, but so cold, and still shaking uncontrollably, so he laid her down and held her tight, pressing his full length against hers.

Gradually he felt her grow calmer. 'Get the blanket right round you. Good. Now roll yourself in those furs. You'll soon warm up and then you can sleep.' He released her and began pulling away, but she grabbed a fistful of his shirt and held on.

'No. Don't go, James. Stay with me . . .' The shaking started again, just as violently. He saw her eyes, wide and glittering in the lantern light. 'Sleep here, with me. I don't care . . . *Please* don't leave me.' She refused to release his shirt, and the blankets fell away again and he saw she was wearing only a thin shift. 'And hold me again.'

There was an animal fear in her eyes.

He hesitated. Good God—! Then he reached out and extinguished the lantern, and pulled the wet shirt over his head. 'Come on then.' And he took her in his arms again, and pulled the stinking furs back over the two of them. Her arms went round him like icy bands, and they lay there, fused together, and silent.

Slowly, as warmth spread between them, he felt her shivering subside and he began chafing her back, feeling the delicate wing bones of her shoulders, the ladder of her spine – and then down to the hollow of her back. He found himself loosening the plait of her hair and spreading it to dry, then later sweeping it aside to feel the smoothness of her neck in his palm. Then his hand slid down her back to the hollow again, and only by sheer force of will did he venture no farther. And he felt her relax and grow still.

And then his holding of her was no longer what it had been, and the stillness became expectant.

He had never intended to kiss her, but he could not stop himself. And once begun— With an effort he forced himself to pull away and he lay on his back, still holding her, her head now tucked beneath his chin, her hair spread across his chest. *God, what a fool.* Half-child she was, but she had responded to him as a woman would, although she had no understanding of where it might lead. But he did— And there was only a thin layer of cotton between the two of them. He rolled onto his side, pulling the blanket over them, turning her so that her back was against his chest, her body fitted into the curve of his. His arms encircled her again. How small she was! And lovely— He would leave just as soon as he could, and he bid her to go to sleep. She gave a soft, muffled response, and he threaded his fingers with hers and crossed both their arms over her breast. This way he could still hold her, and by locking his fingers with hers, his hands could no longer explore. 'Sleep,' he ordered, and buried his face deep in the smell of her.

———

She was still asleep three hours later when dawn awoke him. He lay there a moment then carefully extracted himself from the skins and blankets and looked down at her. She slept like a child, her hair all a-tumble and her lips parted – and he felt an ache deep inside as he recalled the night. Carefully he pulled on his shirt, and its icy wetness brought him rapidly to his senses. *Fool!* He tucked the blankets round her so that the cold would not waken her when he moved, and slid to the entrance of Skinner's tent.

He was untying the flaps when she awoke.

'No. Don't go. Or wait and I'll come too—' She sat up, clutching the blanket with one hand, and reached the other out to him. Then she seemed to remember. 'But I can't. All my clothes are in our tent. And they'll be ruined—' She pulled the blankets up under her armpits and ran a hand through her hair. And smiled at him—

He frowned in response. 'I'll go and light the fire, then see what I can find.'

'James—'

He continued to frown, distancing himself. 'What?'

'If you hadn't stayed with me last night I would have died.' He snorted, and turned back to the ties. 'I know I would. I was terrified once I was alone.' She reached out to him again and then recoiled from his wet shirt. 'It's soaking! You can't possibly wear it. Take it off.'

'Leave it be—'

But she laughed at him, and tugged at it.

And then his shirt was off again and he came back to her, back to where he had been before, except they were both awake now. And warm—

But as reasoning began to desert them both she twisted in his arms, and looked up at him: '*Clementina*. I'd forgotten! How could I have done—'

This time she let him pull away, and he wrapped the blankets tight around her, pinning her arms to her sides. 'I'll go and see.'

'Then come back—'

Chapter 24

The shirt was even more unpleasant to put on a second time, and the cool air seemed to freeze it to him as he stood up outside the tent, and he shivered. A pale light was filtering through the trees and its shafts revealed the destroyed campsite. Dear God, what a mess! He stretched to get the kink out of his back, pulled his shirt down, stretched again, and inhaled deeply.

Then stopped. Tobacco.

He turned, and saw Larsen had emerged from his tent and was looking steadily back at him, his pipe in his hand. They stared at each other, then James went over to him. What else could he do?

'How is Lady Melton?' he asked.

Larsen drew slowly on his pipe. 'She stirred, spoke a few words, and now she's sleeping.' He regarded James with a thoughtful expression but made no further remark.

'That's good.'

Larsen nodded slightly, still considering him. It was a grave expression but not hostile. 'And Evelyn?' he asked.

'She's fine.'

Larsen nodded again. 'That's good too—' And they stood in silence, looking out over the camp.

'Did you get some sleep, sir?'

'A little. Enough. Any chance of getting a fire lit? We could all do with a hot drink.'

Half an hour later the party, with the exception of Lady Melton, were sat around a listless fire, huddled close to absorb what little heat it offered, eyes smarting in the smoke. Water had been heated and Larsen felt warmth from the thin coffee coursing through him. He was cold and he was tired and he was cramped – and he was also very alarmed.

He looked across at Evelyn with deep misgivings. James had found her a dry pair of Louis's trousers, a spare shirt of his own, and a belt which somehow managed to hold the whole ensemble together. Her own boots had been salvaged from the crushed tent, and she had a blanket draped around her shoulders. Overnight her hair had dried into wild curls which she had tied back with a piece of twine, and there was dirt down the side of her face where she had swiped at a horsefly, a dark bruise on her forehead – and an expression in her eyes which would have chilled her father's heart.

For the young man had become her lodestone and her eyes followed his every move. And James, hide it as he might try, was very well aware of the fact.

Oh God!

Skinner had looked in on Lady Melton and had come out much relieved, having exchanged a few words with her. He had summoned Tala who, he informed Larsen, had medicinal skills, and the Indian had cleaned the wound on her head and then disappeared into the forest, returning with a plant whose leaves he pressed to the broken skin on her brow. It was, after all, only a superficial wound and, despite concerns last night, nothing was broken. But the poor lady was still as white as a sheet and tearful, complaining of a pain in her chest, perhaps a cracked rib or two, and needed no persuading to stay where she was.

He and Evelyn had then gone in to see her, and Evelyn's appearance had raised a wan smile. 'You look like a brigand too now—'

'I've wanted breeches since I was a child. These are Louis's, and rather large. The shirt,' she said, with heightened colour, 'belongs to James.'

Larsen had not let her stay long, seeing that Clementina was dropping back to sleep, and had led her back to the fire. It was smoking rather less now and beginning to put out more heat. Dry logs had been recovered from beneath one of the canoes and James was preparing breakfast. The oats had got wet too, he explained, but lumpy porridge never harmed anyone.

Larsen glanced around and saw that no one was in earshot.

'So—' he said, knowing he had to speak now while he could but this was not a task he relished. 'You two . . .' And there he stalled.

Evelyn flushed crimson and James stopped stirring the porridge and looked across at her. 'She was cold, sir, and frightened. Nothing more.'

Larsen looked back at him, liking his directness. It made things easier. 'And you are, after all, well acquainted.'

Evelyn froze, but the young man held his look. 'How do you know?'

'Dead bird's feathers.' He watched James's face. 'Only a member of Ballantyre's household would know that raven or jackdaw feathers might substitute for those of a long-dead macaw.' And he saw the young man's expression change as he remembered.

Evelyn looked from one to the other. 'You mustn't say anything, Mr Larsen . . .'

'I know, and I won't.'

'James is innocent—' Evelyn had sat forward, urgently, letting the blanket slip from her shoulders.

Larsen put up a hand. 'I know that too.'

'What do you know?' James asked.

'Enough.' Larsen turned to Evelyn. 'Your father seemed to anticipate some sort of trouble so he left me a letter. I read it yesterday when you were down by the river.'

'A letter?' Evelyn grabbed at Larsen's sleeve. 'Why would he give you a letter when he's coming back today? In fact, he'll be back at any moment—'

'I know he will, and there's no cause for concern—'

'But why a letter? Let me see it!'

James handed Larsen a plate of food and called the others over, thus sparing him the need to respond. But Evelyn continued to frown. 'When will my father be back?' she demanded of Skinner as he came over and took his plate.

'Why, jest as soon as he can, missee,' he replied. 'The river'll be fast now, after the rain, so don't you worry.'

'And the others?' enquired Larsen.

'Same applies.'

They huddled around the smoking fire and discussed what now needed to be done. Skinner agreed with Larsen that as soon as the others returned, they would pack up and start back, but he was phlegmatic about having been washed out. It had happened before. 'Couldn't have guessed about that tree, though, but jest so long as everyone's alright . . . And that monster'll still be up at Astra's Pool waiting for you next time, mister,' he added, nodding towards Larsen.

'If it lives another summer.'

And if he did. This trip was taking years off him—

Skinner got to his feet and went over to the crumpled mass of tent and broken branches, picked up the axe again, and handed it to James. 'Jest salvage what you can,' he said. 'It won't be much, and I think the washstand is done for.'

'Good, it made us ridiculous,' Evelyn said as Skinner walked out of earshot.

James grinned briefly. 'Now that the fire's got going we can spread out your clothes and get them drying.'

Evelyn gave him a look which made Larsen belch again with anxiety, and they watched him start chopping away at the smaller branches where the entrance of the tent had been, and lift up the sodden canvas.

They would be lucky to retrieve anything from there, and the sooner they got back to civilisation, the better.

'I'll check on Clementina again—' he began but Evelyn put a hand on his sleeve.

'I want to see this letter.' James had pulled out a pile of damp furs and clothing and was now slinging a rope between two trees. Larsen wished that he would come back over. The young man was displaying an unexpected competence in dealing with matters. 'It's addressed just to me, my dear, and I'm not sure—'

'Yes, he wrote to *you*, not to me, as he should have done.' Her words were clipped and angry. 'He's told *you* things that he has never told me, which he should have done, years ago.'

Her tone must have carried because Larsen saw James pause in spreading one of the blankets, and look across at them, and then he ducked under the rope and came quickly to them. 'What is it?' he said.

'I want to see this letter.' She let go of Larsen's sleeve and stood up to face James.

James's eyes met Larsen's over her head.

'Let us both see it.'

Larsen looked from one to the other, and then aside to where the two whisky jacks had found the open oatmeal tin. They had tipped it over and were busy raiding the contents, their eyes darting left and right. He felt old suddenly and quite uncertain what he ought to do. Nothing in his life had equipped him for dealing with matters such as these. He drew the letter from his pocket and handed it silently to James, abdicating responsibility. 'But then we must talk. Decide what to do—'

James pulled Evelyn down onto the fallen trunk, sat beside her, and handed her the letter. It began with a bald account of who James was, his innocence regarding the charges against him, and then moved swiftly on to an account of Jacko's killing. He felt Evelyn stiffen as she read a name, and her hand flew to her mouth.

I witnessed this myself, as did my head keeper Robbie McAllister, who was found dead next morning. I had dismissed him that evening and it is my belief that he was attempting to blackmail Dalston, and that Dalston killed him too. I have, however, no proof.

Do you believe in destiny, my friend? I think perhaps I do. Nemesis, perhaps, has had a hand in this for which I am glad, the matter has festered too long, poisoning lives, and I have a chance to resolve it here. Should anything happen to me I wrote out a full account while I was at Skinner's, and this will explain the whole, and it awaits you in Boston. My advocate in Edinburgh already has a sealed document which I lodged with him five years ago. If I am not granted the opportunity to see the matter through, then I ask that you will do so, old friend. And I hope, when you understand what I have done, that you will forgive me . . . Show this to Melton if you must, he is a sound man, but don't let James Douglas take matters into his own hands or he will undo all I have striven to put in place. Look after Evelyn, and believe me, you can trust James with your life, and hers. CB.

Evelyn lowered the letter and stared at James. *'Rupert!'* But he was looking fixedly ahead. Evelyn shook his arm. 'It was *Rupert—*' she repeated. Her father had known this all along and done nothing! Whatever must James be thinking? But he was still staring into the fire, not shocked or surprised even, and Mr Larsen was watching him with an odd expression. Then understanding dawned, and she drew back. 'You *knew* it was Rupert—' Her breath came in short gasps and her head spun. 'You knew all along!'

'Yes. I knew.'

She blinked rapidly. 'But—? How long have you known?'

'Since the killing, and then I recognised him at the station—'

'You mean you *always* knew?'

'I didn't know his name.'

She stared at him in astonishment and swung round wildly to face Mr Larsen. 'And *you* knew! You brought him here—'

'No, my dear, I *didn't* know. Now listen to me—' He raised a calming hand.

But she turned back to James, gulping in anger. 'You knew and Papa knew, all these years, while I—' She clenched her hands into fists and pressed them to her temples.

'Wait—'

But she was no longer prepared to listen. All these years she had lived under the shadow of an event she had been unable to comprehend, and now, to be treated in such a manner— 'It was unforgivable! You knew. And yet Rupert Dalston sat with us, and ate with us, and you sat there *knowing* it was him, while for five years I'd believed it was Papa and you—!'

James took hold of her wrists and held them. '*Wait*—'

Her cries had brought Skinner running. 'What's going on? Fer Christsake, let her go—!'

'It's alright, Mr Skinner,' Mr Larsen spoke with sudden authority. 'Evelyn, calm yourself. Your father must have had his reasons.'

She barely heard him, for another thought had struck her. What did he mean, if he can't see the matter through? 'Is Papa in danger? To have written you such a letter—'

Skinner was looking bewildered. 'He ain't in danger, missee, jest from a passing storm—'

'Dalston doesn't know who I am so nothing's changed—' James held on to her wrists.

She pulled back, resisting, and he released her. 'He was sitting right next to you that night when you talked about fishing flies—! And if Mr Larsen began to guess, then Rupert might have done so too.' She saw James exchange glances with Mr Larsen.

'Will someone tell me what the hell's going on?' Skinner was becoming angry now, and poked a bony finger at James. 'And jest who is it yer supposd to be?'

'Later, Skinner. Mr Larsen will explain. We need to be ready for trouble—'

Evelyn could take no more. She rose and strode across the camp towards the trailhead which led to the landing above the falls. James called out to Tala who stepped into her path, his arms outstretched to stop her, and she turned back: 'I'm going to meet Papa. I can't just wait here and let things happen.'

'And jest what're you going to do, missee?' Skinner was looking from one to another, completely at a loss. 'With the river this high Kershaw might shoot 'em through the first set of rapids and land jest upstream from here. Louis might try the same— So whoever it is you want to meet, you could miss 'em.'

Mr Larsen nodded. 'He's right. You must stay here, my dear.'

'And Clementina might need you,' James added. 'I'll go on to the far landing. Machk and Tala can wait at the near one.'

'And what they got to do when they get there?' Skinner asked, throwing wide his arms.

But while James started to explain, Evelyn slipped past Tala and started down the trail.

———

She could hear James calling her but she did not stop. She had known that he would come after her, or Mr Larsen would send

Tala, and she had no idea how far it was to the landing or whether the trail led directly to it, but anger, and hurt, drove her forward and Louis's trousers gave her a long, unfettered stride— The terror of last night had been followed by an extraordinary sweetness but she was now overcome by fury at the utterly unacceptable revelation of what her father had kept from her. All those years—! And for the last week he had allowed Rupert Dalston to come amongst them as a friend.

And the fact that he had always known that James was innocent defied comprehension. She heard James call again and quickened her step to a run, determined to reach the landing. For James was culpable too – whatever else, he and her father had agreed to some pact this last week, and kept her in ignorance. A moment later he was behind her on the trail, and caught at her arm.

'Not so fast,' James said. 'Be sensible.'

She shook him off. 'How far to the landing?'

'Not far. Half a mile, maybe less.' And he manoeuvred round her, barring the trail ahead. 'Go back to Mr Larsen.'

'No. Let me past.'

'Dalston might get to the landing first. He might be there now—'

'So might Papa.'

'And what will you do?'

She bit her lip, and looked aside. She only knew that she must find him. 'How could you *not* tell me it was Dalston?' she said. 'You just stood by and *watched* him.'

'You think it was easy?'

'But you did, even so—'

'Go back now, Evie.'

'And why has Papa said *nothing*? All these years—'

'We'll ask him. Now go back to Mr Larsen.'

'No.'

Deadlock.

They stood on the trail, facing each other. Then he shrugged, released her arm and stood aside. 'So be it. But be prepared for anything—'

The path was wide enough for them to have walked beside each other, but he let her walk ahead, and they continued in silence. Through breaks in the trees, she could see steam lifting from the damp forest, and as the sun rose it warmed the foliage, releasing a warm smell of balsam and spruce. Above them the clouds thinned to reveal a stark blueness, and she felt the anger drain from her and slackened her pace, allowing James to come alongside.

'I just don't understand—' she said.

'Nor do I.'

They walked on. It felt as if the very foundations of her life had cracked apart and all her certainties hand drained away. How could her father have abandoned every principle of justice and integrity, everything that he held dear? It had almost been easier to believe him a killer.

She paused and turned to James. 'What has Papa said to you?'

'Only that it was always his word against theirs, and that he has no proof.' She had a fleeting vision of the moment when she had flung open the study door and seen the man sitting in the armchair, smoking calmly, while her father stood at the fireplace, his face like thunder. It must have been Rupert's father.

'But why has he never spoken out?'

James looked across at her, but said nothing. The reason, he believed, was quite simple, but it pained him to tell her. At the bottom of it all, somehow, Ballantyre had been defending his own, just as Jacko had always said he would. *They'll do anything, him and his cronies, to preserve their own interests, and safeguard their right to rule* . . . But under Ballantyre's roof James had forgotten that essential truth. *He'll send me down time after time, when he catches me, because if he freed me he'd have to free the next man, and where would that lead? For all his charities and largesse he'll always uphold the system which secures his position – the rest is just a sop for his conscience—*

His conscience.

And so Ballantyre, despite everything, had kept silent about Dalston. Behind the façade of philanthropy, self-interest flowed through his veins as strongly as any man of his rank and wealth. But his daughter still believed in him, or wanted to, and the anxiety which now puckered her bruised brow told him just how very *much* she wanted it. But he could not help her.

'He was always so pleased with you, so proud.' Evelyn's words broke into his thoughts, and he scowled; she could have been talking of one of the race horses. 'And yet he let everyone believe that it was you . . .' He made no comment. 'How much you must hate him for it.'

Hate was too simple a word, but it stood beside bitterness and anger. And betrayal— And it had been Larsen's forgiveness Ballantyre had asked for in the letter, not his.

Then he heard something and he went on the alert. Voices— He pulled her off the trail but then realised that the sound came not from ahead of them but from downslope towards the river. The sound came again – raised voices, shouts above the river's roar, and then a familiar whoop. Louis and Marcel *were* taking them through, and with the river in full spate! He sprinted forward, knowing where he might get a glimpse of the river. 'Wait here!' he said and ran on, leaving the trail to cross a treeless shoulder of bedrock and scramble down the decline. He had no fear of being seen, every eye would be fixed on the boiling river, every nerve drawn tight, and the noise of the rapids would mask any sound. He slithered to a halt on the wet earth and lay on his stomach, watching the river glinting through the trees, and was just in time to see the canoe charging forward as Louis guided it through the rocks, incapable of resisting a challenge. James saw him, standing there at the stern, shouting instructions to Marcel in the bow and the Ojibway men on either side with their paddles raised at the ready. He stayed to watch, seeing the light craft bucking and dipping, throwing spray up from its sides, and heard Louis's irrepressible whoops as they cleared the rocks.

And in the middle of the canoe sat Melton, beside Dalston.

He went back to Evelyn. 'Tala and Machk will be waiting for them,' he said. 'Your father won't be far behind, so if Kershaw does intend to try that same trick, we need to be up there at the landing to signal to him. So, quick now, press on.'

Chapter 25

Larsen told Skinner as much as he felt he needed to hear, and from the look on the old man's face this left him just about as bewildered as before. All that seemed to concern him was that although James Douglas was a wanted man, he had not been harbouring a criminal, and would not come under the scrutiny of the law. Having established that fact, and that it was Dalston, and only Dalston, that he had to watch out for, he was content to follow Larsen's suggestion that they await developments and do nothing until they had to.

'But be at the ready, Mr Skinner.' He explained matters to Tala too, enough to enable him to warn Louis, and to put him on the alert. He then went and looked in on Clementina, brought her some tea and helped her to drink it, answering tearful enquiries about when she might expect her husband's return. 'And then can we go home?' she pleaded, and he reassured her then left her to sleep. At least she was speaking coherently, he thought as he stepped out of the tent, and her face was no longer quite so ashen.

He went back to sit beside Skinner at the fire, just the two of them, two old men who had only come to fish. Skinner looked more shrunken than he had a week ago. 'Did you ever hook that monster up in Astra's Pool yourself?' he asked, steering the old man onto familiar territory, and he had the satisfaction of seeing his wrinkled face lighten.

'More'n once! And he's got a mouthful of hooks and trailing line, must have jaws of steel. But no one's hooked him this season, far as I know, so either he's got too wily or he's dead. But I like to think he's still down there. And I tell you another thing . . .' and he was away, and all Larsen had to do was sit there and nod, and be impressed – and suppress the anxiety of waiting.

———

It did not seem very long before his wandering thoughts were brought sharply back to attention. He heard voices down towards the river, and then suddenly they were there. Melton appeared first, moving fast. Tala must have told him what had happened, but he was brought up short by the sight of the campsite and the torn shreds of tent trapped below the tree trunk, and his face drained of colour.

'Oh God,' he said.

Larsen rose quickly. 'She's fine, George. In my tent. Sleeping now but fine . . .' Melton gave him a brief nod and headed for the tent. Dalston was next, and he too stood and stared about him, whistling softly. The others followed, arms full of fishing tackle and sodden gear which they dumped down beside the fire, and began talking to Skinner. Larsen watched Louis cast an appraising glance across the camp and mutter something to Marcel, then he looked across at Larsen. They held the look between them for a moment, and Louis gave a quick nod. So Tala had passed on the message.

It was only then that Larsen noticed Dalston's face. An ugly bruise stood out red and angry on his cheek and his eye was swollen and rimmed with black. 'I thought we had it bad,' he said, coming across to join Larsen, throwing himself into a salvaged chair beside him. 'Tent came down in the middle of the night so we had to crawl under the canoe. God, what a night. Is there coffee in that can?'

'Let me get you some.' Larsen got to his feet and found a mug, watching as Dalston continued to survey the camp.

'And so the ladies had a narrow escape. Poor Clem,' he continued, lighting a cigarette. 'But Evelyn's alright, is she? I don't see her—'

'They were born under a lucky star, those two,' said Larsen, handing him the drink, and a bottle. 'The tree fell between the two cots and the trunk was held above them by some branches. A few inches either way and—' He described in some detail how they had managed to get the two women out while Dalston continued his survey.

'Evelyn's in with Clem, I s'pose,' Dalston interrupted, taking a swig, and it occurred to Larsen that it was not the first recourse to brandy he had taken. So early in the day—?

'Will you eat something? There's some porridge, I believe—'

'God, not that pap again! Anyone who offers me porridge— Ah, George!' Melton emerged from Larsen's tent. 'How is she? She's a sport, is old Clem. Have some coffee.'

Melton stood a moment looking down at the flattened tent, the canvas filthy now and torn, covered with twigs and pine needles, and he made no reply. Then he raised his head, his expression sober. 'My dear Larsen, what a night you must have had of it. Clementina says she can't remember a thing, and I can only imagine what you went through. But Evelyn's quite unhurt, I gather?'

'She was trapped for a while, and frightened, of course, but just got a slight blow on the forehead.'

'Where *is* Evelyn?' persisted Dalston. 'I thought she was in with you and Clem.'

Larsen could prevaricate no longer. 'She's gone down to the portage landing to wait for her father.'

'Not on her own, surely—' said Melton, then he broke off, and all heads turned.

'Good God!'

Ballantyre had appeared as if from nowhere and stood at the edge of the campsite, not at the end of the portage trail where he might have been expected, but at the spot where the other trail led up to Astra's Pool. He stood, rigid with horror, with two unknown Indians flanking him, and stared at the remains of the razed tent, with the tree trunk still lying across it, and then across to Larsen.

'Niels! Where's Evelyn?'

Larsen went quickly to him. 'She's fine, Charles. Everyone's fine. A narrow escape but everyone's fine . . .'

Ballantyre closed his eyes and put a hand on Larsen's shoulder, as if to steady himself. 'And Clementina?' He looked across to Melton.

'Took a bang on the head. Nothing more. They were lucky.'

Ballantyre surveyed the scene. 'So where are they?'

'Clementina's in my tent,' said Larsen. 'Evelyn went down to the portage landing to wait for you to get back. She was anxious—'

Ballantyre frowned slightly. 'She's alone there?' His eyes flickered around the campsite and came to rest on Larsen's.

'No.'

Ballantyre held his look and gave a slight nod. Then Skinner came over and pulled him towards the fire, and gave him a blow-by-blow account of the events of the night, sparing him no details, and Larsen watched the horror spread across his face—

'Sweet Lord!' Ballantyre said when Skinner paused to draw breath, and he gave Melton a hawkish look. 'But Clementina really is alright?' Melton responded with a quick nod. 'And what about you? You had a time of it upriver, I imagine.' He glanced at the ugly bruise that was discolouring Dalston's cheekbone, the swelling which half-closed one eye. 'How long have you been back?'

And then everyone was talking at once. Everyone except Dalston who, Larsen noticed, was still looking around the camp, but his expression was unreadable, distorted as it was by his bruising.

———

The portage landing was empty when James and Evelyn reached it, as was the river for as far as they could see. A virgin forest crept halfway up the cliffs while, below it, were the rocks and then the dark water itself, swirling as it flowed over submerged rocks and fallen trees. Clouds, spent vestiges of last night's storm, moved swiftly across the sky.

Evelyn stood a moment then sat down on a log beside the water and fixed her eye on the bend in the river.

James stood a little apart, watching her. There was nothing to do but wait. Then he too sat, his elbows resting on bent knees. And he thought of that very first day when he had seen her, on the terrace at Ballantyre House skipping beside her father, a little scrap of thing – and then the next day when McAllister had dragged him through the house, and she had half-raised her small hand in greeting from the gallery. He thought of the riding lessons too, and of the rides which had come to sweeten his days – until all had been shattered on that unforgettable night, when her eyes had fixed with fear on the blade of his knife.

She had been there, part of his life, throughout it all—

And now she was here, sitting just a yard away from him in Louis's trousers and his shirt, looking like a gypsy with her dirty face and wild hair, more boy than girl. What if she was right, though, and Dalston *had* begun to suspect? What would he do? But Dalston was marooned here just as they all were. And any show of violence would be a declaration of guilt. If he only knew what Ballantyre had been planning—

———

'What will you do, when all this is over?' Evelyn knew that he was watching her. 'Will you be able to come home?'

'I am home.' It was an answer she might have expected, but not the one she wanted to hear. Since last night, there had been no time to think, and the thought was unbearable. But he was his own man here, and he would never give that up.

So what other answer could he give?

She hugged her knees to her, crossing her ankles, head averted so that he could not see her expression. And what other answer could there be? If he returned home, the distance between them would be unbridgeable, defined by class and prejudice. He would be slotted firmly back into his place, held there, and the rest would follow. But while here – he could determine his own future. There was an awful irony, she thought, resting her cheek on her knees, that it was the injustice he had suffered at her father's hands which had allowed him to escape, and he was free now in a way she could never be, hobbled by wealth and class – and by her sex.

She looked back up the river, towards the bend, beyond which she could not see. For her, there was no choice. She would return home to the sanctioned *spheres of womanhood*, back to Ballantyre House to a life which Clementina had promised to take in hand. No man would ever put her name on a newly charted map; there would be no Lake Evelyn.

'I don't want to return home either,' she said, turning back to him. 'I'd rather stay here.'

He looked up but said nothing.

How could she ever hope to break away and become part of the affairs of the world? It would be better to be poor, with nothing to lose, and then she could be like the smart shop girls in New York, or the women striding down the boardwalks in Port Arthur, with their skirts a-swinging as they confronted the challenges of life. But her father would not be able to comprehend such desires.

'Mr Larsen says that there are women running businesses in Port Arthur—' she said after a moment.

'Aye. Bars and brothels.'

She frowned at him. 'He said one woman is running a lumber yard—'

'A lumber yard?' He smiled but the smile did not reach his eyes. 'Ask your father to set you up with one.'

She lifted her chin and deepened her frown. 'When I come into my mother's money I can do what I like.' Perhaps—

'Is that so?' He stretched out on his back on the smooth rock, his hands folded behind his head, and gazed up at the sky. 'And you plan to go into the lumber business. I'd no idea . . .'

His tone, detached and scornful, provoked her. 'Running a lumber yard must be better than what's awaiting me at home. If I stayed here, in Port Arthur, maybe I could find work to do.'

She wanted to gain his attention, to *make* him listen, but he only rolled his head to look at her. 'Work.'

'Why not?'

He returned his gaze to the sky. 'Do I need to answer that?'

He was deliberately distancing himself from her, and she recognised the tone. It was the one he used when she asked him things he did not want to answer, about Jacko and his old life. But that would no longer do, not after last night. 'Or I could stay here, with you,' she said. He made no response. 'Last night—'

'Last night you were cold and you were frightened,' he said. 'And, like I told Larsen, that was all—'

Then the only sound was of the current of the water flowing rapidly away from them.

'No,' she said. 'There was more.'

He rolled onto his side and propped his head on his crooked elbow, and looked back at her.

'I want to stay here,' she repeated.

'Evie—'

'Papa cannot *force* me to go back.'

'He can.'

'I won't go.'

He rolled onto his back again, lifting an arm to shield his eyes from the sun. 'So what would you do, Miss Ballantyre? Bed down between Louis and me in some cheap boardinghouse over the winter, cook our food and take in washing? Or should we put you out onto the streets so you can earn your keep?' She was not sure what he meant, or why he was suddenly so angry. 'Poverty isn't a game, you know, like sleeping outdoors on a summer night. It means endless cold, hunger, and humiliation. Begging for work, and begging for food when there is none, and then stealing it when you can. Believe me, I know. And hunger and cold here are killers—'

'And is that what you'll face this winter?' she asked. 'Not if Papa—'

'You think I want to take his help, or his money?'

'But you must! You must demand it, and then take it. It is the only thing he has left to give—'

'I've plans of my own.'

Yes! James could make his plans, but she could not make plans for herself, in a world where she could no more decide her own destiny than fly. 'So I must return with Papa, and then go and stay with Clemmy and hope I'm lucky enough to find another Rupert Dalston, who isn't a murderer— That's what you're saying, isn't it?'

He did not reply but the thought brought her abruptly back to the moment, and she looked back up the river. It remained empty.

'What do you think Papa plans to do?' she asked as the fierceness left her. 'About Rupert—?'

'He says he needs a confession from him.'

'He'll never make one—'

'He will.'

She looked up at his tone. 'But surely if it's forced from him, he can retract it later, in court.'

James sat up slowly, and he too looked up the empty river. 'I don't see him going to court.' The edge to his voice made her stomach lurch. 'No court will hang an earl's son, however much he deserves it.'

. . . *don't let James Douglas take matters into his own hands* . . .

'But if charges are dropped and a settlement made – would that not be enough?' He threw her a scornful look. 'If you do anything outside the law . . . it would have made you into what you are not.'

'If I kill him, you mean?'

Something clutched at her heart— 'You aren't a killer, James.'

He gave her a narrow slanting look, squinting into the sun. 'But you thought I was, Miss Ballantyre. For five years you thought it—'

She looked back at him, and spoke slowly. 'But now, after all that has happened, if you told me that you were, I don't think I would care.'

Chapter 26

'So who's with Evelyn?' Dalston asked, when all that needed to be said about fallen trees and flattened tents had been said. 'The Scot?'

'Yes,' Larsen replied, glancing across at Ballantyre.

The young man began to get to his feet. 'Then I'll go and tell her that you're back.'

'Thank you, Dalston, but I shall go myself.' Ballantyre rose but had only taken a few paces before he was stopped by Melton, who stepped into his path.

'Charles—' he said, quietly. 'I'd like a word. I'll walk with you a way, if I might?'

His face bore a strange expression, and Dalston turned in his seat. 'George!' he said, his eyes glinting. 'This is not . . .'

But Larsen saw that Melton's expression had changed to one of stubbornness. 'You must allow me to deal with the matter as I see fit, Rupert—' And Larsen saw that he was looking deeply unhappy.

'But, dammit, man, I spoke to you in confidence—!' Dalston spluttered, half-rising from his seat.

'Nevertheless.'

'Ah.' Ballantyre paused, then looked slowly from one to the other. 'I see—' He turned back to the fire and sat again, his hands folded calmly on his lap. 'My dear Melton, please proceed—'

'*George*, for God's sake!'

But Melton shook his head again. 'You made some very serious allegations—!'

Larsen had not seen Louis and Marcel move, but somehow they were there, right behind Dalston, and the atmosphere had become charged. Too late now to remember that the little pistol he carried everywhere was in his pack beside Lady Melton in the tent.

'Charles, in private, I think,' Melton said.

But Ballantyre remained seated, quite still, and he gave Dalston a twisted smile. 'I'll admit that you've astonished me again, young man,' he said. 'But for once I believe we are in accord! It is indeed time to finish the matter.' Dalston flushed as Ballantyre gestured Melton back to his seat. 'And there's no need for privacy, George, because I know what you're going to say to me. You're going to ask me whether it's true that I'm sheltering a man wanted on two charges of murder. And the answer, my friend, is yes, I am.'

Melton looked astonished, and unsure of his next step. Ballantyre, however, slowly lit one of his cigars, flicked the match into the fire and gestured again to the seat. 'Please, George, do sit, as this might take a little time.' Then he addressed Dalston again. 'I'd give a lot to hear what else you felt compelled to confide.' Dalston flushed deeper, and a nerve in his bruised eyelid began to twitch. Larsen guessed that this was not playing out as he had intended.

Then Ballantyre looked across at him. 'And something tells me that you, my friend, felt the need to read the letter I left you?'

'I did.'

'Good. Very percipient of you, as always. And now I wonder if I can trouble you to show it to Melton. It will save time in explanation, and if accusations are being bandied about then perhaps we should have them all on the table.'

Larsen went quickly back into his tent, retrieved the letter, and took a moment to check that his pistol was loaded, and to slip it into his pocket. Clementina, thank goodness, was breathing deeply, still fast asleep. He paused at the entrance of the tent and listened as Ballantyre continued. 'But I believe you intended that George keep your little confidence to himself until we were back in Nipigon, did you not? Then you could arrange for James's arrest— Rash of you to tell him now, perhaps, but then you prefer action to *reac*tion, do you not, and you'd no idea what I might be planning.'

Larsen heard Dalston's cool reply as he rejoined the group. 'No. Nor how you intend to explain yourself.' He had crossed his long legs, as if in mimicry of Ballantyre, and adopted the same air of studied calm. 'I have no idea why you and your daughter have been playing this game of pretence. It took me a while to puzzle out who the man was, but I knew something odd was going on—'

'Very astute of you,' said Ballantyre.

Larsen handed Ballantyre's letter to Melton. Dalston frowned and watched him closely as he read it while Ballantyre drew on his cigar, narrowing his eyes against the smoke. Larsen saw Melton's expression change as he reached the critical point in the letter.

Dalston sat forward. 'I don't know what's written there, George, but it'll be a pack of lies. Here, let me see—' Ballantyre gave a wave of consent and Dalston snatched the letter, skimmed the contents, and his face suffused with colour. 'Good God! So that's it, is it?' he snorted. 'Do you imagine anyone is going to believe this, Ballantyre? It's quite absurd! Laughable, in fact— You use *me* to cover up your filthy behaviour and protect your . . .' He broke off and his lip curled in disdain.

It was a good performance and Larsen saw Melton's frown deepen.

'Aha!' Ballantyre raised his eyebrows. 'So you *were* party to that element of the plot, were you? I often wondered – but I was unsure whether that bit of embroidery was something just between your father and myself. How very interesting! And you've enlightened George, have you?'

It was now Larsen's turn to be perplexed, but Melton's growing discomfiture was all too evident, and he raised a hand. 'Wait. Stop there. Before we go any further. If we are to have this matter out, then James Douglas should be here so that he might account for himself.'

'I'll go and get him,' said Louis, who had been watching the proceedings without expression.

Dalston scoffed. 'And give him the tip-off to run again— I think not—'

Melton looked about the camp, mentally dismissing each individual in turn. Then: 'Mr Skinner, could we trouble you to go? And I ask you to say nothing, except that everyone is now safely back in the camp. But—' He turned back to Ballantyre. 'Charles, consider! You won't want your daughter to hear—'

'Evelyn will hear only the truth from me,' Ballantyre replied. 'And she *shall* hear it— Bring them both back here, please, Mr Skinner.'

—————

By the time Skinner arrived at the landing they had moved off the rocks to a softer place, where low plants and fallen leaves made a cushioned spread beneath them. If asked, James would not have been able to say how they got there, but it was enough that he was holding her again, her hair a sweet blend of woodsmoke and balsam, her skin smooth beneath the shirt—

Skinner hawked noisily and then spat.

'There's no time fer *that*.'

James spun round and sat up. '*Skinner!* Christ—' He turned back to Evelyn, shielding her while she buttoned her shirt, her head averted and her hair falling forward.

'Yer pa's back, missee,' Skinner said, looking pointedly the other way. 'Came back overland. The others 're back too.'

James's mind came swiftly back from the sweet place it had been. 'They sent *you* to fetch us?'

'That's right.' Skinner did not meet his eyes.

'So everyone is there? And Dalston. He's there?' he asked, glancing at Evelyn.

'He's there. One eye closed.' Skinner chuckled. 'Got into a fight with Marcel upriver. Not seeing things so clearly now.'

James got to his feet, pulling Evelyn up beside him, keeping her close. 'Why were they fighting?'

Skinner could never resist a story. 'They saw a bear with cubs across the river, see, and Marcel told him not to shoot it but Dalston did anyways. So then Marcel had to shoot the cubs, and that made him mad, and he wouldn't cross the river for the skins, which made Dalston madder. Louis said he threw the first punch.'

'Idiot—'

Skinner nodded sagely. 'Maybe Louis shouldn't have pulled Marcel off him, and then things would be simpler—'

James stopped and looked at him. 'Skinner. What's happening back at camp?' Evelyn stood close, her hand gripping James's arm. She had attempted to tie back her hair, but it was coming down again, and there were pine needles down the length of her.

Skinner shook his head but his jaw was working anxiously. 'Jes' come back with me now. You too, missee. That's what yer pa said. Jes come back. Both of you.'

Chapter 27

At first glance the group at the campsite appeared quite normal. They were gathered around the fire as if it were any other day when they might be discussing their catches, the strikes and losses, or the speed of the river.

Evelyn looked for her father and saw him sitting there, relaxed, a cigar in one hand, a tin mug in the other, and he was talking to Larsen, who sat beside him. Rupert was with George, as was usual, and he was talking intently to him, though George was half-turned away. Louis and Marcel stood just behind the two of them, and then she saw that their stance was anything but relaxed; they were like pointers, straining at the leash— Machk, Tala, and two strangers sat a little way off, but their attention too was fixed on the group by the fire.

Louis was the first to see them emerge from the trail. His expression lightened at her appearance, and he gave a grin, then her father looked up and rose to his feet.

'Evelyn, my dear—' He bent to kiss her on the forehead, lightly touched the bruise there, then scrutinised her apparel, eyebrows raised. 'How very practical,' he said. 'You've had quite a night, I hear, and must tell me about it.' Then he looked across to James. 'And I understand that I'm in your debt, young man, for expediting matters.' He searched James's face. 'But now we must deal with a storm of a different sort – matters have come suddenly to a head, you see.' Evelyn felt her stomach turn over and she looked across at Rupert, who muttered something in an aside to Melton. 'So sit

down, will you, and Evie, take my seat beside Niels.' Mr Larsen
stood, reached out to take her hand and squeeze it as she sat down
beside him. And he held on to it.

Her father remained standing and James's face was wooden as
Ballantyre addressed him again. 'Having worked out your identity
it appears that Dalston has endeavoured to win support by giving
Melton a version of events—'

'Not a *version*, Ballantyre,' Dalston interjected.

'— a version that differs from mine,' her father continued. 'And
while we don't have twelve good men and true, we have men of sound
judgement here, who can perhaps consider the matter for themselves.'

'This is absurd!' Dalston gave a credible appearance of bored
indignation. 'George, for God's sake! Tell the man he ain't in some
Kelso courthouse. Skinner, how soon can we be back down to civilisation where this man can be put under guard and the matter
dealt with by the proper authorities?'

'There is no authority here today, Dalston, other than mine' –
the words, spoken softly, charged the atmosphere – 'and you *will*
hear me out.'

The words sent a shiver through Evelyn, and suddenly she was
afraid. She had known her father remote, she had known him sardonic, and she had known him angry, but she had never seen the
expression he now bestowed on Rupert. He was in deadly earnest,
and all heads turned to him—

A flame leapt in the hearth, and then subsided, and it seemed
that the trees began to close in around them to form walls, a wilderness courtroom. A raven flew overhead and gave a guttural cry,
as if to start the proceedings.

———

From his position at the edge of the circle, James watched Dalston's
face grow rigid as Ballantyre accused him first of Jacko's murder,

and then of McAllister's. His tone was cold, factual, and precise. 'I know he shot the old poacher, because I was there and saw him do it,' he said, 'and so did James Douglas. I believe Dalston killed McAllister, my head keeper, too, although there are no witnesses.' Dalston made a sound somewhere between a scoff and a sneer. 'I had dismissed the man an hour before he was found dead. When his clumsy attempts to blackmail me failed, I imagine he tried his luck with Dalston; he was fool enough, and came by his just deserts.'

Dalston rallied and came back at him. 'No witnesses, eh? Awkward for you, that.' He gestured to the letter which had fallen on the ground. 'And no proof either, you say so yourself.'

Ballantyre gave him a grim smile. 'But nonetheless it is the truth.'

Dalston's good eye slid around the gathering. 'One shooting, four witnesses, of which three give the same account, one differs. Then one slit throat, no witnesses. *Very* awkward, in fact.'

'A slit throat, you say?' interjected his adversary.

Dalston ignored him and continued. 'My father, McAllister, and myself all saw James Douglas arguing with the poacher on the far side of the river, we heard a shot and saw the man fall. Ballantyre saw it too. And then he' – he indicated James – 'ran off into the woods. My father will swear to this, and he has a statement written by McAllister to the same effect.'

'McAllister himself was killed the same evening. How do you explain that?' Ballantyre enquired.

'Douglas killed him too, of course, then stole a horse – or was given it, more like – and made off. It's all really very simple.'

Melton frowned. 'Was *given* it?'

'Pa and I always thought he had help getting away. How else did he disappear so completely? He was penniless! Maybe Ballantyre arranged for him to come over here straight away. Stands to reason, he had business interests in these parts, and no one would think to look—' He seemed to be warming to his invention.

James opened his mouth to protest but Melton put up his hand. 'You'll have your chance to speak in a moment.'

Dalston was not done. 'Why don't you ask Ballantyre why he has never offered this alternative version until now, five years after the event?'

'And I might counter by asking you why McAllister would feel the need to give your father a written statement, rather than wait to present it at a trial?'

Dalston hesitated for a second. 'Because he knew you would try to protect this . . . this man.' He waved a contemptuous hand in James's direction.

'And why would I do that, Rupert?' asked Ballantyre. 'Why protect a man who had committed murder on my own estate?'

James watched Dalston carefully. He was hesitating again and looked like a man about to gamble all on a single throw. 'Melton knows why, Ballantyre,' he said, his swollen eye twitching. 'I told him, you see. Everything. He *knows*.' The emphasis was given with a sneer.

James looked from Dalston to Melton, and then back to Ballantyre. Knew what? Somewhere he had missed something— Melton was looking deeply unhappy, and he saw him glance anxiously in Evelyn's direction. 'That aspect need not be addressed in public . . .' he said

'Like hell!' James retorted. Were they closing ranks? Even here—! '*How* was Ballantyre protecting me? And why—'

Dalston's eyes darted between Ballantyre and Melton, but it was Ballantyre who answered, his voice flat calm. 'Because, Dalston claims you had long been my . . . my Ganymede.' James looked blank. 'He accuses me of sodomy, James, and asserts that I had used you as my catamite ever since that first day when I took you under my roof, a child of thirteen. It was his father's invention, to buy my silence, and McAllister was only too happy to concur.'

———

Seconds ticked by in shocked silence, and Evelyn sat in a daze. Then her father's meaning became clear and she stopped breathing. Ganymede, the beautiful shepherd boy whom Zeus had seen on the mountainside, and had carried off to Mount Olympus to be cupbearer to the gods— She felt the colour flooding into her face, and looked across at James.

———

James felt his guts absorbing the kick as Ballantyre's words found their meaning, and he stared across at him in disbelief. Then fury roared in his ears, but it was a double-edged fury. 'So you were protecting *yourself*, in fact. Your reputation—'

Ballantyre held his look. 'That was the threat which bought my silence, and my compliance. So – yes, I was.'

James felt sick. So he had been right all along, except that Ballantyre had not been defending his own, but *himself*. Defending his wealth, his position, his standing in society against an allegation which would have destroyed him. And to do so Ballantyre had simply thrown him to the wolves—

Ballantyre's next words gave confirmation. 'I was told that one word from me to the effect that Rupert Dalston, in a moment of madness, had shot dead an unarmed man on my land, and that was to be the story splashed across every newspaper in the land. I would be branded a sodomite and a liar, accusing an earl's son of murder to protect a depraved wretch, a poacher's brat, who was my paramour. McAllister, it seemed, was only too pleased to sign a confirmation of the allegation, on receipt of a significant sum, and so settle old scores and punish us both – in fact, it suited him very well.' A deep thrumming sounded in James's head. Ballantyre was right; McAllister had never missed the opportunity to abuse him whenever he could get under the stable master's guard, defying Ballantyre, and this opportunity would have delighted him.

———

Larsen had felt Evelyn stiffen beside him as her father spoke, surprised that she had understood; then he remembered Ballantyre's pride in her classical education and realised that her father had chosen his words carefully and with delicacy, so that she *would* understand—

But, dear God, even so, she could have no idea what such an accusation would have meant! And her father would have been vulnerable to such an attack, easy prey, as he was well known for his passion for reform amongst the orphanages, for his work in boys' reformatories and penal establishments. He had made enemies amongst the less enlightened, and his inclusion of the poacher's young apprentice into his own household had, as Larsen understood, caused a considerable stir amongst his neighbours who had thought such behaviour, at best, eccentric. So Stanton had acted with ruthless acumen, twisting an act of high-principled generosity into a weapon. It was altogether fiendish. Ballantyre would have lost everything, his reputation shredded, and, with all likelihood, he would have ended up imprisoned. And with McAllister's sworn statement he would have had no defence.

Then he recalled, with growing clarity, how many years earlier, in those heady days of railway investment, her father had used Ballantyre House to secure a large loan from Stanton. And in the event of Ballantyre resisting him, that loan would surely have been forfeit – and he would have lost the estate too. He stopped, his mind jarring as another, very different thought flew out of nowhere like a black-fletched arrow to lodge in his brain, and slowly a wider understanding began to dawn.

He glanced up to find that Ballantyre was looking back at him, as if reading his mind, and Larsen saw the muscles tighten in his cheek. 'My friend Larsen will tell you that I was, at the time, in partnership with Earl Stanton, and heavily in his debt; he held mortgages on my estate, so he was able to promise me financial ruin as well as arrest. But we both knew that it was the accusation of sodomy which would have destroyed me. And mine—' His glance flickered to his daughter. 'So you see, James, he left me quite impotent, powerless to resist.' Larsen looked across to where James Douglas stood, stiff and hostile, arms folded, staring back at him. 'And he'd have seen you hang without a murmur.'

Larsen began to calculate quickly, winding back the years, exploring his emergent thought. Five years— Images began to flash across his mind. South Africa: the appalling risks that Ballantyre had taken, then the steady gain, and eventually the huge profits. Railroads: more risks, then losses, money stretched thin. But not Ballantyre's own money by this time, but the bank's, borrowed and then loaned to a partnership he had with Stanton, then Stanton alone demanding more loans, big ones, and then extensions with guarantees underwritten by Ballantyre, but anonymously. Larsen sat back in horror as it came together in his mind—

Somewhere, from a long way off, James heard Dalston scoff at Ballantyre's words. 'What utter rubbish. All of it. Except for the central, carnal, facts. Ballantyre is a liar, and was a pederast. Probably still is—'

But the words made no impact on James. The red mist of anger was thinning, and as it did he was able to examine what Ballantyre had said. *The accusation of sodomy which would have destroyed me.* He raised his eyes and met Ballantyre's – *he left me quite impotent, powerless to resist* . . . How could that ever have applied to Ballantyre? And it was as if they were alone in a dark place, just the two of them, looking back at each other across five years, once bonded, master and man, but no more. They dealt as equals now. The others faded into blank shadows, and time lost its meaning. And Ballantyre sat there across from him, his very soul exposed, awaiting James's judgement. Not humbled, but calmly waiting—

And in a moment that lasted forever James began to understand, as five years ago he could never have done.

And as understanding came the anger drained away and it seemed that the jagged charge which had leapt across the river between them that day at Skinner's dock lost its power to wound and became another sort.

'For God's sake, man. Look at them. Isn't it obvious!' Rupert's words shattered the moment, and this time James stepped forward, determined at last to smash that face. Evelyn grabbed at his arm, but George was there before her, moving quickly to stand between him and Rupert, holding up both hands. 'There'll be no violence here. These are serious allegations which neither man can make without strong evidence—' George had altered. There was no trace now of the laconic fisherman, the forest clearing had become *his* courtroom— 'Evidence which no one seems to have.'

'Doubtless Dalston's father still has McAllister's mendacious statement safe somewhere.' Her father spoke quietly. 'Stanton showed it to me the night of the murder. But I think you'll find that's all he has.'

'Yes, he has it, I feel sure.' Rupert was looking relaxed, entirely in control. 'So by all means let us test it in the courts upon our return.'

'And you, Charles, what evidence have you?'

Here was the nub. Evelyn watched her father's face carefully, but he still spoke with a calm confidence. 'In the case of Jacko's death, the evidence of my own eyes, which only James Douglas can confirm.' Rupert made a derisive sound. 'But in the case of McAllister, a little more—'

'Rubbish. You have nothing—'

Her father gave Dalston another long appraising look, but she began to feel uneasy. He was surely bluffing— If he had had evidence he would have used it.

'Only three men knew that McAllister died not from a stab in the back, as was reported, but that his throat was cut, from ear to ear. That detail was thought too grotesque to unleash upon the guests who were staying at Ballantyre House at the time, and was suppressed. The newspapers then erroneously reported it as a stabbing, and there were few who knew differently other than myself, the constable, and my stable master, who found him. And, it would appear, you knew as well, Dalston. How was that?'

Rupert shrugged dismissively. 'I've no idea who told me – it was five years ago. My father, probably, when he got home.'

'Yes, you left us late that night, as I recall, although you had only arrived that morning for a weeklong shoot. What was it that called you away?'

He was trying to unsettle him, but Rupert maintained a bored indifference. 'After all this time? I've no idea—'

Her father nodded. Still calm. But his face now bore an intense expression, bright-eyed and watchful. It was an expression which, for some reason, Evelyn found oddly familiar. How could that be—? And then she recognised it, and confidence began to creep back. It belonged to those treasured days when she had accompanied him to the riverbank, carrying his fishing basket; it was the expression he wore when he threw out a line, soft and gentle, to land on the water, light as thistledown, looking for a rise. She had seen it when she used to stand there, enthralled, as the coils of line spun out, catching the sunlight before falling straight and true. But now he was throwing across the wind—

'My memory by contrast,' he was saying, 'is unimpaired. I ordered you off my property that night, Rupert, and your father left at first light after a long and acrimonious discussion. So neither of you saw the corpse or had any reason to know that McAllister's throat was slit.'

Rupert looked only a little discomforted. 'Maybe so. But what does it matter? Stabbed or throat slit – I'd little interest in the case. It had nothing to do with me.'

Her father threw again. 'Sinclair saddled your horse for you that night, just before midnight, and found McAllister's body in the shrubbery when he came to find me on the terrace, to tell me that you'd gone. I remember very clearly, the man's blood was still congealing when I went back with him; McAllister was newly dead.'

It was a weak throw and she began to realise with a sickening certainty that her father, in truth, had nothing. It would only ever be his word against theirs—

Rupert must have thought the same. 'Rot. He was found in the morning. That much *was* in the papers—'

'So you *did* take an interest?' Rupert waved a dismissive hand. 'But you see, Sinclair and I had moved him to an outbuilding that evening, as he was littering the shrubbery and I had guests to think of. This was explained to the authorities, and noted. But he was killed just about the time you left, no doubt when you encountered him on your way to the stables.' His last fly floated innocently away on the current.

Dalston let it drift by. 'For God's sake. What possible reason had I to kill McAllister?' Then, unwisely, he rose to it after all. 'Quite the opposite. He was a key witness.'

'Key to what?'

Rupert looked confused, and his colour changed. 'The case against James Douglas, of course.'

'You were building a case! But why?' Her father tightened the line.

Rupert's good eye blinked rapidly. 'Melton, for God's sake! Must I put up with this interrogation?'

'Yes. You made a serious accusation—'

Evelyn felt a jolt of joy. Was George's position shifting?

Rupert stared at his friend. 'Alright, then,' he snapped. 'But it was obvious that James Douglas killed McAllister, he must have been skulking in the grounds at the same time.'

These last words electrified her, and suddenly she knew that she had something to offer. 'No. He wasn't. He was in Papa's study.' All heads swivelled to her. 'With me.'

'Whatever do you mean?' asked George.

'Oh, for God's sake!' Rupert cried, exasperated. 'Now *this* for the first time too . . . She's just making things up, and I can guess why. Seems to me these last few days young Ganymede's appeal has widened— How old were you, Evelyn? Thirteen, fourteen?'

But she was looking at George and answered his question. 'I was searching for Papa, so I went to the study, but I found James instead, emptying Papa's cash box into a saddlebag.'

There was silence, then Rupert let out a whoop of delight. 'And you offer this in his *defence*? My dear girl!'

The endearment was like acid, burning through veneer, and she looked back at him, fearless now. 'And he had been there long enough to break the window, smash the drawer of the bureau, and prise open the cash box.' Everyone was staring at her but she continued to address George. 'Coins were spilled across the desk when I arrived, and then we spoke for a while. If McAllister died just before midnight, then it wasn't James that killed him. He was with me.' And she looked across at James and saw his eyes gleam in response.

'How can you be so sure of the time ?' George asked sharply.

'I heard the stable clock, and then the fireworks started.' And there was the smell of cordite which had haunted her down the years, but if that moment could now be turned to good use, it would haunt her no more.

Rupert started to get to his feet, but Louis pulled him back.

Rupert cursed him, shrugging off his grip, only then becoming conscious of the two men behind him. 'Melton, this is a travesty! You *know* it is. You've absolutely no authority to question me, nor have these men hold me – for God's sake I had no *reason* to kill McAllister.'

But George's face remained rigid, and he nodded to her father to continue.

His next cast went farther. 'Except to nip in the bud any further attempts at blackmail.'

The frown on Rupert's face suggested that he was becoming confused. Would he rise to that one? He hesitated. Then 'But, for God's sake, *why* would he try to blackmail me?'

Almost.

'Or perhaps you simply wanted to retrieve from his person a draft for one thousand pounds drawn on your father's bank.'

Dalston blanched, and his eye twitched again. 'What—?' Then, with bluster, 'There was no such draft.'

'My dear Dalston, I'd seen it. The scoundrel had shown it to me, and offered to retract the statement he had given to your father if I would double the amount. The draft was found on him.'

Dalston rose angrily to that one. 'It was not. *That* is a lie!'

Follow through, she willed him silently, knowing somehow that he must.

And he did. 'How so?'

'Because I'd—' said Rupert and then stopped.

She could almost see her father's wrist twist on the invisible rod. '— already taken it off him?' He jerked the line hard, and drove the hook in, beyond the barb. 'Thank you, Dalston.'

'No! Damn you. *No*—' Rupert swore furiously, and tried again to stand, but Louis and Marcel between them clamped him to his seat where he thrashed like a trout in the tangle of a net, cursing them, still protesting wildly to George.

Chapter 28

The tension broke with Dalston's curses, and everyone began to speak at once. Larsen got stiffly to his feet, a hundred years older than when he had sat down, and offered Ballantyre his flask. Ballantyre accepted it, although Larsen saw him pause, the flask half-raised, and look across to where his daughter had leapt to her feet and was now held close in James's embrace.

Melton was staring at Dalston, even as Dalston still tried to convince him that it was a pack of lies, that he was innocent of all charges, but Melton just stared back in horror. Skinner remained seated, understandably bewildered by the entire proceedings, but eventually it was his voice that carried above the rest.

'*Jeez*. So. What happens now?'

'Thank you, Mr Skinner. A timely thought,' said Ballantyre. 'I should like Dalston to sign a document which I prepared in readiness some time ago and have been carrying with me, but I'd like you to cast your eye over it first, George, as I'll ask you to witness it. You too, Niels, if you will.'

Ballantyre pulled a paper from his jacket and handed it to Melton, and Larsen read it over his shoulder. It was short, to the point – and entirely damning. When they had finished reading, Melton nodded. Ballantyre took it and handed it to Dalston.

'Read this, and then sign it. It is a true account of that evening, and I intend to present it in court.'

'You'll bring the matter to court?' Melton's expression sharpened, and he looked uneasy. Larsen heard him ask in a quiet aside, 'Will that be necessary? It'll cause an unholy furore, you know. And such filthy allegations against yourself, sir, however untrue—'

Ballantyre looked across contemptuously to where Dalston sat, white with fury as he read the document. 'They would have brought James to court, lied, condemned him, and then watched him hang. If you think I'll agree to some accommodation with Stanton after all this, you are much mistaken.' His gaze shifted to James. 'I owe him that much at least.'

Evelyn felt James's embrace slacken, although his arm still encircled her waist. She looked up at him and then saw that her father was coming towards them.

'Evelyn, my dear—' he said, and then it seemed he had nothing else to say, but he raised a hand to her cheek and brushed it softly. Then he looked at James. 'I shall speak further with you presently—' He turned away again, and in moving aside allowed them all to see that Rupert had calmly folded the document into a paper dart which he aimed unerringly into the centre of the fire.

It was immediately consumed.

'Did you really think I would sign it?' he asked.

Her father looked gravely back at him. 'Perhaps not. Though it can, of course, be redrafted.'

Rupert seemed to be regaining some of his composure. 'Just as you like. But I'll still not sign. You can make all the charges you like when we return to Scotland, but you've not a shred of evidence. Anything you force me to sign will be under duress, and not admitted as evidence. And my family, you know, has powerful connections . . .'

'Yes, I know.'

'And the fact that you, and your daughter, have sheltered a wanted man rather than hand him over to the authorities will hardly play to your advantage. Don't you think?'

Evelyn felt fear clutch at her again, and it tightened when she saw the expression on James's face. He released her and stepped forward, but her father raised his hand. 'Peace, James. The matter is not yet concluded.' He turned back to Rupert. 'I think you'd begun to believe your own story, hadn't you? How extraordinary – no wonder your father sent you on your travels. Only such self-delusion can account for the astonishing audacity you showed in accepting Larsen's invitation, offered to you in all innocence. Did you think I would welcome you? That I had forgotten, and for-given? Or was shooting a poacher such a trifling offence that time had erased the crime, allowing you to pay court to my daugh-ter—?'

'Pay court?' Rupert flashed a contemptuous look in her direc-tion, and then glanced at James beside her. 'Hardly! And besides it would appear the gal's tastes run to—' James made an ugly sound and this time it was she that pulled him back.

'Dalston, for God's sake, man—!' Melton protested, revolted.

Her father waited, then: 'Or perhaps you thought that your father still had some hold over me?' His face was like granite. 'I promise you, young man, the boot is now on the other foot.'

Larsen felt his stomach turn over. He had some idea what was coming, and although it offended his every instinct, he knew he would stand by Ballantyre's actions, and any consequence, even if it left his own reputation in shreds. 'I had planned things very dif-ferently,' Ballantyre was saying, 'over many years. But when I found James Douglas, here in this wilderness place, and then received Larsen's telegram to say that he had invited you along, I knew that the fates had decided to take a hand, and that there would be a dif-ferent resolution after all.' Larsen glanced at Dalston and saw that the bruise around his eye had darkened from red to purple. 'And as of two days ago I am empowered to follow the matter through. Am I right, Niels?'

Larsen started, and then calculated rapidly. Of course. Good God. Yes.

'You are right,' he said.

'And we had expected to celebrate rather differently, did we not, my friend?' Larsen responded to the gleam in Ballantyre's eye and had a sudden image of that moment at Astra's Pool, of sunlight on spinning coils of line as they stood side by side. That instant of perfection.

'As of two days ago,' Ballantyre continued, 'papers I signed in New York took effect and I now have overall control of Mr Larsen's bank. For most of our clients this means very little, but for you, Dalston, and for your father, it means everything. All your family's debts – and they are very considerable – are owed to the bank, you see.' Larsen saw Dalston tense and start to pay attention. 'And if this matter regarding James Douglas is not resolved, to my full satisfaction, then I shall not hesitate to call them in. All of them at once. I had intended to put the matter to your father on my return, but then you walked so arrogantly into my lair—' Dalston's face drained of colour. 'So one more unwise remark and I might choose to foreclose immediately by telegram, from Nipigon station. Believe me, it will be that easy.'

Larsen had the sort of mind which could retain detail; it was a gift which had made him such a successful banker. And it allowed him to recall, and now recognise, each step that Ballantyre had taken as he wove his vengeful plot through the bank's affairs. He had never once had reason to doubt his partner's integrity, and Ballantyre had always been scrupulous in his dealings with the bank's clients. With all clients, except Earl Stanton. And what Larsen had seen as benevolence and friendship he saw now had been a deadly snare, laid five years ago and then tightened at every opportunity with ruthless skill. He belched as he looked at Evelyn, remembering how wildly he had misinterpreted Ballantyre's motives – and

Stanton had never questioned his generous treatment. Had that been from arrogance? He had that a-plenty— Perhaps he too had thought the matter of the poacher a trifling affair, long forgotten. Or had he seen Ballantyre's willingness to lend without security and extend overdue loans as fear that Stanton still held, and might use, McAllister's damning statement? And all that time Ballantyre had been quietly amassing a fortune which made him virtually invincible, and now he had Stanton where he wanted him, in the palm of his hand. Jeb Merlin might hold the mortgages on Stanton's estate, but Ballantyre had everything else.

And then, with that odd ability Ballantyre had to pick up on other people's thoughts, he spoke, almost as if in an aside. 'The final piece only fell into place very recently when I was able to seal the acquisition of the mortgages on the rest of the Stanton estate – the land, farms, and Stanton Hall. ' He turned to Larsen, and added, 'Which was why this little mining enterprise was rather important, you see. The Wizard demanded a high price for them.' Then, in a low voice meant for him only, he said, 'You've a lot to forgive me for, Niels—'

Larsen was rendered speechless. It was he who had told Ballantyre that Jeb Merlin held those mortgages, and then he remembered how Ballantyre had disappeared for a while that night on Merlin's yacht. Good God! He had arranged it there and then, under his very nose; and he quailed at the thought of how much of the bank's capital had been spent to secure those papers.

James saw Louis look up sharply at the mention of the mining enterprise and he shot James a glance. He had entirely forgotten the reason for Ballantyre's recent absence and now cursed to himself. So had Ballantyre somehow outmanoeuvred them too? But James was not the only one distracted by their thoughts at that moment, and so no one saw Dalston slip a hand inside his jacket. And so the shot, when it came, took them all by surprise.

James heard Ballantyre's cry, and then a second shot was fired in the ensuing struggle and it hit Louis in the thigh, causing him to release his grip on Dalston. Larsen, who later had no memory of pulling his own pistol from his pocket, fired it without thinking. It hit only the back of Dalston's chair but that was enough to put him off his aim. And so Dalston's third shot, aimed at James, went wide.

And then all was confusion. Dalston swung the butt of his pistol into Marcel's face then shouldered him in the gut and sent him sprawling into the path of Tala and Machk, who tried to seize him. Panicked screams from inside Clementina's tent added to the chaos, distracting Melton's attention. Firing randomly, Dalston's next shot hit Machk, then he turned to run for the river.

James went swiftly to Louis who was grasping his thigh.

'*Laissez-moi. Vite!* Go after him!' James glanced up and saw Evelyn bent over her father. He cried out to Skinner to come to Louis, then pelted after Dalston.

His quarry had reached the river's edge by then and was pushing one of the canoes over the shingle and into the water. He turned as James leapt down the incline, aimed again, and shot. Pain seared across James's shoulder, and then Marcel, his face streaked with blood, tore past him.

The canoe was already pulling away by then and Dalston was paddling hard. He glanced just once over his shoulder at them, then turned back, all his energies concentrated on keeping the canoe heading across the river, fighting the current, heading for the opposite bank. James considered, then dismissed, the idea of following in another canoe.

'*Imbecile.* He'll never make it.' Louis joined them, clutching his bleeding thigh, and they stood at the water's edge and watched.

The current midchannel was strong and they saw the canoe

taken broadside. If Dalston did not paddle hard, it would take him with it, down towards the lower falls. But so far he seemed to be making steady progress towards the opposite shore.

'My God, he's going to do it!' said James.

'But then what?' said Marcel, with scorn. He was right, of course, Dalston would soon be lost in thick impenetrable bush, miles from civilisation with only the river as his guide. 'And we would find him—'

He broke off as another shot rang out, but this came from behind them and whistled over their heads.

———

Later Evelyn had no memory of picking up the rifle. She had seen it, propped against a tree, and seized it, ignoring her father's roar, and run after the men with the vague idea that they would need it. She had halted at the top of the rocks and saw that Dalston was getting away. Too late to give the gun to them now – so she fired it from where she stood, falling back and crying out at the recoil.

Perhaps she missed her mark, but it was enough. Out on the river she saw Dalston flinch and duck, breaking his paddle stroke, and allowing the bow to swing round and the canoe to head downstream, gathering speed. The current had him— They saw him straighten, unhurt, and start paddling again, but wildly now, desperately swapping stroke from side to side as the river bore him on.

There was nothing any of them could have done, even had they wished to, they could only stand and watch as the current bore the canoe along until it disappeared around the bend of the river, towards the falls.

Chapter 29

A thick pall of white smoke rose from the fire, and it hung there, low over the clearing, fumigating the campsite. No matter where Evelyn sat it seemed to find her and her eyes were soon smarting and sore. Her father sat close beside her, his face scarred by the bullet that had seared his cheek. He was almost as pale as the gauze she had applied to the wound, but she fancied that some of the lines had smoothed away and he looked younger. Drained and infinitely weary, but younger.

She held on to his hand, tightly.

Part of her wanted to leave this place at once, but this was also a moment to savour, for here, at least, the world, with all its complicated trappings, was held at bay and matters which had festered too long had at last been settled, and in a way that made sense. As soon as they started the journey home everything that had occurred here would be questioned and explanations demanded.

It was too late to start the journey back to Skinner's lodge to-night, though, especially with so many of them injured or hurt. Clementina had taken a great deal of calming down and was even now sobbing quietly in Larsen's tent, with George beside her. James's and Louis's wounds were not serious and had been attended to, while her father had dismissed his own as trivial. Machk was the most badly injured and would require medical attention when they reached Nipigon, but Tala had made him as comfortable as possible and said that he was not unduly concerned. The men who had accompanied her father back to camp turned out to be Achak's men, and they had agreed to stay on and help the shattered party get back down the river and were even now restoring the camp so it could be used for one last night. James was helping, one-handed for the most part, refusing any suggestion that he rest his injured shoulder. Amazingly it was still only midday.

———

'Was that shot fired on James's behalf, or mine?' her father asked her, breaking a long silence.

She looked back at him, and did not answer at once. Then: 'I think it was for five lost years.'

He grunted. 'Well, whatever and for whomever, I'm glad you missed.'

Tala had taken Achak's men along the trail downstream to below the falls where they had found the canoe, damaged but not destroyed, thrown against the rocks below the falls. They had pulled it ashore and agreed that it could be repaired, and had left it to collect later. A little farther downstream they found the paddle, but it had taken longer to find Dalston's body— Then they had seen a foot, wedged between two rocks which had held him, vise-like and below water, at one side of the falls. With difficulty they had released the body and pulled it ashore. There was, amongst a range of other cuts and bruises, no trace of a bullet wound, so they had covered it with a tarpaulin, and piled rocks on top to keep away animals, and left it there to collect tomorrow. Her father had nodded with satisfaction when they reported this.

He smiled at her and then he turned to Mr Larsen. 'I hope one day that you will be able to forgive me, Niels, but I could not bring you into my confidence.'

'No—'

'Everything had to be in place, you see, before I could light the fuse and bring Stanton down.'

'I'd have felt compelled to stop you.'

'I know.'

There was another long silence. 'And now? What happens now, Charles?'

Her father sighed and ran his hand through his hair, wincing slightly as he pulled at his wounded cheek. 'Perhaps my appetite for vengeance has been assuaged—' he said. 'I'll use my leverage to see to it that Stanton clears James's name, of course, which will mean he must admit to Dalston's guilt. As the scoundrel said, his father has powerful friends, but I doubt they'll stand by him once the facts are known, though they might help him hide the dirty linen. They'll do that much— Dalston is dead and there is little to be served now by causing a scandal. And so we can, perhaps, keep the bank's business out of it.' Mr Larsen looked profoundly relieved. 'Stanton's older son, his heir, is a sound man and has done me no harm, so I'll not ruin him, as I would inevitably have done. His father is finished, though, and can live out his years knowing that he is at my mercy— That, perhaps, will be enough.' He squeezed Evelyn's hand. 'And we shall go home, my dear.'

They would. Of course.

'Did you really not know that James was here?' she asked him, after a moment.

He gave a half-smile and shook his head. 'I've had men looking for him for five years and I see now why they could find no trace of him. But somehow I always knew he was alive.'

She digested that in silence. So he had been searching— 'But how was bringing Earl Stanton down going to help James? How would he have known?'

He smiled at her. 'He would have known, believe me. I was planning to light such a flare! It would have blazed the truth across every newspaper, and I was counting on the fact that the ensuing furore would bring him out of hiding, and I could then start to set matters right. But it would not have caused a ripple out here on the Nipigon, and so he might never have known.'

Then he looked around him, surveying the wreckage, and began to talk: 'That night, I couldn't believe what Dalston had done, shooting the poor wretch in cold blood. I think he must have been unhinged, or drunk— His father was furious but decided at once, without compunction, that James would take the blame. I was stunned, and then outraged that he dared propose such a thing! James Douglas was under my protection, I told him, and perhaps it was that which gave rise to his monstrous plot. He became very inventive – by evening he'd worked out the whole infernal scheme, bought McAllister's complicity, and I saw at once that he could make the accusation of sodomy stick.'

And this must have been the scene that she had broken in upon in his study.

'And you know what? Looking back on it now, taking James in all those years ago was not the philanthropic act I believed it to be. I was pitting my principles, my morals, against Jacko's, demonstrating to him that what I had to offer was in every way superior to his vagabond ways.' He rubbed the heel of his hand on his forehead, and winced again. 'But by the end of that evening with Stanton I'd learned that my own class had no more principles than a pack of sewer rats.'

And Evelyn, for five years, had believed the same of him. 'Papa—'

He ignored her, and continued. 'I like to think I stood against Stanton for as long as I could, but I could see that he meant business. And then, at that pivotal moment, *you* flung open the door and came flying in, so distressed and so fragile, and stood there in front of your mother's portrait.' He gave her a twisted smile. 'It was then that I faced the stark reality of the situation, and saw that I had no choice— If James was caught he would hang, regardless, while if I agreed to Stanton's terms, and James managed to get away, he had a chance. His only chance— It was so clear then, you see, so simple. And, I tell you, Niels, it was the oddest thing, but I had a sudden image of Jacko's face as he had looked at me across the courtroom on that occasion I told you about.' He turned to Evelyn. 'He once told me that the justice I peddled was self-serving, and that he would only ever be governed by his own conscience. And I began to see that if there *was* to be justice, it would be through adopting his morals, and abandoning my own. And so I resolved to get justice for the old reprobate, even if it took me years.'

She only partly understood but saw that Mr Larsen was nodding.

'In fact it was Jacko who saved us all. He'd already taught James the skills he needed to survive, and that day in court he taught *me* how to act to save James as well, by trusting not to the law, but to my *conscience*, for there would be no justice any other way. The weapons Jacko used against an unkind world had been the snare and the net, while mine would be money and reputation. And they were weapons that I understood—'

He looked over to where James, one-handed, was packing those provisions which had survived the storm. 'And then, less than a week ago, James Douglas came paddling down the Nipigon River towards me, bathed in evening sunlight, the very embodiment of my unquiet conscience.' He shook his head again, as if in disbelief. 'And next morning Dalston was delivered to me at the station, all packaged, bound hand and foot, ready to stand his trial. I tell you, it was an extraordinary feeling—!'

Then he rose, stretched, and his eye fell again on Evelyn's apparel and he said, in a lighter tone: 'Not only practical, my dear, but rather becoming.'

'They're Louis's,' she said, not knowing what else to say. 'And I shall have a pair made for riding at the very least.'

He laughed, and drew her to him, cupping his hand to the back of her head in the old way, and dropped a kiss on top of her wild curls. 'You shall indeed. And now, my dear, I think perhaps you should go and see if Clementina requires anything. It would be a kindness if you stayed with her for a while and gave poor George a break from these endless vapours.' He held her at arm's length. 'And if you'll forgive me one more time, I have business to attend to.'

———

James looked up as Ballantyre came over to where he was, with difficulty, closing the lid on one of the portage boxes. Between them they sealed it.

'Does it give you much pain?' he asked, gesturing to James's shoulder.

'No,' he lied. 'And your face?'

'It's nothing. Larsen reckoned Dalston had been drinking, for which we must be thankful, otherwise he'd have had your heart and my brain—' He looked across to where Louis sat with his back against a tree trunk, his wounded leg stretched out before him. 'And what about you, Louis?'

'For me, it would have been more serious,' he said.

Ballantyre laughed. 'And my daughter is wearing your spare trousers, I understand. I'll see that you get them back. Although,' he added, 'I imagine, you'll soon be able to afford a dozen pairs.'

Before Louis could respond, Ballantyre swung back to James. 'I promised myself that I would fish Astra's Pool again before I left, and it appears that this evening will be my last opportunity. So if your shoulder really isn't paining you perhaps you'll join me up there in a little while? Give me half an hour, then come.'

James looked at him, but as usual Ballantyre's expression gave nothing away. Until now his visit to Achak had been entirely forgotten, but his remark to Louis could only mean one thing—

Its significance had not been lost on Louis either, and he watched Ballantyre as he went to assemble his fishing gear. 'He knows it was us,' he said.

'Yes—'

Together they watched him set off up the trail and disappear amongst the trees. 'Has he said anything to you?'

'Nothing.'

Then Evelyn came over to them. 'He's gone *fishing*?' she said. 'He told me he had business to attend to. I thought he meant—' She broke off and looked from Louis to James.

'He wants me to join him in a moment.'

Evelyn took hold of his good arm. 'Good. He can *help* you, James, and you must let him. Whatever he offers you, you must take it.'

He extracted his arm, gave another nod, but this time in Louis's direction.

————

Half an hour later Evelyn stood beside Louis and watched James head up the shadowed trail after her father. They needed this time together, she knew, and yet once more she had been excluded.

She became aware that Louis was watching her, whistling softly between his teeth. 'And so, mamselle, all is resolved,' he said. 'And you will return home.'

'Yes.'

'James has told me about your fine big house, and your father's lands. You are very fortunate.' There was a mocking tone in his voice, and she resented it. 'So you will go back there soon, and then enjoy forever the sweet taste of raspberries.'

She frowned at him and he held her look. 'And what else should I do?' she demanded.

He gave his maddening shrug, then gestured up the trail. 'I think milord Dalston's father came just a little way close to the truth.' He took in her puzzlement and smirked. 'There is a bond between those two, I think, that goes deep, and now, up there, it is the strength of that bond that will decide things. And for me too—'

'What do you mean?'

'— perhaps James will tell you,' he said, and eased his position, his hand on his wounded thigh. 'But will he be held by old bonds, or new ones, I wonder? Your father will cool his bad conscience with fine offers, as you said. But what will James say?'

She did not like Louis in this mood – his eyes were dark and angry. 'I've no idea.'

'No? Your fate is being decided up there too, I think. Will you not try to influence them? I cannot.'

He gestured to the bloodstained bandage around his legs. 'I am *hors de combat*. But you, mamselle, in those fine *pantalons* of mine, you could go after them . . .' And with that he leant against the tree trunk and closed his eyes.

———

Astra's Pool was a tranquil spot fringed by trees, resplendent now in their autumn colours. Whoever Astra had been was long forgotten, but for anglers, she was immortalised here. The pool was fed by a pretty bridal veil of a waterfall, and was drained at the other end by a stream which tumbled over a set of smaller falls and rapids before it joined the river. The surrounding cliffs gave the pool shelter, and today it was flat calm as James emerged from the trees.

Two or three yards from the shore he saw Ballantyre standing in the water, flicking his rod back and forth, sending the coils of line through the air, as if he stood beside his own stretch of river. Wherever his fly landed, overlapping ripples caused the reflections to blur. There was beauty, and artistry, in his movement, and James stood a moment and watched, his shoulder throbbing, and his heart very full. Next time Ballantyre cast he saw James, raised a hand, and began to reel in. He came over to the shore and propped his rod against a rock. 'Let's sit a moment, shall we?'

As they sat a fish rose to an incautious fly, real this time, not counterfeit, and Ballantyre cursed it briefly. Then he turned to look at James. 'There is nothing more I can say to you, by way of explanation or apology—'

'I know.'

It was true, and they sat in silence.

After a little while Ballantyre spoke again: 'Jacko once preached to me on the difference between natural and unnatural justice, in my own courtroom, no less.' James smiled slightly, imagining the scene. 'And I reviled him.'

'But he would have been satisfied by today's outcome.'

'You think so?'

'Yes. Better that the river took him.'

Ballantyre nodded, staring out across the lake as the ripples flattened into calm again. 'Perhaps so— Stanton will retract his false statement, I promise you, and so there will be justice for you as well.' James nodded. 'And will you then come home?'

And James replied as he had done to Evelyn. 'This is home now.'

They sat in silence again after that, but it was a companionable silence, and James thought he sensed Ballantyre's relief at his answer. And then into the stillness came a strange whirring sound, and they looked up to see a ragged mass of large birds, flying with necks outstretched and their long wings flapping. 'Sandhill cranes,' he said, 'following the geese, heading south.' They watched them pass overhead, seeing the low sun shining through the wing feathers.

'Yes,' said Ballantyre, then his tone became more brisk. 'The season advances, and tomorrow we too will follow them.' He turned to look at James. 'And so, to business, my friend. It appears that you and your friends played me for a fool! And did a fine job of it.' James stiffened, wary now. 'You can imagine my surprise when I told Achak that I was travelling with Skinner, and he asked about the three of you—' He glanced briefly at James but away again at once. 'He was a charming and intelligent man, don't you think?' James made no response. Whatever else happened now he had Louis and Marcel to consider. 'Several things then fell into place, and after some further discussion we were able to reach a settlement between us.'

A settlement. James felt the stirring of a sick anger, but Ballantyre was continuing. 'I'd a prior agreement with Achak's father, you see, as a result of Kershaw's prospecting. Nothing signed, of course, but after some debate Achak agreed to abide by it. As a matter of honour.'

After all that had happened, all that had been said, Ballantyre still felt he could talk of honour?

'In the end we were able to agree to terms very similar to those you three had negotiated with him,' he continued. 'Fair and reasonable terms, I might add, which protect Achak's interests and will still turn a good profit. Kershaw now has a fairly good idea of the extent of the outcropping, and the potential of the area is much larger than you might imagine. Not only gold, you see, but copper and iron ore. Diamonds maybe— The claim that you three negotiated with Achak is not central to my plans, and if Kershaw is right, the outcropping there is thin, and will require considerable effort to extract it—' James turned to him, confused now, but still wary. 'As a single enterprise it will be an expensive undertaking, but as part of a wider concern—'

'What are you saying?'

'— although even as a single enterprise, if you choose to continue in that way, it will yield you worthwhile results.' Ballantyre turned his head then and contemplated him with an odd expression. 'Did you really think that I would try to take it back?'

He gave a grunt at James's silence. 'I suppose I deserved that you did.' Then James saw that a smile was twitching at his lips. 'Once I'd recovered from my surprise at your collective guile I was actually rather impressed by it. You, James Douglas, for all my efforts, are Jacko's spawn, with the heart and soul of a poacher.' He pulled out his cigar case. 'Jacko would have been proud of you. First my grouse and my salmon, and now my gold mine. Does your thievery know no bounds?'

At the end of five minutes James sat staring at Ballantyre in astonishment. 'From my point of view it would work well,' he concluded, tapping ash onto the rock. 'I like your friend Louis, he understands human nature and would handle the workforce well. Marcel's temper might become less of a liability if his job was to liaise with Achak. I will pay them well, have no fear. I suspected you would not wish to return to Scotland, so I'm inviting you to be my partner in this, James. I will retain seventy-five per cent ownership, you get the rest.'

James continued to stare.

'If your own partners wish to negotiate some other deal regarding the operation of your claim, then I'm happy to discuss it,' he continued, 'but that's up to the three of you. And Achak.' He paused and relit his own cigar. 'This arrangement will suit me very well, you see, otherwise I would have to employ foremen, overseers, and the like who might try to rob me.' He paused again, then added, 'Something I don't recommend you try—' He raised his eyebrows, as if seeking a response, but James said nothing. 'In fact it was your impudent little claim-jump that started me thinking. Very enterprising, and legally quite unimpeachable, as I had signed no documents, so it was, on your part, opportunistic and admirably incisive. Good qualities to harness, I think.' Then he added in a different tone, 'And it provides me with a God-sent opportunity to start to put things right between us, James Douglas.'

———

Somewhere in the trees nearby the song sparrow resumed its song. There was no other sound except for the breeze rustling through the trees, and James felt its coolness on his face. He got to his feet and went to stand beside the still pool. In a week or so ice would begin to form at its edges, and in a month it would be frozen solid, and animals would cross it, leaving tracks in the deepening snow.

It was an incredible offer—

But he would be Ballantyre's man again. He might be three thousand miles away but he would still be there, in control, pulling the strings, determining fate and future. He would be no more free of him than Evelyn—

He tossed the half-smoked cigar into the water.

Evelyn.

The thought of her slipped into his head, unbidden, smooth and warm, like the feel of her skin beneath his palm, and his pulse began to race. And he stood there, stock still beside the pool, and let the idea take root and grow. Perhaps there was, after all, a deal to be struck—

He turned back to Ballantyre. 'Thirty per cent,' he said.

'What?'

'Thirty per cent to me. And thirty to your daughter. The rest you retain.'

Ballantyre stared fixedly at him. Then: 'To Evelyn?'

'Yes.'

His expression did not waver, and James returned it evenly. 'So you think to have Evelyn too?'

'That's up to her.'

'And thereby gain a controlling interest in the mine.'

'To hell with the mine. Her share would remain hers, whatever happened. It gives her independence and freedom.'

Ballantyre ground out his cigar on the rocks. 'To come to you?' A chill had entered his tone.

'If she'd have me. Yes.'

'Evelyn returns home with me.'

'I know.'

'She's not yet twenty.'

'But she won't always be.'

Ballantyre continued to stare at him, then he turned away and looked out over the pool of still water, his profile as rigid as the surrounding cliffs. James held his breath as the silence between them lengthened, staggered at his own audacity.

When Ballantyre turned back his expression was unchanged. 'I cannot help thinking that if I had sent you straight to Rothmere House ten years ago, I would have spared myself a good deal of trouble.' Or was it subtly altered—? 'You'd have the estate too, I daresay!'

'I don't give a damn for—'

'I might remarry. Breed sons!' There was now a glint in Ballantyre's eye.

'I'd wish you joy, sir,' James replied.

'*Ha!*'

'I only want Evelyn. But she'll come to me of her own free will – or not, as she chooses.'

Ballantyre shook his head from side to side, as if in disbelief. 'I was right – there *is* no end to your thievery. But Evelyn returns home with me, nevertheless, where she stays until she comes of age, or to her senses. Whatever you might think, she is a child still—'

He broke off as Evelyn herself appeared at the edge of the forest, still wearing James's shirt and Louis's trousers. She stepped out of the shadows and paused, her hair lit by a shaft of sunlight flickering through the trees. They both watched her as she came towards them.

———•———

She had stopped at the end of the trail and looked towards Astra's Pool, and saw them, standing beside the water, talking. But James had his arms folded high across his chest, and her father had his shoulder half-turned away, and her heart sank. What had Louis said about a bond?

They caught sight of her and she went closer. 'Not fishing?' she asked, looking from one to the other.

Her father was contemplating her with a strange expression. 'You will return home with me, Evelyn. You do understand that? Whatever has happened in my absence between the two of you, you will return home.'

Her eyes flew to James's face and she felt colour flood her face. What had been said?

But James was shaking his head. 'Of course she returns with you, sir. I ask only that your offer is framed as I ask.'

So Louis was right. Matters had been discussed, and decided.

'Your father has made me an offer, a business offer. A share of his mining enterprise' – James glanced across at him – 'an offer which he might well now withdraw.'

'Unworthy, James,' said her father softly.

James shrugged. 'But I will only accept it if he agrees to my terms.'

'Which are what?'

'That he gives you a third share in the business as well. Yours forever. Which would leave you free to choose your own path.'

She looked back at him, thinking of the place by the river where Mr Skinner had found them. 'What business?'

'Not lumber—' he said, with a slow smile. 'Mining.'

'But I know nothing of mining,' she said, and her eyes met the smile in his.

'Nor do I—'

She felt her father looking from one to another, and then she sensed something change. The tension seemed to go out of him. 'So you both have a great deal to learn,' he said, and she saw a smile reach his eyes. 'But James will learn his business here, earning his twenty-five per cent share, and you will return home with me. And in a little over a year when most young ladies receive pearls and other jewels to mark their coming of age you, my dear, will also receive a twenty per cent share. What you do with it, Evelyn, will be your entirely own affair.' He turned to James. 'Satisfied?'

'I said thirty. To each of us.'

'I know you did, young man. But this is the deal I offer.'

James turned to her. 'Evelyn?'

A strange new feeling was taking wings within her, like the beat of a hundred geese soaring high above them. 'If you said thirty, then I don't think you should back down.' Her father looked astonished. 'And perhaps the contract should state that an additional per centage will be passed on when' – her nerve failed her – 'a certain level of profit is reached.'

James smiled at her: 'Or on some other fitting occasion—'

Her father's eyes narrowed as he looked back at her. 'I said you were a child still,' he said slowly, 'but I believe I am mistaken. You were, after all, willing to shoot a man—'

Out in the middle of the pool there was a splash and sunlight caught the rainbow hues of a mighty trout as it arched, leaping clear of the water, scattering silver droplets as it rose. And as it fell back the old fighter shattered the surface of the pool, taking with it a jaw full of hooks and trailing lengths of broken fishing line.

Acknowledgments

The characters and events in the book are entirely fictional. The River Tweed flows through the lovely Scottish Borders, but Ballantyre's estate along its course is imaginary. The Nipigon River also exists, although not as it did in 1893 when it drew 'Gentlemen Anglers' from across the globe to fish for the legendary brook trout. Since the 1920s hydroelectricity has altered the river beyond recognition, though fishermen still enjoy fine sport there. I am enormously grateful to Betty Brill at the excellent Nipigon museum (nipigonmuseumtheblog.blogspot.com) not only for all her help in pointing me to early literature about the river, but also for her helpful correspondence on the natural history and wildlife in the area. I hope that she, and others, will forgive the liberties I have taken with the town and geography of the region. Of those articles to which she drew my attention, 'Days on the Nepigon' by E. E. M. (1917) and 'Up the Nepigon' by Elizabeth Taylor (1889) proved invaluable sources. *A Historical Walk Through Nipigon* by Bonnie Satten (2003) describes the town in past years, and John R. M. Kelso and James W. Demers's *Our Living Heritage: The Glory of the Nipigon* (1993) tells the story of that small town's fascinating history, while Thomas Waters's *The Superior North Shore* (1987) describes the natural history. Thunder Bay Library staff are also to be thanked for sending me a copy of Hiram Slack's 1887 account of a fishing trip up the Nipigon and for dealing with other enquiries during my visit there. Joseph Mauro's informative and well-illustrated book, *A History of Thunder Bay* (1981), provided insights into the days when Port Arthur was set to become the 'Chicago of the North,' as did Tania Saj's *The Last Best Places: Storytelling About Thunder Bay's Historic Buildings* (2009), while Elinor Barr's *Silver Islet – Striking It Rich in Lake Superior* (1988) tells the extraordinary story of that mine. Information on the Chicago World's Fair was gleaned from many sources, but the Fair was brought to life by the illustrations in Neil Harris, Wim de Wit, James Gilbert, and Robert Rydell's *Grand Illusions: Chicago's World's Fair of 1893* (1993). Henry David Thoreau's *Walden; or Life in the Woods* and his essay 'Civil Disobedience' provided inspiration for developing the character of Niels Larsen, and also for the views of Jacko and Charles Ballantyre. All these sources provided inspiration and period background but do not alter the case that *Beyond the Wild River* is a work of fiction.

On a more personal level I am grateful to an old friend Cliff Samson, now an antipodean fly fisherman, for pointing me in the direction of *Red Palmer: A Practical Treatise on Fly Fishing* (1888) by Taylor James, as well as answering other questions. The Scottish Borders, near Kelso, have special memories for my family, and my sons came with me to rediscover cherished childhood days spent in northwestern Ontario. They bore me company in Thunder Bay and for a memorable few days in Nipigon where, as we drove back one night along the road beside the river, a tree fell across our route in one of those sudden storms. One fell in the campsite of the Prince of Wales (Edward VIII) during his fishing trip to Nipigon too. The days when Nipigon drew such exalted figures to fish there might be over, but the history of that region still fascinates. It might not be as wild as it was in 1893, but it is still a very beautiful, if little known, part of the world, where the trappings of civilisation seem to fall away.

History

By Sarah Maine

I have two prints on my wall. One is a hand-coloured wood engraving by T. Weber dated 1890: *Vue Prise sur la Rivière Nipigon* which shows the lower reaches of a mighty river flowing past pine-clad cliffs and down to the north shore of Lake Superior in Canada. The other is a black and white photograph of one of the islands in these lower reaches and is dated 1893 – spot on for the year in which Charles Ballantyre, a wealthy Scottish landowner, brings his party to fish on the Nipigon. The photograph shows a fishing camp with three or four tents, a cleared area and figures down by the shore. And one of the figures is a woman! There she is, an intrepid soul, living under canvas and enjoying the sport and the thrill of the river, and I have since read accounts by these Victorian rule-breakers that offer passionate descriptions of the river and the freedoms it offered.

In 1887, the magazine *Forest and Stream* dubbed the Nipigon 'the finest trout stream in the world' and it drew wealthy 'gentlemen anglers' there in pursuit of the river's legendary brook trout. In 1919, it even lured Edward, Prince of Wales, to try his luck – although by then the river was already famous. There is nothing to see now of the wooden hotels that housed these early tourists or of the outfitters who supplied them, but the excellent little museum still commemorates the world-record-breaking brook trout caught in 1915, weighing in at 14.5lbs. Nipigon seemed to have been set for glory and there were hopes that the railhead of the transcontinental railway would finish at the large wharf constructed there in optimistic anticipation. But it was not to be and Nipigon is now a quiet little town, still supplying fishermen who come to fish below the great railway viaduct.

I later discovered that the photograph on my wall had come from a book entitled *America's Wonderland* (though Nipigon is, of course, in Canada) produced to coincide with the Columbian Exposition in Chicago in that same year. This inspired me to use the Exposition as a pivotal point in the book where Evelyn Ballantyre muses not only on the lot of women as she gazes at the murals in the Woman's Building, but also begins to understand the difference between illusion and reality. Those classical buildings she so admires lose something of their lustre when she learns that they are straw and plaster on steel frames and won't last the winter. And 1893 is, of course, the year of The Panic when finances crumble and the characters who people the sleek steam yachts moored at Chicago are going spectacularly bankrupt.

Evelyn has grown up on an orderly Borders estate, living the sheltered life of a late-Victorian girl emerging into womanhood. She sees only tranquillity in the pastoral scenes before her, listens to the gentle babbling of the river Tweed at the end of manicured lawns – and yet the scent of roses is stifling her.

Events take Evelyn, with a party of her father's guests, first to Chicago and then through the Great Lakes to what is now Thunder Bay. In 1893 the city was still Fort William, once a Northwest Company fur trading post, and a booming port, Port Arthur, which shipped grain brought east by the railways onwards through the Great Lakes system to the St Lawrence seaway. Port Arthur was dubbed the 'Little Chicago of the North' and one or two buildings, notably the Whalen building, still survive to mark that high ambition. In 1911, my great grandfather was chief engineer on a steam yacht, not unlike Larsen's yacht in the story, owned by the entrepreneurial James Whalen; this, too, fed into the story.

Do you wish this wasn't the end?

Join us at www.hodder.co.uk, or follow us on
Twitter @hodderbooks to be a part of our community
of people who love the very best in books and reading.

Whether you want to discover more about a book
or an author, watch trailers and interviews, have the
chance to win early limited editions, or simply browse
our expert readers' selection of the very best books,
we think you'll find what you're looking for.

And if you don't,
that's the place to tell us what's missing.

We love what we do, and we'd love you to be part of it.

www.hodder.co.uk

@hodderbooks

HodderBooks

HodderBooks